BLACK
LIST

BLACK LIST

GENEVA LEE

QUAINTRELLE
PUBLISHING • BOOKS

A branch of Geneva Lee, LLC.
www.GenevaLee.com
First published, 2020.
Special ed. ISBN: 978-1-945163-43-2
Cover design © Date Book Designs.

In Memory of Trish

1

STERLING

Rain splatters the succession of black Mercedes-Benzes and Bentleys arriving at the cemetery. Everyone in attendance pulled their most somber sedans out of the garage this morning. There are no flashy red coupes or ostentatious sport utility vehicles today. Rich people know how to put on a show, and today is all about show. But despite the dark clothes and the umbrellas, not a single tear rolls down a single face as attendees climb out of their cars and make their way toward his grave site. The rain cares more than anyone present, myself included.

A woman stumbles, her heel catching in the mud, and my arm shoots out to break her fall. She glances up, murmuring thanks. Everything is gray around us—the sky, the rain, the headstones. Even her copper hair looks almost silver in the clouded light. The world is a hundred muted shades of nothing, except her eyes. They are bright glittering emeralds against the day's gloom. Even after five years, I'd know them anywhere. A lot has changed. I've changed. Maybe she has, too. But those eyes are the same.

Nothing registers on her face as she turns to accept the hand of her companion. He leads her to the front of the crowd, where she belongs. *With them.*

I skipped the service and the viewing. I'm not here to pay my respects. I came to see him put in the ground. I came to smell the dirt as it hits his coffin and seals the fate of the MacLaine family. Business can be attended to later. I want the pleasure of watching a man fade to nothing but a legacy—a legacy I intend to destroy. But that's not the real reason I'm here. It's a perk that I made it back to town in time for the funeral.

A priest says a few words. The rain continues to fall. When the ceremonial dirt hits the coffin, I'm watching the redhead. She doesn't flinch. She doesn't look away. I guess she didn't change after all.

Adair MacLaine.

The only woman I've ever loved.

That bitch? She's the real reason I came back.

An hour later, I pull into the paved, circular drive of Windfall, the MacLaine family estate, and hand the keys of my Aston Martin to a parking attendant. Judging by the slight bulge protruding from the left side of his cheap blazer, he's doubling as security. He scopes out the Vanquish appreciatively before his eyes skim over my Italian wool suit, pausing at the Breitling on my wrist and sweeping to the black Berlutis on my feet. Nodding toward the house, he steps to the side. It seems the only identification they're checking is material status.

That's a mistake.

Mourners are distracted. Some by grief. Some by a preoccupation with social responsibility. The MacLaines suffer from the latter.

People hosting a funeral have blind spots. Ever wanted to see inside someone's house? A funeral is a perfect opportunity. Thieves, paparazzi, and assassins all know it's an in. Need to get to a high value target? Kill someone close, but easier to reach, and wait for their funeral.

Not that I killed Angus MacLaine. Even though I would have liked to. I'm guessing I'm not the only one.

The former senator had no shortage of enemies. Some he'd made on his own. Others he had inherited along with the family newspaper empire. For every legitimate bit of journalism he had, he owned ten tabloids. His television networks ran more propaganda than an army recruitment office.

But it wasn't his business practices that made me hate him —although they didn't help his case. It's that he was a soulless son of a bitch. Maybe he'd had a heart at some point, but he sold it for a fortune that amassed five billion dollars. Then he'd gone to Washington to protect it at all costs, like his father before him. That was then. This is now. And I'm the devil come to collect.

A smile crooks across my face as I survey the kingdom I'm about to take. The MacLaine estate sprawls as far as I can see in every direction. Thirty years ago, Angus MacLaine built it for a couple million dollars. Today it's worth ten times that, and yesterday I bought the lien on it. I read once in an interview that he wanted his family home to recall the glory of the Old South without all the baggage of the past. I assume he meant slavery and the Civil War. It was just like a MacLaine to believe he could simply erase a problem. The architect had managed the feat, creating an estate that occupies fifty acres in

Valmont, Tennessee—the most prestigious enclave outside Nashville. Stone columns rise from the veranda to support a second story porch that runs the length of the main house's front. Unlike traditional antebellum homes, the house extends to wings on each side. The east wing houses the family bedrooms and private areas—places I was once not allowed to enter. The west wing is comprised of a solarium that empties into the grounds. Those are completely blocked by the behemoth white mansion, but I know it won't have changed. Past the outdoor kitchen waits a swimming pool, tiled in Venetian glass. His and hers pool houses offer a much needed, if entirely bullshit, air of propriety. Then there's the tennis court, and, if you walk far enough, stables that shelter the family horses.

I don't give a fuck about the house, though. Or its tennis court. Or its swimming pool. I'm not here for the modern art coveted by collectors throughout the world. I'll sell all of it, eventually. Just not yet. That's the difference between reciprocity and revenge. Reciprocity evens the score. Revenge, when done correctly, is slow, like lovemaking. It lingers. It builds. It lacquers pain, coat by coat, until you crack.

I'm in the business of vengeance.

The inside of Windfall is more extravagant. MacLaine was unfamiliar with the concept of *too much*. Most American homes could be parked on the marble floor inside the foyer. The ground floor boasts all the standard rooms—the dining room, a sitting room, the kitchen—and then some: a ball-room, the staff kitchen, the breakfast room, a gentlemen's parlor, and God knows what else. I stare for a moment at the split staircase that curves toward the upper rooms, remembering the first time I set foot in this hellhole. Adjusting my tie, I swallow the thought into the pit I use for past memories.

MacLaine would be pleased at the turnout, even if half the

people here despised the bastard. People you'd recognize from *Forbes* magazine covers or television, if anyone still watches it, mill throughout the ground floor. It's a sea of black, groups moving in surges from one empty conversation to the next as easily as they run through the canapés.

A man near the bar glances in my direction, his face blanching paper-white. I've been recognized. Not that he'll tell anyone who I am. Then he'd have to admit that he knew me— that he knows what I do. I move past him without a second glance. He won't be any trouble—and I have bigger prey to hunt.

"I don't believe we've met," an older gentleman says when I pause in the dining room.

I know who he is, but I feign ignorance. He wouldn't appreciate it if I told him we were acquainted. Not Mr. Moneybags who paid to have the barrier to his takeover of his largest competitor permanently removed last year. No, he wouldn't want me to tell him that we've worked together *distantly*. Not in such a public gathering of self-proclaimed people of importance. Instead, I shake his hand, locking my grip firmly. Statement enough.

"Sterling." I'm not listening when he introduces himself. My thoughts are elsewhere in this house, memories warring with desire as I wait for her to make an appearance.

"What do you do?" he asks.

"Asset management." I snag toast with caviar off a passing tray and pop it into my mouth.

"What firm? My man is retiring…" he continues on and I resist the urge to walk away. Death can't stop networking. Not with people like this.

"I'm a private contractor."

He waits for more information—maybe a business card. I

don't offer any. So like a good member of the greatest genera-
tion he fills the void between us with mindless market chatter.
I nod enough to look like I'm listening—and then I feel it
—*feel* her—approaching. The room is electric, humming with
the undercurrent of static building toward a strike—and the
inevitable crash.

ADAIR

This isn't happening.

My mother once told me that having MacLaine blood running through your veins meant being able to walk through fire like you set it on purpose. Given how often MacLaines start shit, it's a valuable skill to have. Today, though, even in the pouring rain, I felt the heat the moment he touched me. It burned through me like wildfire. That's how it had always been with us. No one was responsible for the devastation. It was an act of God, some natural force that couldn't be prevented once it started. There was no controlling it. No denying it. All I could do the moment our eyes met was turn away and hope I made it out unscathed. Unlike last time.

That's the thing about being a MacLaine, we may walk through fire but that means we're all hiding scars.

The moment the limousine pulls into the drive, I'm out and up the steps. I don't have to go far to find a bottle of whiskey. Not at Windfall, the family estate my father built. My finger traces the label. *West Tennessee Whiskey*. My father's favorite. I pour a glass with unsteady hands, hoping to wash the memories away.

"It's been five years," I remind myself quietly. But while five years might be long enough to bury secrets, it can't erase mistakes.

The house will be full of people soon. Mourners come to pay their respects, or rather gossip about my father and his fortune. They're here to play the guessing game torturing the rest of us: who gets the money? The land? The company? What will happen to the MacLaine legacy? It's all I've thought about for months. Years, if I'm being honest. Ever since daddy got sick. Ever since…

And then? Sterling Ford shows up at the funeral.

Which can only mean one thing: a reckoning.

I tried to play off the encounter. Five years had passed. Neither of us were kids anymore. I'm not certain I've changed much. At least, not as much as him. When I first met him, Sterling was a lean but wiry six feet. At the time I'd wondered if he was an athlete, but his physique then had come from a very different source.

"Maybe it wasn't him," I say to the empty room, even it doesn't believe me. I know it was him like I know I'm breathing.

A shiver rolls through me as the memory of his skin, slick and hot against mine, flashes to mind. My body had recognized him before my brain did. He's no longer the boy I remember, but I would know him anywhere. I am chills and fire—a feverish reconstruction of the woman I was when I woke up this morning mixed with a girl who fell for the wrong man. I knew today would be the end of me. I thought I might have a choice in who I would become after this. Now I know I was wrong. We never really rid ourselves of the past, no matter how deep we bury it.

"Adair!"

I quickly down the remaining whiskey. I know my sister-in-law's voice by the edge of perpetual panic it holds.

Taking a steadying breath, I leave the bottle on my father's desk. Exiting the study, I find Ginny in the foyer, struggling to hold a squirming heap of black taffeta and limbs.

"Could you?" Desperation glints in her chocolate brown eyes. "I need to speak to the caterer."

"Of course." I scoop my niece from her arms. Ellie instantly ceases her struggle, smirking up at me.

"Ellie, keep your skirt down," her mother orders before smoothing her own black sheath. Ginny can't stand a wrinkle out of place. Her copper hair is knotted into a chignon, not a hair daring to escape the tight coil. Her porcelain skin is buffed to perfection, a complimentary shade of rose dusting her cheeks. She is exactly the trophy my brother wanted on his arm. The only kink in her life is Ellie, who was born a bundle of determined chaos. She hurries off toward the kitchens, patting her perfect hair delicately as she goes.

I place the little girl on her feet, bending down to talk to her. Unlike her mother, Ellie's strawberry blonde curls are tangled and windswept. I frown as I recall the argument I had with her parents last night. I told them she was too young to attend the graveside service. With them it's always about appearance. How would it look if Angus MacLaine's granddaughter were absent? I'd nearly bit my tongue off trying to keep quiet. Now Ginny is put out that Ellie was misbehaving. "You were pulling up your skirt?"

"Watch," she tells me seriously. Taking a baby step back, she holds out her arms and spins in a wild circle. Her dress flares out, rippling around her as she twirls.

"Very nice." I clap as she slows, dizzily stumbling over her own feet like she's had too much to drink. I steady her and smile down at her. "Whoa. That's pretty cool, but do you know why Mom doesn't want you to do that?"

"Cause it's granddaddy's *fumeral*." Her eyebrows crease together like she's been through this before and recently. She tips her head, her gaze full of questions and I brace myself. "What's a *fumeral*?"

"Funeral," I correct her gently. I always get stuck with the hard questions where Ellie is concerned. "It means goodbye."

"Why are all these people here for goodbye?" She holds up her hands to emphasize how everything about this is weird. "Why can't we just wave to him when he goes?"

I curse Ginny for not having this conversation with her. This is supposed to be her job. She's her mother. I know what will happen if I bring it up. She'll flutter like a wounded bird and tell me that Ellie doesn't ask her those things. We've been here before. There's no point bringing it up. Ginny and I aren't exactly close. Not anymore.

"He already left," I tell her softly, "and this is a party for us to remember him."

"Is there cake?" she asks hopefully.

Ellie might wait to ask me questions, but clearly that doesn't mean I'm any good at answering them. If Ginny could skirt the issue, so could I. "Probably."

A grin lights up her baby face, then falls away. "He left? Do you miss him?"

Ellie's earlier questions were tricky. This one coils around my heart and squeezes. It takes me a moment to answer, because I'm not sure. She waits patiently and I know what I should say. "Yes."

"We should find cake," she says gravely, "so we feel better."

"It's a plan." I take her small hand in my mine. It's warm and soft, thawing some of the ice that's encased my heart since this morning. It's hard to focus on the bad when she's nearby and full of life.

That positivity leaks from me like a slowly deflating balloon when I enter the sitting room, hand in hand with Ellie, and see him. Up until now, I hoped I had seen a ghost. I don't realize I've dropped her hand until she tugs at my sleeve impatiently. Her hand slips back inside mine but this time it doesn't feel comforting. It feels like an anchor—another family obligation binding me to this house.

He's in our adjoining room, strong hands gripping the back of a mahogany dining room, discussing something with an older man, some friend of my father's. I try not to stare but I can't help drinking him in, looking for some clue as to why he's here. When I first met Sterling, I wondered how he was so muscular compared to other guys our age. I wouldn't have thought it was possible for him to fill out even more. Before, he was formidable. Now? He's *intimidating*. Even from here, I know his suit was custom tailored to fit his broad shoulders. The dark swirl of a tattoo peeks out from the cuff of his sleeve. That's new. Gone is the sweep of black hair in favor of a crew cut that showcases the hard set of jawline and slight stubble. I watch as he lifts his hand and rubs it across his chin. The world seems to slow as his gaze flickers from his companion, across the room, and lands on me. His index finger pauses on his mouth and I can almost swear I see his teeth nip his lower lip.

I've been caught staring, but I can't tear my eyes away.

Ellie's hand tugs free of mine, jarring me back to the present and my responsibilities.

"*Auntie Dair.*" She's pointing to the spread the caterers have laid on the dining table.

Of course, he had to be here, and I had to agree to cake.

Would he think I was coming to talk to him? Was I the reason he was here? Maybe it was a fluke.

Don't be stupid. Sterling didn't show up today, of all days, out of the blue.

Maybe he worked with my father. Stranger things have happened. Except not really. My father might have worked with the devil himself to close a deal, but somehow I doubt Sterling would get in bed with a MacLaine.

Or rather back in bed with one. Not after everything that happened.

Then again, we were adults now. He probably never even thought of me after he left Valmont. And he is obviously successful judging from that suit. Still, I can't help but wonder where he's been the last five years.

While I've been trying to convince myself that this is the world's most unlikely coincidence, Ellie has been attempting to pull me toward the desserts. No doubt she's spotted the chocolate cake.

I breathe a sigh of relief when I spy my brother, Malcolm. Marching her to him, I interrupt his conversation, which sounded like business talk anyway. Maybe politics. I'm not sure which topic is worse at a funeral but discussing either is like a MacLaine. "She wants cake."

He doesn't bother to look at me—or her. "Get her some." Then he turns back to his discussion.

"She's your daughter," I say icily.

His answering glare is somehow even colder. I hate seeing my green eyes staring back at me from his face. Are mine that empty? Malcolm has my father's dark hair and brutal looks, but we both have our mother's eyes. Ellie has gone completely silent at our feet. She isn't tugging at my hand anymore. I glance to her and hate myself. I tell myself she's little—that she doesn't understand what's going on—but she gets more than I want to admit. A rock would pick up on the tension between me and my brother, but that's not the worst of it. It's become a game to pass Ellie off like we're playing hot potato. It's been worse with the funeral plans. I couldn't tell Malcolm or Ginny no when they needed an extra hand after Daddy got sick. That was a year ago, and I've been playing part-time nanny ever since. That's why Ellie usually lands with me. I suspected it made her mother feel better to dump her with family instead of a stranger. Her baby lips trembles and I realize she understands so much more than either her parents or I give her credit for.

"Let's get cake," I say in a strained voice. "Apparently, Daddy doesn't want any."

I keep my sights on the table and lead her there, pretending to be completely absorbed in every request she makes—partially due to guilt, but mostly in an attempt to ignore my proximity to Sterling. It doesn't matter. My body vibrates with barely suppressed awareness. I can feel my memories of him. They dance across the back of my neck, rippling through me and raising goosebumps along my skin. I don't even realize I'm picking up one of each item Ellie has pointed to until the plate is heaped with sugary confections. A sugar high might teach her parents not to dump her with me.

I don't have to look over to know Sterling is watching me now. I feel his gaze sweeping over me, penetrating my act, past the wall I've built so carefully over the last five years.

Ginny appears, casting a disapproving look at Ellie's plate. She looks even more stressed than when she left. That's par for the course with her. Her anxiety ratchets up a notch every minute of the day. Even the small pharmacy worth of pills her doctor prescribes isn't helping anymore. She wasn't always that way. Times change. Not always for the better.

I leave Ellie with her now that she's been placated with

sweets. Commanding myself to look ahead, I manage to avoid Sterling. I want to look. I want to move closer. I won't let myself do either.

But today isn't one for escapes. Cyrus Eaton enters the front room, slinking through the crowd. He also moves like Sterling, graceful and serpentine, his dark eyes sweeping the room for his prey. When he spots me, I half expect him to pounce. His orders come from his girlfriend and my best friend, Poppy. She's stuck in Paris, so she sent him to guard me. If she only knew.

I made a mistake. Several, if I'm being honest. Who hasn't?

Cyrus is in front of me. Sterling behind me. I have to brave one of them. For a moment, I consider climbing through a window. They're certainly large enough, but I'd probably set off an alarm. I have to make a decision. I've never been very good at that.

I want to know why Sterling is here. I want to know where he's been. I have a million questions and a few accusations for him. But getting too close is more dangerous than knowing the truth. That's exactly why I move toward Cyrus. Better the beast you know. I have no idea who Sterling Ford is anymore. And Cyrus? For better or worse, I know exactly who he is. He never left. Like most of the people in my life he's been a fixture in my world. Like Poppy and our friends. Like my brother and his family. Even my father.

But Sterling? There is a morbid symmetry to his reappearance. He'd been here when my life started falling apart. Then he'd pieced it back together.

I suspect he hasn't come to save me twice.

3

STERLING

Indecision grips her features and she pauses long enough for me to study her. Adair MacLaine was a slip of a girl when we first met. The girl was pretty. The woman is stunning. Her once slender body has ripened into a soft fullness, lush and tempting. A black dress hugs her generous hips and dips low to show the swell of her breasts. Her head tilts up, nose in the air, and I wonder if she ever found the confidence she so desperately flaunted five years ago but never really felt. Maybe she bought some with daddy's money.

She pivots on her Louboutins and starts toward the door with a smile on her face. I turn to discover she's headed for an old friend. I'm ten steps closer and a foot taller. I catch Cyrus Eaton before she can reach him. Now she has a real choice to make. Fight or flight. Maybe she's finally shed her skin to become the woman she wears like a glove. Adair hesitates before backing away and disappearing into the crowd.

Maybe not.

I'm not surprised. Cyrus, on the other hand, is. He takes a second to process me before his hand claps on my shoulder, dragging me into a hug. "Sterling Ford. What the fuck?"

Trust him to get straight to the point.

"How long has it been? Five years?" he continues as we break apart. "I didn't know you were back in Valmont."

"Nashville, actually," I tell him.

"Visiting?" Cyrus can mine someone for information more efficiently than a computer virus. It's his particular talent and one he's put to good use on the stock market. Unlike most men I'd met who'd made their name in day trading, Cyrus shows no signs of stress or premature aging. Likely because he would never need the money he made there. Playing the market is exactly that for him: a game. Not a high stakes one like poker or black jack. Investing millions was no more than Monopoly to him. His mess of blond hair is closely cropped now, stubble dusts his jaw, but his smile is feline and familiar.

"I have a place off Broadway." He didn't need to know more than that. Cyrus isn't on my list, but that doesn't mean I trust him.

"We should do dinner. Poppy should be home from Paris later this week. She went to the spring shows with her mother." He shrugs as though this is a perfectly normal thing for a grown woman to do. For people here, it is. I have nothing against Cyrus or his girlfriend. As far as I'm concerned, they're the closest thing to decent humans this town has ever produced. That doesn't mean they're in touch with reality.

That's the real problem with Valmont: it exists within its own bubble of exclusivity. Close enough to Nashville to commute but with enough space to spread, it attracts the rich, the refined, and the renowned. It also has the real estate market to match. The average home price is well over the million-dollar mark. In my time here, I'd seen the elitism first hand. They passed off the snobbery as high society, and even the kindest among them, like Cyrus and Poppy, had no perception of reality. When you're born with a trust fund, vacation homes, and household staff, how could you?

There are two tricks for surviving the Valmont enclave. The first is to understand them—what drives them, what scares them, what informs them. The second is to never become them.

I might have made a fortune since my time here, but I will never be one of them. Not that they would ever let me.

"This is terrible, isn't it?" Cyrus lowers his voice, watching someone over my shoulder. I know exactly who has his attention without having to turn. He always watched over Adair. There was a time when I appreciated that. Now I want to shake some goddamn sense into him. "Losing her dad after…"

I mutter a half-hearted agreement. Part of me agrees with him. The rest of me is over it. Lots of people lose their fathers. Lots of people have sad stories. Why does hers matter more than the rest?

"At least she had time to prepare," he says.

"Was he sick for long?" I ask, pretending like I don't already know. When I had heard the MacLaine family patriarch was ill, I'd celebrated at a two-star Michelin restaurant and ordered champagne for the house.

"A few years. It was good of you to come, especially after you left things with her." He claps a hand on my shoulder, its weight heavy with implication. He knows more than most about how my relationship with Adair ended, but he doesn't know everything.

"The past is exactly that." I mean it. I have no interest in the boy I used to be or the girl she was. But I'm invested in what happens next. Too many people think revenge is about the past. It's not. It's about the future. You can't destroy the past. All you can do is ruin what's to come.

"I should…" He trails off, leaving an invitation hanging in the air.

"I came to pay my respects," I tell him. "Adair doesn't even remember me."

"I'm sure that's not true."

"Then she doesn't want to see me," I say. Cyrus looks like he wants to contradict this but can't. We both know it's true. She had her chance five years ago. She knows I'm here. I caught her looking at me. Maybe she's trying to place me. Women like her throw away men as though we're disposable. "Is she seeing someone?"

"Many a man has tried." Cyrus grins conspiratorially. "Money's tried a couple of times."

I smother a growl. There are things I missed about Tennessee— hot chicken, good music, and muggy, summer nights—but I have never once missed Montgomery West.

"Still no love lost there, I see," Cyrus murmurs.

"Bygones," I force out. I have reasons to hate "Money" West that would sway even his oldest friend. I keep them to myself. Information is only currency when it's in one man's pocket.

"I should check on Adair. I promised Poppy," Cyrus reiterates his mission. "We should get together, though. I want to hear all about what you've been up to the last few years."

Translation: he wants to know how the poor scholarship kid, who lost everything, is standing in front of him in a two thousand dollar suit. That's a trade secret, but Cyrus might be my most amiable contact here. If I'm in with him, opportunities will present themselves. Money might buy open doors, but friends could as well.

I slip a silver business card holder from my jacket and hand one to him. Cyrus studies the linen card and its simple embossed information for a moment before pocketing it. A million questions scroll through his eyes, but he doesn't ask a single one. "I'll give you a call."

"Do that," I say absently, noticing something interesting. Malcolm MacLaine and a handful of other men are heading toward the opposite wing of the main level where the offices sit empty. Cyrus excuses himself to find Adair, giving me the chance to follow them.

The benefit of a flexible moral code is that I'm accustomed to remaining unseen when need be. As the men disappear into one of the MacLaine family's conference rooms, a snort of laughter escapes me. Trust a MacLaine to hold court at a time like this.

I slip into the large executive office that Malcolm and a half dozen other men entered a few minutes ago. I'm intimately familiar with Windfall's rooms. I have rather fond memories of the table the men have gathered around, in fact. But I'm not here to skip down memory lane. I have an offer to deliver. Some might consider it a threat. I suspect the heir to the MacLaine fortune will see it as an opportunity.

They're already down to brass tacks—voices raised, first round of whiskey drank—so no one notices when the door clicks quietly shut behind me. I know a fair few of MacLaines' associates, mostly by reputation. The family lawyer, Judd Harding, and I have our own history. The rest of the men are here for the same reason that I am: money. Angus MacLaine had died mired in debt after being forced to retire from the State Senate—a move that hadn't endeared him to the powers that had put him there.

"I know my father's death leaves unresolved issues, but my bid for the Senate this fall is a sure thing." Malcolm is exasperated, raking his hands through his hair. "However, without the company to back up my run, we're all going to lose."

"Now isn't the time to discuss this, Malcolm," Harding

says not bothering to smother the weariness in his voice. "Once the will has been executed, we can handle these matters."

"I don't need the goddamn will to be executed to know that my father's stock in the company is mine!" Malcolm's hand slams against the conference table rattling the crystal Waterford whiskey glasses in front of each of his associates.

"My uncle has a vested interest in MacLaine Media." Even from behind, I recognize Luca DeAngelo's languid baritone. His index finger taps the table softly. He's the only man I know who can be bored while delivering a threat to someone. It's one reason that he's one of my best friends in the world. I find it's best to keep Luca close. "Without the family's assistance, your father's last run for the Senate"—

"Excuse me," Malcolm cuts him off, but he isn't begging his forgiveness. He's spotted me. "This is a private meeting."

"Conducting business during a funeral?" I volunteer a sneer. Malcolm MacLaine is the kind of man who probably conducted business over his father's death bed. The bastard gene runs in the family.

"And you are?" His eyes narrow, trying to place me. When he can't, he smiles apologetically at the men in suits. "I'll have security"—

"That won't be necessary," I cut him off, striding into the room toward the bar cart. "When you hear my offer, you'll be glad you invited me to stay."

He doesn't respond.

I'm not a man who needs an invitation into another man's office or to his belongings. Not when I already own them. Helping myself, I pour a glass before turning back to the group. Malcolm hasn't moved an inch toward his phone and the other men are watching me with a mixture of curiosity and trepidation. Luca's dark eyes shoot me a look that clearly says *took you long enough.* I shrug as to say *it couldn't be helped.* It's not like he doesn't understand the value of a dramatic entrance.

"Help yourself." Malcolm's lips thin into a line.

There's an empty seat at the table—the one on the far end, opposite where he stands. With one hand, I unbutton my suit jacket before settling into it. Heads swing from me to Malcolm and back like metronomes, but he can only stare. I might as well have walked in and peed on the rug. I'm marking my territory with no regard to his claim over the space, and he knows it.

"They can leave." I gesture to the others. Luca gets up to excuse himself while the rest turn various shades of scarlet, protesting. Except Harding. He's flipping through his mental contacts list. I see the pages turning in his guarded expression. His head tips in surprise when he lands on the answer but he covers his reaction quickly. Past the suit and past the years, he sees who I am. Or who I was. No one here knows who I am now. I like that, and I plan to keep it that way.

"I don't know who you think you are," Malcolm seethes, igniting a wave of furious commentary from the others.

I swirl the whiskey in my glass, watch it coat the sides, and wait.

"Do as he says," Harding advises over the protests. He doesn't look happy about it.

I hadn't expected him to go to bat for me, but even an unwilling ally makes things easier.

Men shuffle out of the room, bested by a better man or, at least, a bigger cock. I ignore the curious glances thrown my way. They'll know who I am soon enough. Not one of them speaks. Malcolm glares at me in gloomy silence.

Brushing my fingertip along the crystal tumbler's cut edge, a soft vibrating chime fills the air. "Cheer up. It's a funeral."

"Are you going to drink that or did you come here to play?" Malcolm asks dryly.

I stop fiddling with the whiskey and lean back in my chair. That's both a good and bad question. I did come here to play but not in the way that he means. My game is a bit more interesting than fucking with a room full of dickless loan sharks. I've been maneuvering my pieces into the right places for years. MacLaine wants answers. I want to savor the moment.

"You're wasting my time." MacLaine's chair pushes away from the table as he rises to his feet.

My gaze stays trained on the spot he just vacated. "Sit."

"If you think"—

"Sit." The command booms from me. He lowers into his chair.

I let him stew in his cowardice for a moment—let him linger in the humiliation of accepting my command. It's better than I imagined, bringing a MacLaine to heel. He's not the one I want at my feet, but he's delicious practice.

"Those men don't know it yet, but they no longer have an interest in MacLaine media or your family's assets," I inform him.

Green eyes bug from their sockets before he can rein himself in. He clears his throat, his fingers loosening the silver tie at his neck. "I'm not sure my investors"—

"*Your collectors*," I correct him. "The day your father died all partnerships and subsequent financial arrangements died with him. But you know that, don't you? Mr. Harding would have advised you as much."

Malcolm glances, stricken, to the man at his right. Later, Harding will explain who I am and how he knows me—I wonder if he'll tell the whole story—but even he isn't up-to-date on current events.

"No Senate seat to dole out favors," I continue. "No almighty media network to stir the pot. Not after the fines from the FCC and the loss of half your family's newspapers to bankruptcy. Do you know how many of your papers have been liquidated recently, Mr. MacLaine? *I do*."

"That's none of your business." His voice shakes as he speaks. He's putting on a front. I can't exactly blame him for that. I would in his position. Although, I'd never be in his position.

"It is my business. As of this morning, I hold a significant share in MacLaine media." I pause to let the news sink in and relish his shock. The pleasure is second to only one thing, and, before long, I'll have her just where I want her, too. "Your father divided his interests poorly. I'm sure Harding told you that."

"How much?" He mouths the words more than he speaks them.

"Enough, I imagine."

There's a flash of triumph in his eyes at this revelation. "You don't know what he left us."

"No, I don't, but I do know that forty-nine percent of MacLaine Media holdings were sold off by your father before his death. Care to guess how much of it I bought?" God, I couldn't enjoy this more if I had Adair bent over the table so they could watch the family getting fucked in more ways than one.

Even across the room, I see the slide of his throat as he swallows this information. Maybe Harding hasn't broken all the bad news yet. Silence roars between us, deafening in its implications. I've always been comfortable alone with my thoughts—comfortable weighing my words before I commit them to the world. Malcolm doesn't share this characteristic.

"That's impossible," he explodes. "Harding?"

The lawyer's lips press into a thin line. It's answer enough even for Malcolm, who seems the type that needs things spelled out for him.

"I want to see the will tomorrow," Malcolm mutters.

"The reading is set for"—

"I don't give a damn. Make it happen. Now," he snaps.

Harding's head shakes as he exits the room. I almost feel sorry for him. He's exchanged one tyrannical business man for another, but this is worse. Malcolm MacLaine is a class below his father. From my research, he's half as shrewd and nowhere near as cunning. Still, a snake in the grass can bite.

Neither of us speak for a minute after the lawyer is gone. Malcolm is smart enough to weigh his words. There are no witnesses to what happens here. He knows that. Normally, that might induce him to tell me off, but now there are other considerations. I can almost hear the wheels turning in his head. If I'm telling the truth—if I'm in possession of a significant portion of the MacLaine assets—it won't be hard for me to snipe his business associates. It won't matter what he claims happened between us. Money talks. Money speaks a language of lies, greed, and betrayal and everyone wants to be fluent in it.

"What do you want?" He manages to say evenly, although white-knuckled hands clench the table edge.

It's a loaded question. There's what I'll tell him I want and what I really came for, but the two desires are inextricable from one another. I hesitate to look as though I'm considering. I've planned this moment, waited for it, and perfection can't be rushed.

I know all about Malcolm MacLaine. I know he went to Valmont University and graduated *summa cum laude*. I know that his education was purchased, courtesy of a time when the wealthy could still buy their children success. I know how he met his wife. I know her secret. I know his secret. I make it my job to know the dirty truths people try to hide. The only thing more valuable in this world than money is knowledge. The right information is a never-ending paycheck. All of my research on Malcolm MacLaine tells me that he rivals his father for heartlessness. But even the heartless have vulnerabilities. His father's was his children, whether or not they saw it. Malcolm's weakness is his wife. He'll protect her over all else, but Ginny MacLaine isn't the type of woman to stay with a ruined man. If he loses his fortune, he loses her. We both know it.

That's why I know he won't have a problem with the MacLaine asset I've come to claim.

"Your sister. I want your sister."

There's a long pause as my demand sinks in. "My sister isn't for sale."

It's an admirable show of chivalry, but we both know his refusal reeks of bullshit. Business is business or we wouldn't be sitting here now.

"Malcolm." I lean back in the chair and regard how he flinches when I call him by his first name like an old friend. "We both know that everything is for sale, even Adair MacLaine."

4

STERLING
THE PAST

V almont Tennessee is nothing like the city. In New York,
every street is crammed with life. It bursts out of cracks
and alleys. It assails your senses. Tourists find it overwhelming.
To me, it's as close I get to feeling home. At least, it was *before*.

Before Francie got ideas in her head about my future.
Before my test scores came back and my teachers took notice.
Until that point, I was just another foster kid living on time
borrowed from the state. After, people started tossing around
words like genius and university.

I filled out the applications to make Francie happy. I'd had
enough shit foster moms to know things with her were as good
as it was likely to get. I didn't expect the acceptance letters.
Not from the schools I applied to, even with the high test
scores and the decent grades.

When she walked into our cramped kitchen in Queens,
clutching an envelope with the Valmont University crest on it,
her eyes glistened.

"We can't afford it," I said flatly. That was my plan all
along—set the bar impossibly high so it was easier to just duck
under and continue on with my life—the life I'd built here. I'd

cleaned up my act enough that I'd gotten to stay here for three years. I wasn't leaving now. "Community college is fine."

"You're too smart to get stuck here, Sterling. You don't belong on the streets."

That's when I'd noticed she was actually crying. I couldn't stand it when she cried—and I had made her cry a lot. I'd broken more than a few foster parents in the first few years I was in care. That's how I wound up with Francie in the first place. I never understood why she kept me. But every time I'd come home with a bloody nose, she'd gotten me cleaned up, washed my clothes, and got me a hot meal. Then she'd laid down the law.

There were rules in Francie's house. Rules that my friends hadn't had. Good grades—and I'm talking there had better not be a minus behind that A—were expected. Dinner was at six. On Sundays, I escorted her to mass at Our Lady of Mercy. For that, she didn't kick my ass out. I'd barely managed to meet those expectations my first year with her. She'd been more lenient back then. Over time, I'd done more. I listened when she told me to take harder courses, even though it meant taking shit from the guys. I let her read some of my stories, but not everything I wrote. Some things didn't need to be shared. This is where good behavior had gotten me. Despite my frequent street fighting, which was inescapable in our neighborhood, I'd kept my grades up and had taken the stupid college entrance exam—without actually planning to go. Until the fucking score came in the mail. I should have known by how excited she was that she expected me to go. Or when the guidance counselor called me in to her office to have a serious talk about my future.

I never decided if I'd failed to set the bar high enough or if Valmont University had lowered it to accommodate me. I'd read the brochure, but I didn't buy what it was selling. It was a bit too glossy, too photoshopped to be believed. It wasn't a world I belonged in. Valmont may be a half hour outside Nashville, but it has one foot firmly planted in the past while the other tries desperately to drag it along toward the future.

I'm not stupid enough to believe my scholarship covers the entire cost like she claims. Watching her eat off the dollar menu on the fourteen-hour drive confirms my suspicion. That's why Francie is different. She could have kicked me out when I turned eighteen, but she didn't. It's also why I've agreed to give Valmont a try. One semester and I'm out. Before we hit the Tennessee border I'm already checking local help-wanted listings on my phone. I doubt she can afford this, no matter what she says.

When we reach campus, certainty replaces doubt. I've been on college campuses before. NYU sits in the middle of the goddamn city, after all. But this isn't a cluster of buildings crammed into Manhattan, it's an entire city itself. Thick, wrought iron gates open to University Drive, and overhead, oak trees form a canopy of shade as dappled, emerald light dances off the hood of our white Mazda.

"This is the oldest remaining stone street in the city," Francie informs. She's been devouring every bit of information she can scrounge up on this place. She sighs, drumming her long, brown fingers on the steering wheel. "I'm jealous."

"Of what? The shitty road? It hurts my balls."

Her smile wilts at the corners of her mouth and she casts *that* look at me—the one that says my attitude is not appreciated. I've flattened her mood, one skill I'm particularly adept at: hurting good people. It must be genetic. My piece of shit father was the master of it.

"It's nice," I say, trying to muster up some enthusiasm. The stone street really does hurt my junk. I wonder what kind of sick fuck decided to keep that delightful bit of history around.

"With that enthusiastic endorsement," she says with a groan. I can hear it in her voice. She can't wait to get rid of me.

"You could have just kicked me out," I mutter. It would have been easier. I had friends in New York that I could squat with. I ignore the hollowness inside me. It started as an ache then formed a pit when we reached the Pennsylvania border. By the time we reached Tennessee, I was nothing—just a void.

"Why would you think that?" she asks quietly. For a second, I think she's read my mind. Francie's freaky like that. Then I realize, she's responding to what I said.

Why did I say that? I don't know? Because she packed up all my stuff, shoved it in the trunk, and plans to drop me nearly a thousand miles away? Just a guess. The easiest way to solve a problem was to get rid of it. That wasn't what was really bugging me though. It was how she'd gone about it. Forcing me to take the harder classes, making me sign up for the entrance exams, paying for my applications—she didn't want to simply be done with me. Francie doesn't solve problems like I do. She fixes people.

She's too blind to see that I'm a lost cause, and fuck if she's not going to pay for that mistake. I'd seen how much Valmont University cost. "You aren't obligated…"

"Like hell I'm not. If your"—she cuts herself off. Whenever she's tempted to talk about my family she stops herself. It's her rule—never speak ill of your family. She told me about it when we first met. I was allowed to resent them, be angry at them, even hate them, but she drew the line at trash talk.

Words become actions, she'd tell me.

I know a thing or two about that.

Valmont University looks like the brochure. Large oak trees line the road that winds past the main campus. We pass building after building named after what I'm assuming were old white guys with deep pockets. Beauford Hall. MacLaine School of Journalism. Eaton Library, across from which a smaller, brick building sits: Tennyson Hall. The home for the English department is named after a famous poet. Go figure. There's no money in books. Past the ivy-clad halls, the largest building of all reigns over the others. A sign post pointing in its direction declares it the West Student Union. Students spill from each building we pass, bags slung over their shoulders. Classes don't start for another week. I wonder what its like to be so fucking eager to learn that you're walking around on the first day with your books already. It's all a little too perfect. I guess a college is always selling some version of ideal—the ideal campus, the ideal career, the ideal future.

"Greek row is down there." Francie jerks her thumb in the opposite direction.

"So?" The location of the university's fraternities and sororities is so low on my list of interests it's practically off the list entirely. If I'm being honest, I don't mind knowing where the sororities are. That's useful information. I just don't see why she's pointing it out.

"You could rush. It would be a way to meet friends."

I raise an eyebrow, biting back more commentary. She won't appreciate it. I know she's just trying to help but sometimes I think Francie has lost her mind. "I'm not really the frat type."

That's the nice way to put it. I had a group I ran with back in New York, but even my best friends didn't qualify as brothers. I'd be a brother once I knew it was more than a secret handshake and keg access on the weekends.

The residence halls are outside the main campus. Cars are parallel parked in front of every dormitory despite signs declaring *Fire Lane: Violators will be towed*. The curbs are so tightly packed we can't find a single space near my building.

"We're going to have to hoof it," Francie announces wearily after we circle it twice. "I'm glad you don't have much to carry."

I shrug. That's an understatement. When she finally pulls into a spot at least a quarter of a mile from the closest dorm, I jump out of the Mazda and pop open the trunk. My whole life fits in the compartment. I didn't come to Francie with much —just the clothes on my back and a bruised left eye. I'm not leaving her with much either. Grabbing one of the two boxes to my name, I swivel to find her watching me. Tears stream down her face.

Francie doesn't look a thing like my mother. At least, not as far as I can remember. My memories of my mother exist in shades of black, white, and red. They're ugly and harsh. Her face is the only beautiful part of them. Pale with luminous eyes and ink-black hair that fell silkily over my face when she would bend to kiss me. Francie's dark skin and riotous curls are as far from my mom as possible. But for one second, I see my mother looking back at me. I hate what I see shining in Francie's eyes:

Pride.

I've done nothing to deserve it—from either of them. Shifting uncomfortably, I zero in on the dorm at the top of the hill.

"I don't have all day." I hope I sound bored. Disinterested. Anything to get her out of here faster. She's done her part, fulfilled the role the state gave her years ago. She doesn't have to keep at it. The sooner she leaves, the better it will be for both of us.

"You have all week," she reminds me, falling into step beside me, the other box in her arms. "Orientation starts tomorrow according to the email I got. There's going to be fun icebreakers and…"

She rattles off a list of activities that she knows I won't bother with. I have a schedule and a map. There's no way I'm going to sit through whatever fun-filled activities they're hocking to parents. Instead I focus on navigating the gauntlet of idiots crowding the sidewalks. Everywhere I turn a mom is sobbing and clutching an uncomfortable teen. A few dads watch these embraces with equivalent discomfort, their eyes darting to the street and their illegally parked vehicles. A long-ignored emotion wells in my chest but I shake it off.

"This is it," Francie says brightly.

"Thank God you were here. I would have kept walking." I shift the weight of the box to my left knee as I try to reach for the door handle, but I lose my grip in the process. The box falls to the sidewalk as the door swings open. The guys coming through it jump out of the way. Cold, gray eyes glare at me.

"Watch it," a dark-haired guy barks. He's wearing a worn Ramones t-shirt and jeans I suspect cost more than the total value of the contents of the box at his feet.

Anger bubbles inside me and I open my mouth to release it. Before I can, his friend punches him in the shoulder.

"Don't be a dick." He rolls his eyes as he bends to retrieve the fallen box. "Let me help you, man."

"Thank you." Francie sounds a bit too enthused and I wonder if its because she expects Southern politeness or because he's good-looking. I hope the flush on her cheeks has more to do with hauling a box up that hill. Her attitude cools when she glances to the other man even though he's equally handsome, I guess. Much older men had frozen under that icy stare, but if it bothers him it doesn't show.

"Money," the one who picked up the box addresses him with the bizarre nickname, "what have we discussed about being around other humans?"

"Now who's being a dick, Eaton," he bites out, but he lifts the box Francie is carrying from her arms.

Eaton. Now that sounds familiar but before I can place the name, Francie says, "There's the Southern hospitality I expected. Thank you, *gentlemen*."

I cringe at Francie's emphasis on the final word. It's a typical move on her part. I've deemed them calls to action. She doesn't believe either of these assholes are gentlemen, but that won't stop her from forcing them to act like ones.

"What room?" The nice one asks, holding open the door.

"226," I mutter, wishing they wouldn't accompany us farther. I don't need Francie trying to impose etiquette lessons on my peers, even if they need them.

He exchanges a look with his friend. "Mystery solved."

"I tried to tell you," the other says with bleak amusement as he passes the entrance.

Francie caves to curiosity before I do. "What mystery?"

"I'm in 226, too. We're roommates. Cyrus," he says. He sticks his hand out and I carefully shake it around the box.

"Sterling," I introduce myself. "And this is Francie."

"That's Montgomery. We call him Money," he continues.

I don't want to know why.

Cyrus studies me with more interest now. I know what he sees: a threadbare t-shirt that was once black, old ripped jeans that are a bit too loose on the hips, and the poor kid wearing them. Francie bought me some new clothes before we left, but she hadn't been able to afford much. Compared to him, we're total opposites other than our height. My black hair is an untidy mess from hours in the car. He's combed his blond hair into artful submission. I hadn't bothered to shave the last two days and dark stubble itches along my jawline. He's clean-shaven, highlighting aristocratic cheekbones. His near-onyx eyes are his only dark feature just like my blue eyes are unusually bright. Unlike the rest of us, he isn't dressed casually. He's wearing tailored pants and a button-down shirt. He doesn't look like a college kid. He looks like a CEO.

"You're staying in the dorms?" Surprise flashes across Francie's face. I can't blame her.

"His father is teaching him a lesson," his friend says and I can hear the sneer in his voice as he leads us toward a stairwell.

"He wants me to have the typical college experience." If he's bothered by this teachable moment, he doesn't show it.

I take the steps two at a time, ready to get this over with. It's bad enough that my roommate is clearly rich and privileged. Now I've inherited his jackass buddy, too. As soon as Francie is gone I can look into a different room.

"He wants to torture you," Montgomery corrects him.

"It's no big deal," Cyrus says. "I'll probably crash at the house after rush week."

Yet another reason to avoid Greek row. Cyrus is okay, but I'd bet money most of the frat members are more like his friend. With any luck, they won't be around much. He might be nice, but if his dad's idea of a life lesson was doing something average like living in a dorm room, I expected we didn't have much in common. My own dad didn't even know I was in another state starting school. He didn't deserve to know. Yeah, I was nothing like either of these guys.

Our dorm room is the definition of average. Cinder block walls painted a sickly neutral beige and cold tiled floors, probably brimming with asbestos greet me, from under the edges of an expensive rug. One bed is already made up—a bit too neatly—and there are no boxes in sight. Either my new roommate is seriously OCD or his mom has been here.

"Magda chose the bed closer to the window. I hope you don't mind. She said it was better for circulation." He shrugs like he doesn't buy it or care.

"Is Magda your girlfriend?" Francie asks.

He blinks, temporarily confused, but Montgomery laughs, dropping the box carelessly to the hard floor. "Magda is his maid. Daddy might be forcing him to slum it, but even he's not that cruel."

Withholding the help is punishment to my new acquaintances. Where has Francie sent me? Hell?

"I hope you don't mind," Cyrus looks genuinely concerned and I wonder if it's because now I know he has a maid or if it's because he'd rather jump out the open window than continue this awkward introduction. He looks between me and Francie and back to my boxes. "Do you have more? We can help."

Montgomery flinches at being volunteered but he doesn't speak.

"That's it," I say, trying to sound like I don't care that all my worldly possessions fit into two boxes while my roommate's maid has already unpacked his and made his bed for him. I'd known I would feel like I was in a different world when I'd accepted the Valmont scholarship.

"Let's grab a bite," Cyrus suggests to his friend. "We'll let you get settled."

"It won't take long," Montgomery mutters.

I can tell him and I are going to be close—close to killing each other. I keep this thought to myself. Francie doesn't need to leave her worried that I'm going to be fighting the first opportunity I get. But I suspect I'll be delivering a welcoming right hook to Montgomery's face sooner rather than later. When they take off, I relax. I hope Cyrus is right and he winds up going Greek.

Francie seems to read my mind. "Maybe you should check out this house your roommate is pledging. He seems kind."

He seems *tolerant*—at best. I want to tell her that guys like Cyrus and Montgomery and guys like me don't have anything in common. From their bank accounts to their problems, we live in very different worlds. But when I turn to her and see the hope written across her face, I swallow it all down.

"I'll consider it," I lie.

The door to the dormitory opens and Cyrus strides in grinning apologetically. "Forgot my ID."

"He's not used to paying for things." Montgomery leans against the doorway, a wolfish grin taking up residence on his face. He knows what he's doing. He's not going to establish dominance over me, but he'll make sure I know how far beneath them both I am. "Just drop your last name, Cy. You don't need money."

"Shut up," Cyrus orders him as he digs in his top drawer.

"Come on." A pale hand appears on his arm, tugging at it. The owner of it comes into view slowly. Slender arms, dusted with freckles flow into a willowy body clad in a short, summer dress that showcases long legs. She's dressed for the heat, but despite that her cheeks glisten pink with a slight sheen of sweat. Strawberry blonde curls tumble over her shoulders. She looks over to me, her emerald gaze sparkling intensely. One second is all it takes. She takes me apart with those green eyes, studies the pieces, and then turns to Cyrus. "I have things to do. Can we get going?"

Cyrus doesn't introduce us. He grabs the ID card and heads toward the door. It swings closed between me and his world—his friends. Then it cracks back open and his head pops through. "Party tonight at the Beta Psi house. You in?"

My thoughts flash to the girl. I want to ask if she'll be there. I have no idea what she saw inside me, but I want to know. "Sure."

He leaves without giving me more details. Already I'm reconsidering. There's no way to know if she'll be there and if it comes down to spending more time with *Montgomery*, I think I'd rather drink Clorox.

Beside me Francie is practically vibrating with excitement. She doesn't need to know going to the party is a gamble that the girl will be there. I don't need her obsessing over that factoid. It's bad enough that she heard me make the plans.

I start to tell her that I've changed my mind, but her face is lit up like I've just handed her a winning lottery ticket. "Promise me you'll go to the party."

There's no goddamn way out of that, and she knows it. My past is a collection of broken promises. If she asks me to give her my word, I have to choices: refuse or keep my promise. I won't make a promise and not keep it.

"Fine," I agree. It's one party.

"Don't isolate yourself," she says. "This is a chance to be anyone you want to be."

"Like myself?" I ask dryly. But we both know the truth. About who I am. About who I was born to be. Violence is written in my DNA. Dragging me a thousand miles from home won't erase my past, and it won't change my future. A girl who runs with rich boys isn't going to be interested in me. Not for long, anyway. Some truths are inescapable. I was born a bastard. There's no changing that.

5

ADAIR

Frat houses smell like someone is trying to mask dirty laundry and stale beer with bad body spray. It doesn't help that the ground level of the Beta Psi house is packed with undergrads all suffering from various degrees of intoxication. My own cup remains untouched. Cheap beer tapped by a guy wearing his clothes inside out isn't exactly my poison. But the red cup is like a security blanket, a sign that I belong here. Well, not here exactly. Not in a frat house. But at college—at Valmont. With the Solo cup in my hand, I'm just an average freshman. As long as no one asks my last name, that is.

"It's so big," a wobbling brunette squeals, clutching my arm as she passes and spilling some of my drink. "I've never been in a house so big."

"Thanks for clearing that up," I yell over the crowd, swiping at the beer on my dress, but she's already gone. My mind hadn't exactly jumped to the size of the house when she spoke. To me, the Beta Psi house isn't that big. Of course, it might feel a bit more cramped with hundreds of bodies crammed into it.

She did no favors for my outfit, a bodycon dress that

wraps slinkily around my shoulders and hips. Thankfully the bright floral print masks the spill, but I doubt beer and silk are a good match. I groan as I realize my feet are wet. My red sandals boast a four-inch heel, delicate criss-crossing straps and absolutely no protection for my toes. My first official college party is off to a fantastic start. I don't know why I expected it to be different from when I crashed them with my prep friends. I'd hoped it would feel like I'd crossed a bridge, moving from one point in my life to the next.

Except it's all the same.

Maybe it always will be. I'd wanted to leave Tennessee for college. I had even defied my father and applied to several schools on the East Coast. When I'd gotten in, he'd played his own card: I attended his alma mater or he didn't pay. There was no way I would qualify for financial aid. He had known the whole time. Mom had tried to reason with him, but Angus MacLaine gets what he wants, especially where family is concerned. Now I'm stuck here, doing exactly what I was doing last year. I don't even get to live in the dorms.

I have to clean this up, because I can't handle having wet feet. Bypassing the living room and its walnut paneled walls, complete with a half dozen couples procreating against them, I head toward the stairs. There's a bathroom down here, but the line will be too long. There's another one next to Montgomery's room. On the few occasions when I've been dragged here before, his sister, Ava, and I have snuck up to use it. I have no idea where she is now. I've lost her to the crowd along with my best friend. I wonder if I made a mistake not rooming with Poppy when she asked. Not that I had a choice. But I can't help feeling like Ava and Poppy are leaving me out.

The second and third floors of the Beta Psi house don't pretend to be civilized like the main floor. There's no tastefully upholstered furniture, no framed portrait of famous alumni, no polished wood. As soon as my hand slips from the walnut railing and I step into the hallway, I'm in a different world entirely. The faint scent of aftershave, sweat, and pot lingers in the air. Empty bottles clutter the floor, and there's a hole where someone has clearly punched the wall. I can't imagine what it would be like if they didn't have a full time housekeeper. I feel sorry for the poor woman who has to put up with these boys. I step over a passed out guy slumped next to a door but instantly feel bad.

Bending I check to make sure he's breathing.

"He's alive," a deep voice startles me with the announcement, and I press a hand to my chest. Then *he* steps from the shadows. It takes me a moment to place him because he doesn't belong here—and knowing how snobby Montgomery is he won't be invited to join. I don't know Cyrus's roommate. We haven't even been introduced yet, and he already nearly scared me to death.

"What are you doing up here?" I snap defensively. I realize how it sounds too late.

His eyes narrow. Washed out by the dim hallway light, they look silver. Even blanched near colorless, they're bright—and burning with hatred. It steals my breath and I scramble to collect myself. Overreact much? But it's harder to appear poised in his presence. I'd glimpsed him earlier and liked what I saw. Now? *Wow* doesn't quite cover it. His black hair sweeps over his forehead, artfully unkempt. He's wearing the same old t-shirt and jeans from earlier today along with a scowl. He clearly doesn't care to impress anyone.

"I have more of a right to be here than you do." He shoves his hands in his pockets and leans against the wall.

"Is that so?" I challenge, my heartbeat ticking up. Who does he think is? "Why is that?"

"Necessary equipment."

That catches me off-guard. I stare blankly at him. "Huh?"

He snorts before gesturing to his crotch.

Oh.

"That qualifies you to wander around a frat you don't belong to?" I shake my head, hoping that it's dark enough that he can't spy the heat staining my cheeks. I feel them burning with a mixture of embarrassment and rage.

"I was invited," he says stiffly.

I've struck a nerve. I should stop. Instead, I dig the needle in farther. "That doesn't mean you belong."

A low rumble vibrates from him. His body, now rigid, ripples with effort as he tries to suppress it, succeeding only in making his muscles strain against the thin fabric of his shirt. Plenty of guys I went to school with were athletes. In our circle, appearance is as important as the balance of your bank account. None of the guys I know look like this. There's something feral about him, a savagery that peeks out of those angry eyes that's only intensified by his large body.

"You think you're better than me? That you can play the spitfire and look badass? Because I see right through you," he bites out. "Daddy's lucky little princess born sucking on a silver spoon."

The words slice me open and now he's not the one who's struck a nerve—not like me—he's split me open, gutted me. Somehow this total stranger has found my weakest point. I don't want it to be true. I can't deny that it is. Being at Valmont is proof of that. I didn't go off to school. I didn't have anywhere better to be tonight than alone at a frat house in expensive, beer-splattered shoes.

There's no way in hell I'm going to let him know that.

"Jealous much?" I plant my hands on my hips like I'm daring him to continue. Why not? I'm already bleeding. He can't do much more damage.

I hope.

He opens his mouth but before he can speak the drunk guy on the floor falls forward and pukes on my feet. I jump back, a scream escaping me as the hot sick coats my skin. The night has officially gone from crap to the ninth circle of hell. It can't possibly get worse.

Then he laughs.

I was wrong. My blood boils and now the premature hatred he'd exhibited earlier floods through me. I don't even know his name, but my mind is already imagining a dozen vicious karmic paybacks. Everything from drunk dude getting to his feet only to lose it again all over my companion's perfect face to spreading a rumor that he's packing a cocktail Weiner in his pants. I suspect that one's not true, but he'd deserve it. I would be doing the entire female student body a favor.

I'm not going to do it and the drunk guy isn't going to get up and this dickhead isn't going to get what he deserves. Pushing past him, I head toward the bathroom still fuming.

"You can't say that you didn't have that coming," he calls after me—and he sounds almost… *friendly*? If this is how he makes new friends, he needs a serious lesson in interpersonal skills.

I don't respond. Beelining for the bathroom, I slam the door behind me and lock it. I slump against the wall and inspect the damage to my shoes. It's almost as bad as the damage to the rest of me. He doesn't know me. That should be enough. I haven't exactly put my best foot forward. I grimace thinking of my shoes—or even worse, my feet—again. But he had started it, hadn't he?

I've already suffered a lifetime of people thinking they know me. People assume the MacLaine children haven't worked a day in our lives. All we do is work. Our father's love isn't free. Everything we have cost us something. I'm not spoiled. Not in the way he thinks.

There's something rotten inside me though, and I can't deny it. It shows itself when I least expect it—when I least want it to—and tonight it found a playmate.

I force myself to confront the task at hand. My shoes are ruined. Unstrapping them, I toss them in the garbage before shimmying up my skirt so I can wash my feet under some running water. I consider looking for soap but a college boy's shower will make you lose faith in humanity. How could living creatures be so gross? Sticking my leg carefully into the stall, I turn the knob so I can wash tonight off. The shower head hisses, pipes rumbling, and then cold water shoots directly into my face, my dress, my hair. I try to cover my face with one palm while I search for the knob, half-blinded by the assault. When I finally manage to shut it off, I'm dripping wet. Drenched silk clings to my skin and soaked strands of hair fall limply on my shoulders while water puddles at my feet. Air conditioning blasts from a floor vent making me wet *and cold*.

A fist pounds on the locked door and I freeze.

"You okay in there?" a muffled voice calls.

It's him. That's when I realize that I'd screamed when the water hit me.

"Fine," I bite out through shivers.

"You screamed."

"Go away!" I want to tell him exactly where to go and what he can do when he gets there, but I have bigger problems.

I grab a towel hanging nearby and dry myself, trying hard to ignore its tell-tale mustiness. Swiping at my face and hair, I drop the towel to the ground. Tonight could not get worse.

The mirror proves me wrong on that count. Smudged mascara rings my eyes, my lipstick is smeared at the corners of my mouth—I look like a drowned cat. It takes me a few minutes to wipe the ruined makeup off. Pulling a scrunchie off my wrist, I knot my hair into a messy bun, which is a minor improvement. It's no use trying to save the dress. I need a savior. Someone who will brave the asshole in the hall to rescue me. A knight in shining armor.

I take my phone out to call Poppy, who is way more dependable than a knight, and realize I don't have service.

I'm stuck shoeless and soaked, wanting to shrink into nothing and sneak out of this hellhole. But I'm a MacLaine, so I don't. Who cares about the rude boy in the hall? It would take an act of God to impress him. No one else is going to notice me. They'll be too drunk or trying to get laid. All I have to do is walk out the door. August in Tennessee is hot and sticky. I won't miss my shoes and my dress will be dry by the time Ava or Poppy finds me. I just have to hold out. I think of the drunk guy in the hall, passed out in a pool of his own vomit, and decide things could be worse.

When I crack open the door, I brace myself. Any hope that I might be spared the humiliation of facing him is dashed. He had not gone away as ordered. In fact, he's leaning against the wall, staring at me. His cocky gaze scans me up and down, and then one side of his mouth tugs up. It's the slightest move-ment, but it's enough to push me over the edge.

"Freaking hilarious, isn't it?" I shout. "First, you get me puked on and now I'm soaked."

He straightens up, his eyebrows knitting together. "*I* got you puked on?"

"You didn't stop him." My accusation is as limp as my hair but I put as much conviction behind it as I can muster.

The smirk falls completely off his face replaced by a scowl, which suits him more. "Oh, sorry. I'm fresh out of barf bags."

"You just left him on the floor." This is the hill I die on

apparently. I don't know why it's so important to blame him. It just is. Because he's here and he's infuriating and he *laughed*. Southern boys—even the arrogant, spoiled ones I'd known my whole life—would never do that. If it had been Cyrus or Money or any other local guy here they would have offered their assistance. "You're not a gentleman."

"I'm not a gentleman…" he repeats back the words like they taste funny in his mouth. He steps toward me, his movement sending a rush of cool air around me and I tremble. I tell myself it's from the chill, but I'm not so sure that's true. Closer up, I realize how tall he is. He's got a foot on me at least.

"No." I tip my head up. I will not let him talk down to me. I will not be intimidated.

"How are you getting out of here, Princess?"

"Don't call me that," I say coldly.

"I bet that's what your daddy calls you, isn't it?" He moves until our faces are inches apart. I can smell his cologne—spicy and strong—and mint on his breath. There isn't a trace of alcohol on him. "You're not a lucky princess?"

My father has never called me 'Princess' a day in my life. I force my face into a blank slate—indifferent and disinterested. "What did your daddy call you?" I ask. "Or let me guess, you don't have one? Is that your story?"

There's a crack I don't quite understand, but my body does because I shrink against the wall he's just put his fist through. When he pulls it out of the plaster, it's covered in blood and dust. He shifts forward to press his palms to the wall, ignoring his maimed hand, his strong arms caging me to the spot. I stare at the boy who's just put a hole in the wall. A boy as vicious as my empty words. He's beautiful poison. I want him to stay away. All the warning signs are there. But somewhere deep inside me, I want to take a drink. I'm not sure why. Maybe because I hate myself as much as he hates me. This close I can see his eyes are a blue as bright as a sunny sky but colder than midnight. I'm locked in place, afraid to move. I am a butterfly, fragile wings pinned to the wall, and I don't know if he wants to watch me struggle or if he's going to crush me. I only know I'm at his mercy.

"Don't open books you can't read." The warning is laced with dark roughness. But then his arms fall and he moves away from me. He doesn't look at me when I scramble away from him. I guess a predator always knows where his prey will run.

I'm nearly to the front door when Poppy's British lilt calls my name. I don't stop. I can't. Picking up the pace, which is easy to do barefoot, I race down the front steps, past the front lawn until the sounds of the party fade and night swallows me whole. I turn, half-expecting him to have followed me, but there's no one behind me. The evening air is heavy and humid, filled with distant shouts and cricket song. I'd acted on instinct when I ran. Now, halfway down the block with no shoes on my feet, I feel a little silly. Why had I run out of the party?

I have lived in Valmont my whole life. My friends are at that party. My family name is on more than one building on this campus. *I* belong here—at that party. And to make things worse, I probably scared the shit out of Poppy. Whipping my phone out, I discover I have service and ten missed calls. I feel like screaming, but someone would probably call security, and I don't need the night to end with a visit from the campus police.

But the calls aren't from Poppy. Eight are from my brother, Malcolm. Two from his fiancée. A terrible coldness creeps through my veins. They'd been trying to reach me half the night. The calls are time stamped from about the time I got to the party. I don't know how long I stare at my phone, torn between calling back and waiting for it to ring—dreading both possibilities.

"Adair!" Poppy's panicked voice startles me and I nearly drop the phone.

I owe her an explanation, I think, but as she draws closer, I notice her eyes are wide and frantic.

"I'm sorry," I say quickly. "I just—"

"Your brother is trying to reach you," she cuts me off as more of our friends join us.

Cyrus and Ava and Money.

Even *him*.

Somehow I know what she needs to tell me. I feel it. Out here in the night, away from the chaos of the party, the night is clear and I can see it in her face. I want to tell her not to say it. I want to run again.

I just stand there, vaguely aware of a rock under my bare foot, phone shaking in my hand.

"Your parents," she finally manages.

I shake my head not wanting to hear more. My hands go to my ears as though I can avoid that truth if I block her out.

Poppy takes my hands gingerly in her own before squeezing them tightly. "You need to go to the hospital."

"I don't have a car." Or my purse. Heat stings my eyes and I realize my cheeks are wet.

"I'll drive you," Money says, lurching toward us.

"You're drunk," Poppy accuses. "We're all…"

I look at them, staggered protectively around me, and realize the horrible truth. My friends have been drinking at the party all night—the party at the house with the terrible reception. The reception that kept me from getting the calls from my brother. Oh God.

"I'm not." He steps from the shadows, calm, his eyes cast to the ground.

I open my mouth to say no—that I can't accept a ride

from him—but I can't bring myself to say it. I'm not sure I have a choice.

"Take mine. It's in the student lot." Cyrus tosses a set of keys toward him, and he catches them easily, even in the dark. He really is the only sober one. He's all I have.

I wait for him to laugh and drop the keys. I wait for the cruel boy to come out to play. I'm weak, vulnerable—easily defeated. Instead, he strides forward and grabs my hand like I need an escort.

Poppy bites her lip before throwing her arms around me. "We'll be there soon. Go!"

I don't have the chance to ask her to come with me before I'm being dragged away—away from my old life toward the unknown.

"Where are your shoes?" he barks as we reach the street that leads toward the dormitory parking.

"They were ruined." Someone else answers. I don't recognize my own voice.

He stops and opens his mouth, probably to lecture me on how stupid and frivolous throwing away a pair of shoes is, but he doesn't speak. He studies me for a moment, his face unreadable. What had he said about not being able to read a book? He was right. He's written in a language I don't speak. So I don't expect it when he sweeps me off the ground and into his arms.

"**P**ut me down!" Her fists beat my back and I have to twist to avoid a well-aimed kick. She might be beautiful, but she's hard to like.

"Stop that shit," I order her, "or I'll drop you." I mean it, even if she feels good in my arms, like picking up sunshine—if sunshine had an attitude and too much to drink. This isn't the time to think about that. This girl deserves to have her ass handed to her, or to have her ass meet the cold pavement, at least. Another time.

Earlier, she was being a bitch for no reason. She has a right to be one now. Cyrus told me about the call from her brother. I don't know why I tagged along to find her or why I volunteered to drive her. That's the hazard of staying sober, I'm always cleaning up messes. It's how it was in New York. Why would Valmont be different?

"You shouldn't have picked me up in the first place," she argues, but she stops physically resisting me. Probably because she believes my threat.

Good. It's fucking hot enough in Tennessee without fighting her. My t-shirt is already sticking to me like a second layer of skin. Her body pressing against mine isn't helping. Another time, this might be romantic. Valmont is removed far enough from the city that the stars blink brightly overhead. Flowers perfume the muggy air. I dare a glance at the girl in my arms. She's tucked her chin against her chest. I can't see her eyes. Is she crying? She seemed tough earlier, but she's not standing up to a stranger now. She's facing most people's worst nightmare. I want to tell her that she'll survive it, even if she might not want to, but I keep silent instead. She doesn't care what I think and tonight? She's not going to be okay tonight.

I continue to carry her, knowing I'm way out of my league with this situation. I don't know this girl, let alone this city. Why had I volunteered to drive her? I don't know where I'm going—where the hospital is. Cyrus said they took her parents to Davidson County General. Hopefully, my piece of shit phone can pull up a map. Francie insisted I have a new one before I left but all we could afford was the free option, which is not what anyone would consider new. Now I'm supposed to drive the princess to who-the-fuck-knows-where with it as my guide. We reach the parking lot and I realize I have a bigger, more immediate problem. I have no clue what Cyrus drives. I fumble the key fob, trying to see it in the dark without losing my grip on her and start randomly pressing buttons until a car alarm goes off.

No fucking way. I can't believe anyone in his right mind would give me the keys to that. Then again, all evidence up to this point suggests these people have more money than sense.

She doesn't comment on my method or that it takes me a couple tries to silence the alarm. She doesn't even say anything as I drop her into the passenger seat. Instead, she curls into a ball, tucking her knees against her chest. She doesn't buckle up and I'm not about to fight her on it. Circling around the car, I allow myself a split second to appreciate it: a Jaguar F-Type convertible. This car costs more than I'd make working full-time for five or six years. He had just thrown me keys to a hundred-thousand-dollar sports car without a second thought.

Sliding into the leather seat, I discover there's no ignition. I flip on an overhead light and glare at the steering column, but there's definitely nowhere for a key. I feel her green eyes watching me, still not saying anything. After a second, she leans over to press a button. Her breasts brush my arm sending a jolt of electricity to my dick as the engine roars to life.

"No one drives in New York," I grumble. I don't know what bothers me more: that she had to help me or that my pants are suddenly too tight.

She doesn't respond, and I wonder if I accidentally tripped her mute button.

"I'm just pulling up a map," I explain as I google the hospital. I have no idea why I'm giving her a play-by-play. Maybe because each second that passes in silence is worse than the last. I'm probably the last person she wants around right now. I sure as hell don't want to spend my night like this, but what am I supposed to do? When that girl tracked down Cyrus she was having a full-blown meltdown, and she couldn't find Adair.

That's her name—the girl next to me. The reason I went to the party. The reason I was about to leave the party. I only know it because shit got real. No one questioned me when I told them I'd watched her run out of the house. I left out that she was running away from our argument, and when they went after her, I followed them out of some type of morbid obligation. Why? These people are complete strangers. So far the majority of them appear to be a special breed of asshole. Now I'm playing taxi cab to their Queen Bitch.

Because Francie would expect it from me, even a thousand miles from home. Even if Adair doesn't deserve it.

The map finally loads, and I mutter a curse when it tells me we're half an hour away. This is going to be a long night.

Adair stays quiet as we make our way off campus into the sleepy college town. Porch lights and street lamps illuminate pristine streets dotted by well-kept houses and picket fences. Flowers blossom in every yard. I'd bet money there's a goddamn chicken in every pot. Even the smaller homes whisper privilege. Or maybe it's so far outside my comfort zone that I can't wrap my mind around it. In Queens, people live on top of one another. If you want to see grass you better head to Central Park. Even at this hour, New York is alive with people rushing to parties and jobs and home. Here? It feels like we're the only two people in the world. We don't see another car until we hit the highway.

She continues to watch out her window as I watch the clock. The benefit of the Jaguar is that it's fast. In town, I felt like I'd put it on a leash and it was tugging for freedom. As soon as we hit the freeway, I press the gas and let it loose. I don't have much experience driving. Hell, I don't even have a license, but I'm pretty sure this is the vehicular equivalent of sex.

"Why are you doing this?" she asks so quietly that I almost don't hear her over the beast of an engine.

"Your friends were drunk." She can't argue with that.

Still, she looks puzzled like this isn't the answer she expected. A pained expression crosses her face, her freckled nose scrunching a little as she spits out two words. "Thank you."

Forced gratitude. I don't want it. She doesn't want to give it. I grunt—an acknowledgment of our shared, if obligatory, social niceties. I hope she knows I'm not her knight in shining armor. Just like I know she's no damsel in distress. Help is not salvation. I'm not saving her.

I keep my hands tight on the wheel. "I wasn't drinking."

I'm surprised when she doesn't ask why.

"Neither was I," she murmurs. She doesn't volunteer more information.

Now I find myself wanting to ask *her* why. It feels like I'm trapped in a maze and every path I take is a dead end. We're strangers. I can't even call her a friend. I'd planned to talk to her. She's the reason I'd gone to the party when Cyrus invited me. But my skin started crawling the second I walked inside the frat house. Someone pressed a Solo cup full of beer into my hand and...I'd lost it. I should have walked out the front door. Instead, I headed to the second floor.

Everything went to hell so fast that I still don't know what happened. I don't know why she'd gone upstairs, either. A girl like her probably doesn't hate crowds. I imagine they part for her—that people bow down as she passes. There had been hundreds of people stuffed into that house, drinking and dancing and being generally stupid. That's not my scene.

"I wasn't doing anything wrong." It's out of my mouth before I even know I'm going to say it.

She turns vacant eyes on me. "What?"

Why do I have to bring this up now? "Upstairs. Tonight. I got lost."

It's a stupid lie, but it sounds less dumb than telling her the truth.

"I didn't say you were." She's already lost interest, returning her focus to the view from the window.

"You implied it." All I need is one uppity bitch to decide I'm up to no good. Yeah, I have a scholarship but good things are rarely permanent, in my experience. One wrong move and it's back to New York for me. I wouldn't mind, but it would kill Francie.

"You aren't a member." She says it like this explains her behavior.

"Neither are you."

"You made that point earlier," she says dryly. She squirms in her seat until she's facing me. She relaxes against the door. Her hair fans out over the window glass, glinting red like little sparks in the light of passing cars. "I don't even know who you are."

"I thought Southerners were supposed to be polite," I mutter. If she's going to be rude, I can dish it right back. I might not have much experience with her type or college frats or small-town America, but I'm all stocked up on surliness.

"Where are my manners?" she scoffs with a hollow laugh. "I'm Adair MacLaine and you are?"

"Like the journalism school?" I ask, caught off-guard by her last name.

"And the senator and the media conglomerate," she says sourly.

"Cheer up…" I stop before adding princess again. She's got enough going on. "You're lucky. You'll never have to work a day in your life."

Does she even know how easy she has it? Apparently not if she's going to sulk about having a last name that's so important it's carved into stone on a two-hundred-year old university building.

"And you think I want that?" Anger flashes in her face, her cheeks flaming as brightly as her hair. It's the second time tonight that I've made her blush. Now I know two ways to get a rise out of her.

I like it a little too much, so I egg her on. "A little."

"You don't know me at all." The ferocity in her tone says she means it.

"No, I don't," I admit, deciding that given the circumstances I should play nice. "I'm Sterling."

She doesn't respond.

"Sterling Ford," I add.

No response.

So now we're back to not speaking to each other. I'm being punished. At least I've taken her mind off where we're heading, even if I've replaced worry with fury. My eyes skim over her reflection in the rearview mirror so she won't know I'm looking at her. That's when I notice her lower lip is trembling. Maybe I haven't distracted her as much as I thought. "Adair." I try her name out and find I like how it feels on my tongue. "Look, I'm sorry I was a jerk."

"Was?" she repeats.

I can't argue with that, but I'm not going to explain myself. She's behaved just as poorly as I have. She might have a get-out-of-jail-free card but that's not enough to excuse her every sin. She jumped to conclusions earlier. She says she doesn't want her family name but she still acts like I'm beneath her. So, yeah, I can be nice. For now. The circumstances require it. But I'm reserving final judgment on Adair MacLaine.

"Thank you." This time her gratitude is small and tinged with apprehension instead of being forced.

"It's no problem." I wonder if she's thanking me for driving or for talking to her. The truth is I don't know how to distract her, because there are things I should say to her before we get to the hospital. I should tell her that it's going to suck — walking into the hospital. I should warn her that there's no way to brace herself for the possibility that her life might change forever tonight. An ache I haven't felt in a long time settles on my chest.

For a split second, I consider turning the car around and

driving in the opposite direction. Driving until she's so far away from here she forgets where we were headed. I want to give her the beautiful oblivion no one gave me.

Instead, I lie to her. "It's going to be okay."

This pries her attention away from the world outside. Adair shoots me a disbelieving look. Can she hear the lie? Does she already know what's waiting for her?

I think deep down you always know.

I search for some topic of conversation that can take her mind away from the worry.

"Did you grow up here?" *Way to go, Sterling. What an original subject.*

Disbelief turns to mild annoyance, but whether it's because she wants to take her mind off things, too, or because she actually can be polite, she answers, "All my life." She's not happy about it. There's a grudging moment of silence before she asks, "You?"

Valmont strikes me as the kind of place where everyone knows everybody. She has to know I'm not from around here. Then again, maybe she's never spent time with the lower classes of humanity.

"I was born in New York." I don't want this to turn into talking about me.

"And you grew up there?" The question rises from her. Until now every sentence she's uttered has been flat and lifeless. Not this one. It curves and peaks into interest.

"Yeah." *Fuck.* I don't want to talk about my past, but here I am opening a door I'd rather keep shut.

"Why did you come here?"

"That's a long story." She waits for me to tell it. I change the subject instead. "What are you going to study?"

First day of college and I'm already falling back on clichés.

Now I know why people resort to them: it's safer to talk about nothing than face real questions.

"I don't know." She shrugs, her attention fading back to the night outside. I'm losing her again. It doesn't matter. I'm not going to martyr myself to divert her from thinking about her parents.

"What do you like?" Apparently, I *am* going to keep trying to force small talk.

"What are you? A shrink?" She sighs like I'm burdening her with my presence.

"I was just asking." Annoyance surges through me. Why does she make it so hard to like her? She's gorgeous. Obviously, she's rich, given her last name is on a freaking building. She grew up in Perfectville, USA. What does she have to be angry about? A shrink is exactly what she needs to deal with the crazy bitch inside her.

"Fine." Her answer catches me by surprise. "English, maybe."

"Like books?" I ask.

"Like books," she repeats like she's talking to a toddler.

"What's your favorite book?"

She pauses. "That's a very personal question."

"That's not an answer," I say.

"What if I don't have one?" She might be playing coy, but she isn't thinking about her parents, so I move this over to the win column.

"You want to study English but you don't have a favorite book?" I'll goad her into answering.

"I didn't say I don't have a favorite book," she hedges. "I said what if I didn't."

She likes to play games. That much is clear. Well, little princess, you might be a player, but I'm the coach. I didn't survive seven years in the foster care system by following rules.

"No favorite book? I'd say you're going to be a shitty English major."

Something incredible happens. Her head tilts back, auburn hair spilling across the supple leather seat, her mouth opens and she laughs. It's a rainbow after a storm. It's bird song on a spring day. It's a beautiful sound. "I probably will be anyway."

"I bet you could get by if you focus on finding a favorite book."

"I don't think I have just one," she says honestly.

Now we're getting somewhere.

"If you had to tell me to read one book, what would it be?" I ask.

"*Harry Potter*." She's dead serious.

It's really too bad she's such a bitch.

"Read it." I tap the steering wheel. "Suggest something I haven't read."

"*Pride and Prejudice*," she says smugly.

"Read it." This time I smile.

"You have?"

I glare over at her incredulous look. "Does that surprise you?"

"Yeah," she admits. "You don't seem the type."

"What type do I seem?" A siren goes off in my brain. We're closing in on dangerous territory. Do I really want to know what a girl like her thinks about me? She doesn't strike me as the type to spare my feelings.

"Do you really want me to answer that?" She crosses her arms over her chest, which draws my attention to her breasts.

Not that my attention has ever really wavered from them. Not entirely. Not with her wearing that dress. It doesn't matter how she treats me. It doesn't matter that I'm driving her to a hospital. It doesn't matter that she's clearly a spoiled brat. I can't turn off my awareness of her. In the cramped cabin of the vehicle, it's probably impossible. Not with the air conditioning blowing her perfume in my face. She smells like magnolia blossoms, freshly peeled oranges, possibilities. Intoxicating. Tempting. It calls to me. I want to taste her. I imagine burying my face between her tits and drinking her in.

"Not the type that reads books," she continues finally, killing my fantasy.

And that's what she thinks of me.

"Did you think I got to college because of my looks?" I ask.

"Well, it wasn't because of your charm." She shakes her head. She seems to realize she's offended me, because she quickly adds, "Most guys I know haven't read anything besides what's assigned in school. Actually, they don't read that either."

"I like books," I confess.

"Even Jane Austen?" She still doesn't believe me.

"The more I see of the world, the more I am dissatisfied with it," I quote.

"And you memorized it?"

Is it just me or does she sound a bit impressed? "I remember bits that strike me."

"And that struck you?"

"I can relate to that sentiment." I'm not about to explain why.

Her mouth hangs open for a minute before she shuts it. She wants to ask why. Maybe she's scared of my answer.

Now she's learning.

This is how it should be between us. Shallow and meaningless and utilitarian. I drive her to the hospital. I distract her. We stumble into each other's circle on occasion. More than that? No way. Adair MacLaine is money. I'm only here because someone like her pays full tuition. I'm the charity case. She's the debutante. It's as simple as that.

A green highway sign reads Davidson General. Its arrow points ominously at the off-ramp. I glance over to find Adair staring at it, too. This is the end of small talk and polite conversation. Her eyes shift to the floorboard and linger there.

"I don't have shoes," she says quietly.

I hear what she's really saying. She isn't ready.

"It's going to be fine," I tell her. It's a lie. What is it about her that makes me want to pretend like life doesn't suck? Like the world isn't one big disappointment after another?

"Promise?" She turns wide, round eyes on me.

"I never make promises," I say quietly. Promises are too easy to break even when you don't mean to. I'd rather lie than break a promise.

"Please?" The request is so small, so desperate that all my reasons go out the window.

I know I'll never be able to keep it, but I say it anyway. "Promise."

Davidson General is packed considering it's nearly midnight. It's the first sign that Nashville might be a real city, after all. A dozen or so people wait in uncomfortable chairs under harsh fluorescent lights for their turn to be seen. The hospital smells like bleach and hopelessness, as though it's been scrubbed free of not just germs but life altogether. I consider offering to carry Adair again but I know she'd never allow it. Still, I can't help but stare at her bare feet as she makes her way across the linoleum floor to the help desk.

"I'm here for the MacLaines," she tells them. "My brother… called me."

The crack in her voice breaks me open and it's all I can do to barricade the memories threatening to flood from me.

"There should be information soon." The woman doesn't look up from her files. Business as usual. "Have a seat."

Adair pauses and I expect her to unleash unholy fury upon her. She doesn't. Instead, she starts toward a bank of blue plastic chairs.

"Where's your brother?" I ask, joining her.

"D.C." A hysterical edge taints her words. "He's interning for Senator Woolritch. He lives there with his fiancée."

I didn't expect this. I thought she had someone waiting for her. But she's alone, left to wait for answers. How long will that take? Minutes? Hours?

"He's getting the first flight out," she explains.

"I'll stay with you," I say, surprising both of us.

"You don't have to do that. Poppy texted. She's on the way with…"

I stop listening. Her friends are sobering up. She doesn't need me, and I can't blame her. But it chafes a bit, especially since I can't leave until they get here. "Then I'll wait until she gets here."

Indecision races over her face before her expression settles into a mask of indifference. "Suit yourself."

Fine. It's easier than pretending or making small talk. I can sit here and ignore her. In the chairs across from us a woman cradles a toddler, murmuring things we can't hear before kissing his forehead. She brushes his downy hair from his eyes and begins to hum softly. Adair watches them with hungry eyes like all she wants is to climb into the mother's lap and be small and safe again. My arm's around her before I consider what I'm doing. I stiffen, expecting her to slap me or jerk away, but she settles against me. I breathe in her scent, but I don't let myself kiss her forehead. I don't know where the boundaries are between us. We're racing too fast into unknown territory. I can't afford to cross the line.

"What if..." She doesn't finish the thought.

I don't need her to. This is nothing more than survival for her.

"Close your eyes," I command her. "Take a nap. When you wake up, everything will be fine."

She peeks up at me from behind thick, black lashes. "Promise?"

I sell my soul for a second time, hoping it's not a lie, and nod.

A gentle hand shakes me, and I startle to find tired eyes staring down at me. Deep lines etch the man's face but he wears a comfortable smile.

"Son?" His accent is so thick it takes a second for me to process. He presses a finger to his lips, nodding down.

Adair is tucked against me. Her chest rises and falls with a gentle tempo. We'd fallen asleep. I have no idea how long we've been here.

"Has there been any news?" he asks.

I shake my head, wondering who he is. He can't be her father. Or brother. There's no way we've been asleep long enough for him to reach us. Plus, this guy is too old. Maybe he's her grandpa?

"We're here now. You can leave," he says.

His tone is gentle, but I have to resist the urge to tell him to fuck off. I'm not leaving her here with some stranger. Then I realize he said *we're here.* That's when I spot Cyrus and the girl from earlier. My roommate is a disheveled mess, his shirt half-tucked, hair wild. The girl's dark eyes are rimmed red like she's been crying. Cyrus has his arm around her. Tension hangs in the air. They're all here waiting to be whatever Adair needs. My temporary position is no longer required. I should feel grateful to be done with it. I didn't sign up for any of this. I've been in Valmont less than twenty-four hours. I haven't even unpacked my two boxes. I don't require more baggage.

I don't drive Jaguars or have buildings named after my family or get off on being a dickhead frat guy. I'm not part of this world. I don't want to be. I did them a favor. I put up with her for a few hours. Tomorrow, she'll be back to treat me like a bug under her impractical shoes.

Without thinking I look down to her feet, remembering what happened to those stupid shoes.

The old man follows my gaze. "Where are her shoes?"

That's a long story and not my problem, I remind myself. I didn't puke on her shoes. I didn't force her to run away in bare feet. I tell myself she isn't my problem but when I pry my arm from under her sleeping form, her eyes flutter open and for one brief second she sees my face and smiles. I'm pretty sure I know what the earth felt the first morning the sun rose. The smile vanishes instantly. She bolts up, spots the old man and dives into his arms. I watch as she falls apart. I was just a bit of glue to hold her together until she felt safe enough to fall to pieces.

Cyrus stops me at the emergency room's automatic doors.

"Thank you for doing this, man." He claps a hand on my shoulder as the doors slide open and shut and open again behind us.

That's when it occurs to me that I have the keys to his car. I dig into my pocket to find them. Noticing the charge nurse glaring at me, I step to the side to stop triggering the doors.

Cyrus glances at the others. "That's Poppy. We all went to school together. Felix drove us. He's like her dad."

Adair had been expecting Poppy. Of course, she'd needed a ride. That's where Felix came in, I assume. So, he's not family.

Not officially. I think of Francie. I understand better than most what it's like to have a surrogate parent. What I don't get is why. Adair MacLaine has everything. Money. Two parents. Probably a huge fucking mansion somewhere with gargoyles and ivy. Why does a girl like her need a second father? "I thought maybe it was her grandfather."

The age is about right.

"He's her butler," he says meaningfully. Unfortunately, I'm not fluent in trust fund. "Her grandfather lives in the city."

And I can't help but notice he's not here. I'm too tired to try to figure any of them out.

"We got this," Cyrus continues. "You don't have to stick around."

He's probably wondering why I stayed at all. I wonder if he waited for me to drive the car back to campus. I thrust the keys toward him.

Cyrus holds up his hand. "You need to get back. Drive my car. I can call a service if we need a ride."

A service? Not a taxi or a friend. The gap between us widens again. What happens when you fall in? Do they call someone for help or just scratch their heads? Maybe I'm being unfair. He's here. They seem tight—all of them.

"I'll park it where I found it," I offer. He shakes my hand and I half-expect him to thank me for my service.

Dawn breaks over the horizon as I make my way to Cyrus's car. The morning sun paints the sky in shades of purple. The Jaguar waits under the fading parking lot lamp. In the light of day driving it feels like a lie. Or, at least, a joke. I'm sitting in a seat that costs more than I have ever had in my bank account.

I don't make it out of the lot before I decide I need coffee. Cyrus may not mind me driving his car, but he'll probably care if I crash it. This close to a hospital it doesn't take long to find a Starbucks. The line wraps around the building, and when I finally pull to the window, the barista practically falls out the window trying to look at the car. She's pretty, her brunette hair twisted into a knot on top of her head and her lips painted bubblegum pink. I could score her number without even trying. This must be what it's like to have money. People stare. People covet. I consider telling her that I know what it's like to want something you'll never have. I consider telling her this isn't my ride—this isn't my life. Instead, I let her think what she wants and enjoy how it feels. I take my small black coffee, but I don't ask for her number. Instead, I ask her to point me toward a shop. She twists her headset away from her mouth as she gives me directions to a Target. I tip her more than the cost of the drink.

By the time I arrive at the store, I already regret dropping so much money on coffee. There's a couple hundred in my bank account—the result of a summer spent saving with Francie's help—and once it's gone…

I feel especially stupid since I'm already buying something else. Twenty-four hours on my own and I'm dipping into my account twice. There's no choice, though. I think of Adair's bare feet and the cold, tile floor. I head straight to the shoe section, find the cheapest, largest pair of flip flops, so they'll be sure to fit, and buy them before I can pussy out.

At the hospital, Adair is tucked into a corner surrounded by even more people. It looks like she's holding court. Felix the butler hovers nearby watching over them all like a shepherd tending a flock. There's no way I'm walking up to an entire crowd to give their queen bee a two dollar pair of flip-flops. But even from here I can see her bare feet, and I already bought the damn things. It takes a second, but I manage to get Cyrus's attention. He looks even worse than he had an hour ago. The hangover is clearly setting in.

He ambles over, bleary-eyed, and cranes to look out the glass doors. "Is something wrong? The car?"

The booze is wearing off and with it his laissez-faire attitude regarding his car. I can't exactly blame him.

I shove the plastic bag in his hands, muttering, "Car's fine. Give her these."

"Give her what?" Adair asks, coming up behind him. She grabs the bag and peeks inside. She looks up at me, her face a mask of stone. I don't know what she's thinking. I want to crack her open. I want to study her pages, run my fingers down her spine, unravel her word by word. I think she could be my favorite book if I could only read her.

Her teeth sink into her lower lip like she doesn't know what to say. She glances over her shoulder at her friends and back to me.

"You don't have to thank me," I say softly. Another day I'll figure her out. For now, this is enough.

The puzzled indifference shifts not into the vulnerable, scared girl I expect but to an ice queen. Her green eyes glitter like cold emeralds as cold and beautiful as the icy look she now wears.

"You can go," she dismisses me.

I give her a moment—a chance to be the girl in the car who told me to read Harry Potter, the girl who needed me to promise everything would be okay. She groans, rolling her eyes to Cyrus, who's watching us without commentary.

"May I, Your Highness?" I bow to her, sweeping my arm at the waist and flashing her my middle finger.

"I don't know why you think I want these." She holds up the bag. "Or, for that matter, you."

"Of course, you don't," I bite out, funneling my humiliation into rage. "You have a whole herd of sheep to admire and serve you."

I was a means to an end. One she doesn't need anymore. I'm a single-serving friend. She used me and now she's throwing me away. It's the story of my life.

Adair snorts, shrugging her delicate shoulders. She's an illusion. There's nothing weak or fragile about her. No warmth radiates from her. There's no light in her smile now.

"Adair!" Someone calls her name. Neither of us turn to see who it is. We just glare at one another, an invisible, dividing line being drawn between us. Her name is called again and finally, she turns and my gaze follows. A doctor waits by Felix, stripping his gloves off, his eyes cast to the floor.

For a second, her act slips and fear flits across her face. That's the girl whose smile felt like the sun shining on me. She's two people, and I have no clue which one is the real Adair MacLaine. I get my answer when she squares her shoulders and marches toward the doctor without another word.

"Look, Sterling. She's just—" Cyrus begins but I shake my head in disgust.

"Don't apologize for her," I warn him, mustering a weary smile. None of this is his fault. "I'll get the car back to campus in one piece. See you later."

He nods, looking relieved to be off the hook for her behavior. A startled cry rises across the room and Cyrus rushes away. It's not my business what the doctor came to tell her. I resist the urge to even look. I'm not wanted here. Not anymore. She made that clear.

It's a hard truth to learn. The sun never needed the earth.

ADAIR

S ome days are diamonds. I can't get that thought out of my head. I can hear her saying it. Sometimes in a bright, lift-me-up voice when I came home crying about whatever stupid thing had happened that day. Sometimes under her breath when she thought I couldn't hear her. When I was younger I'd asked her what it meant.

"It's from an old song, Dair-bear," she told me. I could wrap myself up in the memory of her calling me that and feel safe for hours. "It means some days are wonderful."

My lip jutted out as I crossed my arms defiantly over my flat chest, which was the current source of my sorrow. That day was clearly not a diamond. Not after what Cyrus Eaton had said in front of the whole class. We were discussing dimensions. The teacher told us the difference between two dimensions and three was that two dimensions were flat. Cyrus yelled out 'like Adair's chest.' I wanted to die. "Today wasn't a diamond! It was a black, dirty piece of coal. It was terrible and I hate school and Cyrus and everyone!"

"Some days are coal," she admitted. "Some days are hard. But you know the difference between diamonds and coal?

Pressure. Don't let the day be coal. Turn it into a diamond." The slight lines around her eyes softened as she gave me an understanding smile.

My mother was beautiful when she smiled. Daddy says it could run the world like a power generator if we could capture it. They say I look like her.

Or rather, looked like her.

Today was coal, and there was no changing it.

I wish they hadn't bothered with the open-casket. I don't need to see her one last time—not like this. Not dead. The funeral home tried to make her look natural in a pretty, floral dress she'd worn to garden parties last spring, her blond hair curled softly and pulled back at the ears like she always wore it. Her lips are painted with her favorite shade: Dolce Vita. I stole her tube from the vanity in her bathroom, but I'm not wearing it. I couldn't even look at it.

Dolce Vita. The sweet life.

Not anymore.

It's been a week since I got the call—a week since my life shattered into pieces so small I'll never put it back together. I want to erase the night. I want to forget everything about it. I want it to have never happened at all. But I can't erase the black dress I'm wearing or the memory of this morning's open coffin.

Someone must have given them a photo to help the undertaker prepare her body. They've gotten everything right, except that smile—the one that could power the world. I know now that it was never the smile, but the light behind it. It's missing. No, not missing. Gone. Extinguished, just like her.

The house is full of people, but, despite the lingering summer heat outside, I feel so cold I sneak off to find a jacket. And take a break from the well-wishing strangers, some of whom I've known my whole life. My room is in the east wing but at the top of the stairs, my feet carry me in the opposite direction. I find myself in her bedroom. Everything looks like it did that morning. The maids haven't been cleaning in here. I would guess my father had warned them not to, and no one goes against Angus MacLaine's wishes. That probably means I shouldn't be in here either. If he found out...

Slipping into the closet, I tell myself she would have a more appropriate jacket than I do. Half my closet is still prep school uniforms from last year. The other half is haute couture. I had to borrow a black dress from my brother's fiancée, because Dad said I couldn't wear one of Mom's. He'd kill me if he knew I was in here now. My fingers trail across the neatly hung clothes, rippling the fabrics and releasing the scent of her: lavender and vanilla and a hint of Chanel No. 5. It's all color-coded, the clothes flowing like a rainbow in the large walk-in, ending in a pool of black. Mom owned black clothing, no doubt for events like this. But she never wore it daily, unlike most women. She preferred color, everything from muted creamy yellows to audacious scarlet red. You could always spot her in crowd of her peers, blooming like an exotic flower in the midst of their sophisticated neutrals. I bypass all those and focus on the darker stuff in the back. Coal black pieces that feel like my heart, except they're still intact.

I grab a cashmere sweater and pull it over my shoulders as heat pricks my eyes. Swiping at it furiously with the sleeve, I catch her scent again and now there's no stopping the tears. Part of me wants to sink to the floor, surrounded by her, and fall apart. But I don't. Instead I force myself out of the closet. The sooner the reception is over, the sooner I'll be one step closer to the end of the second-worst day of my life.

Pausing at the mirror, I take a moment to collect myself. But it's my mother's face staring back at me. We have the same wide forehead dusted with freckles no makeup will cover up. My light copper hair might be the same color, but it's not nearly as well-behaved as hers. I had to shove it into a ponytail this morning when it wouldn't cooperate. I got my green eyes from her. It hurts to look at myself. Because no matter how much I might see my mom looking at me from the reflection, I can see the truth. My cheeks are too round to be her high-angled, regal cheekbones. I've never gotten the hang of eyeliner. I'm a half-baked version of her at best. And now there's no one around to help me finish growing up.

It takes effort to force myself out of the room, but as soon as I'm in the hall, I walk straight into someone snooping around.

"What are you doing up here?" My heart pounds against my rib cage like a bird trying to escape a snare. Inhaling deeply, I will it to calm, but before I can even hope to catch my breath, I realize I've made the same mistake twice. Why do I keep finding Sterling Ford where he doesn't belong?

His eyes go wide, as if I've yanked him back in time to the moment we met, too. They're no longer full of the casual arrogance that had burned in them the first time we met. He is still infuriatingly hot, though, even dressed in a borrowed black suit and tie. I can tell they aren't his by the way the cut hugs his torso. His muscles strain the fabric a bit too much. The pants are a smidge too short. It's far too expensive a suit to be poorly tailored. No, it doesn't fit him any more than he fits in with the people downstairs. I like him better in jeans with a chip on his shoulder.

He has potential, though, beneath that hostile frown. Even full of poorly suppressed disdain, his eyes are brilliant blue, the color of the sky on a clear summer day. He's tamed the black mop on his head into obedience, smoothing it behind his ears, so I can actually see his face. The transformation reveals the chiseled curve of his jawline, a long, straight nose, and a pair of full lips drawn into a cupid's bow at the top. The night we met is a blur, but I realize my memories of him didn't do him justice. He'd smirked at the party. Smiled at the hospital. He'd tempted me before. Now as he stands before me scowling, he's irresistible.

He's also the last person I want to see. I don't want him to be part of this world. But he's mixed up with that night and I don't know who he is any better than I understand why any of this is happening.

"Looking for the bathroom." It's a reasonable excuse.

I'm just not feeling terribly reasonable. "Look at this place. There are bathrooms downstairs."

I emphasize the plural.

"So sorry to intrude, Lucky." I feel the hate in his words, and it's both strange and good.

I'm sick of my body being one dull ache of nothing. Hate isn't nothing. It seethes and twists and squeezes. It whispers all the secrets I try to hide. I want more. I want every bit of loathing he can feed me.

His mouth—that annoyingly perfect mouth—opens, but nothing comes out. There's a battle raging in his eyes, turning the sky blue orbs into stormy seas. I don't expect it when he says, "I'm sorry about your mom."

He has leashed the hatred he displayed moments ago. It's still there, tugging at its bonds, wanting to be freed. Instead of feeding my darkness, he's offering me pity. I didn't want it the last time I saw him. I don't want it now.

"Why are you here?" I demand.

"I came with Cyrus."

I forgot they're roommates. Of course, Cyrus told him what happened. I wonder how many details Cyrus shared about the car crash that killed my mother and put my dad in a wheelchair. I know what my friends think. I heard them talking when they thought I was tuned out. Whispered rumors practically shout at you when you're the source of the gossip.

"I've known Cyrus Eaton since we were in diapers," I say, "but I can't believe he brought a stranger to my mother's funeral."

A muscle ticks in his jaw when he finally speaks, his words are strained. "I asked to come."

"Why?" I don't know how I hope he'll answer this question.

"Because I missed your perverted strain of bitchiness and thought I'd get a fix." He spits the words at me.

I plant my hands on my hips, glad I'd worn my soon to be sister-in-law's dress and my mother's sweater because I don't feel like some girl at a party being laughed at or some girl in a hospital begging to be coddled. Maybe it's a borrowed sense of power, but it's one that I'm not giving back. "Do you get off on funerals? Or just death? Is that why you stuck around the hospital?"

His eyes close for a second and he takes a deep breath. "I think we got off on the wrong foot."

"Really? You don't say." I have no idea why he feels the need to make amends. Doesn't he feel alive letting this out? "I don't really care. Just don't sneak around my house."

There's a flash of something different across his features. I don't have the word for it, but I know it. I've felt it. Before my anger-hungry glee can morph to embarrassment, it vanishes from him and the restraint I'd sensed in him evaporates, freeing the brute under the surface. His beautiful mouth curls into a mocking sneer and his words drip with cruelty. "Afraid I'm going to steal your shit? What's that painting worth?"

"More than you." I'll push every button until I find the right one.

"I can't be bought." I hear it in the final word as his raging ocean eyes sweep past me and down the hall. The hate is back. It's contempt, really. Not aimed at me exactly but rather at all of it. The thick Persian rugs beneath our feet, the sparkling crystal lights overhead, my mother's beloved paintings hanging on the wall. "Did you think I came for you? Maybe I was just going to rifle through your mom's drawers. It's not like she'll be needing any of this."

The truth knocks the air out of me and I gasp no longer fueled by venom. He's right. She won't.

Mom could have hung those paintings anywhere in the house. She could have shown them off to guests. Bragged about how much she paid for them. I'd seen enough of my friends' parents engage in artistic pissing contests to know that's how it was supposed to work. But art wasn't about status to her. She hung them there because she loved them and wanted to start and end her day with beauty.

And all that was gone now. In its place is a void, and Sterling Ford just knocked me right back into it.

"Screw you." I can't get my voice to rise louder than a whisper. It's physically painful to speak. How dare he come in here and judge *her*? All he sees is money, but I know the truth.

"Wouldn't you like to?" There's the arrogance again. Mixed with the cruelty, he's less man than Molotov cocktail.

I can sense it radiating off him. He's not like the guys in my circle. He's not like his new friend Cyrus. There's no practiced civility for the sake of a future trust fund. No expectation of good behavior so daddy won't take away his Porsche. He's different. Find the right button, give the right code, pull the pin—he'll detonate. I bet he's destroyed other girls. I know he could destroy me. Part of me wishes he would. The part of me that wants to feel anything other than this bone-deep throb in my soul.

"I don't kiss frogs." I take a step closer. "And I definitely don't fuck dogs."

It hits the mark. He takes a step toward me and I freeze, wondering what someone like him will do to me. I know cockiness. You can't grow up with the heirs to the thrones of a half-dozen global brands without enduring it. That arrogance comes from entitlement. It's hereditary. Passed down from father to son like a perverse family heirloom.

Violence shades his arrogance. He won that pride, and I don't want to know how. Except that I do. Is that why he's all sharp edges and hewn muscle? Where did he come from, and why is he here? What made him into this walking grenade of a man?

If things had gone differently, I might have asked him all of this. But I don't need a knight in shining armor, I need a sword.

"Look, you don't fucking know me. You've never met anyone like me." Venom coats each word. "You can say whatever you want."

He moves toward me, and I back away instinctively. I found the button. I pressed it. Something tells me I'm not ready for the fallout. Now I'm the one at war, wondering what it would feel like to collide into him even as my brain orders me to run far and fast. Anxiety strips away my confidence. I don't know who I'm playing with—I have no clue who Sterling Ford really is.

"I can see it. Right here." A rough-tipped finger jabs the bridge of my nose before trailing down and tapping its tip. "Fuck or flight. What's it going to be?"

"Don't you mean fight or flight?" I say coolly, hoping I'm the only one to catch the tremble in my voice.

"I said what I meant." He steps back and shoves his hands in his borrowed suit's pockets.

Relief washes over me but when it's cleansed the anxiety, I'm surprised to discover it's left something behind. Something raw that claws at its cage. My hand closes over my stomach as though I can trap it there before it escapes. I don't want to know what monster he's awoken. I don't want to admit that part of me responds to someone like him.

Or that he has me trapped. I don't dare push past him. Touching him...seems like a bad idea. As if he can see my struggle, he steps to the side. Which one is he: the hero or the villain? Both watch me from his guarded eyes.

"Where are my manners?" He gestures toward the stairs. "You have guests."

Suddenly, all those strangers don't feel like intruders. They feel like safety. Rushing past him, I try not to look at him, but I can't help it. He pulls my attention like a magnet. The scowl is now a permanent fixture on his handsome face but it stops at his eyes. I don't pause to consider what I see there until I reach the first step. By the time, I reach the last one, I've convinced myself I was wrong. It wasn't pain in those stormy eyes, and if it was, it was my own reflecting there. I'd imagined it. I couldn't let myself do that again.

I thought Sterling was just a poor boy dressed in a rich man's suit. I was wrong. He's a wolf in sheep's clothing.

❦

"There you are!" My best friend's arms circle me tightly, but my eyes—and thoughts—are on Sterling. Poppy doesn't notice, which is no surprise. She's perfected the art of convenient ignorance. Her philosophy is why deal with something unpleasant if you can avoid it? Sometimes I wish I could be more like her.

Right now, I wish I could be her, instead of the girl

running from the wicked boy upstairs or the girl whose mom just died.

"Are you okay?" Her voice drops to a whisper, and I remember why we're best friends. Because that convenient blind spot of hers doesn't extend to me. She sees me clearly. Probably even the stuff I don't tell her. Like about the night before mom died. Or about the smug jackass I met at the coffee shop before...

We're best friends, but it's not like anyone can ever really know you. Not entirely. We all have secrets—parts of ourselves that are better hidden than shared. Sometimes even from ourselves. We're born alone and we die alone. The last few days have made that clear to me.

"Fine." I shrug off her concern, hoping she doesn't press the issue. She doesn't.

Instead, she seems intent on distraction. "Everyone's in the solarium, hiding from mum and dad."

She clasps my hand and drags me in that direction. I don't want to hang out with them. The guys will make stupid, insensitive jokes. The girls will fawn over me, but I'm not stupid enough to believe it's anything more than an act. But it's better than staying put and running into him again, so I let her lead me away.

Poppy prattles on about changes to her parents' trip to the Seychelles. "Dad's been called back to London..."

I'm barely aware of the update. I've heard it before. The Landrys were constantly planning a vacation they never took. Mr. Landry always wound up being called to London and then Mrs. Landry would fly to Palm Springs and have an affair. The world kept spinning and the Seychelles remained untainted by their lousy marriage. Poppy is proof that good things can come from bad places, like a flower growing through a crack in the cement.

She's kinder than she has to be, given her looks and upbringing. With her black curtain of hair, amber skin, and willowy, dancer's body, she could be like most of the other girls we know: all beauty and money with a big empty spot where her soul should be. She could cut and belittle and dehumanize. Instead, she threw a party for her gardener when he got engaged and plays with the maid's daughter to give her a break. I have no idea why. Maybe it's because she has that convenient ignorance. Maybe she refuses to focus on all the bad in our world.

I'm considering this when I realize that she's moved on with her gossip. "He's from New York. Scholarship of some sort. I can't believe brains come with his body."

No. I've been so caught up in stewing over my confrontation with Sterling that I'm only now considering that he came here with Cyrus. *Cyrus*, who is part of my inner circle, even if he used to tease me about my flat chest. Cyrus, who will be in the solarium with everyone. I doubt Mr. Personality is out making new friends with my mom's bridge club.

I just taunted the wolf, dangling fresh blood in front of him. Now I'm going to walk into his den.

"I'm not feeling so well," I lie, hoping to extricate myself from the situation.

Poppy studies me for a moment, tilting her head, her eyes crinkling, in a way that reminds me of my mother. My stomach flips over, grief churning through it. Now I'm not lying. I don't think I can face my friends any more than I can stand to see that boy again.

Judging by the way Ava and Darcy are huddled in the corner, there's more gossip to share—more trivial, meaningless information. I wish they hadn't come. I wish I could turn around and go back to standing silent in my father's shadow as he shook hands and made small talk.

I'm too late. A dark-haired boy with cold gray eyes spots us, a smile cracking his face. His tie is already loose at his neck, his top button undone. He tosses back the drink in his hand. Shaking his head, he calls out, "Where have you two been?"

I manage a tight smile. Trust Montgomery to treat this like any other party. It takes effort to convince my body to move toward my friends. He is holding court between Cyrus and Oliver Hawthorne, who's still finishing up his last year of prep. There's a half-empty bottle of West Tennessee Whiskey waiting on the table for the next round.

"Thank you for coming." I've been prepped to say this to everyone—raised by old-fashioned parents who expect their kids to have a shred of manners. That etiquette comes out in public, even among friends.

"I wouldn't miss it. Your dad always has the good booze." Montgomery's thoughtless humor slices through me.

"Don't be a dick, Money." Cyrus smacks the back of his head but I see his barely concealed smile. He's better at pretending not to be a walking sack of hormones than the others, but not by much. He's as tall as Montgomery— meaning they tower over me—but that's where the similarities end. Cyrus is fair-skinned, fair-haired, and mostly fair-minded. Of course, he has ambitions to follow his father's path into politics, but not before he takes over the family's global hotel chain. He's lucky he looks like his mother, a Swedish model turned trophy wife.

"I was complimenting her family," Money says, slurring slightly. This clearly isn't his first bottle. Big surprise. He swings for Cyrus's shoulder, misses and slops his drink all over him.

Cyrus jumps to his feet, glaring at him, as he wipes off what he can. "This is Brioni, for Christ's sake." His vision shifts to the doorway. "Sterling, come help me drink this. We're cutting Money off."

Sterling. I don't turn to see him enter. Their new friend. My new nightmare.

The other girls—who didn't bother to look up at my entrance—are very invested in the appearance of Sterling. I can see what draws their attention, even as I dread the next few weeks. They'll talk about him nonstop. If I'm lucky, some other guy will prove more intriguing.

I've talked with Sterling. I've looked in his hurricane eyes. There's not a chance in hell anyone half as interesting winds up at Valmont University this year.

Clutching Poppy's hand tightly, I will her to read my mind. But when I look over, her black eyes are trained on Sterling. She didn't meet him that night. He didn't insult her. He didn't stick around once she arrived with Felix. Now I've lost her, too. I make a mental note to warn her about him at the first opportunity. I can only imagine what a jerk like that could do to someone as sweet as her. For now, I drag her toward the other girls, pretending that Sterling doesn't exist.

"Fresh meat," Ava purrs in a low voice. She's the female version of Montgomery. Usually opposite-sex siblings don't look so much alike, even if they are twins. The West twins could be an advertisement for genetic engineering—beautiful, perfect halves of the same soulless coin.

"He's poor," Darcy says, but she's staring at him with the same lusty expression. She twirls a ringlet of hair on her finger as though she's considering how low she's willing to go. She's not a bitch so much as a pragmatist. With three older brothers, she'll get a much smaller piece of her parents' pharmaceutical company. She started her final year of prep this week, too, and she made no secret that she's headed to university to catch a husband. She's the only person I know studying to ace the

SATs to ensure she goes Ivy League—where the big bank accounts send their sons. In her mind, getting out of Valmont ensures a fresh stock of potential marital possibilities.

"He's also a complete jackass," I inform them.

"That's no way to welcome him to Valmont." Judging from Ava's interest, she plans on welcoming him to town with a private tour of her panties.

There's no use supplying them with the details. Poppy will listen to me, but Ava and Darcy collect boys like stamps—licking them and sticking them before moving on to the next find.

Ava pats the arm of the wicker chair beside hers. "Sit. We need to catch up."

I want to run. To flee the memories of my mother watering her plants. To avoid Sterling. To hide. To pretend life hasn't changed forever.

I sit.

That's all the invitation they need to continue with their gossiping.

"Cyrus said he's a scholarship student. From Queens or something," Darcy tells us. "I didn't think Valmont gave many scholarships outside sports recruits, but he doesn't play football according to Cy."

"Maybe he plays lacrosse," Poppy offers. We all turn to stare at her. Sweet girl. As though there are a lot of inner-city lacrosse teams. She returns our stare with a blank look. "What? A lot of good players graduated last year."

"I have a feeling he's more into one-on-one sports," Ava says, adding, "At least, I hope he is."

"Why don't you ask him?" I slump farther down into my chair.

She turns sparkling eyes on me. "I will."

"Adair."

I look up to find Cyrus lording over me. His eyes zero in on my neckline and I realize he's staring down my top. Pushing up and out of his line of sight, I swivel around to him. "Could you be..." My rebuke dies on my lips when I see he brought Sterling over.

"I wanted to introduce you all to my roommate and Adair's savior the other night." He glances between us expectantly.

This is the part where I play the grateful girl and welcome him, thank him for coming, fawn over his chivalry. I don't move.

"I shouldn't have come," Sterling mutters, showing a shocking amount of insight.

He shouldn't have come. I wish none of them had, but him more than the rest. He doesn't belong here. Not today. I hate him for coming. I hate him for confusing me. I hate him for hating me.

I hate how he makes me feel. I hate that I like it.

"Nonsense. I promised to show you the town. Introduce you to the Court," Cyrus says dismissively, and I wonder if Sterling counts himself as one of us. If he thinks he belongs to the silly clique of rich kids sticking together more out of habit than affection.

"Are we still going by that?" Poppy asks.

We're not the Court anymore. How can they think that? We're not the kids who stole from their parents' bar carts and drank away the weekend in each other's pool-houses. Everything is changing in ways that have nothing to do with starting college next week or who lives in the dorms and who prefers morning maid service at the family estate. Can't they feel it?

"We could divide up by those stuck in the dorms and those still living in the lap of luxury," Money suggests, malice glinting in his eyes.

"Some of us wanted our freedom," Ava reminds her brother, but her next sentiment is aimed at Sterling. "Freedom means getting to do *whoever* you want."

"It means you aren't wanted around," Money says drolly. "You could be the unwanted. What do you think, Poppy? Does that suit you better?"

Poppy tenses. She never built an immunity to Money like the rest of us. Her parents insisted she live in the dorms along with Cyrus's. She'll spend the summers drifting between the city and the various Landry houses. It hardly matters. Her parents are never home anyway. That's the price of running the world's leading tech company. Fortunately—or maybe unfortunately—that means they can buy Poppy the best in life, including an education at Valmont University. In fact, the only thing they don't give her is their time.

"You, darling, are not unwanted," Cyrus soothes her. "I'll take you anytime. You know that."

Her eyes narrow at his advance. "I think I'll stick with the dorms."

"Anyway," Cyrus says heavily, "I couldn't leave him to languish. I thought we could show him a good time."

Languish? A good time? I can't find words. They're stuck boiling in my throat, burning it raw. I don't know if I want to cry or scream. This is different. It's not the passionate, hate-driven anger Sterling released in me. This is sour and rotten. This is betrayal. I don't know why I expect them to care. They never have before. Still, I cast a frantic look at Poppy, hoping she'll save me. She's the only one I can always count on, but she's mesmerized by Cyrus's new pet like the rest of them.

It's as though none of them remember why they're here, except the one person I wish didn't. They begin planning what to do next, peppering Sterling with questions. He answers them. They watch him. He watches me. His eyes scan and dissect, taking me apart piece by piece like I'm an experiment. For a few minutes, I sit there and let him.

"What do you think, Sterling? We could go to the pool house." Ava leans toward him, angling her curvy body to flash him some cleavage.

His gaze stays glued to me. "I want to know what Adair thinks."

Heads swivel in my direction, proving they'd forgotten I was even here—and son-of-a-bitch Sterling wanted me to know it.

There's not an ounce of social nicety left in me as I push to my feet, tottering on my heels, flushed with their betrayals. They're acting like we're just hanging out. Cyrus brought along a new friend. Said friend is a grade-A jackass, taunting me at my own mother's funeral, and every Southern belle in the room wants to show him her welcome wagon.

"I think you can go to hell," I say.

His eyes flash. Everyone freezes. Except me. I'm already across the room. I should go back. I should apologize. That's what my mom would want me to do.

Except she's dead—and I seem to be the only one who cares.

"Let her go," I hear Sterling tell them. "She's upset about her mom."

No one comes after me. The Court has a new king.

I never asked for them to come. I don't want them here. I don't want *him* here, so why do I feel so alone?

The will is being read—and I quote—in the comfort of our own home. What a joke. In fairness to our legal team, most people would consider Windfall comfortable. They see the 10,000 square foot mansion with its house staff, garden staff, tennis courts, swimming pool, and guesthouses, and they make assumptions. I had the *privilege* of growing up here, which means I know better. Windfall is anything but comfortable. My father built the house to intimidate. It wasn't until I was older, and had more experience of the world, that I realized he wasn't trying to intimidate strangers or potential business partners. We were his target. His family. His wife and children.

And it had worked.

Hindsight is a gift and a curse. I wish I could look back on my childhood and remember only the lavish birthday parties and over-the-top holidays, but the sounds of empty bottles breaking and screamed arguments overshadows those memories. I can't summon one happy moment without being inundated by a thousand that broke my heart. That's the truth behind Windfall's name. It wasn't built by good fortune. It was built on cruelty.

But despite that, I'm still standing in front of the closed doors to my father's study, dutifully wearing black and playing the part of the good daughter in mourning over her beloved father. I pretend my world isn't composed of egg shells that leave me terrified to make a move. But I know it's more fragile than glass and any moment, something—or someone—will shatter it.

Ginny joins me without a word. I force a smile even though she's dressed for a business meeting in a white blouse, collar turned up at the neck, and high-waisted, electric blue pants that are so tight they're like a second skin. My niece is off with a nanny. It's her mother's job to see to both their fortunes. Actually, Ginny is going to work by her standards. Being married to my brother, planning his future Senate run, and hanging delicately off his shoulder is a full-time job. People often assume we're actual sisters with our red hair and pale skin. She may not be a MacLaine by blood but sometimes I think she's more suited to it than I am.

"That color washes you out," she informs me, fiddling with the clasp of her gold tennis bracelet.

"Black?" I say flatly. "We're in mourning, remember?"

"And what a spectacular show you're making of it. I commend you," she says, "but let's not pretend you didn't hate your father."

"I didn't." I don't know why I'm defending myself to her. Ginny can believe what she wants. She knows more about this family than most, but she never understood that I loved my father nearly as much as I disliked him.

"I guess we'll find out if he loved you soon enough." She returns her attention to the closed doors.

I bite back a half-dozen sarcastic responses, knowing that if my brother inherits Windfall, it will be up to her if I'm allowed to stay. She's wanted me gone for years, ever since things fell apart between us. She hates that I stayed when she wanted me to go. She never understood that I didn't have a choice.

"How long are they going to drag this out?" She checks her phone for the time and sighs as though it's a huge burden to spend the afternoon inheriting millions.

Malcolm has been holed up inside for the better part of the week, a revolving door of attorneys and accountants coming and going. He must know what's in the will, even though it hasn't been unsealed yet. What else could they be discussing? My father groomed him to take over and planned my brother's run for the state senate. They both had sights on D.C. Surely that meant Malcolm had been privy to my father's plans for the estate and his assets. That's what worries me. What need does my brother have to consult so many legal experts? A cocktail of dread and fear churns inside me as I consider the possibility that Malcolm is meeting to discuss me and my inheritance.

I don't know if I want any of it, but there's no way that I want my brother to decide that for me.

Felix appears by my side, his grey, striped trousers neatly pressed with a perfect crease running down each leg and brass cufflinks shining on his blazer. He no longer wears the white gloves like when I was a little girl, a concession to my insistence that he modernize a little. Today, though, it's a comforting sight to see him dressed in his butler's uniform.

"Miss MacLaine, how are you feeling this morning?"

I manage a tight smile. When my mother died, I'd gone to Felix for comfort. He'd been by my side when the doctor gave us the news. He'd held me as I cried. This time, I haven't needed him. Has he noticed my lack of tears? What does he think of me?

I force myself to answer him, aware that Ginny is eavesdropping. "Tired."

"Maybe you should get her some coffee," she suggests.

Felix shifts uncomfortably on his feet. "Actually, I was asked to attend the reading."

"Of course." Ginny shakes her head. "Angus won't have left you out. You're part of this family."

My eyes dart to Felix, who doesn't look convinced. Ginny is right. The man practically raised us. A good man would reward his loyalty.

No one can claim Daddy was a good man.

When the door to my father's private study finally opens, Harding looks like he hasn't slept in days. He gestures for me to enter along with Ginny. She barely looks at me as we enter. That's what I am to her in the presence of others: invisible. It wasn't always like this. Not when she first started dating Malcolm. I was going to be a bridesmaid in their wedding until they eloped to avoid scandal before Ellie was born. Both our futures looked so different then. Unfortunately, the thing that brought us together—the thing we have in common still —is what drove us apart. It's what destroyed my mother. It's what's kept me here in Valmont. I'm supposed to be proud of my family name. Instead, it hangs like an albatross around my neck—a burden I can never escape. There's no avoiding the MacLaine family birthright. It's not something we're blessed with. It owns us.

My father's study is a testament to appearance making the man. Oak panels polished daily to maintain their glossy luster run the perimeter of the room. Behind his generous executive desk, a picture window looks over the rolling hills behind our estate. The MacLaine name owns the world as far as the eye can see. It's proof of our family's wealth—proof of our unofficial reign over Valmont, Tennessee. For most men this kingdom would be enough, but not my daddy. He'd never been a fan of limitation. Not when it came to women, to liquor, or to power.

I take a chair near daddy's desk, Ginny and Malcolm at my side. Felix squeezes my shoulder as he moves to the back of the room, fading into the shadows.

"If everyone is present," Harding begins. He shuffles a stack of papers and looks around expectedly.

"We are." Malcolm sounds exasperated like Harding has already worn him down.

Judd Harding is a man who sticks to the rules. It's a wonder he held his job as my father's attorney for so many years, given that Angus MacLaine wasn't one to follow any rules. I suppose since my father didn't have a conscience, he had to employ one. Now Harding is Malcolm's censor, and my brother doesn't look happy about it.

I shift in my chair, crossing my legs at the ankle. A perpetual, and seemingly inexhaustible, energy vibrates in my bones. It's been buzzing through me for the last week, and I can't seem to release it. Even now, moments before one of the most important events in my life, I can barely hold still. I want to believe it's a symptom of grief, but it hadn't started the day my father died. It began at his funeral. It began with an entirely different problem and that problem has a name—one I won't allow myself to think, even though I can't get him out of my head.

"Stop fidgeting," Ginny hisses under her breath. "I swear you're as bad as Ellie."

"It's a MacLaine thing," I say sweetly, knowing she hates it when I remind her that she's not an actual MacLaine.

"This is the last will and testament of Angus MacLaine,"

Harding reads, oblivious to us. "To my son, Malcolm, I bequeath the following…"

My brother tenses with anticipation. In a way, this is the ultimate Christmas morning and we've been on the verge of it our entire lives. Every present my father bought himself is now up for grabs, including this house. We've spent our entire lives toeing the line, like most children do, in anticipation of Santa Claus. Better watch out. Better not cry. Our father was always watching. Now we would see which one of us did a better job. I hold no illusions about which of us held our father's favor.

"My collection of cars except for the Roadster. I also leave to him the office in Nashville. A fifteen percent stake in MacLaine Media, and my membership at the following clubs…"

It's not what any of us expect. Malcolm clutches the arms of his chair, white-knuckled and rigid waiting for Harding to finish the list of memberships. When the lawyer pauses, Malcolm asks in a strained voice, "Is that all?"

"There's more, of course." Harding uses his best stay-calm, lawyer voice, which only indicates Malcolm should worry.

Maybe it's my father's last test of patience. Dangle the ultimate carrot over our noses and see who snaps at it first.

"To Adair, I bequeath the 1956 Jaguar XK140 Roadster, the penthouse at The Nashville Eaton, Bluebird Press, and a fifteen percent stake in MacLaine Media."

Some of my inheritance I expect. Some of it I only wished for. The question remains, though, what about the rest?

"What about the house?" Malcolm demands, sounding torn between anger and confusion. "You've only accounted for thirty percent of his holdings. What about the rest? What about the house in Tuscany? The flat in London?"

Harding's lips turn down in a grim smile. He doesn't sound nearly as calm this time. "There's more."

"Your father wished this to remain a secret until the reading of his will in the hopes that the situation would be resolved before his death. Most of his real estate assets were liquidated over the last few years to buy back as much of the company as he could. Unfortunately, death holds no respect for unfinished business." He pauses, the silence ominous. "As of right now, forty-nine percent of MacLaine Media is in the hands of private investors."

"What?" This finishes Malcolm. He jumps from his chair and begins to pace the room. "Forty-nine percent?"

"I told you that MacLaine Media divested itself of some of its holdings," Harding explains. He slips off his reading glasses and stares at my brother.

"No one warned me how much he'd sold," Malcolm seethes. "Who bought these shares?"

"I believe you met one of the parties at his funeral last week."

Considering Malcolm's obsession with the family business, I understand his shock. Who spoke with Malcolm at Daddy's funeral? Why had he kept this from me? My father prided himself on retaining MacLaine Media for the family. It's one of the reasons we remain privately owned.

"He said he'd never allow the family to go below a sixty percent stake in the company," I say slowly. Fifty-one percent: that's all we have left under our control. One wrong move and we'll lose the majority share and, more importantly, the majority vote. We could lose control over the company entirely if that happens.

"Why would we sell any of the company?" Ginny asks.

Malcolm's nostrils flair as though angry that she deigned to speak.

"It was the only way to survive in the wireless age," I explain, recalling the journalism class I'd taken at Valmont

University my first year. "Newspapers were never going to compete against social media. If we wanted to keep the company privately held we had to bring in venture capital so we could diversify. It was the only option."

"You're an expert on this now?" Malcolm says with disgust. "I don't remember seeing you at any business meetings."

"Was I invited?" I ask coldly. "You and Daddy assumed I didn't keep up with the family business."

Realization registers on his face. His kid sister isn't a total idiot. Apparently, he'd forgotten. "Did you know about this?"

He still manages to draw the wrong conclusion. "No. I haven't been to any business meetings, remember?" I shake off the accusation. "What does this mean for our remaining interest?"

Dread digs a pit in my stomach. If we no longer hold the majority interest we can be outvoted. I've watched it happen to my father's friends. I've seen empires crumble, brought down by one mistake.

"That our father gave away nearly half of our family's remaining stake in the company." Malcolm stands and searches the room. *Christ.* Felix, where are you?"

Felix moves dutifully to the bar cart and pours Malcolm a drink. He always instinctively knows what we need. Is that why he needs to be here today? Are we going to need a steady supply of alcohol to cope with the damage?

Malcolm accepts the tumbler from him with a terse thanks.

"But the family controlled sixty percent of the company. Angus said so!" Ginny clearly isn't following the math. I know she could, though, because I've seen the woman shop a sale at Saks. "I don't understand where the forty-nine comes in."

Malcolm flashes her a scorching look. She shrinks from it as if he's actually burned her.

"*It means* we could lose everything." He abandons his empty glass, pressing his index fingers to his temples.

"But—"

"He lied, Ginny," I tell her bluntly. After all these years, I don't know how she's surprised by this.

"It's possible another party could buy a majority share in MacLaine Media, but unlikely," Harding confirms.

"But who would do that?" I ask. "Why would anyone want control over a struggling media conglomerate?"

Malcolm rounds on me, bending down to get in my face. "I know the MacLaine name doesn't mean anything to you, but you could pretend to respect it."

"Our father had to jeopardize the entire family's stake in the company to keep it afloat," I point out. "It's obviously failing. This has nothing to do with me."

I don't shrink like Ginny. The men of this family allowed this to happen. I should have pushed harder to be in the boardroom, to be part of these decisions. How did I not see this coming? The number of closed-door meetings and business dinners my father held had increased exponentially during the last year of his life, even once hospice care had begun. Had Malcolm really been kept out of the loop, or did he not realize what was going on? I'd trusted him to have the best interests at heart for our family. Now I feel stupid for blindly believing anyone was looking out for the rest of us.

"It has everything to do with you," Malcolm mutters.

Now I'm on my feet, level with him at last. "What does that mean?"

"I think you should tell me."

We stare each other down, him trying to elicit a confession and me trying to figure out what the hell he's yammering about. It's not as though we have secrets in this room. We've all paid a price for this family. That bond, forged in blood and sacrifice, is supposed to protect us for our past sins. But my participation in the family's perverse narcissism has never been enough for Malcolm. Why should it be now?

"I don't think there's cause for concern," Harding interrupts us. "All my research on the buyers suggests multiple individuals purchasing. I don't think it's anything to worry about."

"So, wait…" Malcolm turns to Harding, but if he thinks he can change the subject, he's mistaken.

"Why would this be my fault?" I step between them. I'm not going to decipher his riddles. I hold more stake in the company than he does. I have more to lose. Knowing Malcolm, he didn't fail to notice that.

He pretends not to hear me. "Did he leverage the house? He didn't leave it to either of us."

That possibility hasn't occurred to me until now.

Harding looks briefly at each of us as if seeking an ally. When he doesn't find one, he reaches for his briefcase. "The good news is that the house remains in the family."

"That is good news," Felix says. He waits for someone to agree with him. When they don't, he manages to find his smile anyway. "Malcolm. Adair. The house is safe."

He's trying to be encouraging, but bad news always accompanies good news. Are we on the verge of losing it, too? Even worse, do we have to split it? I can almost imagine Ginny gleefully dividing every object and room in the estate down the middle with tape.

It's worse than that. "To my only grandchild Elodie MacLaine…"

Ginny stiffens at the slight. None of us missed the subtle reminder that he'd only had one grandchild. She'd failed him in that regard.

"To be held in trust under the supervision of Felix Gabriel."

"Felix?" Ginny gasps, clutching her seat as she sways in her chair to look at Felix.

He goes perfectly still, except for the smile falling from his lips. I search his face for a sign that he'd known about this but find nothing except confused detachment, as though he's contemplating the same question. Was it something he did? Had daddy indicated this might happen? Felix can't see the answer to those questions, but looking to him now I understand why my father put him in this impossible position. I see Felix through the eyes of Angus MacLaine.

Felix, the cheerleader.

Felix, the father figure.

Felix, the one everyone runs to for help.

And for my father's eyes alone: a rival. It's revenge plain and simple. With one cunning move, my father has turned him into something else entirely: Felix, the enemy.

I know why Daddy did it. It's not going to work on me. Malcolm I have less faith in. I tear my eyes away from Felix to see how my brother reacts.

Malcolm's stony scowl isn't leveled at Felix. It's aimed at me. "Did you know about this?"

"What?" I nearly falter under the weight of his accusation. "Why would I know about this?"

"You've always been closest to Felix," Malcolm accuses, "and then there's the fact—"

"But then Windfall is ours, right? If it belongs to Ellie?" Ginny interrupts.

A rage claws at me like poison attacking my blood. Neither of them cares about how Ellie fits into any of this. They only care about how her inheritance affects them. I should be surprised. I'm not. I am, however, plenty angry over it.

"There are a number of special instructions for Felix to follow," Harding says.

"She can't live here without her parents!" Malcolm storms back to the whiskey. For a moment, I don't see him. I see my father standing before me in denial, reaching for the bottle to wash away any doubt he has about the control he holds over the situation. I blink away the memory. Malcolm isn't him—but for how long will that be true?

"What kind of special instructions?" Ginny asks softly, tears well in her eyes. They spill over, cracking the polished veneer she clings to and revealing what lies beneath the facade of her perfect life. Gone is the trophy wife, the harried mother, the catty sister-in-law—the roles she's played for years. In their place is a girl I knew once, but she's no longer the same. I see Ginny MacLaine for the first time in that moment.

"I'm afraid only Mr. Gabriel is privy to that information," Harding says. "Your father left explicit instructions as to a number of potential scenarios which could change his wishes before Elodie inherits the property on her twenty-fifth birthday."

"She's my daughter, I deserve to know about her inheritance."

Harding doesn't budge. He's still working for Angus MacLaine. He's always taken that job seriously. "All I am able to share with you, according to your father's instructions, is that Windfall should pass to your daughter on her twenty-fifth birthday along with the remaining stake of the family holdings in MacLaine Media."

"Twenty-one percent," Malcolm says with a dull laugh. "More than we got."

"He hoped it would be more if the financials resolved in the family's favor before his death," Harding says. "Twenty-one percent is something."

"Twenty-one percent of nothing *is nothing*," Malcolm seethes. "Is the house really secure until then? Can you tell us that?"

"It's debatable," Harding admits. He presses his lips into a thin line. He's bound by his legal obligations to his client. Judd Harding doesn't work for the family. He works for my father, even in death. It's not a simple matter of refusing to tell us more—he can't do it. He can't tell us why Elodie got the house or why he divvied up the remaining holdings among us in this way.

This whole time, both Malcolm and I have been cautiously making our beds, knowing we'd have to sleep in them one day. The trouble is we were in the wrong room the whole time. Maybe even the wrong house.

Ginny gets to her feet but stumbles like her legs won't work. Before she can fall, Felix catches her.

"Let's get you a cup of tea," Felix suggests.

Ginny stares at him, accusation etched on her face. Her eyes flash to Malcolm, but his attention is out the window—on the kingdom he's lost. If he noticed her distress, he doesn't care. Ginny's gaze finds the floor and she allows Felix to lead her toward the kitchens.

Is this how things will be between us now? Will we question everything Felix does for us? I watch him guide her away, hand on the small of her back to steady her. She doesn't deserve his kindness. None of us do. My father might have played us against one another, but there's a critical error in his calculations. Felix might become the enemy to Malcolm and Ginny but he'll always have Ellie's best interests at heart.

Harding follows them with his briefcase in hand. There's a bounce to his step. He walks like a man who's just shed fifty pounds of dead weight. In a way, he has. He delivered Angus

MacLaine's final blows. He's as free from the man as any of us can ever hope to be.

The room empties save for Malcolm and me—Angus MacLaine's lesser heirs. The ones who had worked for our father's love and still failed to win it. Maybe that's the problem. Our true inheritance isn't property or stocks. It's our father's final, unintended lesson. Love isn't a game. In love, you can't win or lose. Not when it's real.

"Did you know about this?" Malcolm asks again. He sounds tired as though he's ready to collapse at the end of a long race.

"No, I didn't." I'm not going to try to prove it. He can believe me if he wants.

"Even in his grave, the man can find a way to fuck us."

"Yep." I snort, realizing we've found common ground at last.

"I should check on Ginny. She's probably stress shopping online." Malcolm starts toward the door.

But there's something still nagging me. "Malcolm," I call and he stops at the door. "Harding said you spoke with one of the investors at the funeral. Who was it?"

"I don't know him," he says. "He came to me with a proposition, one I need to consider." He pauses, fading away for a moment as if lost in his thoughts before he zeroes in on me. "There might be other interested parties though."

"You'll tell me when you know more?"

"Of course." But he wears a politician's smile—the one passed down from father to son. He's lying. The question is: why?

9

STERLING

Twelve and South rises like a shard of glass in the heart of Nashville. Outside, the morning sun dances off the luxury high-rise over two blocks of restaurants and shops. Farther east, a string of famous bars boasts the best music in town. Inside, the views from the twenty-fifth floor are even more impressive. Unbroken windows wrap the entire exterior of the building's penthouse apartment. It feels like walking on a cloud—if a cloud had marble floors and a fireplace.

"There's not much privacy," the real estate agent titters. Even in her Burberry scarf with Gucci hanging off her arm, she's out of her element in the multimillion-dollar property. That isn't stopping her from trying to appear knowledgeable. She walks through with a critical eye, clucking over all of the apartment's best features.

"It's all the privacy I need, Ms. Summers," I assure her. It's a good thing she's the trophy wife of a Tennessee Titan, because she's hopeless at closing a done deal on one of Nashville's most expensive bachelor pads.

"Of course, you are on the top floor, so I suppose people can't see *everything*." Her heavily lined and lashed gaze zeroes in on me. She's too prudish to say what she's really thinking. "I suppose you could get some curtains."

If it wasn't at the top, passersby could see every inch of this place. Even the master bath boasts a wall of windows so you can see the city from the shower. The only privacy it affords is the walk-in and two toilet closets. In truth, someone would have to be standing in a building opposite us—there are none this tall in the Gulch area—or looking through binoculars. Given what I do, it might be prudent to have a more private space. But that's the trick with money and crime, it's not about hiding, it's about being seen. Show the world what you want them to believe. For me that boils down to showing three things:

I'm rich.

I'm ruthless.

I'm at the top of the food chain.

The penthouse screams all those things.

I turn a crooked smile on her, my mind already half on finding the right people to handle the rest of the details. Shoving my hands in my Armani slacks, I can't resist playing with her despite already reaching my decision, "I have nothing to hide."

"Of course, I only mean at night or when you're in the s-s-shower," she stammers.

"I don't mind if someone sees me stepping out of the shower." I could stop there, but why not complete the dots? "I have nothing to be self-conscious about."

Her eyes skip down my form, a deep red blush painting her cheeks as she stares. They stop on my crotch, her hands seeking the marble counter behind her for balance.

Yep, you're doing the math right, sweetheart. I know what she sees because I spend two hours in the gym every morning —a practice drilled into me from basic training and one that's netted more than a few bodies in my bed. I could have *Ms. Summers* on the kitchen counter if I wanted. We both know it.

Her lips part, her tongue darting past her brilliant white teeth to lick her coral-painted lower lip. I suppose most men might go for brunette with curls as voluminous as her curves. Maybe I would have in the past. I've been around plenty of women like her over the last few years: bored housewives and overlooked trophy wives whose full-time profession is being a showpiece for their wealthy husbands. Husbands who don't bother to appreciate the effort, leaving them to look elsewhere for fulfillment. They see two things when they look at me: youth and money. If one doesn't satisfy, the other will. But I don't want more, I want less. I want bare skin with freckles showing, hair that falls wild down her back, lips naked and waiting to be kissed.

I shift on my feet, my slacks suddenly feeling a bit too strained. A small gasp escapes Ms. Summers, reminding me that I'm here now with a woman who is nothing like that, living in a world where that girl no longer exists. I stifle a groan and stride toward the kitchen.

She whirls around, suddenly and intensely focusing on the appliances. "It's a chef's kitchen. That's a gas oven. Two pantries to your left, one for wine. Then again, you probably don't cook."

I don't bother to correct her on this. In actuality, the gourmet Wolf range and Subzero fridge are two of the things that drew me to this listing. She doesn't need to know this. No one does. I don't care if someone sees my naked body or women coming and going, but the fact that I prefer to cook my own meals? That I take my coffee black and fresh-pressed? Those aren't part of the face I present to the world. I have my reasons.

"There's access to the building's fitness center and sauna on the third floor." I've left her to fill in the silence and she's doing her best to rattle off as many features as her poor, over-whelmed brain can recall.

An incoming call interrupts her sales pitch, and I hold up a finger to silence her. Checking the screen, I can't help but grin. "I'm sorry," I say to her. "I've been expecting this call. Give me a minute."

"Of course," she simpers. "Let me"—

But I'm already walking into the empty bedroom. "Mr. MacLaine, to what do I owe the pleasure?"

"I've been meaning to call you," he says smoothly. Such a politician. "I hope it's a good time."

"I'm just wrapping up a real estate deal."

There's a pause on the other end. "I'd love to hear about that."

I bet he would. No doubt he's wondering how close to home I'm landing. "We should get together."

"Do you have dinner plans?" He thinks I'm extending an olive branch. He's too greedy to pause and investigate. He'll have it in his grubby little hands before he realizes that it's poison ivy. That's exactly what I want.

"Tonight?"

"Unless it's too last minute," Malcolm says. I imagine him squirming in his Aeron chair, loosening his tie, checking his own calendar.

I enjoy it, but playing coy is a woman's game. "I was going to grab Hennie's and head back to the Eaton."

"I think we can do better than that," he says.

I seriously doubt he can beat the best hot chicken in Nash-ville—one of the few reasons I'm actually enjoy being back in the city. But rich people love their pageantry and place settings. Real people prefer good eats. "When?"

"Say seven o'clock at the house?"

"I'll be there." I cut off the call and look down to the city below the window. Nashville stretches before me like an old friend. From here I can see all of Broadway from the Art Deco lines of the Frist down to the bars. There's hardly any foot traffic at this hour as the street rests up for another raucous night. When the moon takes over for the day shift, the world below will be a neon blur of life and music. There's a lot to love about the city. It's not New York, but in some ways it's more of a home than I ever knew there. But I'm not looking for a home, I'm looking for a kingdom. I'm going to be the law of this land. This is the perfect castle in the sky.

Ms. Summers drops her lipstick back into her purse when I return to the kitchen. "Would you like me to show you the joint amenities"—

"I'll take it," I cut her off. I'd known I would before I scheduled the showing, but I'm not one to pay commission without making an agent work for it.

"I will start all the paperwork and I assume you have financing in place?" She chews on her lipstick as if she's been burned at this point before.

I'm about to make her year. "It's a cash purchase," I correct her, checking my watch to discover this took longer than expected. "Text me when you're ready for me to sign. I need to get to an appointment."

She blinks rapidly like she's about to pass out. Her fingers search for the printed listing she left on the counter when we arrived. When they find it, she holds it out to me. "It's three million dollars."

"I can read," I say coolly. It's not the first time a person has assumed my bank balance based on my age.

"Who are you?" she asks before quickly recovering her

wits, "I mean, what do you do? I'll need to know where the funds come from for the paperwork."

She needs to know because she's dying to find out how a 24 year-old has three million to drop on a penthouse.

"I manage bank portfolios, personal assets," I tell her. She doesn't need to know more than that.

And her first question? *Who I am?* That's something I don't show anyone.

The Barrelhouse is empty at ten o'clock in the morning. The lights are off, chairs still on the tables, and its famous stage empty. The glow from a large neon music note casts a blue hue over the dark space. Its hum fills the quiet with unmistakable tension as though any moment the silence will shatter and spill over with life. At night, it transforms into a blues club that's equal parts rowdy and respectable. Everyone —and I mean everyone—has played the Barrelhouse. It's the kind of place where Mick Jagger might stop in and jump on stage for a set unannounced. The place is a landmark in the music industry, and the first club where I ever heard the blues played when I arrived in Tennessee five years ago. Then I was a kid being dragged to hear a musician I'd never heard of in a place I didn't know existed. Today, its new owner is an old friend.

A man bustles from the back kitchen, a bottle of whiskey in each hand. Even here in his own club, Jack Archer moves like the military—efficient but aware of the entire room, his broad shoulders squared and ready for anything. That's probably why he instantly spots me, a wide grin splitting his brown face, and holds up a bottle. "Took you long enough. The hard stuff?"

He knows better than to ask. I shake my head anyway. "It's not even noon."

"Luca will be disappointed," he says. "Coffee it is."

"Luca should have gotten here first."

"I did," Luca says sourly behind me.

Turning, I find Luca DeAngelo sitting in the shadows. Jack might move like a lion surveying his kingdom for potential threats, but Luca sticks to the dark corners. He waits in the shadows for the right moment to strike. Individually, we all have our strengths. Now that we're all here together, we can relax. The tension fades as we drop our collective guard. Jack retrieves ceramic mugs from below the bar and Luca stretches his arms overhead before lounging back lazily in his chair.

"I told you he wouldn't drink with us," Luca says. "This isn't Cairo, after all."

"Cairo was a different story." I grab a chair and spin it around. Straddling it, I drop into the chair and wish he hadn't brought that particular mistake up.

"Most people don't start their day with a shot of West," Jack defends me as he pulls a shot from the La Marzocco. The espresso machine is a concession to the number of people who need coffee when a long night of drinking turns into a mad rush home as dawn breaks. "Still take it black?"

I nod.

"You know how I take it," Luca says.

Jack frowns but pours a dash of Irish whiskey into Luca's mug. He joins us at the table in the corner.

"It's like old times," I say, taking my cup from him. "The three of us sitting in the dark drinking coffee."

"The coffee is better here," Jack says.

"The weather, too," Luca adds.

For all we bash the Middle East, I suspect none of us mean it. We might not miss the heat. But the people? The experiences? Our time there affects us still. I see it every time I get together with my best friends. We can't stay still. We can't fall into normal life. We're always waiting for ground fire or marching orders. At least, Luca and I are. Jack is another story.

"How's the label?" I blow on my coffee, waiting for it to be cool enough.

Jack, who has always had an inhuman tolerance for heat, takes a sip of his without waiting. "Fine."

"That means it's shit," Luca guesses.

"The record label is fine," Jack repeats.

Luca continues to ignore his coffee, concentrating on Jack instead. "If you need help—"

"I have everything covered," Jack assures us quickly.

We all know where the foundation of our current success was laid, but Jack is determined to change direction, even if it means losing every dime on dreams of building his own record label. He's been cautious, starting small with buying the Barrelhouse from its elderly owner last year and turning the hole in the wall landmark into a place to see and be seen. From there, he spun off a small, upstart label: Archer Records. "If I take money, then what happens when someone's niece *needs* a record deal? Suddenly I'm stuck producing the next pop princess?" He shakes his head as if the thought is too painful to bear. "There are a lot of talented artists out there who deserve to have records."

"It's like you're fucking allergic to money," Luca says with disgust. Even with the addition of Irish whiskey, he seems uninterested in his coffee.

"I have everything I need." Jack shrugs. He's never chosen to be flashy with our self-made fortune, and I've never asked him what he did with it. There's no way the Barrelhouse or Archer Records cost him all of his take from the old days. He's just never seemed to need more than to follow his passion. Still, he knows better than to debate this with Luca.

Trusting Luca DeAngelo is like sticking your hand into a black box. He might reward you. He might bite. After all these years, it's still impossible to know which to expect, even as his friend.

When Jack doesn't take his bait, he turns on me, "So, are you still going through with this?"

He should know better the question my resolve when it comes to the MacLaine family. "I just bought a place on Twelfth Avenue."

"The Twelve South Towers?" Jack whistles in appreciation. Unlike Luca, Nashville is in his blood. "Those are pricey."

"Come back to work with me," Luca suggests to him, "and you can move out of that shithole you call home upstairs."

"I like that shithole," Jack says.

Luca isn't buying it. "Bullshit."

This is how it always is with them. Physically, they're about as far apart as possible. Jack's golden brown skin and black eyes are the extreme opposite of Luca's hazel eyes and olive-hued skin. But from the way they go at it, they sound like brothers. I'm the one stuck mediating their constant bickering. We may have come from different mothers, but for all intents and purposes, that's what we are: brothers.

"What's the plan, Sterling?" Jack asks, getting back to the point of this meeting. He'd been happy when I called him until I'd told him whose funeral I was coming to town for. It didn't matter if he had known it was coming. Now that it's here, he seems to be rethinking the situation.

"Getting cold feet?" I ask.

"No," he says and he sounds sincere. He studies me for a second. "Are you?"

Neither of them questioned me when I asked them to buy

equal interests in the suddenly available personal holdings of Angus MacLaine a few months ago. The old man had leveraged his family's personal stock against his failing media empire in a desperate attempt to buy his freedom from the DeAngelo family, among others. He'd bought short-term relief, but lost the gamble he'd be around long enough to buy back what he had sold. I'd been investing quietly in MacLaine media for years under a shell company, careful not to draw too much attention to myself. Now, between the three of us, we're in possession of nearly half of MacLaine Media.

"I still don't understand why you need us?" Luca says. His particular brilliance isn't in the financial but rather the mental aspects of the game. Basically, he knows how to fuck with people until they crack.

"Isn't it more fun this way?" I ask. I could explain, but that's what he really cares about.

"Malcolm MacLaine has no idea who holds the interest in his company," Jack explains. "When he starts to look, he needs to think there are three major players, not just Sterling."

"What's fun about that for you?" Luca asks me. "It's not usually how you operate. You prefer to go for the jugular."

"I guess I'm taking a page from your book," I tell him. Luca prefers to play with his prey. It's more about slowly torturing someone until they self-destruct than blowing them up.

"Having a lot of money wrapped up in a failing company isn't my idea of a good time. No matter who I'm fucking with," he says dryly.

"Not everything is about money."

"That's not the Sterling Ford I know." Luca narrows his eyes before he finally shrugs. "*Suum cuique.*"

Translation: he'll respect my wishes. Despite his more sociopathic tendencies, Luca can be democratic as well. I don't know what fire burns inside him or what fuels Jack. I know enough about my friends to guess what drives them, and I know they have my back. They've never questioned why I hate the MacLaines. It's enough that I do. We each have our own black list of names. We don't have to explain those lists to one another. Not after what we've been through together. Not with the secrets we share.

"When do you want us to move on it?" Jack asks. I know he's less comfortable with this arrangement despite what he says.

"We wait. I'll decide what we do with them later."

"What does Sutton think?" Luca asks.

Jack bites back a grin. He knows Luca is purposefully goading me.

"Sutton has nothing to do with this," I say, straining to keep my cool. It will only fuel Luca's enjoyment of his little joke to do anything else.

He doesn't hide his disappointment nearly as well. "In that case, there were other matters to discuss. I spoke with my uncle regarding the London accounts."

"That's my cue." Jack stands. "I need to get the bar ready to open."

We still haven't gotten used to Jack's desire to stay out of our other business affairs. There was a time we partnered on everything, but we've been going our separate ways for a while. I went independent years ago. Luca went back to his family. Jack is trying to be legit. That's going to be harder while Luca and I are in town.

But as Jack reaches for our dishes, he looks at the tattoo on his forearm. The one he knows is under my shirt sleeve. Luca's, too.

Nothi in infernum.

We might have made good, but we still have debts to pay.

Luca and I discuss the issues concerning his uncle, Marcus DeAngelo, who I'd only left in London a few weeks ago. "He doesn't need to worry. There's no way to trace that account."

"That's what I told him," Luca says.

"He says that MacLaine is reaching out, trying to find out which private investors are holding the shares Angus sold. He wants to invite them to Windfall to discuss options. Apparently, Malcolm MacLaine wants the estate and the company to remain with the family."

"He's going to be disappointed," I say calmly.

"He's trying to figure out who the largest holder is so that the family can regain a majority of the holdings."

"He's going to be disappointed when none of the investors will sell."

"Rumor is that he isn't looking to buy." Luca's mouth twitches. "He's apparently old school. He's offering his family's reputation in trade."

The bastard had gotten the idea from me. "I guess he isn't above selling his sister."

"Did you ever think he was?" Luca scoffs.

"He seemed to think so." I hadn't bought Malcolm's gallant display of fraternal concern for Adair then. He's not looking out for her now. He only wants to make certain he's hooking the biggest catch.

"If he finds out about Jack or me?" Luca asks.

"He's not going to find you," I say, fiddling with my cuff-links. I'd carefully run every transaction through back channels. No one can question my discretion when it comes to ensuring client anonymity. I suppose Luca's concern lies with whether I'm being careful with my own privacy. He doesn't need to worry. "At least, he's not going to find anyone I don't want him to find."

"He assumes the DeAngelos have some of them. Marcus

told me as much. He wants me to deal with it." Luca's stormy eyes glitter with possibilities.

"How convenient." This could be fun. I have plans for Adair MacLaine. Plans that include an altar and a white dress and broken hearts. But there's plenty of time to play with her until then. "Ready to play a game?"

He doesn't need to consider. "Always."

10

ADAIR

B y the third day of the Cold War between me, Malcolm, and Ginny, I'm craving an escape and a friendly face, which is why I agree to a shopping date with Poppy. I need serious best friend time even if it means the mall. How she can still want to shop after being in Paris doing just that a week ago is beyond me. But Poppy is a shopper. I am not. She's a hugger. I am not. She sees the world through rose-colored glasses and I prefer to keep things a focused twenty-twenty. She's also exactly what I need to balance my tendency to be a bitch. That means if Poppy Landry wants a hug, mimosas, and three new pairs of shoes, I'm in.

I volunteer to drive, even if it means picking her up at the condo she shares with Cyrus in downtown Nashville and circling back toward the outskirts of the city, because it's always safer when she's not behind the wheel. Poppy sweeps out of the building in a yellow chiffon sundress that wraps around her swan-like neck, accentuating her bronze shoulders. She looks like she just stepped off a Parisian runway in nude Louboutin sandals that circle her ankle gracefully. In my black Converse, I'm going to be nearly a foot shorter than her, but I reserve heels of that height for business meetings and charity functions. I'd never survive a trip to the mall in them. She slips into the Roadster, arranging her skirt so that it won't blow up when we hit the highway.

"Darling." Despite the slight console separating us, she throws herself across the wide bench seat to hug me. When she pulls back her eyes shine with tears. "How are you?"

I blow a stream of air from my lips and shrug. "I don't really know."

"I'm sorry I wasn't here," she says.

I've heard a lot of apologies in the last few weeks. Everyone it seems is sorry for my loss. Maybe it's the fact that I'm not entirely certain I share this feeling. Maybe it's that I've had so much time to process it due to the length of daddy's illness. Or maybe it's that I've gone completely numb—my heart an anesthetized organ in my chest, functional but deadened. But I'm tired of hearing them. It's too much to process—Sterling, my father, the will.

"Don't be sorry for living your life," I say, turning the key in the ignition.

"I wasn't here when you needed me."

"You're here now." And that's enough. "I just need a friend."

"You always have a friend," she promises. "And you don't have to go shopping for me to be here."

"I want to." Strangely, I mean it. I can't help being in a good mood when she's happy.

"Does that mean I get to pick things out for you?" she asks mischievously eyeing my gray t-shirt.

That could be dangerous, given the uncertainty of my bank account and the fact that my daily wardrobe is mostly jeans, t-shirts, and the occasional sundress. "I don't need anything."

"Shopping isn't about needs. It's about relaxation." She studies me with a critical eye. "Have you been sleeping?"

"Yes," I say defensively.

"What about a dress for the auction?" she suggests.

I cringe. I've been trying to get out of going to the fundraiser for months. It's bad enough to go alone, but I know my brother plans to attend. "I don't know if—"

"You are not getting out of this one," she informs me. "You volunteer with the shelter!"

"That doesn't mean I have to go." But I know that it does. Poppy might have hatched the plan to host a charity gala to benefit adoptions for the Valmont Animal Rescue but she did it because she knew I was worried about loss of funding. Putting on a dress is the least I can do, even if I'd rather hang out at the shelter with the puppies. "You can pick out my dress, okay?"

She lights up like neon at nightfall, immediately launching into the current drama surrounding the gala she's been planning for the last three months, yelling over the rushing wind. I'm mostly caught up when we arrive at Valmont Gallery, which isn't a shopping center, but an experience. The mall sprawls over five acres of land, housing dozens of luxury brands, restaurants, and department stores.

A valet greets us at the parking station near the West entrance, and I hesitate in the driver's seat.

"Park her in a big spot away from other cars," I advise, knowing the classic car is a lot wider than most modern vehicles.

He nods, tearing off a ticket, and I can't help wondering how many times a day he puts up with this request.

"Please," Poppy interjects. She's already out of the car, giving me a look that reminds me of my mother. "She meant to say please."

"Please," I add, feeling properly chastised. Another reason I need her around.

We head straight for Bottega Veneta. Poppy is giggles and rainbows as she gives me the play-by-play on her trip to Paris. It takes effort to leave my worry behind with the car, but I do my best. The truth is I'm not sure I should be shopping even if I need something for the fundraiser. Yes, Daddy left me an inheritance, but I can't help wondering if it's made of fool's gold. Malcolm's reaction led me to believe that everything is on the line. I can't tell Poppy this, though. I can't tell anyone. If we do lose Windfall, if we do lose MacLaine Media, what happens to my family?

I've had a perpetual stomach ache since our meeting with Harding. I can't think about it.

Meanwhile Poppy gushes over a dainty, racing green colored purse with the sales associate. "It's beautiful," she says like she's taking in a masterpiece. "But I just bought a spring bag in Paris."

He immediately launches into all the reasons one spring bag isn't enough. "This is an exceptional shopping tote." He opens the flap as if to prove this. "It will fit all your necessities but not be too heavy. That bag is better for lunch dates."

They banter about this for twenty minutes before she gives in.

"And you?" He studies me for a moment, no doubt trying to determine if I'm a lost cause.

I consider it for a split second, wondering if I can buy a few minutes of happiness. In the end, I decide for him, patting my small cross-body Louis Vuitton that I've had for years. "I'm good."

We leave the bag to be properly wrapped for pick-up later. I lose track of Poppy's purchases by the third store. I can't seem to mindlessly fall into the rhythm I usually enjoy in her presence.

"Okay, spill. What's wrong with you?" Poppy demands.

I study a display of silk scarves intensely, trying to look like I'm enjoying myself. "Nothing's wrong."

"You can talk to me," she says, "unless…"

"Unless?" I murmur absently. Did Cyrus tell her that Sterling is back? Does she remember what it was like four years ago when he left? Has she forgiven me yet?

"Unless you're upset that I missed the funeral." She chews on her lower lip. "I feel awful. I should've come home."

I shake my head quickly. The trouble with being in a bad mood is that good people always think they put you there. "You didn't need to be there."

"I know that's what you said. But a best friend should be there even when they're *not needed*." She's quoting me and the conversation we had when I called to tell her it was over. Trust Poppy to know that what I say and what I actually want are often two very different things. We've been friends long enough for her to see through me like that.

The truth is that I wish she'd been there, but not for the reasons she thinks. I hadn't needed her until Sterling showed up. "It's really not about the funeral."

I can't decide where to start. In the end, my recollection of the day tumbles out of me. I tell her about Sterling. Poppy's expression grows from interested to horrified as my story continues. When I get to the part where my ex is talking with her boyfriend, she gasps.

"Did he say anything?" I ask.

"No! Good lord, Adair, do you think I would have spent all morning worrying about buying a purse if I'd known Sterling Ford was in town?" She grabs my arm and yanks me toward a small, indoor café. We take seats and I don't protest when she orders two white wines before noon.

"Tell me every detail," she demands when the waiter leaves to get our drinks.

"That's all." Frustration bubbles inside me. How many times have I relived seeing him at the gravesite? Seeing him in Windfall? "I never thought I would see his face inside my house again. Honestly, I never thought I'd seen his face again period. It's been years and he walked through the door like it was yesterday. I don't know why he was there."

Poppy groans, rolling her brown eyes dramatically, before turning a playful but withering glare on me. "You don't know why he was there?"

"He didn't talk to me!"

"Please! He came to see you." She says it like it's a settled matter.

I can't admit that I want that to be the truth. That after all these years convinced that I hate him, seeing him once makes me doubt that I do. But it can't be that simple. Nothing with Sterling is ever simple. "If he wanted to see me, he would've come back four years ago, right?"

Poppy hesitates, a battle playing out across her face.

"What?"

"It's nothing." She shakes her head.

Poppy is a great friend, but a terrible liar. When she tries to lie, I half-expect her nose to grow like the old fairytale. She's that bad at it. "Spill."

"He did come back." The confession bursts out of her.

The waiter arrives with our wine to find us sitting in stunned silence. Well, to find me sitting in stunned silence. Poppy looks like she's about to throw up.

"What do you mean he came back?" I ask softly after a minute.

"After you left for Cambridge," she confesses. "He was only here for a few days. I didn't see him."

"How do you know he came back?"

"Cyrus told me."

I close my eyes and let myself ask the one question that I've tortured myself with for the last four years. "Did he say why?"

"He said he came to get his things before he shipped out. Cyrus said he gave him your letter."

That didn't explain anything. It only hurt more. Sterling had returned to Valmont. He had the letter. Cyrus told me he gave it to him, but he failed to mention it was in person. I thought it had been years since Sterling set foot in Tennessee. I was wrong.

"Well, then he didn't come back for me." It's the harsh truth. Because even if I hadn't been gone, even if he had known where I was—if he read that letter, he should have come after me.

"I promised Cyrus I wouldn't tell you," Poppy says, still looking queasy. "I didn't want to hurt you. You'd moved on— left for London…"

"I did move on," I lie. It's so easy to lie about London now that even I'm starting to believe I was happy there.

It isn't her fault that Sterling came back then—or now. It's no one's fault.

"What are you going to do?" Poppy asks.

"Live my life?" I shrug, wishing that idea rolled off my shoulders instead of landing like a lead yoke around them. "What am I supposed to do?"

"Hunt him down," she says, "and demand he tells you why he ignored your letter."

"He ignored my letter because he didn't care." I need to

come to grips with that. I've had four years to let go of him. Seeing him successful and indifferent is the final blow.

Poppy clearly doesn't share this revelation, because she slams a fist on the table. "Okay, hunt him down and cut off his balls."

The group of older women next to us falls silent at her explosion, casting disapproving looks in our direction before getting up and moving across the café.

"Sorry," Poppy calls, her British half getting the best of her. Under her breath, she adds, "Nosy old birds."

"At least, they'll have something to talk about," I say dryly.

Some things don't change. Sterling Ford and I have always been something to talk about.

11

STERLING

Windfall has shed its mourning garb, welcoming life and spring back to its tree-lined drive and manicured gardens. The guard is back on duty at the gate. He steps from the security booth, hitching up his belt with his hands as he scans my car. He can't be more than a year or two out of high school. He has that wet behind his overly-prominent ears quality. No one's told him that, though. Maybe it's the gun in his holster boosting his confidence, but he leans down to the window and waves his hand.

"Can I see your identification?"

I've no doubt Malcolm informed the guards of my invitation, but this kid isn't going to let me go without checking off his entire list. He takes my driver's license and studies it carefully. "New York, huh?"

"Yes." Thank God, he can read.

"Old picture. You musta been what? Eighteen?" He says this like there's a huge gap between my eighteen and his nineteen.

I tilt my Ray-Bans to stare at him. Am I on Magnolia Lane or Memory fucking Lane? "Does that matter?"

"It's about to expire is all. Have a nice evening." He waves me through the wrought iron gates and closes them behind my car.

The sky ebbs into dusky purple as I near the house. There are still a handful of gardeners out, using up the last few moments of twilight to finish their work for the day. Adair once told me it took dozens of staff to keep the property looking like a private resort. It's ironic, really. Angus MacLaine nearly lost everything before he died, but he'd managed to cling to appearances until the very end—a tradition his children have chosen to keep alive, by the looks of it.

At the funeral I'd seen a number of new faces among the house staff, but an old, familiar one greets me at the door. Felix betrays no recognition as he opens the door to the house. The man was ancient when I first met him and the years have left their mark. There's a tremor in his step as he moves to the side to allow entrance.

"I'm expected," I say coolly, wondering if his memory is going along with his body.

"Yes, Mr. Malcolm, pardon me, sir, Mr. *MacLaine*, is in the sitting room," he corrects himself. It must be hard to give an old dog a new master. "He asked that you join him for a drink before dinner."

It's impossible to judge whether his ignorance of me is deliberate or not. Butlers have a peculiar sense of decorum even with old friends, and truth be told, I always liked the old butler. I have no idea how he puts up with the lot of them. But loyalty is a tricky thing. Sometimes it's only habit. Sometimes you don't know better. Like any relationship, sometimes you stay when you should go.

He shows me to the sitting room, which I could find on my own. Like most of Windfall, nothing's changed. An oil painting of the family hangs over a carved Italian marble hearth. Despite the warm weather outside, a gentle fire burns in its grates. The room's temperature remains perfectly controlled, naturally. The MacLaines aren't the type to worry about energy efficiency. It's all part of the traditional Southern image they project. Felix moves to stoke the fire as Malcolm rises from a leather wingback. He's abandoned his suit and tie for a checked shirt, rolled at the sleeves and crisp khakis. It's all the very picture of gentility.

He extends his hand to shake mine. "Mr. Ford, I'm pleased you can join us. Can I get you something to drink?"

"Whiskey over ice," I say.

"Felix, did you open that bottle of West Reserve?" It's an order masquerading as a question. Malcolm MacLaine doesn't serve drinks to his guests no matter how important they are.

"Yes, sir." Felix moves to a bar cart in the corner and begins preparing my drink. Ice cubes clink in the Waterford tumbler. I can't help but notice how his hands shake as he drops them in one at a time.

I move closer as causally as possible, taking the drink when he turns to deliver it. I won't watch the old man spill.

"Aged fifteen years," Malcolm brags as he takes a sip of his. "So complex. You can taste the oak and sherry in it."

I nod in agreement, unsurprised that he doesn't seem to notice that I'm not drinking. People rarely do. Accepting the drink is the important part of the transaction between men with money. I learned a long time ago that powerful men see the world and its people through their own filters. Some men, like Felix, exist to serve. Most men exist to be intimidated, kept carefully under thumb. Other men might be useful but there's always a test to be sure. Those are the types you offer a drink. Acceptance is simply the first step toward partnership. I've shown I'm willing to take something he gives me. Now what other offers will he make?

"I'll send you a bottle," he says. A gift? A bribe? There's hardly a difference to a MacLaine. "Tell me about this real estate transaction."

He manages to hide the panic in his voice but a small note of anxiety sounds in the background.

"A penthouse," I tell him. "I need a place to stay in the city."

"So you won't be staying in Valmont?" It's a loaded question. He wants to know how close I'll be to the dragon's hoard he's trying to protect. Or if it's already too late.

He doesn't need to know the truth. "I prefer the city."

"I don't blame you. It's harder when you have a family." He glances at a framed picture on the mantle. I recognize his wife but I've never seen the dark-haired girl before. "My daughter, Ellie. I don't think we could coop her up in an apartment."

"Better to give her fifty acres to roam," I say, my words an innocuous reminder that I'm well-schooled on this estate.

"Indeed." He reaches to straighten a tie that's not there, tugging loose the top button instead. "I'm sure dinner is nearly ready. My wife will be joining us."

He rises and I follow suit. I don't ask about Adair. Malcolm MacLaine knows what I'm after, which means she'll be there, too. He doesn't need to know how much or why. Not yet.

When I don't prod him for more information, he adds, "And Adair, of course."

"I'm glad to hear it," I murmur as we make our way toward the dining room.

"You never told me how you know my sister?" He stops for a second. "You do know my sister?"

Bless his heart. This was the best Angus MacLaine did as a replacement. It's going to be far too easy to ruin the entire family. "I attended Valmont with her."

"Oh, you're a Viper." He references the school's mascot like the overly devoted former frat boy he is.

"More or less. I started at Valmont, but I finished my education elsewhere."

Wheels turn in his dark eyes as he ushers me into the dining room. An arrangement of roses and tulips in various hues of pink rests artfully in the middle of the table laid with crystal and gold-rimmed china. Malcolm MacLaine is showcasing his wealth to remind me who I'm getting into bed with. But it's more than a performance, he's trying to figure out who I am. He thinks I've given him a clue. I have. When this is over, I want the MacLaines to know exactly who ruined them. I want them to know there's no mercy coming from me. I want them to remember sitting down to dine with the enemy.

12

ADAIR

Poppy distracts me from thoughts of Sterling as best she can for the rest of the trip, but I don't sell my enthusiasm very well. In the end, I buy a handful of new tops she forces on me, her version of therapy always defaulting to the retail variety. The only item I put real consideration into is the gown for Poppy's upcoming charity auction.

After trying on what feels like hundreds of dresses, a red silk one finally meets her approval. It's the last gown I would have considered, considering my hair, but she's right about it. The color sets off my copper locks rather than clashing with it. It's elegant and sexy without being too much for a room full of philanthropists.

Our bags and boxes fill the Roadster's trunk by that evening. Poppy shoves at a bag to get the lid to close before collapsing against the car. "I'm starving. Do you think Felix will feed me?"

I force a smile. Felix has been avoiding me the last few days, or I've been avoiding him. It's hard to tell in a house as big as Windfall. "I'm sure he'll feed *you*."

As we head back to the estate, Poppy lets out a shriek. "Kai is going to make it to the auction!"

Finally, some good news. Usually, I dread these parties, but it's been too long since I've seen Kai Miles. "I haven't seen him in ages."

"He's going to be the celebrity emcee," she tells me. "There was a conflict but he moved things around."

"I'm sorry I haven't helped you with this." It's been eating away at me for months that she's doing this on her own, especially since she's doing it for me.

"You've had a lot on your plate," she says, dismissing my concern.

"You wouldn't even be doing this if it weren't for me."

"And that's not a good enough reason?" she counters. "They need to raise the funds, and I can help. It's not your job to fix everything. Your dad was sick, honey. You were needed at home. *But* you're going to put on that killer dress, come to this party, drink too much champagne, and actually enjoy yourself."

"Is that so?" I can't help laughing at her determination.

"The last few weeks have been hell, and you deserve to have a good time."

Poppy might be the only person in my life who believes I deserve anything. I have no idea why. If she peeled back a few layers of me, she'd probably reverse her position on that.

My life has been hell for more than the last few weeks, which is why she never tries. I've done my best to hide it over the years, but when my father's health took a turn for the worse, it became not only impossible but also, for the first time, acceptable to be open about it. No one can fault a daughter suffering while her father is on his deathbed. It only made me look like the dutiful, obedient child he'd always wanted. He had known why I was really around, playing my part. Just like he knew why I had come back from Cambridge to Valmont after my short-lived escape. The world assumes I came home to be by his side. I let them believe that. Sometimes the lie is prettier than the truth.

"I need to remember to get tickets," I say, making a mental to-do list in my head. I no longer have a dying man to care for, it's time to take back my life.

"Malcolm already bought a table," Poppy reassures me. "Or his secretary did."

That sounds more like it. I'm not thrilled to share the evening with my brother, but a charity event in Valmont never runs out of booze. There will be enough social lubricant for the both of us.

"Do I have to bring a date?" I ask.

"Absolutely not!" She casts a coy look in my direction. "There will be plenty of bachelors from all over Nashville there."

I've known ninety percent of Nashville bachelors since grade school. "I'm not really interested in meeting someone. I just don't want to look like a loser sitting alone."

"No one is going to let you sit alone," Poppy says. "I have plenty of people I want to introduce you to."

Her matchmaking won't be denied. "Do you have selective hearing?"

"Only when it comes to you denying your happiness," she says.

I can't blame my best friend for wanting to see me happy. Her matchmaking has been on the uptick since she and Cyrus began discussing rings. Why do happy people always try to force everyone around them to be happy, too?

I turn the Roadster down Windfall's private drive. The magnolias have begun to bloom, the delicate pink blossoms perfuming the sultry, spring evening. I need to pick some for mama's grave before they wilt. They never last long enough.

A black Vanquish is parked in the circle drive, which means Malcolm has guests for dinner. At least, I'll have an excuse to eat in the kitchen now. I park the Jaguar in the garage and we pile our purchases as Poppy continues to fill me in on the details of how the auction will work, down to her conflict over the centerpieces. "I want to do something cute and on theme."

"Like?"

Her arms are full as she continues, "Little dog bones or something, but my mother says it's tacky."

Miranda Landry believes anything less than Waterford crystal spilling liquid gold and diamonds is tacky. It's going to take effort to persuade her to go with a theme.

"Why not a traditional centerpiece with little dog bone cookies at the table?"

"That's genius. She can't argue with that." She nearly drops her bag as she struggles to get her phone out to make a note. I hold open the back door to the kitchen while she types it out.

We deposit our bags in a heap on the corner desk where Felix usually plans menus and grocery lists. I turn in time to spot excited, blue eyes pop up over the back of a stool at the counter. "*Auntie Dair*, you're home!"

Warmth spreads through me at Ellie's greeting. She's probably the only person in this house to genuinely miss me when I'm gone. In fairness, she's the only person in this house that I miss most of the time, too. Her eyes skip to Poppy, growing from quarters to saucers. "Auntie Poppy!"

I can't compete with my best friend for her affection, though.

"There is my little darling," she coos, going over to give her a hug. Her slender, amber arms circle the little girl and

Ellie melts into the hug. Poppy loves her almost as much as I do.

"I got you something," Poppy tells Ellie. She produces a bright red bag emblazoned with a star.

Ellie leaps out of her chair, knocking her glass over as she reaches for the American Girl bag.

"You spoil her," I whisper to Poppy as Ellie unwraps the doll she brought her.

"I love it!" Her tiny arms wrap tightly around her new treasure before she releases the doll to study it more closely. She analyzes it with the intensity of an astronomer discovering a new star. "She's so beautiful."

"Someone should." Poppy mutters so only I can hear.

Enough said. Poppy gets away with it, though, since she's not family. It's harder when I try to spoil Ellie. Malcolm doesn't like it when I bring her gifts. He says it's not my place. It's not as though she wants for anything. Ginny has filled her room with beautiful objects and books and clothes all with a particular place they must remain to "look right." It's like stepping into a page from a catalog. Ginny throws her lavish birthday parties, just like my father used to give us. Those objects appear in Ellie's life, showing up in her room in place of her mother and father. Those parties are full of people she doesn't know, occupying her parents' time. It's moments like this that the little girl craves. A simple surprise. A loving gesture.

"Why is she eating down here?" I ask Cara, the night nanny, who's taken our arrival as an opportunity to play a game on her phone. She looks up and answers with some hesitation, "Mr. Malcolm has a guest at dinner."

"Oh, I forgot." I'd seen the car, but it's just like my brother to send his daughter to the kitchen while he entertains a business partner. It's what our father did. Our mother never allowed that when she was alive. She said supper was family time. My father's soft spot had allowed that. But when Ellie was born, he hadn't wanted her at the dinner table. A sentiment his son parroted and her mother didn't fight. I'd hoped that she'd be welcome there now that there was an empty spot at the table.

"Well, we'll join you," I tell Ellie.

"You, too, Auntie Poppy?"

"Of course." Poppy grabs her tiny hands and they twirl around the kitchen.

Cara puts down her phone, looking nervous. "They've set the table for you," she tells me. "I'm supposed to ask you to head up as soon as you're home."

The underlying implication is clear. I'm expected to be at dinner. I'm expected to play my role in this family.

"Is that so?" I stride out of the kitchen until I find Felix in the butler's pantry. He's prepping what looks like the second course.

"There you are! Your brother wants you at dinner. He's been asking where you were since I served the salad."

"My brother should have invited me to dinner," I say through gritted teeth. "I'm an adult. I might have other plans."

"I told him so." He nods sympathetically, and I feel bad for avoiding him. None of this is his fault. "Adair, there's something—"

"Can you have Lindsay set two more places at the table?" I interrupt.

"I'm not sure that's a good idea," he warns me. Felix has always looked out for me, but things need to change. Malcolm can't order me around like our father did. I'm not about to trade one tyrant for another.

"I have guests of my own," I say.

He glances over at his soup, and I can see he's calculating how to split it with the sudden addition.

"Unless there's not enough," I say quickly, realizing too late that once again my brother and I are burdening someone else's life with our childish disagreements.

"I can make it work," he says. "Ginny never eats anything anyway. I'll give her a smaller portion."

I make my way back to Poppy and Ellie. Bending down, I lift the little girl onto my hip.

"Miss?" Cara asks.

"She's going to dinner upstairs," I inform her.

It's time for this to stop. If that means making a scene and shaming Malcolm into being the father I expect him to be, then so be it.

"Felix is setting a place for you, too," I tell Poppy. "Will you stay?"

So maybe I need a little backup to wage this war.

She reads between the lines. "Of course. You can give me more brilliant ideas to sell my mother on the theme. Malcolm won't mind?"

"I'm sure it's just another one of daddy's old buddies. Malcolm is trying to sort out the family estate." I may have filled Poppy in on the funeral, but I left out the details of the will. It's not that I don't trust her with them, it's that I know she'll worry. Knowing her, she'll try to get the money from her parents to help us buy back the stock we lost. It doesn't matter if she's my best friend, a MacLaine doesn't take charity.

"I hope you don't mind, but I brought guests to dinner," I announce, unable to keep a smug smile from spreading over my face as we enter the dining room with Ellie in tow. The arrogance oozes out of me when Malcolm's guest turns to greet us.

"I don't mind," Sterling says from his place at the table.

I can't think of anything to say in response.

"Oh fuck," Poppy murmurs next to me. Clearly, she's not been rendered speechless.

"Auntie Poppy, you said a bad word." Ellie's voice is hushed with surprise at her angelic idol's faux pas.

Poppy scoops her from my arms, and I'm too surprised to stop her. "Yes, I did. How silly of me."

She carries the girl to the opposite side of the table, sitting next to her in two of the available seats and leaving the seat next to Sterling empty.

She said it best.

Fuck.

13

I have her attention. Adair MacLaine is on the hook, and I'm going to enjoy watching her wriggle.

"We started without you," Malcolm says without a hint of apology.

It had been clear to me when we started the soup course that Malcolm hadn't invited Adair to dinner. He had assumed, like the privileged asshole he was, that she would simply be there. I was annoyed earlier. Now? Seeing her sort through several stages of surprise makes her late arrival worth it.

Poppy does her best to appear oblivious as she deposits Malcolm's daughter into the seat across from mine. I know she recognizes me. I expect Cyrus told her I'm back in town. It's neither good nor bad to see her. Her presence is just a distraction for Adair. Still, while I've never hated Poppy, her ability to stay politely neutral annoys me. She's always been a diplomat, more concerned with keeping the peace than standing up in her friend's defense.

She seems to have flourished. Jetting off to Paris, wearing haute couture, she's become the Valmont stereotype. Unlike her, Adair is in jeans and a t-shirt, her attitude as fiery as her hair—until she saw me. This Adair is at odds with the woman at the funeral. She reminds me of the girl I met years ago. The question is: which one is the real Adair? Does she even know?

I turn back to my meal, confronted by curious, round eyes. The little girl is hardly tall enough to see over the table. From here, it looks like two wide blue orbs hanging over a soup bowl. I wink at her and her eyes scrunch up with a smile.

"Why don't you eat some soup, love?" Poppy suggests, nudging a spoon into her tiny hands. The girl looks down at the bisque and her face screws into a grimace.

"What is it?" she asks in her tiny voice.

"Lobster. Just eat it, Ellie," Ginny snaps.

Ellie drags her spoon through it but doesn't take a bite. "I want dinner not *wobster*."

My thoughts exactly. I'll never understand why rich people have to eat in courses for hours.

"It's coming," Poppy promises her.

"Are you going to join us?" Malcolm asks Adair, who is still standing in the doorway watching this play out.

I see a tremble roll through her body, hardly noticeable to anyone who doesn't know Adair's body like I do. Her shoulders square, her head tilts, pointing her button nose toward the ceiling, but her eyes fall on the empty seat next to mine. She might act high and mighty, but she has no choice. Soon that will be true about more than her seat at the dining table.

"I guess you didn't get my voicemail about dinner," Malcolm says, disapproval dripping off him as he surveys her casual attire.

This snaps Adair out of it. "Was I supposed to wear a ball gown?"

She saunters toward the table, yanks her chair back and drops into it without the slightest acknowledgment of my presence.

"We've never worn jeans to the table in this house." It's a simple observation laced with warning. For a second, Poppy and I lock eyes. We're two Christians in the Coliseum, and the MacLaines are on the verge of a battle.

"I assumed daddy's rules died with him."

Malcolm's mouth opens, his nostrils flaring, but Ginny jumps in.

"We have a guest," she reminds Adair, but it's a reminder for Malcolm as well.

"Yes," Malcolm says through gritted teeth. "Adair, do you remember—"

"I think so." Adair shoots a puzzled look my direction as if she's trying to place me. "Freshman year?"

So, this is how she wants to play it. She can pretend not to know me. Maybe she'll even sell Malcolm on her charade, but it's written all over her body in a language I've read before. She doesn't know what to do with me.

My fingers close over my butter knife, but I slip on an easy smile. "Seems like forever. Seems like yesterday."

"Feels like forever," she murmurs, picking up her spoon.

"Mr. Ford is interested in MacLaine Media," Malcolm says, each word heavy and purposeful. By now, the entire family knows that their legacy is on the line. There's no need to be more overt with his warnings. She knows what they stand to lose.

"It's Mr. Ford now?" Adair sips bisque from the tip of her spoon with delicate calm.

"Sterling," I correct her. "Old friends don't need to be so formal."

"Cyrus mentioned you were back in town." Poppy's interjection is met with a grateful smile by Ginny, whose been watching Adair and me with the paralyzed fear of a deer on the highway. "I told him we must do dinner. I feel terrible he's not here."

"Cyrus Eaton?" Malcolm is genuinely surprised.

"My old roommate," I explain.

I see something click into place in Malcolm's mind. Does he really think I came around asking about his sister on a whim?

"That's right," Adair says. "I'd forgotten you two had a dorm together."

"Good man," Malcolm says. "Did you room together all four years?"

"I left during my freshman year," I say nonchalantly. Next to me, Adair's spoon freezes midway to her lips. It's only for a second—a pregnant pause—and then she goes back to her feigned indifference.

"That sounds like a story," Malcolm says.

"It is." I recognize an invitation when I receive it, but I'm not about to tell any of them what they want to know. They're not getting through this that easily.

"I've been thinking, Adair," Poppy continues her attempts at small talk. She's always been good at sensing tension. "We should have a photo booth. The Clarks had one at their wedding, and everyone loved it."

"That's a good idea," Adair says, side-eying me and then looking away.

"A photo booth for what? Are you and Cyrus getting married?"

"No!" The nervous laughter accompanying this clarification suggests that's not down to her desires. "My family is hosting a gala for the local animal rescue. Adair has been helping me with a few last-minute details."

"A gala?" I emphasize the words, so my interest is clear to all parties. "Sounds fun."

Malcolm immediately seizes the opportunity. "You should come. It will give you a chance to see old acquaintances. If you knew Cyrus, then you'll know several people there. Being new to town, it might be a way to reconnect."

"*New*," Adair scoffs under her breath. I ignore her.

"Of course," Poppy says looking flustered, "I'm afraid you have to sponsor a table."

This is the moment I've been waiting for. My chance to dangle my wealth like a prize over the MacLaine family's heads. "That's not a problem. I can write you a check right now."

"Tables cost $7000," Adair says with a note of challenge.

"Seems like a worthy cause. Naturally, being *new in town*," I emphasize the phrase her brother used, "I won't have a full table to invite."

"Join our table," Malcolm says. "We'd love to have you."

Adair's spoon clatters into her soup bowl, splashing bisque on the tablecloth.

"I don't think—" she begins.

But I take advantage of her surprise. "I'd love to."

I turn my attention to Poppy, not wanting this to undermine my earlier effort. "You can count on me for a table fee regardless. It's better this way. Everything will go to the animals."

"That's very generous of you," Poppy says pleadingly, her entreaty directed at Adair, whose scowl could kill a man.

"Sometimes, I think I like dogs better than people," I say, meaning it. Dogs are loyal. They don't test you or manipulate you or leave you.

"Do you have a dog?" A tiny voice pipes up from the chair swallowing her across the table.

"Ellie," her mother says in a strained voice, "what is the rule at the table?"

"Children should be seen and not heard," she squeaks, her eyes turning down to the full bowl at her place. She drags her spoon again. No one's noticed that she hasn't had a bite.

The hollow place inside me that I've learned to ignore groans for recognition. She has so much of the things I never had but she's missing out on the one thing I'd always wanted, too. I lean across the table to see her better. She has her daddy's hair. "I don't have a dog. Do you?"

Her gaze darts between her mother and father. She doesn't dare answer until Ginny nods. "No. Mommy won't let me get one. She says dogs pee on the carpet."

"That's quite enough," Malcolm cuts her off.

"This is why we don't have Ellie at the table," Ginny laughs nervously but she's glaring at Adair not the girl. "She doesn't understand how to behave appropriately."

"She's four," Adair spits back.

A nerve has been touched, and now I'm stuck in the middle of a passive-aggressive tournament of champions. I suspect this is about more than the little girl coming to dinner.

"She's happier in the kitchen with Cara at dinner," Ginny disagrees. The two women glare at each other.

"She doesn't enjoy eating the same things," Malcolm explains to me, trying to distract me from the fight between his wife and his sister. "I suppose I didn't have much of a palate then either."

"Then bring her food up here," Adair says.

Ginny turns away from her and gives me a brittle smile. "It's just so important for us to have adult time."

"That's all you ever have," Adair murmurs.

While the adults argue, the glum frown on Ellie's face deepens as she pretends to play with her soup. She can hear everything they're saying. She knows they don't want her here.

Maybe her aunt does, but Adair has never had a talent for going about things the right way.

"Regardless, when we have company, she doesn't belong at the table." Ginny reaches for her wine. She's on the second glass of the evening, but it isn't mellowing her a bit. Every word from her mouth is clipped, strung as tightly as she is. One wrong move and she'll snap.

Tears well in Ellie's eyes and I try to think of something to say or do to end this that won't result in hurting her. Someone should fucking consider that. I turn to Adair, my jaw clenching tightly as I try to think of what to say. Despite her antics, she seems to care the most about the girl. When our gazes lock, I see it there: the trapped, wild look she always wore in this house when we first met. It's like a bird caught inside beating against the window for release. I start to open my mouth—to demand she do something—but before I can she mouths one word:

Don't.

Another time I might enjoy ignoring this plea, but this isn't about us.

Adair pushes her chair roughly back, its legs catching on the Persian rug. "I'll get her ready for bed."

"That won't be necessary. You're not her mother," Ginny says, her voice as smooth and cold as glass. But she doesn't move to stop Adair as she circles the table. "Cara!"

"I said I would do it," she repeats, lifting Ellie into her arms.

"Adair," Poppy calls to her friend softly, "why don't we—"

"It's not your place," Ginny hisses, abandoning any pretext of forced civility.

A woman appears dressed in a pressed, white dress that makes her look like she just stepped out of the goddamn nineteenth-century. She halts at the table and waits with her arms behind her back. "Cara, please put Ellie to bed."

"Yes, ma'am." She reaches for her and waits for Adair to release her. When she does, the nanny exhales in relief. Adair leans over and kisses Ellie's forehead.

"I'll come in and read you a story in a little bit," she whispers.

"I think we're ready for the main course," Malcolm says to Ginny who sits like a seething volcano at the other end of the table. She's on the verge of eruption.

"I'm not hungry," Adair says, and Ginny moves to stand.

For a second, I think that I might actually be privy to a chick fight, but before it can come to blows, Poppy interrupts. "Oh, I didn't realize it was so late. I need to go!"

"Yes, you do. I'll walk you to the door." Adair grabs Poppy's hand and leads her out of the room.

"I'm so sorry about that," Malcolm says. "MacLaine women are feisty."

Ginny sniffs as though she suspects this doesn't apply to her. Now that Adair is gone, she looks as though someone dumped water over her anger. It's still there smoldering, but it can't do anything but slowly fade.

Malcolm presses forward as the entrees arrive. It's as if nothing happened. "I'll have my secretary send the details over about the Gala. I think it's in…"

"The second week of May," Ginny says dutifully.

Ginny MacLaine is a walking calendar—and little else—to her husband, except maybe an accessory to hang from his arm at parties. It's hard to believe they even procreated given the constant chill between them.

"I look forward to it," I say. Lifting my napkin from my lap, I stand. "Would you mind if I use the restroom?"

Malcolm directs me to the nearest one. I don't need it, but

I do need to put some much-needed distance between the two of us. I pace the length of the hall until I reach the solarium doors and stop. It doesn't matter how far I go. I can't escape my thoughts.

I should be thinking about Adair, about forcing Malcolm to make a deal with the devil, planning how to humiliate one of them at the gala. Instead, my thoughts are with the little girl thrust into the family rivalry. Where the child is concerned, there's probably always drama. I know what it's like to be caught in the middle between warring parents, even if I never sat at fancy dinner tables with too many forks while my parents argued bitterly about having to put up with me. But I do know what it's like to want to crawl under a table and hide —to hope you turn invisible. Maybe it's not the same for her as it was for me but I saw the look in her eyes when her mother and father apologized for her existence.

I know what it's like to be unwanted.

"What are you doing?" Adair's voice breaks into my thoughts.

I turn to her slowly. She's regrouped and climbed back atop her pedestal, but her haughty demeanor feels forced. There was a time when she ruled over this house. Her reign is drawing to a close, and judging from the fear she's trying to hide, she knows it.

"Looking for the family silver," I tell her. "You know I have sticky fingers. All these years, I've been waiting for a chance to get at it."

Her lips flatten to prove she's not amused. "What are you doing *here*? Back in Valmont? Surely, you've moved on from petty theft."

"Investing." If she wants to play coy, then we will. "I'm diversifying my portfolio."

"Suddenly, you're interested in telecommunications?" She

doesn't buy it, but I never meant her to. I want her to see me coming. I want her to dread it.

"Communication is the future, Lucky."

If looks could kill, Adair MacLaine would be facing murder charges by morning. I'm the only person whoever called her that. Now even I don't get that privilege.

"How can you even afford—" She stops mid-sentence. She didn't mean to voice this question out loud.

"Of course, that's what you're wondering. How did I become wealthier than you?" I circle around her. She might be on her home turf, but I'm the one in charge. "How did Sterling Ford, the boy who couldn't compete with your trust fund, buy into your father's company? Isn't that what you really want to know?"

She doesn't answer immediately. Her silence echoes in the empty space around us, louder than anything she can say. In the end, she whispers, "I never asked you to compete with the trust fund."

"No, you didn't." That's the problem. She never even gave us a chance.

"Is that what this is about? You have a lot of nerve acting like this is my fault."

"Oh, it is." I take a step closer, savoring how she backs away. It feels so good that I continue herding her, until she's flattened against the wall. There's no where for her to run. No escape. Leaning closer, I press the palms of my hands to the wall, caging her to the spot. I want to know her attention on me is absolute. "You had a choice to make. Did you make the right one, Adair?"

She chokes on her denial. "I never—"

"Hasn't anyone ever told you it's unbecoming to make a bed you refuse to lie in?" She still wears the same perfume, notes of magnolia—honey-sweet but hiding a subtle tartness —bloom in my nostrils, awakening memories I'd locked away.

"I'm not interested in being a lady," she whispers.

I'm close enough to kiss her. Her body strains toward mine despite her pretense that she hates me as much as I hate her. There'd be no fight if I unbuttoned her jeans and slid a hand down her panties. My hand drops to her hip, on board with this plan. Adair stills in expectation, not moving to stop me. I slide the tip of my index finger along her waistband.

"That's probably wise," I say. "You were never any good at it." My head angles, drawn to the curve of her neck. I pause before my lips touch her skin, lingering in the temptation of her scent, feeling the heat of her this close to me. For a moment, her green eyes search mine looking for the answer to some unknown question.

"Why did you come back?" It's no longer an accusation on her tongue.

I know what she wants to hear.

I hate that it's the truth.

"For you."

14

STERLING
THE PAST

T his isn't what I imagined when Cyrus invited me to an off-campus *house* party. When he drove toward Adair's neighborhood, I had realized this wasn't going to be some college gathering. The gated entrance is open when we arrive, thrown wide to welcome us to the Garden of Eden. Ferns and palms clutter the grounds, their midnight-green shadows cast by precisely placed lights, and lush trees line the path. It empties into a small parking lot, already half-full of luxury vehicles. Cyrus shows me inside, stopping for hugs and high fives every few feet. He introduces me to everyone who stops us, but I'm too overwhelmed by the size of the place to remember any of them.

"Let's grab a drink," he suggests, nodding past the packed living room that's so full I can't even see furniture.

I glance over my shoulder at the crowded kitchen that looks like it's straight out of *Architectural Digest*. The stale smell of spilled beer and the clashing colognes from overheated bodies doesn't match the polished quartz countertops and stainless steel appliances. The crowd swallows Cyrus and I'm left searching for his blond head among the other party-goers.

Behind me, a grunt catches my attention. I shift to see two guys hauling a keg into the middle of the room. Perspiration drips down its aluminum sides as some genius tries to tap it and fails.

"Let me." I shove the idiot away before he winds up wasting half the beer. A few twists and turns and it's ready to go.

"Thanks!" Said idiot fills a Solo cup and hands it to me.

I'm guessing the first beer at a party is an auspicious offering in these parts, so I don't refuse. Instead, I deliver it to Cyrus.

"Very impressive." He sizes me up for the hundredth time since I met him on my first day. I can never quite tell what he thinks of me. I don't fit with his usual crowd, but he keeps inviting me to these things anyway. "We have to keep you around. Where's yours?"

I guess I've proven myself useful again. "Not my thing."

Cyrus arches an eyebrow like he can't make sense of this answer but doesn't press me on it. A second passes before his face splits into a grin. "You can DD then."

"That's why I'm here." I force a smile that I'm guessing comes off as a grimace. He doesn't notice. I'd said no when he first asked, agreeing only after he promised it wasn't another frat thing. Then he'd used the magic word: Adair. She's going to be here along with the rest of his group. It's been a month since her mother's funeral. Maybe she's pulled her head out of her ass by now. I suspect not, considering Cyrus told me she dropped out of Valmont. It's not like she needs or even deserves my pity. She's been a bitch at every opportunity—a bitch who can't take it when I dish out exactly what she's been serving. But I got a front row seat to the shitshow she calls her friends the last time I saw her. I doubt any of them have been checking up on her. Not genuinely, at least.

There's no sign of her, though, which means I'm stuck with Cy. I have no idea if I'm expected to play wing man or babysitter. "So, what's the plan?"

"For tonight? College?" He responds seriously like he's considered both.

Curiosity gets the better of me. Cyrus Eaton, who I've come to find out is the heir to a fucking hotel empire, doesn't need to think too far ahead. Given that every morning he wakes up he's surprised that he has classes, it shocks me to consider he might have done exactly that. "College, I guess."

"New one every night," he informs me with a grin that might suggest he's joking. I know he isn't. I've already come home to a sock on the door a couple times. He's been kind enough to drive them down to his family's hotel in Nashville since I complained about sleeping on the common room couch.

"That's ambitious, mate." I follow his eyes to the throng of people, wondering if he already spotted his prey for the night.

"Not up for the challenge, Ford?"

His words ricochet off me without hitting their mark. It's not the first comment he's made about my lack of bunk buddies since school started. He suspects I'm gay. I'm not, but it amuses me to let him wonder. He doesn't seem bothered by it. Still, he tests me every chance he gets.

"Look, I know these girls. Half of them are still in prep." Cyrus moves closer to me as if anyone could hear us in here.

"For fuck's sake, Cy. Did you drag me to a high school party?" I thought I'd left that particular brand of drama in New York. It's one of the few things I don't miss about my hometown. I have friends there, but my school didn't cater to the likes of people like Cyrus and his crew.

"They're legal, and half of them go to school with us. Beer doesn't discriminate, my friend," he advises me, dropping an arm around my shoulder. "The best part is that they're all looking to screw their daddies."

"I think we're a little young to be their daddies." I'll play along with his game for now. I don't have anything else to do at the moment.

"Metaphorically speaking," he clarifies, spreading his hands in surrender. "They've been told their whole lives that they have to marry up, marry well, marry rich, and then they've been forced to attend the same polo matches and charity fundraisers and schools with the same rich assholes for years. It's their own incestuous mating ritual."

"Aren't you one of those rich assholes?" I can't help but point out the obvious. Cyrus Eaton was born and bred in Valmont on a family estate to parents who inherited one of the world's largest luxury hospitality chains. I'm fairly certain he hasn't so much as washed a dish in his life. Cyrus was born with an inheritance larger than any income I'll ever make even if I had started knocking off banks from the cradle.

"Unfortunately, I am," he says. "But you aren't. This time of year new guys are like blood in the water. They can smell you."

I've met a few of these girls he's talking about. I have no doubt that they could rip me to shreds.

"That simple, huh?" I ask.

"You don't even have to try." He tips his head to the side and I look over in time to catch a few girls gawking at us. "First of all, you're fresh meat and every woman here knows it, and you look like you could rip someone's fucking arms off."

"That's a turn on?" I've known men who could do just that. I didn't see them as role models.

"To a girl who's spent half her life at country clubs and debutante balls, it is," Cyrus explains. "It's unfair. The rest of us have to rely on our charm."

"You're in serious trouble then."

"Come on," Cy prods me. He is not letting this go. "Call one or they're all mine."

I'm not here for that, but there's no way I'm going to explain to Cyrus why I came. He's not gonna back off until I've made a match and what else do I have to do with Adair a no-show? I scan the room, stopping when my eyes lock with a pretty black girl who looks familiar. It takes me a second to place her. We'd met at the funeral, but I don't remember her name. Her fuchsia lips part in invitation, her body angling toward me slightly across the space. "Who's that?"

He follows my gaze to her. "Darcy? This is her place. She's—"

"I think I'll go say hello," I cut him off before he can dispense more well-meaning advice. He stalks off in the opposite direction to begin his hunt.

I like Cyrus despite my reservations, but I'm not stupid enough to believe we're friends. As his roommate, I hold some interest for him. He's already talking about renting a house with Money and some other guys next year, though, and there's no way I'm signing up to live in that viper pit. Not that I could afford it, anyway.

"Hey," Darcy says, fanning her black lashes at me, as I approach. "Sterling, right?"

She remembers me? Maybe Cyrus isn't so far off in his estimation of my fresh meat status. "Darcy." She preens when I say her name, sticking out her chest which is already on display in a low cut, canary-yellow dress that hugs her curves. "Thanks for inviting me."

It seems like the right thing to say to the hostess. Her smile widens even as she feigns humility. "*Of course*. I don't even know half these people. Honestly, it's nice to see a friendly face." Her hand closes over my arm, long, manicured fingers squeezing it slightly. She bites her lip a little before pulling me toward the kitchen. "You need a drink!"

"I'm the designated driver," I say, latching on to the excuse Cyrus gave me.

Darcy shakes her jet-black ringlets, annoyance marring her face. "That is just like Cyrus. He doesn't have friends, because he treats everybody he meets like employees."

"It's not like," I stop her before she gets the wrong idea. "I volunteered. So you two aren't friends?"

"Sorta. Me, Money, Adair—we're more like business partners. He can't treat us like shit because we're..." She trails away, her eyes wide like she's almost spilled some secret. "How about a bottle of water?"

"Sure," I agree. She didn't need to finish that sentence. I know why Cyrus treats them differently. They're rich. I'm not. At least, Darcy Palmer tries to be a little classier about it. But she's aware of my rank in the food chain as much as she's aware of her position at the top.

Darcy bypasses the mammoth fridge in the kitchen and leads me down the hallway. I don't bother to ask where she's taking me. I would need a map to find my way around this place, so I stick close to her side. Away from the crowd, I can smell her spicy perfume, a scent so intoxicating she could be a walking opium den, and made stronger by how closely she saunters next to me. Every few steps she brushes against me. Cy was right, I expect any minute now, she'll begin to circle me and zero in for the kill. I won't have to do any work at all.

And I can't be less interested. She's beautiful, her confidence arresting in its ease. Darcy Palmer isn't afraid to show that she wants me, and I feel like a first-class prick for not wanting her back. The truth is that girls like her and Adair and the rest of Cyrus's feminine counterparts just don't do it for me. After the initial attraction, I can't get past the money. I have no interest in pretending I belong here among them. It's just some perverted sense of duty I feel to Adair, or the version of her I drove to the hospital. She'd been a somewhat decent human being on the way. I'd wanted to watch out for her. Every time I've seen her since, she's been vying for the Biggest Bitch of the Universe title. No matter how many times I tell myself we're nothing alike, I can't accept it. I hadn't seen her fear on that drive. I'd felt it burrow into my stomach coming back to hurt me like an abusive, old friend. Adair and I might not be anything alike but there's no denying that I know her in a way none of the others can. Because despite all our differences, I've been in her shoes.

"I never let anyone come back here. Cook would kill me if she found me in her space," Darcy says, drawing my attention back to her where it belongs. She guides me into a second kitchen, smaller but more practical than the one currently swarming with co-eds. Opening the fridge, she grabs two bottles of water. "But it's not like we can talk out there."

She twists the cap off one and holds it out to me.

We might be different but she's not treating me like the dirt on the bottom of her shoe. If I was as smart as the scholarship committee deemed me, I would focus on her. It's not like I'm looking for forever. Maybe Cy is on to something with his plan to take advantage of the opportunities. What man in his right mind would pass up Darcy?

"What's your major?" she asks.

"Finance." I have a mind for numbers. Francie calls it my secret weapon. It's what got me a perfect score on the SATs math component and into Valmont.

"Oh." Darcy must be good at math, too, because I see calculation in her eyes. "What do you plan to—"

"There you are!" A whirlwind of black and white rushes into the kitchen and grabs Darcy's hand.

"Ava," Darcy says through gritted teeth, tugging free of her grasp. "You remember Sterling."

Ava pauses long enough to breathe a simpering, "Hello."

"We were talking." Darcy begins backing her toward the hallway. I half-expect a voice over to begin documenting the natural phenomenon occurring before me as the two powerful females engage in a ritualistic dance.

Over me.

How the fuck did I wind up here?

"I need you," Ava says meaningfully.

"Can it wait?" The civility does little to hide the tension between them.

"Not if you want your parents' bedroom to remain off-limits," Ava informs her. "But if you want it redecorated with some random dude's bodily fluids, by all means, continue."

"Shit!" Darcy whirls toward me. "I need to take care of this."

"You want help?"

"No, we've got this." Darcy digs her fingernails into Ava's upper arm and drags her away, calling over her shoulder, "I'll be back."

I couldn't be more grateful for fate's intervention. It's a helluva lot easier than letting her down gently. Something tells me she wouldn't take that very well. This is my chance to make a clean break. Cyrus is off on the prowl. Darcy is distracted. It'll only take a few seconds to request a car on my phone's app. Putting distance between myself and them isn't just smart, it's necessary. These people have nothing to lose. One wrong move and I might wind up with nothing just like my father. I need to go, I decide as I leave the kitchen. The back door beckons me from the doorway to the staff kitchen. Two steps and I'll be on my way back to reality. I make it one before I turn to head toward the fray.

15

ADAIR

"You're going out?"

I pause at the door to my closet and take a deep breath. I don't need to see my brother's face to imagine the look of disapproval etched across it. He's worn a similar look since our mother's funeral. He arrived in Valmont and took over when it became clear daddy wasn't up to the task of planning a memorial. He can't disapprove of how our father is handling the situation, so instead he disapproves of me.

"I thought that's what you wanted. You told me I couldn't stay home forever." In truth, I've been trying to get out of this party all day. I'm not ready to act like my life is normal again, but I can't let Poppy down. She's going to worry herself to death over me.

Fleeing the security of the closet, I toss a dress on the bed and do my best to act calm. That is getting harder by the day. Every move I make is analyzed, assessed, and found wanting. But I haven't been given any other options. No one allows me to help. No one allows me to have a voice. The black-sequined bandage dress might be a little much for a Valmont house party. Then again, so am I.

My brother's powerful body fills the doorframe, his dark eyes narrowing on the dress. There must have been more meetings with the board, because he's in a charcoal suit. It looks like he's had a day. His shirt is untucked and wrinkled, tie loose around his neck—his outfit as tired as his wary eyes. "That's not what I meant."

"What did you mean then?"

"You dropped out of school, Adair," he reminds me.

"For a semester." I cling to that fact like a life preserver. Most people thought daddy had forced me to go to Valmont. The truth isn't that simple. Now that mom's gone, I need to get as far away from Tennessee as possible. I considered staying enrolled, but there was no way I could concentrate on schoolwork and get the grades I'd need to transfer schools. It'd be only a few more months until I leave this world behind me and make my own way. Only a few more months until I'm more than Angus MacLaine's daughter and Malcolm MacLaine's little sister. Only a few more months until I escape this hell for good. I'm not stupid enough to believe I can escape the family name, so I'm going to use it to get into my dream school: Cambridge. I'll make the MacLaine name my own by putting an ocean between me and them.

"I just expected you to be a bit more serious about your future." Malcolm's words are a slap in the face.

He's got no idea how serious I am about my future. Just because I'm not lining up to be some idiot's trophy wife or perfecting my political aspirations like him, he assumes I'm worthless. "What do you want me to do? You won't let me help with the company. Or attend board meetings. Daddy acts like I'm a little girl. He wants me to stay here forever, being hopelessly dependent on him—or, at least, his staff. I'm pretty sure he wouldn't let me screw a lightbulb into an empty socket."

"So, instead you're going to screw half of Nashville?" he counters, a dangerous edge taking hold in his voice.

To a man who obsesses over his public image, there can be no greater horror than a slutty sister. The truth is that his concern is never to protect me only to control what people think of me.

"Maybe I am." It's the right button to press to get a rise out of him. Now if I just hit it a few more times, he might self-destruct and leave me alone for the night.

"Christ, Adair. We live in this town." The message is clear: what would people think if Adair MacLaine is spotted drinking and dancing and enjoying herself a month after her mama died?

Exactly what they already think: that I am a spoiled heiress who has nothing better to do than blow through my trust fund. No one in Valmont has any reason to think otherwise. My father's name might be held in reverence by the people living here, but the courtesy doesn't extend to his wayward daughter. Malcolm only started caring what people thought of me when he began maneuvering toward the Tennessee senate. He'd spent his years at Valmont turning weekend frat parties into the stuff of legend. If only people knew the truth about this family.

People assume the MacLaine children haven't worked a day in our lives. All we do is work. Our father's love isn't free. Everything we have costs something. I've no idea what price I'll pay to leave Valmont behind. I have to do it, though. Get out, make connections, and hope like hell I can find a way to support myself abroad. The small inheritance I got from mama, the pittance left from her family fortune, isn't going to get me far. But anywhere is better than here.

Malcolm knows that. We've never seen eye-to-eye, mostly because he was born with a penis, which seems to afford him slightly more privileges in our family. I, on the other hand, have worked for every dime, every ounce of affection, every chance I've gotten. Daddy grooms Malcolm to take his place at MacLaine Media, in the government, even here at Windfall. I'm only brought out for special occasions—a trophy to be displayed at parties and then placed back under lock and key. My brother is the heir to the empire, shaking hands and having drinks. He's being handed the family legacy on a platter, and no one—especially not his baby sister—is going to compromise that.

"Worried I'm going to cause a scandal? Simmer down, bro. All publicity is good publicity." I just want him off my back. "Did you forget how you spent every weekend when you were my age?"

"I didn't forget," he says quietly. "I grew up. Maybe you should, too."

I want to throw my head back and scream. "Double standard much?"

"Things are different. Mama is gone. Someone has to be the lady of the house." He couldn't be more condescending if he climbed onto a ladder and yelled at me from the top rung.

"I'm not a lady." I stomp out of the room to prove it before he can stop me.

I take the Mercedes G-Wagon, because it's my current favorite, and daddy is too drunk to notice it's gone. Back in my prep days, I might have walked, ensuring I could easily stumble home. The Palmer estate is only a half a mile away on the opposite side of Magnolia Lane. But Poppy is stuck in the dorms and needs a ride. I don't blame her, given that Ava is readying Darcy's house to play host, and Poppy can't stand

Being stuck in enclosed spaces with Cyrus. When I pull up to campus, she's waiting on a short brick wall. I whistle appreciatively when she climbs in wearing a black and white striped romper. She's knotted her glossy black hair near the haltered neckline.

"You look amazing!"

"I have made a major decision," she says as I wait for her to buckle up. Then she turns to me with an expression she usually saves for serious matters like celebrity break-ups or PETA campaigns. "I'm back on the market."

"You were off-the-market?" I ask.

"Not officially. But I was looking more than seeking. I'm done waiting around. I was hung up on Cyrus, but he's never going to make an actual move. Why waste this?" She flourishes her hand like a game show hostess announcing the big prize.

This is exactly the girl power I need to channel after my confrontation with Malcolm. It's time to take back our social lives. Mama wouldn't want me to sit around in my room. She'd want my days to be full of diamonds. And I could do that. Live for her, soak up what there is to love about Tennessee before I make my escape.

"Okay, but big favor. Can we pick up a friend?"

"You don't waste time," I tease as she points me in the direction of a boys dorm down the street.

"It's not like that," she says.

"Off-the-market?" I ask.

"We're shopping at the wrong stores," she says meaningfully.

"Gotcha."

Poppy's new friend struts out of his building in a body-skimming gray tee and board shorts more suited to SoCal than Valmont. Bangs sweep his forehead and I can't help but think he looks like a young Keanu Reeves—but with a lot more confidence. I flash the car's brights in encouragement of his runway moves.

"Nice ride," he says appreciatively as he climbs into the back seat.

I swivel around and stick out a hand. "Adair MacLaine. I think we're going to be friends."

"Kai Miles." He takes it. "I am in the market for friends."

Poppy and I share a look before we burst out laughing. Everyone's in the market for something tonight. The question is what are the chances we find much worth buying in Valmont. I've sampled the stock. There's not much around here that interests me.

"Thanks for being a DD," Kai says.

I roll my eyes into the rearview mirror. Wires have been crossed, it seems.

"I'm not DDing."

"Sorry," he says quickly. "I thought Poppy said…"

"We won't need a ride home, darling," Poppy interrupts him. "Adair's place is just down the way. We can crash there."

"Is there room?"

I glance at Poppy. Has she prepared him at all? "We've got the space, but Poppy doesn't drink, so it hardly matters."

"I have wine every now and then," she says defensively.

"When do you have wine?" I've never seen her touch a drop of booze.

"When I visit my Grandmum in Surrey."

"Are you sure you aren't too sophisticated for an old-fashioned Valmont house party?" I place the back of my hand to my forehead and feign a swoon of admiration.

"Shut up!" She bats at me, accidentally hitting the steering wheel and the car swerves, narrowly avoiding a ditch.

"That's why she can't DD," I explain to Kai. "We'll wind up in a ditch even if she's sober. You can crash with us unless you're desperate to get back to the dorms tonight, but you'll be taking your life into your own hands."

"I'll take my chances on your couch."

"We have to sneak into the guesthouse," I warn them. "I can't deal with my brother anymore tonight."

"Maybe you shouldn't go home," Poppy says suggestively.

"Have you been replaced by a sexbot?" I ask her. "Where's my best friend?"

"I just mean—there might be someone you're hoping to run into?" she suggests, waggling her brows. "Someone who gets you all fired up?"

This time I nearly put us in a ditch. "What did you do?"

"Nothing." Poppy is a crap liar. Guilt is practically stamped across her forehead.

"No. There is no one I'm hoping to see." I want to call her out. If she did what I think she's done, there goes the evening. Not to mention that she had to call Cyrus to do it. So much for her resolution to give up on him. I feel the empowerment I'd discovered at Valmont leak away. So I turn up the radio to croon along to a Carrie Underwood song. Kai holds his own, belting it almost as impressively she does. When the song ends, Poppy claps wildly. "Nice pipes!"

"I have my reasons for coming to Nashville," Kai admits. "Not that country music is in need of a gay Hawaiian."

"I think that's exactly what country music needs," I disagree, already mentally going through my contacts list. Kai is seriously talented and Nashville is full of producers looking for the next big star. I keep my mouth shut, not wanting to make promises I can't keep.

Kai fills us in on his musical aspirations the rest of the way to Northern Valmont.

"Then my mother tried to get me on America's Got Talent, but…" The words fall from his lips when I turn onto

Magnolia Lane. He rolls down his window to stick his head out for a better look as we pass the first estate. By the time, we pull into the West's drive, his mouth is hanging open. I park next to a Porsche and Cyrus's Jaguar, earning a disgruntled sigh from Poppy.

"Sorry," I mouth. Poppy might be 'back on the market officially' but not emotionally.

"I thought we were going to a house party," Kai says still buckled in the back seat.

"This is it."

"This isn't a house. It's a museum." He finally climbs out, craning his neck to take in the sweeping terra cotta roof.

Someone's had the genius idea to mount strobe lights on the second-floor balcony's iron railing. Anywhere else the police might bust up a party like this, but Magnolia Lane employs private security. I have no doubt they've been properly bribed to steer clear this evening.

"People live here?" Kai asks.

I can't help but laugh. Already I feel lighter than I have in weeks. I turn to Poppy and wink. "Would we call them people?"

"It's debatable."

"Is your house this big?" he asks me.

Poppy giggles, linking his arm through hers and leading him toward the entrance, an oversized set of intricately carved wooden doors. "Oh, darling, it's *bigger*."

"I need the men's room," Kai says as soon as we're inside. His head tilts backward to the large five-tiered, iron chandelier beset with lights made to look like lit candles hanging in the two-story foyer. He nearly topples over trying to take it all in.

"Straight that way. Find the line of girls waiting and turn on your charm," I advise.

He flashes a winning grin and sets off just as Ava catches us. Her black mini dress contrasts starkly with the considerable amounts of peachy skin it displays. The sharp sting of vodka on her breath nearly knocks me out as she teeters on her heels, swaying into a hug. "You came! Poppy told me you tried to back out. She said you weren't feeling well."

"Is that so?" I side-eye Poppy. It's not like her to walk into a lie.

"I feel better," I say, not wanting to give the real reason I'd considered ditching the festivities.

"I should have stayed in." Ava's lips plump into a pout. "There's no one interesting here."

"By no one do you mean boys?" I guess. "This place is crawling with boys."

"No *new* boys, though," she corrects me. "Except Sterling —and Darcy has dibs on him."

"She does?" My voice pitches up in surprise, and I flinch painfully aware how distressed I sound. Ava doesn't seem to notice thanks to her blood alcohol level, but Poppy smirks next to me. This confirms her suspicions.

"She says, but I think he's fair game," Ava slurs.

"I don't think he's interested in Darcy." Poppy casts a knowing look at me.

"Did you guys see the pool?" Kai asks, finally finding us.

Ava straightens at his appearance, holding out her empty hand. As soon as he takes it, she presses closer to him until he's practically holding her up. "I'm Ava."

"I'm gay," he says, blinking over the bundle of vodka-infused girl suddenly in his arms.

She sighs heavily, pastes on a smile and releases her catch. "Oh well. Want a drink?"

"Um, sure." He looks to us for confirmation.

"She doesn't bite," I promise him.

"Unless I'm asked," Ava says sweetly. "Oh, there's Oliver. I need to say hello. I'll catch you all later." She waves, her cup sloshing onto Poppy's romper. She weaves into the crowd without an apology, spilling a trail of vodka in her wake.

Poppy surveys the damage, brushing the liquid from her romper. "Why is she acting like a lunatic party hostess?"

"She's being Ava."

"I wish I was a social butterfly." Poppy watches her go.

"Ava is more like a praying mantis," I correct her. "You are a social butterfly. This just isn't your garden, babe."

"At least Sterling is here," she teases me.

"Who's Sterling?" Kai pushes back the dark hair flopping into his shining eyes.

"Who cares if he's here?"

"I care because he's very pretty to look at," Poppy says, "and you care because you're totally in love with him."

"Poppy Landry! I am not in love with him. I'm totally in loathing with him, but that is it."

"Your voice is shaking," Kai points out.

"Want to try that again with a little sincerity?" Poppy asks.

"Okay." I consider my words, measuring each one before I speak. "Maybe I don't hate Sterling, but I don't like him—*especially* not like that. He was nice and drove me to the hospital, so he can't be a complete asshole. I can't prove that, though, since that's all he's been every other minute I've spent with him."

"You can keep selling, but I'm not buying."

"He is terrible. He's rude, and he's arrogant, and he's—"

"Staring at you," Poppy cuts in.

I drop my voice to a whisper. Telling myself, there's no way he heard any of that in here. Not with all these people. "What?"

"Now he's on his way over," she narrates, "and he looks good enough to lick."

"I concur with that opinion," Kai adds.

"Oh my God." I squeeze my eyes shut. The only thing that could make a conversation with Sterling more awkward is the addition of Poppy's far-from-subtle double entendres.

"Adair," Sterling says. My name is rough on his tongue, grating across it. I open my eyes expecting a glare and find a smile instead. "I was hoping to run into you. I wasn't sure you would come."

"I don't think my attendance was ever in doubt." I force myself to sound cold even as my body heats up in awareness.

"She just needed time," Poppy jumps in like a lifeguard sensing danger. The question is: which of us is drowning? "We met at the funeral. Poppy? I'm Adair's best friend. I'm like a sister but I call her out on her BS."

"I remember," he says. According to Poppy, Sterling took off right after me that day. She saw this as a sign that he'd only come to see me. I tend to think he couldn't stand spending more time with my friends.

"Ignore her. The rest of us do." I shove her playfully. She takes the cue to shut up a little too well.

"I can see I'm not wanted. Let's find you a drink." She takes off with Kai in tow, leaving me with Sterling, both of them making kissy faces behind his back as they go. Later, I am officially revoking her best friend card. I'll give Kai one more chance.

We stand a moment in relative silence, chaos all around us. Finally I blurt out the most obvious thought in my head. "This is uncomfortable."

"It's an improvement. You're usually telling me off," he says.

"And you're usually being a total dick," I say.

His smirk only makes his lips look fuller and more inviting. How can he make me want to kiss him and smack him at the same time?

"Truce?" he asks.

Maybe it's the overly-hot room steaming my brain into submission, but I agree.

"I'm not good with family shit," he explains.

I can't help but laugh—not at him, but the irony. "No one here is. In Valmont, you belong to your family, especially if…"

I trail off not wanting to admit the pathetic truth out loud. I know better than most that girls belong to their families in Valmont. We're practically trading cards, used to close business deals and ensure smooth mergers. Nothing says let's make this work like marrying your daughter off to your company's rival. These convenient marriages never last long, but from there it's usually a matter of finding your next husband and then your third. Freedom is terrifying when you've only ever known captivity.

"Where are her parents?" Sterling asks, redirecting the conversation.

"Fiji or somewhere. They're celebrating their anniversary," I tell him.

"I thought she was still living at home."

"So?"

"I guess if Francie could take off on vacation, she would," he says. "She never left me to go on a trip."

"Francie?" I repeat. "Is that what you call your mom?"

I instantly realize I've said the wrong thing. Sterling bristles, growing taller before my eyes. I sense the distance he's putting between us even though he doesn't take so much as a step away.

"Let's not pretend you care," he says coldly. "I'm a dog, remember?"

He throws my words back at me. They churn inside me until I want to throw up. I should apologize. He might have been rude at the funeral, but calling him a dog? It makes me feel gross and small. Even worse, it makes me feel like a MacLaine. Not like mama who married into the name. Like Malcolm and daddy.

I'm nothing like her. And now I never will be. She'll never teach me to be kind. She'll never coax the genetics she gave me to the front. I'll wind up just another heartless MacLaine.

"Nothing to say?" he pushes. "What a surprise."

He shakes his head, disgust contorting his sharp features, before he strides off, leaving me frozen to the spot.

"There you are! Oliver spotted a girl and I'm friendless" Ava's drunkenly, cheerful voice is at complete odds with how I feel. The grin falls from her face when she gets closer. "What's wrong?"

"Boys are dumb," I croak. Ava and I have never been very close, but this seems to be a universal truth among girls.

She gets it. "Let's get you something to drink."

I don't put up a fight, focusing instead on getting my crying under control.

"Can you get me a beer?" she asks the boy standing next to the keg. He's got to be a couple years older than us, but she dazzles him.

"Sure." It's like she handed him a Christmas present. Bumping another guy from the tap, he reaches for a cup. "Hold on."

He passes it to Ava and she gives it to me. "Fresh air?"

I nod, I need out of here. Why can't I escape these parties and people? *A couple more months*, I promise myself.

"A couple more months until what?" Ava asks.

I didn't realize I spoke out loud. Taking a huge drink, I consider my options. No one knows about my plan to leave Valmont University behind. Poppy will be heartbroken, so I can't tell her. But I need to put it out there. I need someone to know so that I'll be held accountable to my plan. If I stay here much longer, I'll never leave. I'll become like the rest of them.

"Can I tell you something?"

She holds a finger up and points to the back patio.

I nod, being alone seems like a good idea. If the wrong person overhears, it could get back to my father. Ava West doesn't give two shits about anyone but herself. Of course, she's making me question that as we make our way through the crowd. Maybe alcohol softens her sharp edges a little.

We're nearly outside when Ava stops. "There's Money. Let me get him. He can get you to your house."

I want to tell her that I don't need to go home, but by the time she abandons me at the door to catch him I'm wondering if I do. There's too many people here. The room is starting to swim. I step outside and suck in deep breaths of night air. It's still muggy in Tennessee in September but it's still fresh air. It's so quiet outside, everyone is packed in the house where the air conditioning is. The sound of the party grows distant, and the night fogs at the edges as I try to cool down. But I can't clear my head. It feels as heavy as my guilty heart. I take another drink, but the ice-cold beer isn't helping. The red cup blurs in my hands. I try to focus on it, but it slips and spills on the tiled patio.

I turn toward the door, reaching for the knob. I need to find Ava and Money, or maybe Poppy. Someone to take me home, so I can lie down. I lurch it open, but instead of people inside, there is a swirling mass of colors and movement. I blink but it doesn't get any clearer.

"Adair." The voice comes from above me. How did I wind up on the ground?

I try to raise my head to his voice but it's too hard. I open my mouth but nothing comes out.

"Adair." Sterling's voice grows more insistent and then his face swims into sight.

"You're so pretty, even when you're all funny looking," I say. Or I think I do. I'm not certain given the confused look he returns.

"Thank you," he says slowly. He picks up my cup and sniffs it.

"I shouldn't drink that. I'm the DD," I tell him.

"Not tonight." He crouches back on his heels and stares at me, his gorgeous face blurring in and out, then he mutters a string of curses that would make a sailor blush. "I can't leave you like this."

"Then don't."

His face softens, his hands gently brushing back my hair before he scoops me into his arms and everything goes black.

16

STERLING
THE PRESENT

"If I were you," Luca begins, and I brace myself for my friend's particular brand of advice, "I'd stay here. Full house staff. Bar downstairs. Room service. Why exactly would you want your own place?"

"Why don't you live here?" I ask him, handing off the last of my luggage to the bellhop along with a fifty-dollar bill.

"Maybe I will." Knowing Luca, he's seriously considering it.

If it was my first stay here, I wouldn't blame him. We both landed at the Eaton as a matter of convenience. Nashville has plenty of hotels, but the Eaton boasts particularly tempting options for men like us. It's an old-school hotel, catering to a clientele that expected gentility, grace, and, most importantly, discretion. In other words, it's where Nashville's elite go to conduct their affairs—both business and extramarital. The executive floor features suites generously decked out for business meetings with conference tables and reception areas. A Chesterfield sofa in olive-colored velvet sits across from two leather club chairs. In another hotel, the ticking stripe wallpaper might look outdated, but here it fits with the timeless sophistication. You didn't bring a hooker to the Eaton, you brought your mistress, likely a friend's wife or maybe daughter, as proof of good breeding. The whole place smacks of civilized vice.

And it's available to anyone willing to pay its considerable price tag. "I'm not giving this place one more dime than I have to."

"You're the one who suggested the place."

"Because of *the list*," I say with meaning. I toss a folded piece of paper on the bed.

He picks it up and opens it. "You know blacklist is one word not two, right?"

"Everyone's a critic," I mutter, snatching back the hastily written list of people due a visit from karma.

"The more you know," he says with a shrug. He doesn't question my blacklist. He never has. Luca carries his own baggage. If he took any issue with my plans for revenge, he's never shown it. A DeAngelo rarely suffers from moral crisis. Luca is no exception.

"Should I pack my things before you leave?" He fingers a matchbook from the hotel bar. "Is this going to be like Istanbul?"

"Nothing that simple," I assure him.

"Good. Because Italian wool is quite flammable, and you told me to pack enough to stay a while." A wolfish grin slashes across his face as he recalls our ill-fated time in Turkey. Glancing at him in his well-tailored black suit, he might pass more for a local Southern gentleman than a mercenary. Look closer and there's a beast with a cruel sense of humor stalking through his dark eyes.

"I know the owner. He's not the one on the list." Cyrus is due to inherit the hotel and the rest of the chain when his dad finally kicks it, so my retribution regarding the Eaton lands solely at the hotel's long-time manager. Cyrus had been one of my only true friends in Valmont, never bothered by my lack of money, or status, but his charitable attitude hadn't been shared by the staff here at the time.

"How do you want to play it here?" he asks.

Before I can answer him, a knock at the door interrupts us.

"I'll get it." He walks to the door and opens it.

A man in a neat but inexpensive suit and white gloves greets him with a bow of his head, a show of deference I'm certain inflates Luca's overstuffed ego even more.

"Mr. Randolph would like to have a drink with you in his office—to thank you for your stay."

"I'd be happy to join him for a drink," I say loudly and the concierge startles.

"Sir, I'm sorry, I assumed," he stutters an apology. "Both of you are welcome to join him before you depart."

Luca crosses his arms over his broad chest when he leaves. "Drinking with the management?"

"You know I don't drink." I straighten my tie in the mirror by the door. Mr. Randolph won't remember me. I doubt he ever bothered to learn my name.

"Why do you look like the prettiest boy asked you to dance at the prom?" Luca leans against the wall, surveying me with interest.

"Mr. Randolph is on the list. I've been meaning to squeeze in a visit."

"As long as it doesn't affect the service," Luca says dryly. "I'm still staying here."

"I assure you he's mostly a figurehead. Too busy conducting his own affairs to bother worrying about the hotel. He leaves everything to his staff now."

"In that case, I guess it's time to pay him a visit," Luca agrees.

The hotel manager's office is decked out in a style more befitting a king than an administrator. I happen to know that running the city's most exclusive five-star hotel comes with a more than a decent salary. Doing some digging, I've discovered that isn't enough for him. A man doesn't open an account in the Caymans without reason. Nicholas Randolph opened two.

He greets me at his desk, extending a pudgy arm. "Mr. Ford, I've been meaning to invite you for a drink."

The years haven't been kind to him. His graying hair—or what's left of it—is swept pathetically over his shining boulder of a head in an attempt to hide his balding skull. His suit, while expensive, has been fitted to a much leaner man. I can almost hear him screaming at the tailor to make the measurements tighter. Why be comfortable when your pride is on the line? I accept his handshake, not at all surprised at how hard he squeezes. A good, firm handshake is important to men like him. Meanwhile, I barely bother. Touching him isn't on my list of must do's.

"This is my associate, Luca," I say, purposefully withholding his last name. Anyone in the hospitality business knows the DeAngelo family. Learning he's in the presence of a member of the family will either distract or disturb him. I'm not interested in either scenario.

"Thank you for joining me for a little afternoon refresco," he says. Luca barely smothers a laugh, but Randolph doesn't notice. "I hope you enjoyed your stay."

"Immensely. I'd have been here longer but I closed on my condo last week."

"A condo?" He settles into his chair, waving his hand over a spread of house delicacies he's had brought in for the occasion. I shake my head. "How lovely. I like to check in with our more important guests to make certain we exceeded their expectations."

"I try to refrain from having expectations. I'm easy to please," I say, refusing the bourbon he lifts next in offering.

"Well, then, good," he says in a flustered tone, retrieving a monogrammed handkerchief from his suit pocket and mopping his forehead.

"Luca will be staying at the Eaton for some time, though."

"Oh, excellent." Randolph turns his beady gaze on him. "In town for business?"

Luca nods, picking at his sleeve. He's never been one to bother with chit chat.

"And your business is?" Randolph presses.

"The family business," he says in a bored voice.

Getting nowhere with Luca, he returns his attention to me. "And you, Mr. Ford? What business are you in?"

I can't blame him for wondering what the man staying in his most expensive suite for nearly a month does for a living. In Randolph's eyes I'm the sort of clientele he wants to attract. At least, I am now.

"Asset management. I handle *private financial matters*," I emphasize the last part—bait sure to make this fish bite.

"Management," he repeats. "Investments and such?"

"In a way," I say. "I only work with very select clientele. My clients require the utmost discretion."

A light goes on in his yes. "I understand. I wonder if I might talk to you about a little financial issue of my own."

He eyes Luca nervously, trying to figure out how safe it is for him to talk.

Randolph is a money launderer. Not a terribly good one, because I found proof of it far too easily, which means he's just smart enough to know what he's doing but just stupid enough that he'll get caught. *Eventually.* He's been skimming off the top for years. I have proof but it wouldn't take a genius to see his lifestyle doesn't match up with his salary. Loyalty is a funny thing in the South though. I've seen it before. People forgiving those who shouldn't be forgiven. Overlooking crimes to save face. Scandals are as prevalent here as anywhere else, but they tend to be swept directly under the rug.

"You can speak freely," I assure him.

"Are you also in asset management?" he asks Luca.

Luca straightens in his seat, suddenly interested in the conversation. He's never one to turn down a chance to boast about his own occupation. "I'm more of a people person. I handle staffing issues, among other problems."

I toss in an incredulous stare. Staffing issues? It's possibly the worst double entendre for *assassin* that I've ever heard. Randolph swallows, his Adam's apple bobbing with the effort. He clearly gets the idea.

"What he means is that he's discreet," I explain.

"In that case…" He clears his throat, darting nervous glances at Luca. "I recently had an investment opportunity present itself. Very certain returns. I need to figure out where to put the money."

"A mutual fund?" Luca suggests flatly.

"You're never as funny as you think you are," I warn him under my breath. I nod to Randolph encouragingly.

"It would be better if my wife didn't know about it…" he says, adding as an afterthought, "Yet."

"Sometimes separate finances are for the best," I say.

It's a common problem I'm asked to solve. When a rich man bores of his wife and takes a new mistress, he starts to think about hiding his assets. The less the wife knows about, the less he has to share in the divorce. Most wind up still losing a chunk to keeping the mistress happy in the process. But she's on the hook, willing to trade her body for the finer things. A wife expects the finer things for putting up with you. Something Randolph's wife feels acutely, I'm sure.

"I'm sure I can find the right investment for you," I say. "Why don't you and I discuss this further? I'll need to know exactly what assets and so forth you would like moved."

He dabs his nose with the handkerchief, appearing relieved that I seem willing to help. "I always count myself blessed to meet just the right person for a job so often at my own. I'll be certain that the bill for your stay is adjusted accordingly."

"That's unnecessary." I have no intention of accepting his handouts. "Consider it my appreciation for how well the Eaton has taken care of me in the past."

This pleases him to no end. He rises to his feet and shows us to the door. In the lobby, Luca smacks my arm. "You're doing this for *his thanks*?"

"I owe him one," I say darkly.

"Whatever." Bored Luca has returned. He jerks a thumb toward the bar off the lobby. "Drink?"

"I have plans tonight." I check my watch. "There isn't time."

"Dance card's full, huh?"

"I was thinking you might like to join," I say as he walks with me to the valet station. I hand them my slip. Malcolm had sounded reluctant when he'd called with the details and I'd asked to bring a guest to the gala. Once I'd assured him it wasn't a woman, he'd agreed. Everyone is likely to be on their best behavior at the event tonight. Luca's presence will provide some much-needed chaos.

"What do I have to do?" he asks.

I shrug, knowing exactly how to tempt him. "Drink too much and start shit. You game?"

"I thought you'd never ask."

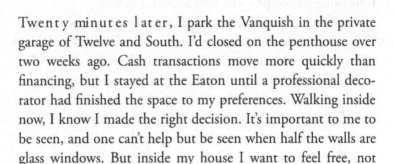

Twenty minutes later, I park the Vanquish in the private garage of Twelve and South. I'd closed on the penthouse over two weeks ago. Cash transactions move more quickly than financing, but I stayed at the Eaton until a professional decorator had finished the space to my preferences. Walking inside now, I know I made the right decision. It's important to me to be seen, and one can't help but be seen when half the walls are glass windows. But inside my house I want to feel free, not only of the expectations of others, but of myself.

The decor is simple—clean lines with nods to my travels. The walls have a fresh coat of bright paint and the wood floors are polished. Everything is arranged to my exacting specifications. An oversized abstract painting I purchased in Holland centers the lone living room wall. There's an L-shaped couch in tan leather facing the window to the city below with two mid-century modern chairs opposite it and a live-edge coffee table stretching between them. The Persian wool rug, my concession to comfort, anchors the pieces.

The focal point of the master bedroom is a king bed on a low-rise platform with a simple wood headboard sourced from a local artisan. A single nightstand from the same maker sits to one side. Two night stands send the wrong message when a woman stays the night. The linens, a favorite, were imported from a London company that also supplies Buckingham Palace. Quality trumps quantity at every angle.

In the closet, my suits hang evenly spaced according to color. A gallery light illuminates a selection of neatly rolled silk ties on display next to them. My shoes, mostly Italian leather, have been polished and lined on an opposite rack. The chest of drawers is filled with silk pajama bottoms, jeans, t-shirts, and the rest of my private wardrobe.

But while most of the house is simple with a stress on minimalism and bespoke pieces, my favorite room is full to bursting: the kitchen. The cuisine at the Eaton was excellent, but it's not a home-cooked meal. I'd learned the value of that in Francie's cramped kitchen in Queens. I'd clung to it in the barracks in Iraq. Cooking has always been my sanctuary, and I spared no expense here. The high-gloss, white cabinets are fully stocked with stainless steel cookware and French enameled cast-iron pots. A column of drawers neatly house every possible utensil needed to create my favorite dishes. The espresso machine is imported from Italy. I've learned how to pull a proper shot over the years. I run my finger along the sharp edge of a Wüsthof knife longingly before returning it to its slot on the block. The kitchen will have to wait, unfortunately.

Tonight's required tuxedo hangs in front of my suits, freshly pressed by the hotel staff this morning. Sometimes obligation gets in the way of pleasure — a truth I've known for a long time. At least, this evening, business and pleasure will definitely mix.

17

ADAIR

The Alumni Club at Valmont University caters to its privileged former students with a palatial private restaurant and ballroom near the campus's football field. In the spring it's rented for weddings and galas. I've been to a dozen private events here since I was a student. Tonight it feels like I'm going back in time, though, because it's the first time I'm going to see Sterling Ford on the VU campus in years.

I almost hate to admit Poppy was right about the dress. I haven't worn a silk gown since my jean size reached double digits. Usually it clings a bit too much to my hips. This dress skims over me, just closely enough to showcase my ample curves without making me feel self-conscious. It's either made of magic or I'm officially delusional, but regardless, I don't care.

Less glamorous is the box of dog treat cookies I'm lugging into the kitchen in my Louboutins. Trust Poppy to remember what she'd previously forgotten at the last second. She meets me at the door, grabs the cookies, and deposits them with a passing volunteer. Poppy, never one to shy away from color, is radiant in a green satin gown that twists over one shoulder.

Matching emerald earrings dangle from diamond hooks, nearly reaching her shoulder. They sparkle against the black curtain of hair that swings freely down her back. I'm about to compliment her when she grabs my arm and drags me into a walk-in pantry.

"He's here," she informs me in a low voice like the walls might be listening. "Cyrus saw him."

"So?" I pretend this news doesn't send my stomach plummeting to the floor.

"You were hoping he wouldn't come," she says.

"But I knew he would."

"At least, you look fabulous." She spins me around to examine her work.

"It doesn't really matter how I look. He's seen me before." I refuse to let tonight become entirely about Sterling.

"He's never seen you looking like this," she says.

Maybe that's why I'm so calm. Yes, I'm back here where everything started between us. But when I slipped on my gown I didn't find a girl looking back at me in the mirror. So, it had taken a fair bit of fashion tape to keep the girls inside the dress's lightly-boned bodice. No panties exist that could be worn with the closely draped silk skirt, but I felt powerful in the crimson number. Usually, I wanted to fade into the background at these events, eager to avoid the same crowd I'd known my whole life. Tonight? I want to be seen. I want him to see me. I want him to face what he left behind.

"Are you ready for this?" she asks.

"As I'll ever be."

We've been having some version of this conversation for the past two weeks. Together, we dissected every moment of the disastrous dinner at my house. I told her about my confrontation with him in the hall, but I might have left out the bit where he admitted why he came back.

For you.

I omitted that part because I've been trying to forget he said it. I haven't had much success.

I don't know what he meant by it. It's not like he's been beating down my door begging for another chance. Every moment I spend with him only leaves me feeling more confused, because until that night in the hall, I wasn't sure I meant a thing to him.

And Sterling?

He's my line in the sand—the defining moment of my life. Nothing was the same after I met him. There's no forgetting him. My mother once told me that you never stop loving your first love. I asked her if she was still in love with the first boy who stole her heart. She'd just given me a sad smile. When Sterling left, I wondered how I would feel if I saw him again. Now I know.

I hate him—and the thing I hate the most about him is that part of me doesn't hate him at all.

"I've been thinking. Maybe you two should talk. Really talk," Poppy suggests. She holds up a hand before I can reject this idea. "Hear me out. There's a lot you two left unsaid."

"He doesn't deserve it. I don't owe him anything," I shoot back.

"I'm not saying you do," she says quickly, sensing my volatile mood. "It's just that if you think he came back because of you — if you think this thing with him buying into your family's company has something to do what happened between the two of you — then you need to get it out in the open."

"He made his decision about us a long time ago." I don't need to remind Poppy about what happened. Sterling left after he blew up my entire world. Now he's back playing some sort of game and acting like he didn't inflict any damage years ago. "He should be begging me for forgiveness."

"Maybe you should tell him that."

I shake my head. "Why should I have to tell him anything?"

"Because he obviously doesn't get it. It's the fatal flaw of men: obliviousness."

"He doesn't seem very oblivious to me." I flashback to Sterling advancing toward me in the hall. My body had synced to his in that moment, moving in tune with him. I'd retreated because I knew he would chase me.

The pantry door cracks open and Cyrus pops his head in. "What are you two doing in here? Everyone is looking for you."

My stomach flips, even though I know he means Poppy. As confident as I feel I can't deny that each passing second is filing away at my already frayed nerves.

"We were just having a chat," Poppy says cheerily, as though we don't have a care in the world, and whispering in pantries is perfectly normal behavior for grown women.

"Are you two ready to rejoin civilization then?" he asks.

I open my mouth to say yes, but Poppy picks this moment to tattle on me. "Adair is dreading Sterling's presence."

"Traitor," I mutter.

"It's completely obvious," she says defensively. "Plus, Cyrus needs to look out for you when I'm needed. Right, darling?"

"Of course—" Cyrus wraps an arm around her waist, "— when I can take my eyes off you."

"Do you two need a moment alone in the pantry?" The last thing I need is to be party to their particular brand of affection. It's so sugary, I feel like I should stir it into some tea.

"Sorry." He doesn't look the least bit like he means it. Cyrus always has something to prove when it comes to his feelings for Poppy. Tonight is no different. "Honestly, Adair, we're all adults now. I'm sure there's nothing to worry about."

Poppy clears her throat and he changes course. "Naturally, I'll step in if necessary."

"Thanks." I swallow back a sigh. I'm so tired of my friends trying to protect me. "But I can take care of myself."

"Still…" Cyrus leaves the offer hanging. He kisses Poppy. "I'll see you out there."

"Why does everyone always assume I need help?" I grumble as soon as he's gone.

Poppy grabs my shoulders. "It doesn't matter if you need our help. Our friendship isn't merit-based. We're going to help because we're your friends. End of story."

"When did you get so bossy?" I ask.

"When you decided to get whiny," she tells me. "You're stronger than this. You always have been. Sterling coming back was unexpected. I don't blame you for being shaken, but now it's time to dust yourself off and remember who you are."

"But," I begin.

"If ifs and buts were candy and nuts, we'd all have a Merry Christmas," she stops me.

I can't help laughing at this. "What does that mean?"

"You can't live your life wondering about the future or the past. There are no buts about it. You are Adair MacLaine, and whatever mistakes you've made, Sterling made the bigger one when he lost you."

"Seriously, what did you do with my best friend?" It's like she's a different person since she came back from Paris.

"I can't help it," she confesses. "I don't like seeing you like this."

"I just don't understand why he came back," I say softly.

"Yes, you do. He came back because he's still in love with you."

"That doesn't explain why he's trying to ruin my family," I say.

Poppy arches an eyebrow. "This is Sterling. Of course, it does."

She has a point. Sterling might love me. Sterling might be back for me. But there's no denying that he's not here looking for a happily ever after.

18

STERLING

"Why do I always wind up in a tuxedo when I spend time with you?" Luca asks, messing with his black tie as we enter the Alumni Club's ballroom that evening. "You're a terrible date."

"Stop doing that, dear." I brush his hands away and playfully adjust it for him, earning me a scowl. His mood is hot and cold as usual. He didn't exactly love filling the last chair at the MacLaine table for the evening. "You love tuxedos."

"It's not the suit that bothers me. It's the fact that I have to spend all night listening to rich people talk about how rich they are," he says, disdain dripping from his words as he surveys the crowd.

"You're rich," I remind him.

"I know. That's the point." He turns his withering stare on me, lowering his voice. "I also enjoy rock climbing, I paint, and, oh yeah, I kill people. Being rich is the least interesting thing about me."

"Perhaps you should bring your interests into the conversation more," I say dryly.

"That would go over well," he mutters, forcing a smile as we pass a couple.

"You might get a few new contracts."

"I only work for the family now." He sighs. "I miss the good old days."

Before I can remind him of the number of times he was in the crosshairs during those good old days, a familiar face spots us. There's a moment of hesitation as the woman in the black lace dress studies me, trying to place where she's seen me before. It's been easier than I expected to blend back into Valmont. Very few members of our old crowd recognize me at first glance. I'm not surprised she does. Her head twists away, moving to whisper in the ear of the platinum-haired woman in a gold-sequined gown next to her. They've both changed considerably, but I recognize them from their predatory gaze. After all this time, Ava West and Darcy Palmer still scent fresh prey when it walks into a room.

They are day and night next to each other. Ava's once dark hair is now bleached platinum blonde, but her porcelain skin and sharp eyes are the same as when we first met. Her crimson lips curl into a wicked smile as she begins to speak to the group of men clustered near her. Darcy has pulled her tight ringlets away from her face, showcasing her regal cheekbones and full pout of a mouth.

Whatever Ava says to the men sends heads swiveling in our direction. Cyrus doesn't look surprised to see me, but Montgomery West and Oliver Hawthorne do.

"I get the feeling you're being summoned," Luca says as Ava wags a finger in my direction.

There's a reason he's with me tonight that has nothing to do with filling a seat. "Ready to meet the rest of the blacklist?"

For the first time this evening, his answering smirk is downright jubilant. "Lead the way."

Our welcoming committee watches as we walk toward them.

"Sterling Ford, as I live and breathe!" Darcy Palmer abandons her poise and hugs me. Not to be outdone, Ava follows suit and adds a full-mouthed kiss for good measure. Malcolm nods hello as he continues his conversation with a few other business types. Money lingers nearby looking slightly bored. He doesn't bother to acknowledge our arrival.

"You finally dragged your sorry ass back to Valmont." Ava leans into me but her gaze skitters to Luca. She's never been one to hide. She hunts in plain sight. "And who is this?"

"Luca," he says before I can introduce him.

"Ava West." Her hand flutters out to him and he takes it graciously, planting a kiss on it. "A gentleman!"

I choke back a laugh. It's his most unlikely cover yet. Of course, Luca always knows how to charm the ladies. Malcolm doesn't look as thrilled at his presence. No doubt he recognizes him. He clears his throat and Ava takes a step away from Luca. It's clearly a warning and a response. Still, the two keep a measured distance from one another. Why is Ava taking orders from him?

"You're saving me a dance," Darcy says.

"I'm not much for dancing."

"You'll dance if I want you to," she informs me, then glances to Luca. "You will, too."

His hooked grin says he doesn't mind at all. "Find me when the music starts."

"I'll hold you to that." Her head tilts, her dark eyes appraising him with a little more interest. I know what she sees: the Rolex, the expensive tux, the money. She grabs Ava's elbow, nearly spilling her champagne. Ava starts to object but Darcy doesn't let her. "Excuse us, we need to make the rounds."

"What was that about?" Luca asks under his breath.

"You're blood in the water, my friend," I explain. "Every woman will be circling you by the end of the night, trying to get a taste."

He frowns. "Was that part of your plan? Bring me along as a distraction?"

"I told you I needed your help."

"I feel so used," he says dryly, snagging a glass from a passing tray.

"I'm sure you'll get over it," I say, noticing Malcolm's eyes have followed Ava across the room. I can't stop myself. "Lost your wife?"

"I have a headache," Malcolm explains, touching his temples gingerly. "Ginny went to look for aspirin."

"Here." Money pulls a flask from his jacket and offers it to him.

"Whiskey and wine are a terrible combination," Malcolm says.

"I can find Oliver. He'll have something harder."

"I imagine he will. His brother always had the good stuff in college," Malcolm says fondly as though the good old days of pharmaceutical drug abuse are happier times.

"Oliver!" Money calls, waving him over. "Got anything for a headache."

"Seriously?" Oliver asks, creasing his eyebrows.

"I know you do." Money turns to Malcolm. "He could always hook up the Beta Psis. Xanax. Fentanyl. Bennies."

He produces a bottle from his jacket. "Man, that was a lifetime ago."

"You helped drop many a pair of panties," Money says.

"Rex was the same. We used to call him Cupid." Malcolm takes the pills Oliver doles out for him.

"I would have thought your bank accounts were enough to do that," I say dryly. Oliver's gaze slides uneasily to me.

"Nobody got hurt." Even he doesn't believe the lie he's telling.

"It was just for fun." Money punches my shoulder. "You were never much for fun, were you, Ford?"

"I guess not."

"I never did see why my sister was so into you." He leans closer, the sharp sting of bourbon on his breath.

"Money, don't you have a date or someone to bother?" Malcolm says, his voice rich with warning. The stroll down memory lane is over.

If Money is distressed at his exile, he doesn't show it. He shoves the flask back in his jacket and lurches to his feet, throwing an arm around Oliver. It's not a surprise that any of them enjoyed recreational drugs back in the day or that they shared them with their conquests. I'd seen what those drugs did, though. Watching them stride away, carefree, I make a mental note to add one more name to my list.

19

S ome party this is turning out to be.

"You're so pretty, even when you're all funny looking." Adair is blabbering, but now I know for sure she's been drugged. There is no way she would ever say that on purpose, but it's nice to have confirmation. I don't mind knowing the truth. I grab her glass and sniff it while she blabbers something mostly incoherent about being a designated driver.

"Not tonight," I inform her. What the fuck am I getting myself into with this girl? A torrent of rage bursts out of me, half-directed at her for being stupid enough to get drugged, and half-directed at whatever asshole did it.

I don't have a choice. Adair might be able to take care of herself normally, but not in this state. Plus, there's the fact that someone at this party did this. I have no idea who. Are they looking for her now? Waiting for the moment when she's finally vulnerable? I crouch beside her, unsure what to do. One thing is clear. "I can't leave you like this."

"Then don't." Despite her condition, I hear the plea in her voice. She wants to be saved, even if I'm the one doing the saving. I brush a lock of copper hair from her forehead. She's going to be trouble. Scooping her into my arms, I barely stand before she goes limp. "Fuck! Adair!" I shake her but she doesn't stir. Her chest moves just enough to let me know she's still breathing. "Fuck!"

I'm not sure how someone so small is so heavy. I manage to pry open the back door without dropping her, my eyes never leaving the slight movement of her chest. I'm not sure what to do once I'm inside. I can't leave her, but I can't carry her into a party like this. She's breathing. All I can do is ride this out until she wakes up. I'd rather not do that here, though.

"If you're up there, I could use some fucking help," I say to the ceiling. Francie's the religious one. I'm not even sure I'm asking right.

"Oh my God!" A shrill English accent answers my prayers. The girl she came here with—Poppy—rushes over to me. "What happened?"

"I found her like this," I tell her. I don't need her jumping to any unwarranted conclusions about how I wound up with Adair passed out in my arms.

Poppy shakes her head like this doesn't make sense. "She wasn't going to drink tonight."

"She should've stuck to that plan," I say dryly, "especially, since somebody slipped her something."

"Should we call the police?" She clutches her chest and looks around wildly as if she expects a villain to appear twirling his mustache. The movement sends her stumbling on her heels.

"She's not in any danger as long as someone keeps an eye on her. I've seen this before." We might not have had mansions to crash in New York, but I'd been to my fair share of parties. Poppy isn't going to be much help, but I imagine Adair has handmaidens or some shit. Surely, there's someone capable of taking care of her. "She's going to feel like shit in the morning, though. Can you get her home? Is there someone we can call?"

Her head shakes so fast she nearly falls over. "Her dad will kill her, and all our friends—"

"Are here drinking," I finish for her. Of course, they're all hitting it hard while I get stuck babysitting their queen bee. "Where was she going to take you when this was over?"

"Oh! Adair has the keys to her family's pool house. You could take her there!"

"Isn't there a gate?" I'd been to the MacLaine estate for her mom's funeral, and I couldn't see how I'd make it past the security, especially not while sneaking princess back onto the property.

"I know the access code," Poppy says, "I can go with you. I'll stay with her."

"No offense, but you're hardly in a condition to take care of her." She's not exactly sober, and I have no idea how much she drank. There's no way I can just leave Adair like this.

"If you think that I'm going to let you take my unconscious friend away without any supervision, then you're an idiot." She plants her hands on her hips for emphasis. Her stance might be more impressive if she wasn't hammered.

"Calm down, Wonder Woman," I stop her. "I'll help you get her there, but I'm just going to stick around if you don't mind."

"Let me find Kai." She dashes back to the party, and I hope she doesn't take too long. Adair is practically snoring in my arms. A couple partygoers pass us on their way out to the pool, eyeing me curiously. No one stops to ask if she's okay or even questions me. Given that half the people here are too drunk to walk, I guess it's not that weird. Still, I can't stand to think what might have happened to her if I hadn't come along. Even though I don't like Adair, there's no way I want someone touching her. Not without her consent. Not at all, if I'm being honest. All the times I'd seen this back in New York, the poor choices leading to a blackout were usually voluntary. The guys I knew there didn't go in for unwilling participation. And fucking with someone's friend or little sister got you your ass beat—or worse. That's the code I live by. I don't have a problem if a girl throws herself at me or if she wants to go. Sex doesn't have to be some type of religious experience in my book, but this shit isn't cool.

Poppy reappears with the guy who was with them earlier. He takes one look at Adair and panics. "Is she okay?"

"She's fine," I repeat. Drunk people can be so paranoid. "But we should get her somewhere quiet and comfortable. She's going to have one hell of a headache when she wakes up."

"Someone did this to her?" Kai asks as they take me to Adair's car. Poppy digs in Adair's bag for the keys, and I nearly drop her when they lead me to the Mercedes. At least if I have to put up with these entitled brats I get to drive all these amazing cars.

"This is her car?" I grunt as I get her situated in the front seat. Kai and Poppy pile into the back.

"Technically, it was her mother's," Poppy tells me.

That makes more sense. I can't help wondering if she inherited it—not that it made up for her mom's death. But it's a helluva nice way to remember her. The drive to Adair's house —which is a ludicrously inadequate term for something the size of Versailles—is way too short.

"This is it!" Poppy cries from the backseat when I nearly miss the turn.

"You weren't kidding earlier," Kai says. He rolls down his window while I enter the gate access code, so he can hang his head out to stare up the drive.

"Get back in the car," I order him. The kid is going to fall out of the car if he hangs his body any farther out the window. He manages to get mostly inside but barrages us with awestruck commentary as Poppy gives directions to bypass the main house and go around to the side.

"How many houses does this place have?" I mutter as we pass more and more buildings. My eyes dart over to Adair. She's slumped against the car door, but she looks fine.

"Oh, that's the gardener's shed. This is just a guesthouse. It's all part of Windfall."

"Windfall? What the fuck does that mean?"

"This is Windfall, the MacLaine estate," she explains.

"You name your houses?" Kai asks. I'm glad he said it for me. Rich people must have too much time on their hands.

"Of course." Poppy sounds as if she can't find anything wrong with this. "My house is so boring. My father's English, so he went with Landry Court. He wasn't even trying."

"That was Darcy's house, right? What's its name?" Kai asks as I park the car near the guest house. It's bigger than my brownstone in Queens. I can't imagine why a visitor would need two thousand square feet of their own just for a visit.

"Las Palmas." I can hear her eyes rolling even though it's too dark to see. "At least they were a little more creative with their name. Of course, if it was me I'd call it the hen house."

"The hen house?" I repeat, sure I heard her wrong.

"Yes," she says indignantly. "It makes sense to name it after Hennie's. Las Palmas sounds like it belongs in L.A. or Miami."

I share a look with Kai, who's helping me carry Adair

inside, while Poppy continues our education in the ways of the Valmont elite.

"Hennie's?

"Hennie's Hot Chicken. The Palmers own the entire chain. Darcy's mom is Henrietta Palmer."

She might as well be speaking in tongues for all I understand of what she just said.

"I've never heard of hot chicken," I say honestly as we haul Adair into a room.

"It's a Nashville thing," Poppy explains, supervising the entire process of delivering her best friend to bed. She stuffs a pillow under her head. "Wouldn't the hen house be cute?"

"I guess," I say absently. It's a little surreal to go from a party to a discussion of the merits of estate names, all while caring for a girl I hate.

Kai doesn't suffer from the same degree of whiplash regarding our circumstances and begins battering her with questions about hot chicken. I barely pay attention. I'm too busy studying the rise and fall of Adair's chest. There's no reason to think she's in danger, but someone has to keep watch.

"Now I'm hungry," Poppy says. "Let's go check the kitchen." She flies from the room like our work here is done, but Kai hesitates at the door.

"Want anything?"

"I want to stay with her," I tell him.

"Good idea." He glances toward Adair, his brows furrowing. "She's going to be okay, right?"

"Yeah." It's enough to reassure him, so he takes off after Poppy.

With them both gone, I look uncomfortably around the room. There's no way I'm climbing into bed beside her. If Adair wakes up, she'll probably clobber me to death with the bedside lamp before I get a chance to explain what happened. Even sitting on the bed feels wrong. All she's had about me since the minute we met are wrong ideas. I can't keep fucking explaining myself to her. In the end, I grab a pillow and make a spot on the floor, close enough that I can hear her breathe.

20

I'm on my second glass of liquid courage before I see him. I remember the first time I saw Sterling Ford in a suit—a borrowed suit. It was the day of my mother's funeral. He looked as out of place there as the suit had on his body. Gone are the days of wearing another man's clothes. His tuxedo is tailored to his body, showcasing his broad shoulders. With the jacket buttoned, his torso narrows to a lean waist. Sterling had the body of a man years before any other guy I knew. Now? I can't help wondering what it looks like beneath those layers of fabric.

He walks with the air of a man who owns the room. Heads turn in interest. The Valmont-Nashville philanthropy crowd is an incestuous bunch. We're born together, grow up together, marry each other, divorce each other, and attend each other's funerals. New blood usually comes by way the trophy wives unwisely imported from the ranks of professional sports cheerleaders and fashion models. In recent years, divorcees who managed to dodge the prenup have taken to being cougars with gusto. After a while, they all blend together, a pack of cougars and lions, divorcing one spouse while hunting for the next in the same pride. Once you're in this crowd, you can't escape.

I can't imagine Sterling ever fitting in with us. He's too jagged, his edges too roughly hewn to wedge into an available slot. I still can't believe he's here at all. He'd never hidden his distaste for the wealthy, a hatred that applied especially to me.

Ava appears at my side, following my gaze to him. "Did you see Sterling Ford is back in town?"

"I have eyes." There's no way I'm letting her see an ounce of my discomfort over his arrival. A West uses psychology like currency, gambling on instinct and doubling down on emotion. They collect reactions and meltdowns and make you pay the price later for showing your cards.

"You knew." She studies me with interest. Ava's too smart to not see through my detached façade.

I cling to it anyway. Shrugging my shoulders, I take another sip of champagne. "He's in the middle of a business deal with my brother."

She'll find out about this anyway. My only chance at retaining the upper hand is to act unbothered by this as if there's nothing unusual about my ex-boyfriend, a poor kid from New York, suddenly becoming a viable financial partner in MacLaine Media.

"If only your father could see him now," Ava says, giving voice to the one thought I've not allowed into my conscious brain. It's been there knocking on the gates, begging to be let in. Now she's opened the door.

"My father was always more interested in money than the man behind it." That much is true, at least.

She smirks, seeing through my indifference. We both know that my father gladly took money from anyone — new money, old money, blood money — it didn't matter. But no amount of money swayed his opinion on a man once it was made. Despite years of charity events and holiday parties, he never trusted a West. Then again, vipers steer clear of their own.

"So, are you planning to saddle that bronco?" She strokes the rim of her rocks glass, watching him. She'd seen him as a potential notch on her bedpost years ago. I'm guessing that hasn't changed. "I would."

The confirmation is unnecessary and produces an equally undesirable visual.

"You have such a way with words," I say, trying to ignore the image of Ava and Sterling dancing around my brain.

"You have a way of avoiding questions," she says.

It's as close as we'll ever get to complimenting one another.

"There you are!" Poppy joins us, grabbing a champagne flute from a passing tray. "My mother is having a meltdown."

"What's new?" I ask. Malcolm has found Sterling and is introducing him to various guests.

"Everything is fine," Ava promises Poppy. "And if it isn't, it's too late now. Have a drink and put some distance between the two of you."

Ava has always been kind to Poppy, but everyone is kind to Poppy. Probably because Poppy can see the good in everyone. The two had roomed together in college for a couple of years. Poppy never minded the parade of men Ava marched in and out of their dorm room. Maybe that's why Ava keeps her claws retracted when it comes to her.

Poppy spots Sterling with my brother. "There he is."

"So was I the last to know he was back in town?" Ava demands, realizing Poppy isn't surprised to see him either.

"I don't see why you care," I say.

"Sterling and I are old friends. Not all of us hold a grudge against him."

"I'm not holding a grudge."

"And the sky isn't blue, I'm not a West, and Nashville isn't in Tennessee." Her wide smile is as feline as her ability to rub anyone and every thing the wrong way. Just like a cat, there's no way to control her. She does as she pleases.

"Let's go say hello," Poppy suggests, linking her arm through mine.

"I don't think" —

"If you want company, I'll go," Ava offers.

"I should say hello," I say, reversing positions. The only thing worse than enduring Sterling's presence tonight would be watching Ava plastered all over him. There's not enough alcohol in the state of Tennessee to cope with that.

She snorts, raising her whiskey glass. "That's what I thought."

It's not unusual for Ava to toy with someone, but she generally has a reason. When it comes to me and Sterling I have no idea why she cares.

Poppy leads the way, murmuring hellos and accepting hugs as we pass various groups of people. Most nod to me. It's a sign that I'm the prickly part of this pair when no one attempts to embrace me. I prefer it that way. My best friend might get joy from hugging, but I feel like it leaches my energy.

Malcolm is busy boasting about some recently received network rating to a group of older men. Sterling couldn't look less interested.

"And the campaign?" an older gentleman asks. I think he's a local land developer. He's definitely someone that knew my father, and clearly he wants to be certain a MacLaine is in the Senate. It's easier to buy a vote when you know a man.

"We're still on track," Malcolm assures him, chancing a look at Sterling.

It's a mistake. Sterling appears not to notice, which is how I know he does. Nothing gets past him. The fact he's pretending proves the information is valuable.

"Poppy. Adair." Sterling greets us as we reach them. It's as much a greeting as I expect, his eyes travel over me. Unlike a moment ago, he doesn't hide his naked interest. He shows that, taking a step closer like an animal marking his territory —a sign of his claim over me to the other men.

Poppy nudges Cyrus closer to me, obviously sensing I need an intervention. Our eyes meet for one uncomfortable moment. I wish she would stop forcing him on me. It's hard to forget past mistakes when they're always near you, and it's especially difficult to do during the reunion from hell.

Malcolm continues his discussion with my father's old associates. No doubt he's busy securing more campaign contributions. It won't be hard. A MacLaine sat in the State or U.S. Senate for the last two decades—up until daddy got sick. There's a vested interest among Valmont's elite to get one back inside as swiftly as possible.

"You look lovely, Poppy," Sterling says to her. He glances at Cyrus. "I hope you don't mind me saying so."

Poppy bites her lip, torn between her nature and our friendship. Nature wins out and she gives Sterling a hug. "Thank you for supporting the shelter."

"It's a good cause," he says smoothly, still focusing all his attention on them. "But what is this for exactly?"

He holds up the paddle he was given at the door. My own is tucked safely in my clutch.

"The auction," Poppy explains. "It's how we're raising money tonight."

"What are we buying?" Sterling asks.

"Souls, I hope." A striking man I've never met joins us, his smile as dark as his eyes.

"That's not the best joke to make with this crowd," Sterling warns him. "You don't want to give them ideas."

"I don't believe we've met." Poppy steps forward and introduces herself. It's just like her to make friends.

"Luca," he says, lifting her hand to his lips. "Luca DeAngelo."

Cyrus stiffens at the gallant gesture. It's not like him to be jealous. Usually, he thinks far too highly of himself to worry that he might lose her. But he's staring at Luca like he's a threat.

"I'm so glad you're here," she murmurs, looking startled but delighted. It's not like her to be so easily charmed by a stranger. Cyrus places a hand on the small of her back, a subtle reminder that she's his and unavailable.

She recovers instantly, moving closer to her boyfriend. "We're doing this to raise money for the Valmont Animal Shelter," she explains. "They brought some animals here for adoption to the highest bidders."

"We're bidding on animals?" Luca shoots Sterling a poison-laced look.

"It's for a good cause," Poppy says quickly. "Funding has been cut recently. The shelter is going to be forced to reverse its no-kill policy unless we can do something."

"How noble." Luca doesn't sound like he believes this. I'm not entirely certain what kind of a man takes issue with raising money for homeless dogs, but I'm not surprised he found Sterling.

Poppy stumbles for something to say before looking across the room. "Oh, there's Kai! I need to make certain he's ready."

"I'll go with you," I volunteer. It will be good to see a friendly face.

"I will only be a second," she says, dismissing me without realizing that she's leaving me to fend for myself with the boys club.

It's going to be a long night.

21

STERLING

I've had dinner with Taliban insurgents a couple hundred feet from me. They were still more comfortable than sitting at this table. It's your typical black-tie affair. Too many utensils. Several bottles of wine with price tags that top the gross national product of a few developing nations. Artfully carved pats of butter. How the hell did I wind up here? Despite Malcolm's attempts to the contrary, Adair has managed to secure a seat across the table, leaving me sand-wiched between Poppy and Luca. I have an angel on one shoulder and the devil on the other. It should make for an interesting night.

Adair is absorbed in conversation with Kai Miles—a bit too focused to be believable. I don't miss how she brushes his arm and laughs at everything he says. Given that Kai is gay, I know it's a show she's putting on for me. She thinks she can make me jealous, and I can't help enjoying the attempt.

"So you two are old friends?" Poppy asks, nodding at Luca. Her ability to innocently turn simple small talk into a loaded question never ceases to amaze.

Luca smirks at me over the rim of his wine goblet. "Do you want to tell the story or should I?"

Interpretation: do I want them to know the truth or a lie? This is Luca's specialty: concocting wild fables on the spot. I never know what to expect when he opens his mouth. I only know it won't be anywhere near what happened. It's useful when you're under-cover and amusing when you're bored.

"You tell it better than I do," I say with a meaningful nod. Permission granted.

"Sterling saved my life," he begins.

This ought to be good.

"Did he? He saved your life?" Adair asks coldly. Her interjection catches the attention of everyone at the table. They fall silent and wait for the rest of the story.

Luca turns a well-honed level of earnestness on her. "He did."

In fairness, I have saved his life —on more than one occasion. It's these little truths hidden in the lies that make it easier for him to sell.

Adair is either not impressed or doesn't buy it, because she snorts and reaches for her wine glass. She's always been a skeptic, especially when it comes to me.

"What an exciting way to meet," Poppy gushes, clearly trying to salvage the tense mood at the table. She shoots a look at Kai, clearly requesting backup.

"How?" Kai jumps in. "Distract me from how hungry I am."

Luca leans back in his chair and shrugs. "My car broke down halfway between London and Edinburgh. No cell service. Walking for help would've taken hours. That much exercise would definitely have killed me." He tosses a winning smile at Adair, who stares blankly at him.

Trust her to be immune to his charm.

"London?" she repeats.

"I have family there," he says casually.

"Oh, maybe I know them," Poppy says. "What's your last name again?"

"DeAngelo. Luca DeAngelo."

Adair rolls her eyes at his dramatic delivery of this information, but I don't miss how several of my table-mates tense when he says this. I knew that dropping the DeAngelo name wouldn't go unnoticed. It seems the businessmen in this town know it. The DeAngelo presence isn't as prevalent here as in major cities like New York — but for those with large corporations the DeAngelo family's reach is well-known. Until now, there's never been a DeAngelo presence in Nashville or its surrounding areas. The arrival of Luca in Valmont is a clear cause for concern. It's much easier to ignore the shadier aspects of doing business globally when your domestic bubble is safe from your less savory international associates.

Poppy, however, is completely oblivious to this and continues on her crash course conversation. "What does your family do?"

"All sorts of things," Luca says. "We don't have a traditional industry, I suppose."

"Are you"—Ginny begins before Malcolm cuts her off.

"How refreshing. A Renaissance man," he says, fingers fidgeting on a salad fork. "Certainly, we could all use a break from business discussions, though."

"Probably. Did I hear you're running for Senate?" Luca asks, managing to find an even more delicate topic.

Malcolm squirms in his chair. No doubt he's wondering what could come of a DeAngelo's interest in his campaign. MacLaine Media always considers the needs of its foreign investors, like the DeAngelo clan, in its publications and programs. However, politically, the family's concerns lie with

Valmont and its taxpayers—or lack thereof, if a MacLaine can help it.

"He's going to win," Ginny says proudly.

"I imagine so." Luca's smile bares a bit too much teeth to be congenial.

"You met in London? When?" Adair asks, dragging the topic back to how I supposedly met Luca. It's not a simple question, though. It's an interrogation. I don't know if she thinks Luca's story is bullshit, but she's going to dissect it until she knows for sure. That much is clear.

"What was that? Four years ago?" Luca passes the ball back to my court.

When you've been in life-and-death situations with someone, you know how to communicate in precarious moments. Luca understands the answer to that question could have serious consequences. Trust Adair to want the particulars.

I tilt my head to him before shrugging at Adair. "Honestly, it's all a blur."

It's a non-answer. It's also the best I can do without knowing why she's asking the question.

Ginny laughs, the tinkle of it falling like shattered glass between us. "That's funny, because Adair was in —"

"Oh! The salad," Poppy interrupts. This time it's not an innocent insertion. I don't miss how she casts a furtive look at her best friend.

The waiters could not have timed it more perfectly. The table partners into private conversation as the plates appear before us. I murmur an absent thanks to the server, but never take my eyes off Adair. She shifts into protective mode, adjusting the face she wears for the world. She chats with Kai, returning to her futile flirtations. Their conversation continues through dinner. Luca feeds an ever-increasing stream of bullshit to Poppy, who drinks it up while Cyrus appears torn between amusement and disapproval. He's never been able to decide what to do with Poppy: invest in her or take his chances on finding a better prospect. It's clear his feelings toward her haven't changed. Cyrus never loved Poppy Landry before. He doesn't now. Love matters less than business alliances in Nashville. Still, there's no rock sparkling on her finger. It's worse because she loves him. Anyone can see it. What I can't decide is whether or not she realizes he doesn't return that love? It's obvious to everyone else.

Luca's drawling baritone interrupts my reflections. "And that's when Sterling says 'I'll buy you a new Rolex, but you have to take care of the camel.'"

I turn my head to stare at him while laughter breaks out across the table. Maybe I need to pay more attention to what he's spewing before his lies become a liability.

"It sounds like you two have had quite the adventures." Adair doesn't sound impressed. She quirks an eyebrow in challenge.

"We have," I tell her. Let her wonder if they involve camels or not.

The main course arrives and I stare at the block of artfully arranged tofu drizzled with a thick, green sauce.

"What happened to chicken or steak?" I ask.

"All the entrées are vegetarian," Poppy says. A glance around the table confirms that we're all eating the same dish.

"This is an event for an animal shelter," Adair reminds me smugly.

"There are some patrons who prefer a cruelty-free menu," Poppy says. Her dark eyes round with concern. "If you want something else..."

I hold up a hand. "It's fine. I'll find something tasty to eat later."

I keep my eyes on Adair as I speak. She turns away, her cheeks flushing.

The food is saved by the sauce and its warm notes of curry, pepper, and coriander. A hint of Kaffir lime blends delicately into it. It's probably better than the boring chicken usually served at these events.

"I hope it's okay," Poppy says, leaning closer as I finish a bite.

"I love curry," I say genuinely. "I ate a lot of it in London and Mumbai."

Adair pushes away from the table so quickly that her chair nearly topples over. "I'm going to the powder room."

She can't cover that she's visibly upset. I know why. I remember how she used to dream of studying in England—of living there. Instead, she's been stuck here in Tennessee, and it's all her own damn fault.

"I should go get ready for the auction." Kai stands and places his napkin on the table. It's obvious that he's going to check on her. I'll never understand all her little lapdogs or how they chase after her. Even after all this time, they don't seem to care how she treats them.

"Kai is emceeing the auction tonight," Poppy says, diverting everyone's attention away from Adair's dramatic exit.

"So how does this work?" Luca asks. "I see a little fur ball that I can't live without and I have to outbid whoever else wants it?"

"No one actually takes pets home" she says, laughing as though this is obvious. She seems genuinely amused at the thought. "It's all ceremonial. It's sort of a runway show of animals combined with an auction."

"No one adopts the animals?" I ask. I will never under-stand rich people. "Why not just ask everyone to write a check instead of all this trouble?"

And expense.

There's a shared look among the Valmont heirs at the table.

"It's nice for people to see where their money is going," Ginny explains.

"The dinner encourages people to donate more," Poppy agrees. "After, you get to take a photo with your pet before he heads back to the rescue."

In other words, it's a chance to seem benevolent to your peers. It hardly matters the motivation. Whether it's the guilt of seeing poor, helpless puppies without a home or just to show off how good of a person you are compared to your neighbor, motives don't matter. It's another pageant of wealth and privilege. I wouldn't be surprised if the evening ends with everyone donning masks and robes while chanting mystical incantations to the gods of banking and finance.

"How charming," Luca says under his breath.

"There are some really adorable animals," Poppy says, oblivious to his sarcasm.

Everyone claps as Kai takes the stage with a microphone in hand. He beams a million-dollar smile at them. "Good evening and thank you to everyone who came out to help us support the Valmont Animal Rescue."

Last year he was nominated for a Grammy, and now he's stuck entertaining socialites in the name of friendship. Kai is just another object in the Valmont collection of treasures, expected to return at a moment's notice whenever they need to use him for a function. He's a crystal vase brought out of the china cabinet for special occasions.

"Tonight, you're going to meet some of the animals you're saving with your adoption money," he continues.

Adair quietly rejoins us at the table. I want to keep her in my sights, so I pretend to be absorbed by the overview of how the auction will work.

"If there's a guinea pig, I'm bidding," Luca warns in a whisper.

"Thank God, they don't let you keep the animals," I mutter.

"I would make an excellent pet owner." He clutches his chest.

"No, you would not." I can't imagine Luca being responsible for another living creature.

"Everyone, say hello to Diamond," Kai says as an older woman in a black satin gown carries a tabby cat on to the stage. She looks uncomfortable, her dress isn't designer or expensive. Undoubtedly, she's a volunteer who has been tapped to parade around the animal population for the amusement of the Valmont elite.

"Diamond started her life on the mean streets of Nashville. She enjoys scratching posts, belly rubs, and catnip. Now don't forget, ladies, diamonds are a girl's best friend." Kai looks pained to say this bit, and I'm about to ask who wrote the script when he hits us with: "The bidding will begin at one thousand dollars."

Luca sits up and stares around. "A thousand bucks for an alley cat? These people have lost their damn minds."

I chuckle quietly. I suspect he hasn't seen anything yet.

When the bidding concludes, Diamond raises just under three thousand dollars for charity.

"I take it all back," Luca says quietly. "This is genius. I wonder if I can get one of these women to adopt me."

Judging from how many women in the room keep glancing in our direction, it wouldn't be hard for him to find willing matrons. Not that he needs the money.

Next up, a small terrier catches the eye of Ginny. Malcolm

grudgingly raises his paddle, looking uneasily at me. He shrugs as if to say women. We both know he doesn't have the money just to show off for philanthropy. That doesn't stop him from driving the price up to $5000, though. He winds up in a pissing contest with another man whose wife is whispering furtively in his ear. It's like their entire reputations rest on what sad dog to fake adopt.

"And now the lovely Adair MacLaine would like to introduce you to Zeus," Kai says, and I'm surprised to see Adair leading a giant black dog onto the stage. Zeus has a brutal look to his muscular body. There's clearly pit bull in his blood. But he doesn't strain against his leash. His tongue lolls comically out the side of his mouth. "Zeus came to our facility after being saved from an animal shelter that doesn't have a no kill policy. It's animals like Zeus that need our help. He was discovered chained up in a yard in East Nashville, but despite his rough beginnings, he's proven to be a gentle giant. The bidding will start at $300."

"Why so low?" I asked Poppy. "Cats are going for thousands for fuck's sake."

"He's a mix," she explains. "They're impossible to adopt—at least to families. Most people don't want their children around that type of dog. We're very selective about potential owners, but he hasn't had a single interested party in the three months he's been at a shelter. He was scheduled for euthanasia at his prior rescue."

I know a thing or two about being unwanted, how it feels to be passed around like people are just taking turns putting up with you. When the bidding starts there's hesitation. A few spare pitying glances, others return to conversations. He's not the adorable puppy that makes for sweet social media photos. Adair whispers something and the dog sits immediately. He soaks up the praise as she pats his head.

"Why is Adair up there?" I ask.

"She volunteers at the shelter. You know how she loves animals."

"Ever since she had to stop riding, this has been her passion," Cyrus adds.

"She stopped riding?" This is a surprise.

"Competitively," Poppy tacks on, shooting daggers at her boyfriend.

There's a story here. A few more glasses of wine and I'll get one of them to spill it. For now, I can't stop looking at Zeus. The bidding has already tapered out. He isn't going to raise more than $400 when it's all said and done.

"Adair adores him," Poppy says, "but she'll never adopt him."

So, she loves him, but he doesn't deserve a place in her heart? Before I realize what I'm doing my paddle is in the air.

"$5000," I call out.

Heads swing my direction. Kai is momentarily gobsmacked. I don't miss how Adair flinches when she realizes I'm the bidder.

But I didn't do it for her.

No one challenges my bid, although a few assholes yell jokes about how I'm bidding all wrong. That's not how I see it.

"Are these animals available for adoption?" I asked Poppy after the bidding moves to the next animal.

"Yes," she says, her eyebrows knitting together. "But—"

"I'll double that bid if you can arrange for them to have his paperwork ready tomorrow morning."

"You don't have to actually take him home," she reminds me.

"For ten thousand bucks, I'd rather have a dog than a picture."

"You old softy," Luca mutters so only I can hear.

When Adair returns to the table, she accepts praise from everyone as though she fucking sold the dog. In a way, she did, but it's not because she's some beautiful soul. She keeps her eyes carefully from mine. She knows why I did it.

"Sterling is adopting Zeus," Poppy announces.

"I was there." The chill in her voice instantly diminishes the mood at the table.

"No, he's actually adopting him." Poppy claps her hands together as though I've made her night.

Adair's mouth hangs open for a second before she clamps it shut. She doesn't recover before the auction ends and the evening progresses on to the dancing portion. Yet another course in the endless buffet of tonight's fuckery.

"You don't look pleased," I say to her.

"It seems like you have something to prove," she says.

"That I love animals?" I offer.

A muscle ticks in her jaw. "I'm sure that's it."

"Why don't you and I dance? I'll explain why I adopted the dog." I stand up and extend a hand across the table. All our companions watch us, waiting to see how she'll respond. She dares a look at Malcolm and I catch him nod his head slightly.

He's given her marching orders. I'm to be kept happy—and these days, Adair always does what she's told. She huffs as she stands and then stomps to the dance floor. I catch her before she reaches it, wrapping a hand around her waist and spinning her into my arms. My other hand closes over hers. It's delicate, her skin cool and soothing to the touch. Adair stares at our clasped hands for a moment as if trying to recall some long-forgotten memory. My thumb brushes over hers instinctively. She doesn't resist as we move seamlessly into a waltz.

"I didn't know you could dance," she comments.

My hand flattens on the small of her back, holding her in

place—close enough to smell the magnolia in her perfume, far enough to resist its temptation. It's the little things about her that press on my memories. "There's a lot of things you don't know about me."

"Like where you're going to keep a dog?" she asks. "Sounds like you're busy running off between Nashville and London and who knows where else."

"Actually," I say, leading her around an older couple who isn't keeping pace to the music, "I just bought a place at Twelve and South."

The color drains from her face, but she doesn't respond.

"I thought Zeus looked like good company," I add.

"If you think that you're going to adopt that dog just to spite me," she starts.

"I adopted the dog because no one wanted it." My voice is low and laced with contempt. She flinches but recovers immediately.

"You're assuming that." There's still nothing she hates more than that, it seems.

"Poppy told me. He's just a bargaining chip. No one wants him. They're scared of them. They think he'll hurt them. They saw the cover and decided his story isn't for them without reading a single word."

"They don't know him," she says quietly.

"And you do?" I ask her.

"Better than you think." Her fingers shift from my grasp and lace through mine. "As long as you're going to take care of him."

"I swear on all the dog biscuits." I spin her in a circle, dipping her backward slightly. She blinks like she feels a heady rush of blood. That makes two of us. I need to get this back on track, and quickly. "You work at the shelter?"

"I have to have something to do." She doesn't sound happy about it.

Someone taps me on the shoulder. We pause to find Kai there. "Mind if I cut in?"

Her knight has come to save her. She looks relieved. I release her into his custody, ignoring how empty my arms feel without her in them. I have to remind myself that Adair is a burden that's too heavy to carry long.

The sun is really, really bright. I scooch up on my elbows and stare around me. Pink walls and a room my mom decorated to feel like the Beverly Hills Hotel greet me. I have no memory of making it back to the pool house last night, but there's a pretty obvious clue snoring on the floor next to the bed. How the hell did I wind up back here with Sterling Ford sleeping at my feet?

My last memory—Sterling picking me up—is where the night ends in my memory. It's as fixed as the period at the end of a sentence. But why him? Moving the sheets as quietly as possible, I creep out of the room, tiptoeing to the door so I don't wake him up. I stop in the bathroom long enough to dig out a toiletry kit— my mother took the whole hotel vibe as far as possible— and brush my teeth. A quick glance in the mirror reveals yesterday's makeup fared about as well as I did. I scrub it off until my skin glows pink, hoping to jar some memories free. No luck. There's just Sterling's worried face swimming in front of me, and then nothing. Full-stop. The end.

Down the hall, I hear someone moving around the kitchen. Another person is singing. Apparently, Sterling didn't bring me here alone. I head down and discover Poppy buttering slices of toast.

"Good morning, darling," she says, dancing over to peck my cheek. "How are you feeling?"

"Like I was run over by a truck," I say, rubbing my temples. "I wasn't, was I?"

For all I know, I might have been.

Kai and Poppy share a look before he returns to the eggs he's frying on the stovetop.

"What did I do?" I demand.

"You did nothing," Poppy says slowly. "You passed out."

"I didn't have that much to drink." In fact, I can only remember taking one drink pre-Sterling.

"That's exactly it," she says. "Sterling thinks someone drugged you."

"For real?" That explains the construction crew hammering in my head. Drugs aren't uncommon at Valmont house parties. Some people want something stronger than alcohol. Some people have too much money. It's a terrible combination. "I'm going to kill Sterling Ford."

He's the last person I remember. Why had I let myself be alone with him? How could Poppy have let him sleep in the same room as me?

"I don't think you should be mad at Sterling."

"He's the last person I was with, and—"

"He found you and then he found me," Poppy cuts in, officially stopping me in my tracks. "He helped us get you here. He even drove your car home. He stayed with you all night like a guard dog."

I didn't expect that. It's not difficult to imagine the hot and cold egomaniac doing something heartless. It's a lot harder to imagine him doing something selfless—and he'd done something selfless twice now. He'd been a dick about it the whole time, but, still, why did he care? Sure, it's the decent thing to do, and if our situations had been reversed, I would have helped him. The trouble is that I didn't expect that of him, which means I'm either completely wrong about who he is, or I'm actually the bitch in this scenario. Neither thought is comforting.

"Also," she adds, "he's really nice."

"Nice?" I repeat. "That hasn't been my experience."

"Maybe you two got off on the wrong foot."

I want to crawl into a hole until my head stops pounding and I can sort through this mess inside it, but before I can Poppy holds out a plate.

"I made you breakfast," she says brightly.

Kai clears his throat. He's been quiet during this whole exchange until now. "You did what?"

Poppy gives a sheepish smile. "Okay, I made toast and Kai tried to show me how to make scrambled eggs."

"How did that go?" I ask, the weight on my chest easing enough that I laugh.

"Thank God, she's an heiress," Kai says as he scoops eggs onto a plate. Poppy drops two slices of toast next to it.

"At least they're edible," she says.

I eat slowly, my stomach still churning with anxiety. If they hadn't been there, what would have happened? It's not like someone drugged my drink by accident. I try to remember who gave me the cup, but I'd never seen him before in my life. I'll have to ask Ava if she knew the guy. It's a long shot, since half the people there were probably new students at Valmont.

"I can't believe someone would do that," Poppy says.

I snort. Even now her glass is half-full. Mine is feeling pretty empty, at the moment. "I can."

"Thanks for letting us crash here last night," Kai says.

"We were thinking of going for a swim. Care to join us?"

"You don't have any suits," I remind her.

"That's the joy of a GBFF," Kai says, clarifying when I give him a puzzled look. "Gay best friend forever. I've decided that's what I am for you two. You don't have to worry about me seeing you naked, because I'm not interested and I think all bodies are fabulous."

"You might have to worry about half of the garden staff seeing you, though," I say dryly.

"We'll leave our underwear on," Poppy promises.

"I'm not sure what to make of that," A gruff voice says from the hallway. Sterling stands there, rubbing sleep from his eyes. His dark hair is tousled on top of his head and there's a hint of stubble on his jawline. He must have to shave every day. I try to peel my eyes away from him and fail. It's clear he's only half-awake, because the minute he blinks he seems to realize he's shirtless. He tugs it over his head quickly, his usual scowl pulling down his lips. "Bathroom?"

"Let me show you." I hop up from the stool, instantly regretting my decision when my head reminds me that I'm still hungover from last night's debacle.

As soon as his back is turned, Poppy pretends to fan herself while Kai mouths *wow*. I glare at them, hoping they behave. I'm careful to keep my eyes in front of me as I lead him down the hallway. They want to wander his direction. Pushing open the door, I dart inside and dig out another toiletry kit. I hold it out to him. "Here."

"What's this?" he asks.

"A toiletry kit." I shove it into his hands but he continues to stare.

"A what?"

"Like you get at a hotel," I say slowly. Is he screwing with me? "You know, a toothbrush, toothpaste, some cotton swabs. The basics, in case you left anything at home."

"Is this a house or a hotel?" he mutters.

"My mom likes to have things on hand for guests," I say, feeling a little stupid, especially when it dawns on me what I said. "She liked to have them on hand."

"Thanks," Sterling says quickly like he wants to avoid making this worse for both of us.

When I return to the kitchen, Kai has made another plate for Sterling, but they're already cleaning things up. "I'll do that."

"Don't you want to swim?" Poppy asks.

"Taking care of this is the least I can do after you got me home and cooked me breakfast." I look back down the hall. I need to talk to Sterling. I need to thank him for saving me once again. This time, I am determined that it will go differently than the last time. That will probably be easier without an audience.

"We'll be out there." Poppy takes the hint and disappears outside with Kai.

My thoughts linger on Sterling's face when he looked at the toiletry kit. Something had flashed in his eyes, but he'd covered it with his usual cruel sarcasm. All I know about him is that he grew up in New York. I know he's read Jane Austen enough to quote it. I know that he doesn't like to talk about his life. I know that he's never been to a hotel that gives you a toiletry kit. I know that I offend him every time we talk. It's like I'm programmed to do it. But most of all, I know how little I know him—and how much I'm beginning to want to change that.

When he appears, his hair is damp like he ran water over it. It falls in dark slashes over his forehead, covering his eyes, and I resist the urge to brush them away. He looks surprised when I hand him the plate of toast and eggs.

"I thought you might be hungry," I admit.

He shrugs like he could care less and stalks to a stool at the kitchen island. "I could have made something for myself."

Somehow, I don't think he spent his time in the bathroom wondering about me. He's just as determined to be obstinate as ever. "Well, you deserve to have someone cook you breakfast after last night. I'm pretty sure we all owe you one."

"You don't owe me anything," he says as he shovels eggs onto his fork. His face lightens when he takes a bite. "This is actually pretty good."

I might be offended if I had cooked it. "You sound surprised."

"I didn't think people like you knew how to cook."

"I didn't cook it," I admit. "Kai did."

"That explains it," he says.

"What does that mean?"

"Just that if you live in a house like this you probably have someone to cook your meals." He's actually not being combative but his words sting anyway. The truth usually does.

"I'm not completely helpless."

"I never said you were, Lucky."

"That again?" Him calling me that is one memory I still have of last night.

"Look around you," he says. "Not everyone is this fortunate."

"My family worked for this." The flush on my cheeks isn't the product of pride though. It's something else entirely. I have no reason to be ashamed of my family. I can't change who I am.

Sterling seems to be thinking along the same lines. "And you were lucky enough to be born to them."

"Stop," I say, holding up a hand in surrender. We're not going to get anywhere if we keep up with this feud. "I don't want to fight with you."

"But we're so good at it." He bites off a corner of toast and grins.

I take a deep breath. I'm feeling light-headed again, and I don't think it has anything to do with last night. "I just wanted to say…thank you."

"Wow, that looked challenging."

"It was," I confess. "I don't like feeling out of control. I know I was last night. Thank you for making sure I got home safely, especially after I've been such a bitch to you."

"No one deserves to have someone do that to them," he says quietly.

"I have no clue who did it."

"If I ever find out who did, they'll be sorry." He looks like he means it. It's oddly touching, given that we don't exactly have a blossoming friendship. So maybe Sterling is rough around the edges, but it's obvious that he's not the dickhead I thought he was.

"Let's start over," I blurt out.

"Start over?"

"We didn't exactly hit it off the first time we met."

"No, we didn't," he agrees.

"So, we'll start over. I'm Adair MacLaine. Nice to meet you." I stick my hand out.

He drops his fork on the counter and takes my outstretched hand. His skin is warm and his grip is so strong it feels like he could crush mine if he only decided to squeeze. Despite that, for some reason, I don't want to let it go.

"Sterling Ford," he says.

"Friends?"

"Sure," he says, but he doesn't quite seem certain about

this. Before I can call him on it, there's an earsplitting shriek outside. He turns toward the sound, alarm on his face.

"Poppy and Kai are swimming. It's probably a little cold," I explain, actually a bit relieved to remember I'm not alone with him here.

"They're swimming in October?"

"Well, the pool has a heater." I'm not sure what to talk about with him. Now that I've gotten the uncomfortable thank you out-of-the-way and we both agreed to give each other another chance, I have to find a way to forget all the ugliness that's occurred between us. I decide to focus on what he did for me. "You didn't have to sleep on the floor."

"I wasn't going to sleep in the bed with you." He sees the look on my face and quickly adds, "I didn't want to freak you out."

"You could've slept in one of the other rooms." The pool house has three bedrooms and a living area. It isn't like the floor was his only option.

"And leave you there like that? I wanted to make sure that you were okay. It wasn't safe to leave you there alone."

Now I definitely feel like a bitch. Sterling Ford might not be a traditional knight in shining armor. Nope. His armor is tarnished and his attitude is just as bad, but he's my savior nonetheless.

"And thank you," I say quietly, "for driving me to the hospital that night. I was terrible to you."

"I think it was understandable, given the circumstances."

"Not really." I shake my head. "I felt helpless."

"We all do stupid shit when we feel powerless." There's not a note of judgment in his voice for once.

I hate that he's right. I nod, still feeling ashamed.

"I'm really sorry about your mom. You okay?"

"I think so. Thanks," I say, my mouth going dry. "I miss her.

You know…that's the first time I've said that out loud. Everyone's avoiding the topic. I think they want to help me move on."

"You don't move on from that." He hesitates for a second. "My mom died a couple years ago."

"I'm sorry," I say. And I am. I know how much it hurts. I know it can't be undone. That's why he came to the funeral. It wasn't out of some perverse curiosity. He came because we were in this together. Most of my friends have lost parents to divorces. They think they understand. Sterling and I share a bond that neither of us want.

"You sure they're swimming and not murdering each other?" he says, changing the subject as the sound outside grows louder.

I'm grateful for the segue. We head out the French doors to find my friends splashing each other in their underwear.

"Well, this is something." Sterling smirks.

"They look like little kids," I say.

"They look like they're having fun," he says.

"Want to join them?" It's the wrong thing to ask, because I barely have time to process Sterling's arm wrapping around my waist before he throws me, fully dressed, into the pool. I come up, spluttering, just in time to see him do a cannonball in after me. Poppy and Kai shout their approval at this turn of events.

"I can't believe you did that," I scream, peeling wet hair from my face.

"Oh shit!" Poppy looks from him to me.

"Sorry, Lucky," Sterling says. "I thought you could use a little excitement in your life."

"Is that so?" I tread water, glaring at him.

"Okay, maybe not excitement," he hedges, "but some fun?" He no longer sounds so sure about this theory.

"I'll give you fun." I dive toward him, throwing myself

against his body. We crash under the water in a tangle of arms
and legs and possibilities.

An hour later, after Sterling's clothes finish drying, the
three of them head back to campus in an Uber. I sneak into
the kitchen through the back door. My father and brother
don't come down here, so it's the safest option. But the heav-
enly scent of bourbon chocolate chip cookies, Felix's specialty,
greets me on entry. He pauses at the oven with an eyebrow
raised.

"Long night?" he asks, scanning me up and down. I'd fore-
gone the dryer in favor of a large, fluffy towel. He looks at the
puddle dripping onto his clean floor and sighs. "I'm not going
to ask."

"I went for a swim." It's not exactly a lie.

"Get changed and come down for a cookie."

I dash upstairs and toss on some yoga pants and a clean T-
shirt. Then I head back down for cookies and advice. Felix is
always good for both.

He's pulling the first batch out of the oven when I arrive. I
reach for one hot off the cookie sheet, and he smacks my hand
away.

"I thought you might need these when you didn't come in
last night," he says.

"Did anyone else notice I was gone?" I ask.

"They haven't said anything to me." He winks.

I swipe a hot cookie off the rack and bite into it. Chocolate and vanilla move across my tongue, but it's the slight hit
of whiskey that warms me up. I groan. "I did need this. You're
psychic."

"Equally good for heartbreak and hangovers," he says to me. "What am I dealing with?"

"The latter," I admit. Felix doesn't need to know the particulars. I'd rather he think I was out having a good time, having a little too much to drink, then worrying that I was in danger.

"It sounds like your friends and you were having a blast this morning," he says.

"Sorry," I say with a frown. "Were we too loud?"

"It's nice to hear laughter in this house again," he says, adding quietly, "Of course, I'm not used to boys spending the night."

"Nothing happened!" Normally, I would have snuck Sterling and Kai off the premises before dawn. It's not like a guy's never spent the night in the pool house before. Plenty of my male friends have crashed there over the years. I'd always just been too afraid of what would happen if daddy spotted them to let them stay past dawn. He's too preoccupied to notice something like that now, but Felix isn't.

"No judgment." That's his way of saying that he's cool. Felix is cool. But he's more like my granddad than he wants to admit. I know he doesn't want to think about me having sex with anyone—not that he has to worry about that.

"I didn't recognize those boys," he says.

"They're just friends," I say, taking another cookie.

"Are you sure about that?" he asks. "I couldn't help taking a peek outside."

"Well, Kai is gay, so I wouldn't get my hopes up there," I warn him in a teasing voice.

"And the other one?"

"Not gay."

"So?"

"I'm not sure," I admit. Felix is the only safe party to have this discussion with. If Poppy knows that I have even the slightest curiosity about Sterling, she'll never stop playing the matchmaker. Until I make up my mind about what I think about him, I can't have that. "He's complicated."

"Do tell."

"He drove me to the hospital the night she died," I say softly.

Realization lights across his face. "I thought he looked familiar."

"I thought he was kind of a jerk."

"And now?"

"Maybe I was wrong," I say.

"First impressions are as reliable as a weatherman — wrong as often as they're right," he tells me.

"So, you're saying I should give him another chance?" I ask.

"It looks like you already have."

I chew on my cookie, considering this. Sterling hadn't made the best first impression but neither had I, if I'm being honest.

"What about you?"

Felix has been seeing a local teacher for the last couple of months. As much as I want him to be happy, I'm worried about what will happen if things get serious.

"We have a date tonight," he says, filling me in on the details. He's bringing her daisies and some of the cookies. I'm left feeling guilty for not wanting things to move too quickly. It's obvious he cares about her, and any man who treats a woman like he does deserves to be happy.

"I guess that means I'm having dinner with the family." I screw up my nose. Family dinners are a lot like a game of Russian roulette. I'm never entirely sure what to expect when I take a seat at the table.

"Look at this as an opportunity," he says. "A chance to reconnect."

I snort at the thought. The MacLaine family has never been connected in the traditional sense. It's more like a collection of dots. If anyone bothered to draw a line from point to point—person-to-person—it might form a coherent picture. Then again, it might just be a mess. "At least, I know they'll be cookies afterward."

"There's something else," he says, handing me another cookie. "I'm not sure how to say this."

I take it, realizing my fingers are trembling. There hasn't been a lot of good news for me lately. If Felix baked cookies to soften whatever he needs to tell me, I imagine it's not good either.

"The mortuary called. Your mother's headstone is in place." His voice is gentle, but the words scrape against the hollow pit in my stomach. I stare at the cookie in my hand, no longer feeling hungry. It seems that there's some heartaches even Felix's cookies can't cure.

I trade the comfort of my yoga pants for a trim pair of black capris, a loose, cream-colored cable-knit sweater that drapes off my shoulder, and velvet flats. It's dressy enough that I won't get a lecture from daddy about proper evening attire, while still being comfortable. But it doesn't matter. I can't eat at dinner. Normally, I love pot roast and mashed potatoes. Tonight I can't find my appetite. I've known it was coming. One of the shocks of burying someone is discovering that it takes weeks for their tombstone to be put in place. One of life's little jokes. Think you're ready to move on? Even just a little bit? Well, got you! Get your ass back to the cemetery and feel the pain all over again.

Ginny is here tonight, talking incessantly about wedding plans. She's marrying my brother in February, the week of Valentine's Day. The only thing that could be more cliché would be a June wedding. Still, she isn't so bad. Her own mother lives on the east coast, so Mom had been helping her with the majority of the preparations. Now that she's gone, we get to listen to all the drama associated with a high society wedding. There's a lot. Shakespeare would be impressed. Hell, he'd probably take notes.

"So, I told them that if Senator MacLaine called the Customs House, we could move the venue in five minutes flat. Suffice it to say, there won't be a golf tournament at the country club that weekend." She looks incredibly smug about this turn of events.

"Good," Daddy says, not bothering to look up from his phone. There's always some new message coming in from Washington. I've sat down to dinner with this man nearly every night of my life, but we're rarely in the same room. He's always elsewhere — his mind focused on other things.

When Mom was alive she'd say gently, "Angus, come be with your family."

"Yes, dear, one more minute." He'd smile at her like she was the moon and sun and stars and then go right back to his emails and business dealings.

At least then we'd had Mom to ask us about our lives. She would tell us stories about how her and Daddy met. Or what ridiculous things the local chamber of the Tennessee Historical Society had up their sleeves now. These days it's just Ginny planning the wedding or total silence. The only other topic of conversation that regularly comes up is Malcolm's hopes for State Senate. Because of this, he's on his phone nearly as often.

I guess that's why Ginny only bothers coming around once or twice a week for dinner. In the meantime, she must be saving up all her energy to try to get attention on these nights.

"Tell me," she says, turning in my direction, "what do you think of lavender bridesmaid dresses?"

"I thought it was a Valentine's Day wedding," I say. "Shouldn't we wear pink or something?"

She waves her hand derisively and laughs, as though it's a ridiculous thought. "That would be cliché."

I want to remind her that she's the one that insisted on planning a wedding during America's most cliché Hallmark holiday, but I keep my mouth shut.

"I guess," I say with a shrug. I could care less what bridesmaid dresses she chooses. It's not like I have a choice about being in the wedding. Back when Mom was alive, she made it fun to talk about the wedding plans. It was exciting then. Now it's just another day to dread. Another day Mom should be present for but won't. Another day to face the gaping hole she left inside me. "Well, we need to make a decision," Ginny continues, not noticing that I'm less than interested in the topic. "We should have ordered dresses weeks ago, but we were so busy."

"Weeks ago?" I repeat.

"They take forever to arrive. Your mother and I had an appointment, but..." She trails away, her eyes darting nervously to me.

I wish I hadn't taken that moment to attempt a bite of pot roast. It turns to ash in my mouth, and I have to force myself to swallow.

"I miss her, too," Ginny says quietly.

I manage a small, but grateful smile.

It feels like business as usual for Daddy and Malcolm. Mom's death is more about damage control than grief most of the time. I know Daddy misses her. I hear him crying in his office with the doors closed. It's just like him not to let us see him vulnerable. Still, I can't find the grace to feel sorry for him. Not after what he did to her. Instead, we're all alone in our grief—locking ourselves in our respective rooms and working our way through the unexpected sorrow alone. But isn't that how death works? We all go through it alone. I guess it's preparation for the day our own comes.

"We could go try some dresses on," I offer. I'm not the least bit excited to do it, but I have to remember that I'm not the only one hurting. The wedding doesn't have to be a sad day. It can be what we make it.

"I'll set something up." Her eyes light up, and I know that at least one person at the table is looking forward to the future. Maybe someday I will, too.

"That reminds me that we need to rebook the photographer for the paper," she says to Malcolm. "They'll want do a feature on our engagement."

"Do we have to?" he asks.

"Of course, you have to," Daddy interjects, reaching for his glass of bourbon. I can't help but notice he has drank more than he's eaten this evening. Apparently, he's on a liquid diet. "Appearances are more important than ever."

Of course, that's why he thinks they should do it. He cares more about what the outside world sees than what any of us feels.

"Why do we have to?" I can't stop myself from asking. I'm tired of every moment in my life being a photo op. "I think that people should allow us time to mourn."

"And they have," he says harshly, peering at me over the cut crystal rim. "But that means you can't get away with doing whatever you want forever."

"What does that mean?" I ask.

"Adair and I already spoke about her returning to school," Malcolm interrupts. He's trying to save me from our father's interrogation, or at least, maintain some peace at dinner, but it's too little, too late.

"Good, because she's returning to school in January," Daddy says.

"About that," I say. "I've been reconsidering staying in Valmont."

"You have?" His voice is dangerously calm and I do my best to stay poised.

"Everyone is so busy with their own lives," I begin. I've been considering how best to broach this. I can't exactly come right out and say that I want to run screaming from the only home I've ever known. "It gets lonely. Plus, I know Mom would want me to go out and see the world."

"Your mother would want you to be near family," he says, adding, "so that we can keep an eye on you."

I cross my arms over my chest, abandoning all attempts at eating. "I can take care of myself."

"Can you?"

Malcolm dabs his face with a napkin. "Maybe we can discuss—"

"Because someone had to drag you home last night," Daddy continues, ignoring Malcolm.

"He was just making sure I got home safely!" I let myself get loud so that the heat blooming on my cheeks will look like anger instead of what it really is: guilt.

"Was he?" He doesn't buy it. "If someone had seen—if someone had gotten a picture—"

"Who is going to follow me around in Valmont?" I ask. Really, he's the height of paranoid. Of course, that's because he knows that he's skirting a very fine line when it comes to our personal lives. If the family draws too much attention—if someone starts to look into the details regarding my mother's death—it could be a huge story. The kind that does more than hurt reelection bids.

"Exactly," he says triumphantly, and I realize that I've wandered into his trap without realizing it. This is why he wants to keep me about in Valmont. We're safe in our little enclaves. It's not that none of our neighbors or friends care what we do. It's that we've all arranged to ignore each other's sins in favor of protecting our own.

"You let Malcolm go to DC," I point out.

"Malcolm needed to go for graduate school and his internship. He's going to be in the Senate someday."

"Maybe I'll run for the Senate," I say.

Both Malcolm and Daddy laugh. Ginny frowns but she doesn't stick up for me. Feminism only goes so far with this family, and we both know it.

"There's not enough room in the Senate for both of us," Malcolm says as though this explains why that would be impossible. And if there's only room for one, it's going to be him.

"Oh, stop dicking around, it's because I'm a girl," I say.

"Language," my father warns.

"That proves my point," I say, shoving my plate to the middle of the table. The maid appears, avoiding all eye contact and removes my plate. No one says anything about how little I've eaten. No one cares. If someone doesn't catch it and put it on the front page of the paper or on a news ticker, it doesn't matter. That's all this family is: photo ops and pretty filters. We keep all of the ugly behind closed doors.

"Since I have you all here," Daddy says, ignoring my outburst, "there's something we need to discuss."

It's downright democratic of him to pretend like any

conversation we have as a family is a discussion. "Your mother's headstone came, and we need to go see it as a family."

"Of course, Angus," Ginny murmurs, placing a hand over Malcolm's. His gaze turns down as he studies his empty plate.

"Why do we have to go together?" I ask.

"It will be a good thing for us to be seen together as a united front," he says, dropping his napkin on the table as though declaring this last bit is final.

"Oh my God," I say, horrified, as I realize what he is up to. "You want it to be a photo op."

"It's important that the public sees how much her death is affecting our family."

"Why?" I ask quietly. How can he cry for her one minute and use her like this in the next?

"You know why," he says. "Our grief is a private affair."

"Doesn't sound like it," I mutter.

He ignores me. "We owe it to the citizens of Tennessee to share our lives with them, but we have to be selective as to the moments that we share."

"You just want them to see you as a grieving widower," I accuse. Our eyes meet, neither of us flinches at the hatred glaring back from the other.

"I am a grieving widower, but I'm also a politician."

I have a few other words to describe him. I consider hurling them like darts at him now.

Alcoholic. Con man. Murderer.

"You will be there," he says. It's as much an order as a threat. "They will see this family united in their grief."

I get to my feet. It feels like the walls are closing in on me. They bear down until I'm sure I'll be crushed. "You own the papers. Just tell them what you want them to print. But don't make us lie."

"Where's the lie?"

"We're not a family," I say. "We're liars. All of us—and you made us that way."

I don't wait for him to respond, although he yells at me as I flee the room. It doesn't matter. I'll go to my mother's grave. I'll suffer through another stolen moment. I'll pretend that anything about the situation is normal. I'll pretend that her death was an accident. I don't have another choice. Not while I'm under this roof. Not while my father controls me.

And he controls all of us.

I head to the kitchen, ready to cry on Felix's shoulders, before I remember that he's gone out for the night. There's a plate of cookies sitting out for me with a note to eat as many as I like. He'd known how dinner was going to go down. I grab them and shove them in a bag. I need to get out of here. Daddy isn't going to let me leave Valmont. Everyone thinks having money is liberating. I know the truth. I live in a gilded cage. I don't have money of my own. I don't have resources of my own. Nothing here is mine. Not even my free will.

I take Mom's Roadster, because it's my favorite and because it pisses my dad off every time he discovers I've taken it out of the garage. Sometimes I tell myself the pretty lie that I'm running away, but the truth is, I know I'm on a leash. I know exactly how far I can go. There's nothing for me in Nashville. All my friends are at school. Poppy will let me crash at her place.

But Poppy doesn't understand. She tries, and I love her for it, but I don't want to be cheered up. I want to wallow. I want to feel this. I want it to be okay that I'm mad—that I'm furious. I want to feel every bit of this pain without someone trying to take it from me, because it's the only thing I have left that's mine.

And I can only think of one person who will let me do that.

I t's been a long time since I made it downtown. Back
when I was a teenager, I would lie and tell my parents I
was going to Valmont Gallery shopping center with Poppy.
Then we'd drive into Nashville, meet up with the others, and
flirt our way into the various clubs before crashing in the
pool house of whoever's parents were out of town that weekend. We'd pick up Hennie's hot chicken on the way home
and stay up all night gossiping about our fellow classmates
and our plans for the future—the lives we thought were
ahead of us. None of those plans worked out the way we
thought they would. And Nashville? As much as things come
and go—new restaurants, new honky-tonks, new street artists
—for the most part it hasn't changed, either. It's still a town
of rebels and whiskey, music and dancing, and dreams dashed
by reality. These days as many people come to Nashville to
try to make it as New York or Los Angeles. The city's
cemented itself in the music scene, but there's a lot more
going on than just country singers and karaoke bars.
Although there's a fair bit of that, too. The memories pull me
in the direction of the Barrelhouse. I drive past, noticing a

sign declaring it to be under new management. Nothing is sacred.

I park the Roadster in front of it, trying to catch a glimpse through the dark windows. It's too early for them to be open for the day. I wonder how much has changed, but before I can look it up on my phone, Shelby from the animal rescue calls. She probably wants me to pick up a shift over the weekend when most of the other volunteers don't want to work. I never mind. There are more adoptions on the weekend. By the end of Sunday, I feel hope for humanity again. "Hello?"

"Adair, I'm so glad I reached you!" Shelby always talks fast, as though any minute she expects an emergency. In fairness, she runs the city's largest no kill animal shelter. That means she oversees a revolving door of abandoned dogs, cats, and everything in between. She's even gotten a few horses dumped in the parking lot.

"What's up?" There's a flicker of movement inside the Barrelhouse. I crane to see, phone pressed to my ear.

"The gala raised over one hundred and fifty-thousand dollars!" she squeals. "I can't thank you enough."

"It wasn't really me."

"It was your friend, and I know you helped." She's not having it. I've never been comfortable with getting credit for using my connections. It feels wrong. "We had one person donate an insane amount, and I'm sure you already know this: Zeus found a home."

I slump against my bucket seat, pushing up my Givenchy sunglasses to press a finger against my suddenly throbbing temples. "I know."

"Oh, don't be sad, honey! This is good news!"

If she only knew. I swallow hard against the rawness in my throat. "I know. I'm happy for him. I'll just miss him."

It's mostly true. I am glad that Zeus found a home, even if

it wasn't with me. I'm just not thrilled about who adopted him. My eyes skip back to the under new management sign in the Barrelhouse window. Sooner or later, you lose everything you don't fight to keep.

"I was hoping you could do me a favor," Shelby says.

"Sure," I say absently.

"I was hoping you could check in on Zeus and his new owner, Mr..." Papers shuffle in the background. "Sterling Ford. I would do it but I thought you might want to see Zeus and things are crazy here."

I really need to learn not to commit myself to something before I know all the details. "Oh, I'm not sure..."

"Honestly, his donation is huge. I'm grateful, but I'd also like to build a bridge there, know what I mean?"

I want to tell her that I burned the bridge between Sterling and I a long time ago. "I'm not sure I should be the one to build it."

"He mentioned you specifically in the adoption papers," she says. "You must have caught his eye during the auction."

"Sure," I say miserably.

"Thank you! And cheer up, I'm sure Zeus is going to be loved."

"I hope so." We end the call, Shelby promising to text over the address.

I'd plan to spend the day popping in to a few favorite shops and working up the courage to visit my unexpected inheritance. Now, stepping foot into Bluebird Press feels like the lesser of two evils if the other is a visit to Sterling. I guess I'll tally that in the win column. I ignore Shelby's text for the moment and pull up Bluebird's address. A few seconds later, GPS directs me to its offices.

The press isn't what I expect when I find it tucked into a back street a block from Broadway. I've always imagined a publishing house sitting atop some lofty high-rise, floor-to-ceiling windows, people bustling about and shouting out deadlines, editors in corner offices making phone calls to authors and agents all day long while girls with coffee carts deliver lattes. Maybe that's how it is in New York.

That's not how it is at Bluebird Press. It occupies the ground floor of a small brick building, and one tiny sign hangs above the entrance. There's no receptionist to greet me at the door. Inside, desks clutter the space, stacked high with manuscripts next to abandoned coffee mugs. A haphazard bookshelf lines the far wall of the room. This is the only attempt at decor. Someone has lovingly lined up the books, facing some out to display them properly. It's obvious even from here this is a place where people prefer to live in the pages of their books. The rest doesn't matter. It's not the frantic, glamorous workplace I'd envisioned; it's better.

It's so close to noon there's only a few people at their desks. No one bothers to look up from their laptops or manuscripts, leaving me free to wander freely. I pause at a desk in the back corner to nosily investigate a manuscript that's lying out.

"Can I help you?"

I spin around, feeling like a thief in the night. "Sorry," I say quickly, "I was looking for the... boss."

"You mean editor-in-chief?" she asks me.

"Yes." I'm off to a great start. I know a publishing house doesn't have a boss. It has a publisher. It has an editor-in-chief. All the happiness I felt moments ago oozes slowly out of me. I don't belong here any more than I belong anywhere else in my life.

"That's me," she says, brushing past me to her desk. She leans over and hits a few keys on her computer, frowning as an email pops up. I stand there trying to think of something to say. She finally looks up at me. "Is there something I can help you with?"

"A job," I blurt out. I'd wanted to blend in today and not look like Adair MacLaine come to survey her new holdings. I didn't plan this. That's pretty obvious given that I'm in jeans and a t-shirt that says Read an effing book. At least, it's on theme. I don't have a resume or a writing sample. I don't even know what job I want.

"A job?" she repeats. She studies me for a second. Sinking into her chair, she waves to the seat across from me. "Sit. I'm Trish."

"Thanks," I say, grateful for the invitation and that we're foregoing last names. I'm not putting my best foot forward, so the fact that she's willing to even talk to me means she's a lot nicer than I am. "Adair."

"What kind of job are you looking for? We're not really hiring," she tacks on in warning.

"I don't know." Isn't that the truth? "I came in on a whim."

Now she's looking at me like I might be crazy. "So, you were just walking by and thought hey, I should get into publishing?"

"Honestly, I've always wanted to work with books. I majored in British Literature at Valmont."

"What have you done since then?" she asks.

She might not be hiring, but it feels like I found myself at an impromptu job interview anyway.

"My dad was sick," I explain. "I haven't really done anything with my degree yet. I only graduated last year."

"The job market for English majors is a pretty slim one." She sounds sympathetic. "What were your areas of interest?"

"I did my thesis on Jane Austen."

The look on her face says who hasn't, but she's nice enough to keep the thought to herself. "What was the topic?"

I'm losing her. I'm just another hapless English major with your standard thesis on Jane Austen.

"I said all of her books were about how much she hated marriage."

Her lips tug into a smile. "But she wrote love stories."

"That's debatable." I'm used to having this argument. Only one professor in my department thought it was a good topic. The rest said I was misreading the text. "Take Pride and Prejudice. Do you really think Elizabeth is happy with Darcy?"

"I think that's the whole point of the book."

"Darcy is a total jerk," I disagree. It had taken me years to understand this. "Lizzie gave into him because he did something nice for her sister. It doesn't change all the terrible things he said."

Trish doesn't look like she's buying it, but she's definitely interested. "It's an original take. I'll give you that. So you don't know what job you're looking for. What would you like to do with books?"

"Read them. Champion them." I quickly add, "Fix the spelling, I guess."

"Here," she says, passing me a thick manila envelope. "This is from a creative writing grad student at Valmont. I saw him give a reading recently and requested he send me his book. Read it. Take some notes. We'll see what you've got."

"I can do it tonight!" I can't help feeling like she just handed me a golden ticket.

"Writers are used to waiting forever for responses." She shrugs and gives me a wicked smile. "It's good for them. Feeds their torturous souls. Take your time."

"Okay." I spare a sheepish glance at her. "Thank you."

"Don't thank me yet. Honestly, the owner just passed away. We haven't heard yet what's going to happen to the press. We might all be out of a job soon. We might get sold or shut down. I'm surprised we've stuck around this long."

"Really?" I hope she interprets the heat painting my cheeks as something other than guilt. I should tell her who I am. But I can't. Why?

"I think the only reason we've lasted this long is because he forgot about us. We weren't important enough to worry about."

"When will you know what's going to happen?" An alarm bell rings inside my brain. I'm making this worse each moment I don't come clean about who I am.

"When someone changes the locks or tells us to pack up, I'm guessing." She looks grim at the prospect.

"Maybe the family will keep it going," I suggest.

"I hope so, but I wouldn't count on it. I've already started sending out my CV."

"I've got a good feeling." I don't know why I don't tell her the truth. That I'm the new owner. That I have no plans of shutting down the press. Maybe it's the manuscript in my hands. Maybe it's the opportunity to make a different first impression—one not based on my last name. Maybe I just need to earn something in life rather than have it handed to me, even if it's only the truth. The reality is that I might be a shit editor. I might not have the eye. There's no way she'll tell me that if she knows my last name.

"You're an optimistic little thing," she says.

No one's ever called me optimistic before. I like the way it sounds. "I guess I am."

I leave Bluebird, manuscript in hand, hope in my heart, and a text with Sterling's address waiting in my notifications.

I've already dodged reality today. I can't avoid him. According to the address, he lives nearby. I should call and see if he's home. Instead, I decide to take my chances, hoping like hell that he's busy doing whatever job it is that makes it possible for him to drop $10,000 at a charity gala on a dog with a fifty-dollar adoption fee. When I arrive at Twelve and South, my curiosity deepens. Sterling Ford lives in the penthouse—and this isn't some standard apartment building. It's a luxury high-rise in the heart of the Gulch, one of Nashville's more elite pockets. There's no reception desk. Instead, in true Southern fashion, there's a bellhop ferrying visitors and residents to their respective floors.

He whistles when I tell him I'm here to see Sterling Ford.

"He just moved in," he tells me as he sends the elevator toward the top floor. "I think that you're one of his first visitors."

I hate that this pleases me. "Is he here?"

I try to sound as disinterested as possible.

He gives me a quizzical look as if to say why would you come, if you didn't know. "Haven't seen him leave yet for the day. He took his new dog out earlier. Sweet boy."

I assume he's talking about the dog. No one would refer to Sterling as sweet—or a boy.

"I wanted to surprise them," I explain, nervous that he'll tell Sterling I was asking questions about him later. I want to make this quick and painless like ripping off a Band-Aid. The last thing I need is for someone to reopen the wound later.

"Old friends?"

"Something like that," I say through gritted teeth. When we arrive at the top floor, I'm surprised to discover that not only is Sterling's new apartment on the highest level, it is the highest level. The penthouse occupies the entirety of the twenty-third floor. The bellhop leaves me in front of his door.

I watch the elevator door slide shut apprehensively. Part of me wants to bail, to call him back, and walk right out of Twelve and South. Then I remember what Shelby said about the shelter needing the money. This is bigger than hurt feelings and a relationship that was over years ago. Sterling hadn't been awful the other night. If he can just behave himself, maybe we can be civil.

At least I know there's one friendly face waiting on the other side of that door. Zeus might be Sterling's dog now, but I'd been his favorite volunteer, and he'd been my favorite dog. When I knock on the door, I hear a muffled bark coming from inside and heavy footfall, followed by the scraping of claws on tile. The door cracks open and the top of Sterling's head pokes through. "Stay Zeus."

I can't help but smile. I can hear Zeus jumping up on the other side of the door. Maybe he's not taking to Sterling as his new owner yet.

"What's gotten into you?" Sterling asks, still not paying any attention to me. "Can you smell the chicken?"

"Fresh out of chicken," I say dryly. "He probably smells me."

Sterling looks up, the mask of smugness he usually wears temporarily displaced by surprise. "Adair?"

"Don't get cocky," I warn him. "I'm here to see Zeus."

"I thought you were my lunch."

He looks at me like he might devour me anyway. Dozens of memories batter against the levee I've built around my heart, bursting past it and flooding through me. I remember those eyes—how they would burn like blue flames when our bodies were slick with sweat, his skin on mine. Moments from a lifetime ago that feel like yesterday. Whatever it was between us, it's here now, dashing any illusion I held that I'm over Sterling Ford.

Some loves never leave you, even after you break each other. Because when two hearts shatter into a million pieces, you can't pick up what's left of yours without mixing it up with some of theirs. Years ago I gathered myself from the wreckage of us, taking some of him with me. And if I did that —if I wedged the mismatched pieces of him into the remnants of my heart—then he did the same with the parts of me he took.

That's how you survive broken love: you accept those transplanted pieces and hope it's enough to keep your heart beating.

Sterling turns his face away, breaking the connection. "I'd let you in, but Zeus won't let me open the door."

I take a deep breath and sternly say, "Zeus, sit!"

The frantic clamoring on the other side of the door stops.

"How did you do that?" Sterling asks, swinging it open, so that I can step inside. As soon as I'm through it, the dog jumps on me and lands a slobbery kiss on my chin.

"Zeus and I have an understanding," I explain. "If he wants love, he's got to treat me with respect."

"Is that how you earn it?" Sterling asks, leaning against the wall.

I bypass the subtle dig. Without his eyes boring into mine, I can think clearly. I'm here on business. Shelby needs me to do this. She needs Sterling to continue supporting the shelter. I can swallow my pride for a few minutes, do my best, and hope he doesn't hold it against them that they sent me as their messenger.

The condo is exactly what I'd expect from what I've seen of the building. Large and open with an airy vibe from the bank of never-ending windows. It's the picture of wealth and success, save for a scattered heap of wet towels trailing into the living room from an open door. Sterling follows my gaze, his mouth carving into a lopsided grin. "I tried to give Zeus a bath."

I raise an eyebrow.

"He might have liked it a little too much," Sterling admits. He points to his attire and I realize his faded jeans are wet with paw prints. His white v-neck is similarly soaked, clinging a bit too temptingly against his muscular torso. I force my eyes back to Zeus, who's got his front paws on my shoulders.

You're here for a reason!

"Valmont Animal Rescue asked me to stop by and thank you for your generous donation." Zeus settles at my feet and I lean to scratch his head. "They also wanted to make sure that you two were getting along okay."

"Do you have to do this for everyone?"

"I think you're the only one who took home his prize," I say. "Usually, people just want to make a show of it at these things."

"Yeah, well, Poppy said this guy was having a hard time finding a home."

The edge of pain undercuts his words. Sterling knows what it's like to be without a home. He knows what it's like to wait for someone to want you—for everything to always feel temporary.

Shame washes through me. I'm so arrogant that I assumed this thing with Zeus was an attack aimed at me. I didn't stop to consider how Sterling might have felt sitting there and watching cast-offs paraded around so that my rich friends could compete to look like the most charitable of the lot.

"I'm supposed to talk you into sponsorship," I tell him, feeling weary of this game we're playing.

"How forthright of you," he says. "How do you think you're going to do that?"

"I have no idea," I admit.

"A brutally honest answer." He saunters toward the kitchen, turning with an arched eyebrow. "Coming?"

Hearing that word from his lips sends indecent thoughts tumbling through my brain. I want to shake them loose before they launch their poison into my resolve. Sterling Ford might be back in town. There might be decent bits inside of him. But that doesn't change anything between us. Not after what happened.

I follow him to the kitchen area and stand with my arms crossed.

"Feel free to make yourself comfortable," he points to a bar stool.

"I'm fine where I am," I say. I need to stand my ground and remember that no matter what, he's still the one who left.

"Suit yourself." He opens the fridge and pulls out a bottle of water. "Did you come all the way down here to beg me for money?"

Something about the way he says this suggests he's hoping that I have. Will that make him more or less likely to donate to the shelter? Considering that he seems to get off on screwing with me, I'm guessing less.

"I had some business down here. I volunteered to do it." So, it's a lie. Sterling has made every move so far. Showing up at my father's funeral, coming to dinner at my house, attending my crowd's charity function. He thinks he can invade my world. I'll show him that I can just as comfortably invade his.

"Business in Nashville?"

"There's not much business in Valmont," I say flatly.

"There's too much business in Valmont. That's always been its problem," he tells me.

"My father left me a small press in his will. I decided to visit it." Why am I telling him this? I'm not friends with him.

He doesn't need to know about my day. It's just that I can't stand him thinking I came down here to get my nails done or have lunch with the girls. Maybe it's his fancy condo or his unexplained mysterious wealth, but I don't want to feel little in the eyes of Sterling Ford.

"How did that go over?" he asks, sounding genuinely interested.

"Good," I say with some hesitation. Sterling owes me nothing—and I'm pretty sure he hates me—which means he might be the best person to confess the awkward position I've put myself in. Poppy will be supportive and tell me whatever she thinks I want to hear. My brother will urge me to sell the publishing house and say I have no business experience. The rest of my friends won't care. Their own families have dozens of small businesses under the umbrella of their corporations. Who really cares what happens to a small independent publisher? "Except that I didn't tell them who I was."

"You just went in there and acted like a creep?" He uncaps his water bottle shaking his head.

"I said I was looking for a job."

"Did you get one?"

"Not really," I hedge.

The bottle pauses on the way to his lips, which twitch at my uncertain response. "You sure about that?"

"The publisher gave me a manuscript to read. She wants to see what I've got."

"That sounds like a job interview," he says. "Why didn't you tell them who you were? You would definitely have gotten hired."

He's teasing but he's also hit on the uncomfortable truth. "I don't know. I guess I just wanted her to see me for who I am —not for the family name."

"Or as her new boss," he guesses.

"Exactly."

"She might not appreciate it when she finds out that you kept it from her."

"It's not like I'm trying to deceive her," I say defensively. "I just don't want her to tell me that I'd be a good editor if it's not true."

"And you think she won't be honest if she knows who you are?" he asks.

"Would you be?" It's a stupid question. Sterling has always kept things from me—always hidden parts of himself away. I never got to see all of him. Now there's even more he's keeping from me—where he was for the last four years, why he left.

"Maybe you should have more faith in yourself," he suggests.

Faith in myself? Like he had faith in me? I can't keep my disbelief from falling out of my mouth. "Are you serious?"

"Why wouldn't I be?" He blinks like he's genuinely confused.

I resist the urge to scream at him that he knows exactly why I can't take it for genuine advice. He's the one who's walked back into Tennessee like nothing changed when everything has. He's the one who left without a goodbye. He's the one who made me question everything I thought I knew about myself.

"So, will you donate to the shelter or not?" I say bluntly. I need to get out of here. I'm falling into old habits. How, after all this time, can it feel this comfortable to talk to him? He's made it clear he has an agenda that involves my family's company. I have no idea how. Maybe some consultant told him it was a good buy. Maybe he did it on purpose. I don't know, and I can't trust him to tell me. I asked when he came to dinner—and his answer? Those two little words have been rattling around in my brain ever since.

For you.

I try not to think too hard about what he meant by that. I do my best to ignore his answer, but it's always there scraping and clawing and trying to get out of my brain and into my heart. I can never allow that.

"Why don't you support the shelter?" he asks.

"I do."

"I mean, if they need money, then you must be able to…"

Is he fishing for information? Does he really not know what position our family is in?

"I have a responsibility to several charities." That's actually true, which makes it an easy lie. I can't afford to give more. Not until my inheritance shows up in my ever-dwindling bank account. If there's even going to be an inheritance. Harding and my brother haven't been very forthcoming with how much to expect. For now, I think I'm supposed to be grateful that there's a roof over my head.

"What do I get out of it?" He slides onto the bar stool next to me. Zeus sits between us, looking back and forth at our faces with interest. The woman who loved him and the man who saved him. If only my relationship with Sterling could be so simple.

"Why did my brother invite you to dinner?" I blurt out the question.

His lips flatten though he's surprised by the change in topic. "He knows I hold stock in MacLaine Media. He'd like to buy it back, I think."

I weigh this answer. Maybe Malcolm is pretending like we have the money to pay it back. Maybe Sterling doesn't know how badly into debt our father drove the company before his death. Either way, I know Malcolm doesn't have a way to pay him. If that's what's keeping Sterling around, telling him the truth could free us both. "We don't have the money to buy your portion."

Sterling stares at me for a moment as if trying to make sense of my remarkably honest answer. He studies my face, his eyes sweeping down me in a way that's both familiar and unsettling.

"I know that," he says after a moment.

"So we're going to be truthful then?"

"You started it." He shrugs as though he doesn't care either way. I'm not going to waste the chance to get more answers.

"If you know that he can't pay you, why play along?" I ask.

He waits a moment as if considering his answer. "He's not offering money."

My heart skips a beat as if it knows the answer already. "What is he offering?"

"You."

"Me?" My lips move, forming the word but there's no sound. I've been silenced, cut out of the deal, and turned into a pawn by the man who claims me as his sister and the man who broke my heart.

"A merger, if you will," he says. "Your family's reputation and connections in exchange for keeping the stock in the family."

"Oh my God," I whisper as I begin to understand what he means by keeping it in the family. "What does he think this is? The nineteenth-century?"

Malcolm thinks he can arrange my marriage and I'll just throw on a veil and comply? I'm not a mail order bride. He can't just force me to take a husband to save the family business.

"And you're considering his offer?" I accuse. For a second, his mask slips and the pain there says the things he should have said years ago. About us. About the future. About what we were. Then it's gone.

"Did you really think I was?" The mask is back in place. The stage show has concluded. Whatever vestiges I thought I saw of the Sterling I once knew disappear, replaced by the smug prick that's been investing in my life like I'm just some prize to collect.

Four years ago, I waited for him to prove me wrong about him. Now I know better. When someone shows you who they are, believe them the first time.

And my brother? I can't keep turning away from who he is becoming. He thinks he can sell me? There's gonna be a pool party in hell before I let any man control me. But why not let them think they can? According to Harding, there is at least three major parties who bought into MacLaine Media. If I can keep Sterling at bay and trick Malcolm, I'll have time to find the other investors, buy them out, and regain a majority hold over the company. Malcolm will be forced to come to me and Sterling won't be able to buy the love he gave away.

"Support the shelter," I say to him, "and I'll do it."

He clearly doesn't expect this response. "You'll do what?"

"I'll go along with Malcolm's insane plan."

"You'll marry me?" he says in disbelief. "Look, I'm not exactly on one knee. I didn't say I was going to accept his offer."

The words pierce my skin, hitting the wall I've raised once more around my heart, and bounce off me.

"I know that," I snap. "But I'm not stupid. There's a reason why you're letting Malcolm believe you'd be interested in his offer."

"And you expect me to tell you?"

"I don't care what it is. I'm not going to sit around and be some pawn in my brother's battle strategy. If he thinks we're together, he'll stay off both our backs. Then you can do whatever it is you're planning and I..."

"What about you? What are you planning?" His eyes narrow. This arrangement depends on my answer.

I don't have to be completely honest with him to sell the lie that I won't interfere with his schemes. I know exactly the sliver of truth that will make him believe that I have a separate agenda. "I'm planning to escape."

24

M alcolm MacLaine's campaign office is located inside
the historic Nashville Customs House. I imagine it
helps grease the wheels of potential campaign supporters to
meet inside the hallowed, if remodeled, walls of one of the
city's oldest institutions. The MacLaines have always
campaigned on Tennessean tradition and family values. Few
buildings feel as unchanging as those beliefs. Naturally, he's
found one.

"Thank you for taking the time to meet with me,"
Malcolm says when his secretary shows me inside.

"Of course."

Our relationship is developing even more rapidly than I'd
hoped. Malcolm understands who he is dealing with now. Or
what's at stake, at least. It's almost been too easy to bring him
to his knees. I'm not foolish enough to believe he's down for
the count though. It will take more to break him entirely. But
it's more than a little satisfying to wonder how his father
would feel if he could see this. Angus MacLaine is rolling over
in his grave as his children hammer the coffin of his dynasty
closed nail by nail.

I take the seat offered to me, refusing a glass of bourbon with a wave of my hand. There's no need to take one for appearance's sake. Not anymore. He pours himself one anyway. If he's not careful he'll wind up like his father. Perhaps, he has better control over his vices. Angus never cared who he hurt as long as there were no consequences to his actions—it's a trait both of his children have inherited by all accounts.

"I'll level with you." He unbuttons his jacket and sinks into his executive chair. He looks more at home here in downtown Nashville then he does pretending behind his father's desk at home. This office is smaller and the view is mediocre. Soon, I have no doubt, he'll take his father's office in the MacLaine Media tower a few blocks away, which probably affords a spectacular view of the Nashville skyline. For now, he's as he was. Less of a man than his father, by all appearances, but following blindly in his footsteps anyway. I'd seen him at the gala, pretending to be someone he's not. His pockets are empty. We both know it. It's amusing to think he's going to *level* with me when we're on different tiers entirely. *That's* why we're here. I've managed to elude his reach. Malcolm's mistake is thinking that he needs to look down to find me when I've already snuck past him to a higher run. By the time he realizes, it will be too late.

"I need to buy back my family's share of the company from you," he continues. "We need to come to an arrangement."

"I already named my price."

"That is going to take time," he tells me, "*and* there might be other interested parties. You aren't the only one who bought into the company."

"I assumed I wasn't," I say smoothly. If he only knew. "Have you spoken with Adair?"

"I don't know what happened between you and her in the past," he says, "but it's clear that we're going to have to come to another arrangement. I can't force her to do something she refuses to do." He doesn't seem to understand why she's not taking orders. The MacLaine men, obviously, haven't gotten any less narcissistic in the last couple of years.

"I've always gotten the impression that Adair is quite pliable when the incentive is right." Malcolm doesn't wield the same control over her as their father did. Pointing this out will only whittle away a bit more of his confidence in himself. The trick with breaking something strong is to weaken it first rather than waste your energy smashing it outright.

"She hates you." He stares at me as though willing me to disprove this. "I, on the other hand, like you. I wasn't sure at first, but you might be just what the company needs—if we could come to an arrangement. A merger, perhaps."

I don't flatter myself that he's reversed his opinion of me. A MacLaine never thinks highly of anyone that's not their own blood. He can't find the information he needs to make a play. I made sure of that. I'm here because he's feeling desperate. He's no closer to figuring out who the other investors are—no matter what he says about *their interest*. Malcolm is so busy looking for other players, he doesn't see that I'm the dealer. I fed him his hand. He can't bluff me.

"You might be surprised about me and your sister," I say to him. "We got a chance to talk at the gala."

The phone on his desk buzzes, and his secretary's voice pipes into the room. "Your sister is here."

Right on time. It's not a coincidence that I wound up here at the same time as Adair. I'd texted her this morning to set a date for our first public appearance as a "couple." She'd told me she was busy—a meeting with her brother, she said. She'd think about it. Faking a relationship might have been her plan, but her hesitation tells me she's questioning it. I hadn't expected her to dangle herself like a piece of meat over my head, but now that I know she will, I can't resist the opportunity. I won't allow her to back out of our arrangement now.

"Show her in." Malcolm watches me as the door opens. He's trying to read me, but he doesn't speak my language.

"You wanted to talk to me," Adair says haughtily. She storms past me without realizing I'm there and plants her hands on the desk, sticking her round ass in my face in the process. My view instantly improves. "We have to have official meetings now?"

"When it comes to business," he says in a warning tone.

"Everything's business. I don't see why we can't just talk about it at the dinner table," she says.

"It will have to wait, regardless," Malcolm says, motioning to me.

She glances over her shoulder casually, freezing when our eyes meet. There's a moment of confusion in those emerald orbs, quickly followed by accusation. She knows she's been played. "Sterling!"

"I stopped in to chat with your brother." Rising, I button my jacket with one fluid motion. "But I confess, I really came to see you."

My honesty is so surprising she stands in shocked silence long enough for me to cross the few steps to her. I act without hesitation, knowing that even a moment's pause will blow this. Before she processes my proximity, I curl a hand around her waist, pull her to me and crush my lips against hers. The kiss lasts longer than I intend. Maybe because I caught her off-guard, so she doesn't fight it. Maybe because I hadn't expected to enjoy it as much as I do. I know she's poison, but she tastes like honey, and I linger on those sweet lips. When I break away, her mouth falls open.

"There's no point keeping it from your family," I say to her. "They'll know soon enough."

Knitting my fingers through hers, I turn my attention back to Malcolm. He looks like he's already planning the wedding.

"I'm sorry I couldn't wait until tonight to see her," I say.

"You two have plans?" He looks to her for confirmation.

I step in before she can conceive a cutting remark in response. "Yes, we have an official date this time. I'm afraid it's going to be a little less extravagant than a gala, Lucky."

The corners of her eyes narrow ever so slightly. The lie. The old nick name. I'm pressing all her buttons and she's got to go along with it—but Adair has always been an excellent liar. She slips into the deception with ease, gesturing to her causal outfit. "I'm not even ready yet. I look like hell."

She's wearing jeans that cut off at the ankles, a worn-in pair of Converse sneakers, and a soft, cotton t-shirt with a deep v-neck that reveals a satisfying amount of cleavage. She doesn't look like hell. She looks like the devil transformed into a woman come to tempt me.

"You look perfect." I mean it. "It's a surprise, remember? We'll have to run by my place for me to change though."

"You should've done that instead of wasting your time coming all the way over here to see me," she says, her words as sweet as arsenic-laced sugar.

"You aren't happy to see me?"

I don't miss the slide of her throat as she swallows back whatever biting remark she wants to make. She pops onto her tiptoes and kisses my cheek. Unlike our earlier kiss, this one is so full of venom, I swear it stings.

"I have to talk to my brother," she says to me. "Let's meet up later."

"I'm sure it can wait." I wrap my hands around hers and look to Malcolm.

"There's no rush." He's lapping this up. I could get him to agree to almost anything right now. Sealing a union between my company and his, by way of marriage, not only keeps the family business in the family, it also costs nothing more than selling his sister's soul. Something he values a lot less than his bank account.

"Are you sure?" Adair asks, clearly looking for an out.

"I should head home early. Surprise Ginny," he suggests.

"Good idea. You have to keep the romance alive," I advise him. There's no way Malcolm is going home to his wife. Not at 4 o'clock on a Tuesday. Not when his regular room is waiting at the Eaton—a little tidbit Luca discovered when digging into the affairs of Mr. Randolph, the hotel manager.

"I was supposed to help her with Ellie, but I'm sure she'll understand. I'll text her and let her know you're coming home." Adair whips out her phone before he can stop her. Apparently, I'm not the only one who knows about his Tuesday night extracurriculars. I might loathe her, but I do admire her. She's backed him into the corner in five seconds flat, punishing him in a way that's almost Shakespearean. "There. Now she knows you're leaving the office early! She's going to be *so* excited."

"Thank you," Malcolm says in a strained voice.

"No problem." She hooks an arm through mine. "We should be going."

"We'll discuss this further another time," I say to him.

"Yes, we have a lot to talk about." He moves around the desk and shakes my hand, his fingers closing over it tightly and holding it in place. "Take care of my sister."

"I'll keep an eye on her." That's a promise I'll make good

on. If her stunt with her brother proves anything, it's that she's too slippery to let out of my sight.

"Let's go." She tugs me toward the door. As soon as it closes behind us, she starts to pull away but my grip on her hand tightens.

"We're not done selling this," I whisper, tilting my head toward his secretary, who's watching us with eagle eyes.

"Have a nice night, Barb," Adair says, snuggling against me.

Our act is starting to wear me down. Pressed this closely to my body, I smell her perfume—tart and sweet just like her. I have to resist the urge to lift her into my arms and carry her to the nearest empty office. I want her splayed across a conference table, thighs around my neck, screaming my name. I want her to know exactly what she's been missing. I want it to be even harder when she loses me this time.

Instead, we continue to the elevator and as soon as we're safely inside, she yanks her hand away.

"What was that about?" she demands.

"We need to sell this. It has to look real. I thought you wanted your brother to believe that we're in a relationship."

"I did," she says, quickly adding, "I mean, I do. You just could've warned me that you would be here."

"This was more natural." I lean closer. "A romantic gesture."

She stares up at me, her lips waiting to be kissed. Then she blinks and moves quickly to the other side of the compartment. "You're lucky I didn't slap you."

"Now why would you do that?" I ask.

"Because you kissed me," she reminds me.

"I knew you wouldn't slap me for that."

"I have no idea why you seem to be so sure of that," she says.

"You know why," I say, advancing on her until she's pressed against the elevator's steel paneling. Her hands grip the bronze safety railing. "You've wanted me to kiss you since you saw me at the funeral."

"You think I wanted you to kiss me?" she scoffs in a breathy voice. I'm close enough to feel the betrayal of her rapidly beating heart.

"Yes, you did want to kiss me. Just like you want to kiss me now. Just like you wanted to kiss me every day for the last five years." I angle my head until my lips are hovering a breath away from her earlobe. "Isn't that true?"

"I don't want to kiss you," she whispers. "Not then. Not now. Not ever."

"Do you know how to tell when someone's lying?" I murmur in her ear. "Their pupils dilate, they breathe faster, but most importantly, their heart speeds up."

"Maybe I'm just scared of you," she says, even as she moves almost instinctively closer.

"You should be," I agree, "but you still want to kiss me." My mouth moves across her jaw gliding toward her lips. As it reaches them, the elevator dings, jolting us apart when it comes to a stop. Adair turns her head, saved by the interruption, and darts out of the doors as they open.

I'm right behind her, catching her hand before she reaches the building's entrance.

"What are you doing?" she hisses.

"We have a date," I remind her.

"No one's around. We don't need to pretend," she says, stopping to jerk her arm free.

"There's a whole city that needs to believe this," I say flatly. "Besides there's somewhere I want to show you." The Adair I've been around since I returned to Tennessee has been stuck in high heels and dresses, forced to play the part of the grieving daughter and doting family member. The Adair standing before me now, in blue jeans and sneakers, reminds me of the girl I met at Valmont years ago.

"Do I need to change?" she says as if reading my mind.

"You're perfect," I say without thinking. "But I might need to."

She crosses her arms, rolling her eyes as she scans my three-piece navy suit. "Do you think?"

"What? Embarrassed to be seen with me looking like this?" I tease.

"I think that's a trick question." Her eyes don't meet mine, but pink circles bloom on the apples of her cheeks. She's learning — adapting to this new version of who we are. We're not 18 anymore. I'm not the poor boy, riding on her credit card. I've changed. I'm a man with money and means now. She knows it. What she wants to know is how much of that boy is left.

Adair follows me out to the valet, careful to keep a safe distance. She doesn't hide her surprise when my car is brought to the entrance.

"Nice ride," she says.

"I knew you would prove." I help her inside, playing the part of the Southern gentleman. It's not something I was born to and I'm unlikely to make the effort often. Tonight though? Two can play this game. I'm Satan himself, offering her the forbidden fruit she can't stop drooling over.

Circling the car, I slide into the driver's seat. Adair's fingers skim over the wood appreciatively. We came from different worlds. Hers one of diamonds, debutante balls, and silver spoons. Mine? All I'd known was the street, how to survive the foster care system, how to leave the ones who hurt you behind and live with the scars of them. Now I've learned the language of her world. I'm fluent in her tongue:

luxury. But we both know I'm not a native speaker. I wasn't born to her world. She wouldn't lower herself to mine. Maybe she thinks I've come back to show her that I belong now.

She's wrong.

That's not why I came back, I remind myself. Why is it so hard to remember that when she's around?

"What does my brother want to talk to you about?" she asks.

"No business talk," I tell her. "This is a date."

"You're really going to act like this is the real deal, aren't you?"

"You bet." I flash her a smile, and despite her best efforts, she grins back.

"So, what are we going to talk about?"

"There was a time we had plenty to talk about," I remind her.

"Times change," she says softly.

I clutch the steering wheel a bit tighter. Like it or not, we aren't the same people we were back then. So much has happened to both of us. I'm not eager to share the last few years of my life with her. She'll expect me to make amends. I don't owe her—or anyone else—an apology.

I decide to focus on her. "That reminds me. Poppy said you're not riding anymore."

She flinches in her seat and, for a second, I glimpse her there, hiding behind the wall she's built between herself and everyone else.

"You used to love to talk about your horses," I remind her.

"I fell," she says. "It was serious. I had to have surgery." Each word comes out haltingly as if she's choosing them very carefully. That's how she works. She decides what to show others. It's why *we* didn't work.

"When was this?" I might have respected that years ago, but I have no patience for it now.

"A couple years ago." She turns to stare out the window, and for a moment, I'm somewhere else in a different time, wondering how to reach the girl who's right next to me. Maybe I never reached her then. Maybe I'll never reach her now.

"And you still can't ride?" I ask, trying to make sense of the skeletal information she's giving me.

"It hurts," she whispers. "There's nerve damage. I can only last a few minutes before it's too much."

"So you gave it up entirely?"

"Wouldn't you?" she says.

"I guess I'd steal a few minutes of happiness over losing something I loved entirely."

"I guess we're different people." She's back behind her wall completely now.

Our circumstances are different. We've become unrecognizable in some ways. But, no matter how high she builds her fortress or how carefully she wears her mask, I see what she's trying to hide. She's still there: the girl who broke my heart.

"Come up with me?" I ask as I pull into my reserved spot under Twelve and South.

She looks as if she's considering this request, her eyes darting to the elevator at the corner. "I'm not sure you can be trusted in enclosed spaces."

"I'll be good," I promise.

"Maybe I should just—"

"I'm sure Zeus would like to see you," I say. Bringing up the dog is a stroke of genius, because she's out of the door before I finish the sentence. She keeps her distance from me, walking with a healthy space between us.

"Keep your hands to yourself, Ford," she warns as we step inside the elevator.

I draw a cross over my heart before hitting the button for the penthouse. We might be on opposite sides of the elevator, but I still feel the energy pulsing between us. I don't have to press against her to feel her heart racing. A small bead of sweat trickles down her forehead. It's hot but not quite summer yet. No, there's another reason she's heating up. When she thinks I'm not looking, she dares a glimpse in my direction. What would she do if I closed the space between us and pulled her against me?

She'd let me. I know it. But I'm not giving her the satisfaction of making the first move. Adair will wind up back in my bed—of that I'm certain. When she does it, she'll practically crawl there and have no one to blame but herself.

When we reach the top, we both move to exit at the same time. I stop, reaching an arm across the threshold to prevent the doors from shutting. "After you."

She looks as though she doesn't quite buy this gentlemanly act, but she does a good job pretending not to care as she saunters out. As soon as we reach my door, there's a scuffle of claws on the other side. It seems my new roommate has heard me come home.

"Zeus," Adair coos, tapping the wood as I slide my key into the lock. "He's not in a kennel?"

"He doesn't need it," I say.

"You're taking your apartment into your own hands," she warns.

"Oh, I know that. He already chewed up one of my slippers. We had a long talk about being a good boy."

"Did he give you any pointers?" she asks dryly.

Zeus greets us by bounding onto his hind legs and licking each of us in turn. He bounces happily between us, looking overwhelmed with joy to get both of his favorite people in the same place.

"Did you miss me?" She scratches his ears and earns another kiss. "I missed you."

"I see where his loyalty lies. Sit Zeus."

He immediately drops to the floor, his tongue lolling out of his mouth. His head tilts back and forth like a metronome as he looks between the two of us.

"So you're getting through to him," she says with approval.

"We worked on it. It's all about mutual respect."

"Is it?" She laughs at the idea as she kneels down to him. "Well, whatever you're doing he seems happy. I can't believe he doesn't need a kennel."

"I couldn't bear the thought of putting him in a cage," I say quietly. I know too well what it's like to be locked away because no one can bother to teach you better.

"Thank you for adopting him." She lifts her face from the top of his head, eyes shining before she shakes off the emotion she's accidentally shown. "I'll hang with him while you change."

"You could have adopted him," I point out.

"Ginny wouldn't allow it," she murmurs. "She didn't want him around Ellie. She said his breed couldn't be trusted."

"A dog is only as good as he's allowed to be," I say softly. She opens her mouth to respond but I'm already turning away. So that's why Zeus was homeless. He wasn't good enough for the MacLaines. Another thing we have in common.

In the closet, I pull out a pair of faded Levi's and a black T-shirt. Slipping into the clothes is like slipping into an old version of myself. I slap some cologne on in the bathroom and brush my teeth. Staring back at my reflection, I see someone I barely remember.

"Oh for fuck's sake, are you going to start writing poetry next?" I ask myself. "She hasn't changed. Remember that."

Now that the pep talk is over, I head out to find Adair and Zeus hanging out on the sofa.

"He's not allowed on the furniture." I tell her.

"Does he know that?" she asks, but she pushes him off to the floor. "Sterling says no."

Zeus slides down and gives me a pitiful whimper.

I cross my arms. Unbelievable. I adopted the dog, but somehow he still seems to belong to her. "Now you're going to make me the bad guy?"

"I think you can do that all by yourself."

We stare at each other for a minute without blinking before I walk toward her. Adair's body goes rigid with expectation, but I stop and call Zeus. "Be a good boy while I'm gone?"

I never break eye contact with Adair as I stand up and head toward the door.

"Do you need to walk him?" she asks.

"I have a girl who comes by to do that," I explain. "He just went out an hour ago."

"You have a girl?" She raises an eyebrow.

"A dog walker. It's nothing nefarious." I open the door for her.

"Good." She walks through the open door. "We need to make this look realistic, right? I can't have people thinking that you're playing me."

"We can't have that," I agree. She's going to make me work for this.

Even on a Tuesday night, the Barrelhouse is full. I can't help but be reminded of an old country song when I survey the crowd. Everyone here is looking for love in all the wrong places. It's obvious that some of the groups are friends, just out for a night on the town, but there's a fair number of singles hanging out at the bar, engaging in small talk, casting glances at other parties, hoping tonight's the night they find true love. It's not my usual scene, even if I know the owner.

"I haven't been here in forever," Adair says, looking around.

"Really?"

"And you have?" she challenges me.

Jack has the timing of a god, because he chooses this moment to descend upon us. He wraps me in a tight hug, smacking my back with his fist. "I never see you at night. You finally decided to poke your head out of your shell and get a life, huh?"

"I had to make a few friends first."

"Oh good, she's just a friend?" Jack eyes Adair appreciatively. He's seen pictures, but a photograph could never do her justice. "Then allow me to introduce myself. Jack Archer."

"Adair MacLaine." Even in the dimly lit club, I can see she's blushing.

"*The Adair*?" he asks.

"What's that supposed to mean?" She directs this question at me.

"You're not as funny as you think you are," I say to Jack. Trust him to skirt the line. He can be as bad as Luca sometimes.

"He mentioned he knew a girl here," Jack says smoothly, his charm distracting her easily.

"I did mention that," I said, "but Adair is more than a friend." I curl an arm around her waist and draw her to my side. She looks like she wants to protest this but thinks better of it. There's no mistaking her frustrated silence though.

"She looks like she might still be on the market." Jack isn't going to play along blindly.

"Give it up, man. Adair Archer? I don't think that's going to work out."

"I'm a modern guy. She can keep her last name."

"Do you two want to know how many goats I can bring to the table for my dowry?" she asks dryly.

"And she's feisty?" Jack's eyes dance as he crooks his head, a wide grin splitting his mouth. "You might have competition for this one."

It's time to change the topic of conversation. "Don't you have customers to serve?"

Jack tips his head toward the bar.

"Let me get you a drink. I'm just playing with him," he says to Adair. "Sterling needs a little help with his sense of humor."

"Truer words have never been spoken," she says.

I poke her arm. "I'm the one who needs help with my sense of humor? Really?"

"I might die before I see you laugh again," she says as Jack circles around the bar and pulls out three tumblers.

"I'd ask what your poison is, but this one is on the house, so I get to choose," he explains. "It's a local distiller. Best stuff in the state."

Adair studies the bottle as he pours. "Those are fighting words in West Tennessee Whiskey territory."

"You're a West girl?" he asks her as he continues to pour.

"Not really. It's just what everyone I know drinks."

What she doesn't want to say is that the West family and her family go way back and that, like everyone else in

Valmont, she's got some incestuous codependence going with them.

"This is better bourbon. I'd lay money on it that you'd agree," he tells her, sliding her a glass.

"No thanks." I hold my hand when he goes to pour mine.

Adair eyes me over the rim of her glass. "Still don't drink?"

"You know that's for the best."

"Thank God," Jack interjects. "I'm tired of wasting the good stuff so that you can just stare at it all night."

"It's rude to refuse," I say to him.

"It's rude to waste whiskey," Jack says. He looks at Adair. "Do you know why he doesn't drink?"

Adair glances at me as if considering her answer before shaking her head. "It's a mystery."

I have no idea why she lies. She doesn't owe it to me to cover this up. She might not know everything—like the fact that I've had a drink since I left town. More than one. But she knows why I stopped drinking in the first place. She knows why I hate the stuff. She knows what it does to some people. It's a lesson we were both taught too well.

But while she understands, she doesn't take the same approach I do. She toasts Jack, their glasses clinking. Her eyes light up when she takes a sip. "Oh, that is better."

"I'll send you a bottle," he tells her.

"You better not send it to her house. Her family is very particular," I explain quickly. "You can send it to my place."

"Can I now?" he says meaningfully.

"Can he now?" Adair repeats with just as significant a tone.

"People are going to know soon enough, Lucky," I say to her. She freezes at the sound of old nickname on my lips. I take her surprise as an opportunity. "Life has a funny way of working out."

"Excuse me," Adair says, looking slightly flustered. I expect her to call me out—to expose the ruse. She doesn't. "I'm going to use the restroom."

"Do you know where it is?" Jack asks her.

"I've been here before," she assures him.

I watch her as she disappears into the crowd, heading toward the ladies room. I can't help admiring her shapely ass as she goes.

Jack whistles. "You didn't tell me she looked like that. You think she'll need a rebound guy when you're through with her?"

I turn blazing eyes on him.

He holds up his hands in surrender. "I'm just joking," he says, adding thoughtfully, "but it sure doesn't seem like you are."

"The plan is the same. I just want to take this slow. Enjoy it."

"Does she really deserve that?" he asks. It's the first time Jack has really questioned my plan. He's never asked for specifics. He's stuck by my side. Sometimes a person goes through things in life that bind them forever to another soul. Jack and Luca? They're bound to my soul. We might question each other. We might fight. But we'll always have each other's backs even if we have questions.

"Trust me, she does." My gaze falls on a bottle of West's behind the bar, and I remember what Money said at the gala —about Oliver and his side gig as a pharmacist. "We have other concerns at the moment."

I fill Jack in on the particulars. Jack doesn't have the same moral flexibility as Luca and I do, but one thing we all share is an intolerance of men who use innocent women.

"I think we should have a private conversation with him," I say to Jack.

"Done. You find a way to get him in here, and I'll make sure we have time alone," Jack says. The past shadows his eyes. I don't see it lurking there much these days. Unlike me, Jack lives in the light most of the time, but some ghosts always haunt you. "Sterling, is it possible…"

"No," I say.

"How is what you're doing to her any different than what this Oliver guy did?"

"I'm not drugging her or lying to her," I tell him. "She knows I don't love her. She asked to play this game."

"And you're okay with her losing? Because that's cold, even for you."

I look to my old friend. He has a right to ask questions if he is going to be involved. "Do you want out?"

"You know that's not what this is about," he says.

"If she changed, she wouldn't have to worry," I say to him. "But she wanted to play—just like old times. She still sees everyone around her as a means to an end."

"How is destroying her going to make a difference?"

"You know what they say about a taste of your own medicine?" I ask. "Adair MacLaine is long overdue for a dose."

He doesn't have time to respond before Adair returns. Jack pours her another drink and she accepts it with an easy laugh as she begins plying him with questions about me and the bar and our history. I don't miss the concerned look he shoots me when she's not paying attention. Maybe Adair can fool him, but I know who she really is. Jack thinks I'm going to be the one to hurt her. In the end, she'll do the damage all by herself.

25

STERLING
THE PAST

I t turns out that one of the perks of being Cyrus Eaton's roommate is that he's never here. Apparently, living on campus means spending most of his time in a suite at The Eaton Hotel in Nashville. At least, on the weekends. He checked in by text to let me know the place is mine for the next few days. I guess he found a conscious girl to take home.

Knowing that no one will bother me or drag me off to a party gives me time to catch up on things before midterms, which are only two weeks away. I don't know how the hell I've been here that long. I still feel out of place. Cyrus is okay, but its not like we're braiding each other's hair anytime soon. After being up half the night checking on Adair, the last thing I feel like doing is going to the cafeteria to eat. Instead, I use some of my precious meal plan money and order a pizza from some place off-campus. Digging out my books, I stare at them, willing myself to find the motivation to crack one and get started. I'm just so fucking tired that I need to reset, so I grab a worn-out novel from the shelf. I've pretty much given up on the idea of studying at all by the time the pizza arrives. I drop the book back on the pile and go to answer it. But it's not pizza waiting for me. Adair stands there. She holds out a bag of cookies.

"This isn't what I ordered," I tell her, but I take the cookies anyway.

"It's a peace offering," she says.

"I think we already agreed on terms." Not that I'm going to turn down free cookies delivered by a pretty girl.

"Can I come in?" Her neck cranes slightly as if she's trying to peek inside my room. She's probably looking for Cyrus. They've known each other since they were kids.

"I'm alone," I say. "Cyrus went to The Eaton until Monday."

"Good." Her response surprises me. "I just wanted to talk to you."

In a 24-hour period, we've gone from hating each other to hanging out together? I move out of the doorway, wishing I'd changed into something better than a t-shirt and old sweats earlier. I hadn't bothered to comb my hair or shave. Meanwhile, Adair looks like a page from a magazine. Her copper hair is coiled in a loose bun, wisps escaping to fall around her heart-shaped face. She's traded this morning's towel for a sweater that slips off her shoulder, revealing freckles I find myself wanting to count. She clears her throat, and I realize I'm just standing there. Apparently, she wants an engraved invitation. I sweep my arm toward my room. "Sure. Come in. I'm waiting on a pizza. Are you hungry?"

Her head moves into a slight shake before she stops and nods. "Actually, I am. I couldn't eat anything at dinner tonight."

"Do you want to talk about it?"

"Yes," she says, "and no."

"Well, as long as you're sure." I don't know what to do

while she wanders around the small space. I find myself trying to imagine what it looks like to her.

I know Adair didn't live on campus before she decided to take the semester off. But she's been here before for a few minutes. Our room is bigger than most dorms on campus, which I assume has something to do with Cyrus. I'm not complaining. It means we have space to keep our beds separate from each other rather than bunking them. In the middle of the room there's a leather couch, also courtesy of Cyrus. Someone's managed to mount the TV on the cinderblock walls using what I can only assume is magic. Again, I don't question my fortune on that count. There's a rug on the floor that probably cost more than all of my worldly possessions. It's about as comfortable as you can make what's usually the equivalent of a summer camp bunker. Still, I always feel a little like I'm staying in someone else's home.

"It's nice." She delivers her verdict with conviction.

"Mostly compliments of Cyrus," I say with a shrug. Not that she couldn't have guessed that.

"Not these." She trails a finger down the stack of novels on my desk. "These are yours."

"How did you know?"

The joy in her answering laugh twangs an invisible string in my chest. "I've never seen Cyrus read a novel in my life."

"This is your favorite." she says, picking up the well-worn copy of *The Great Gatsby* I'd just been reading. She studies it for a moment, her eyes lingering on the call number taped on the spine. She flips it open and reads, "Property of Lincoln High School—is this a library book?"

"You caught me." I drop onto the couch. If I'm going to be lectured, I might as will be comfortable "I stole a library book."

"You stole more than one," she murmurs, scanning the rest

of the stack before continuing to page through Gatsby. Her eyebrows ratchet up with each page turned as she takes in the notes I've penciled into the margins. "And you wrote in it."

"Don't worry. I haven't stolen any Jane Austen," I say.

"That's a mistake," she murmurs. "Maybe next time?"

"I don't steal library books anymore," I assure her.

"Just special ones, huh?"

"Those are my favorite," I say. "I rechecked them out over and over again. No one ever saw the writing."

"You could've bought them," she says off-handedly. There's a pause punctuated at last by Adair turning a horrified look on me. She's just realized what she said. "I mean…"

"It's cool," I say her, feeling oddly exposed. "Libraries are free entertainment."

"I'm sorry, I didn't mean to insult you." She means it, which goes a long way toward keeping me from reacting.

It's not like she understands. It's not like she's ever had to borrow a book in her life.

"I didn't really steal them. I couldn't return them." I find myself confessing—and I'm not sure why. I don't owe her an explanation.

"Oh yeah?"

"I moved. Different school. I forgot to leave them with the foster family. It happened a lot. Pretty soon it just felt like they were mine. I didn't have much else to my name." Why the fuck am I telling her this? Adair doesn't care about any of it. Why should she? It's not like shitty things haven't happened to her. So what if she judges me for taking a book or writing in one?

Adair doesn't say anything for a minute, she just stares at the book in her hands.

"I think it belongs to you now," she whispers.

"Yeah, but only because I stole it," I say trying to sound like I'm teasing. She'd shown up here upset and I'd dumped a bucket of pathetic all over her. It's no wonder that foster parents were constantly shipping me off to a new life. I'm such a joy to be around.

She doesn't comment, instead she picks up a few more books. "You like American authors." It's true. There's Hemingway and Steinbeck and Fitzgerald in that stack. She puts them back down and shrugs. "To each his own."

"I'm guessing it's not just Austen for you?" I say based on her reaction. "You prefer Brits?"

"I'm a total Anglophile," she admits. "I think that's the reason I took up horseback riding. They're always dashing off to visit someone on horseback or a hero is arriving on horseback. I think that's what I imagine England is like still. Just people going off to the country over the weekend to ride horses, drink tea, and read in the library."

"Maybe for people like you." I can't help but laugh at this visual. "I doubt people in the city ride horses very often."

"Hey, I've seen police on horse back in New York," she says. "Horses can be in a city."

"That doesn't mean that most New Yorkers have ridden a horse," I inform her. "I haven't."

"You've never been on a horse?" Cynical, aloof Adair MacLaine is actually shocked at this.

"I don't think it's that strange." I suspect I'm in the majority on this one.

"Around here it is," she explains. "I'm surprised they don't make everyone get on a horse during orientation. Everyone in Valmont has stables. It's expected. And horses? Riding them is total freedom. It's like pausing time. Total magic."

Hearing her talk about them is magic. Most of the time

I've spent with her she's been on the defensive, careful to keep a tough face for the world to see. But it turns out that she has a softer side. I find myself liking both. "I guess I have to go horseback riding."

"I'll take you." Our eyes meet like we're both a little shocked. I'm not entirely certain, but we might have just made a date. Or maybe she knows that I'm going to make a jackass out of myself trying to ride a horse and just wants to see it.

By the time the pizza actually arrives, we're deep into a discussion of British versus American literature. She's wrong. I just need her to see it. When I put the box down, she stares like she doesn't know what to do with it.

"Hold on." I dash down the hall to the bathroom and swipe a stack of paper towels. Passing her one, I lift the lid and grab a slice. She hesitates for a second before she reaches for one, too. It's strange to see her acting like a normal person. Mostly because she makes it look a little awkward and cute at the same time. The whole moment—from the comforting smell of melted cheese to the piles of books to the smart girl sitting cross-legged on the couch—looks like it should be photographed and stuck in one of those brochures Francie used to bring home for me. This is what college life is supposed to be like—this is what they're selling.

And it's not so bad.

"How is it, Lucky?"

She screws up her nose, clearly she still hates the name. "It's so good. I think it's better out of the box."

"How do you eat pizza?" I ask her.

"Off the plate," she says in a puzzled voice as though a plate is a prerequisite for all food.

"Tell me you don't use a fork," I plead.

"I don't use a fork," she says slowly but it's clear from her expression that she does.

"So you do have flaws."

She flinches before her shoulders square. "There's no wrong way to eat pizza."

"Yeah, but there's a right way." I ignore that she's bristling for a fight and grab a piece. "Let me show you how we do it in New York."

"Why do you fold it in half?" she asks, staring at my slice.

"They cut it bigger in New York. Serve it on a paper plate. *No fork*," I explain to her. "You have to do it this way. Plus, it helps you keep everything from falling off."

"Okay." She follows my lead, her eyes narrowing warily. As soon as she takes a bite, a smile dances over her lips. "It's like a pizza sandwich."

I can't help laughing at her delight. "I guess so."

"I have to confess something." Now she sounds a bit embarrassed.

"Don't be shy," I encourage her. "It can't be worse than eating pizza with a fork."

"I'm not sure about that," she warns me. She sets down her pizza, her face growing deadly serious. "I've never read *The Great Gatsby*."

"And you're an English major?" I nearly choke. I force myself to swallow the barely chewed bite in my mouth. "I take it all back. That's worse."

"There are a lot of British authors. I haven't gotten through them all."

This is not an acceptable excuse. "How can you be sure they're better if you've never read the greatest American novel before?"

"Settle down, Ford. I'll get to it."

But I'm already on my feet, grabbing my copy.

"You'll get to it," I grumble as I drop it in her lap. "You have to do better than that."

"I'm not sure I can accept stolen goods," she teases.

"Just read it," I say.

"Why?" she asks.

"Because it's the Great American novel," I tell her.

She purses her lips before shaking her head with frustration. It's not the answer she's looking for. "No, that's not what I mean. Why do *you* love it?"

"I'm not sure I can explain it to someone who's never read it," I say. There's no way Adair can understand Gatsby like I do, but she should read it anyway.

"Try," she says dryly.

I breathe so deeply it hurts a little while I consider my response. "I guess I just always got him. Gatsby, I mean. He never quite fits in anywhere. No matter how hard he tries."

"I get that," she says softly.

I look at her—*really look*. Does she get it? This girl, who has everything, doesn't fit either? It doesn't seem possible. But I've seen the wall she's built around her. The one she hides behind while raining insults and barbs down on anyone who tries to breach it. I saw that wall, but I didn't ask myself why she felt the need to build it.

"Thanks for letting me hang out here," she says, finally breaking the heavy silence lingering in the air.

I force myself to look away from her. "Any time."

I'm surprised to discover I mean it. Adair isn't cold. That's a veneer she wears like armor. I'm not sure what's underneath yet, but I want to know about the girl with the green eyes. She's not easy. She's work but that makes me like her more. There's sunshine underneath her thunderstorm. When the light peeks out from the storm clouds in her eyes, it's all worth it.

For a moment, I consider closing the gap between us. I've held Adair in my arms but that's not what I want right now. I want to taste her. I want to run my tongue over those freckles on her shoulder and then explore her until I've kissed every last one on her body. I want to see if she breaks like a sunrise or shatters like lightning strike.

She bites her lip, turning her face from mine. Can she see it in my eyes?

"They put the tombstone up at my mom's grave," she whispers.

Her words settle like light rain, and just like that there's no sun or storm on the horizon. She didn't come here to hook up. She came here to be understood.

"I'm sorry," I say, meaning it.

"My dad wants the whole family to go so that reporters can see us being sad *together*," she says.

"*What?*"

"I know, right?" She sinks into the couch, drawing her knees to her chest. "We had a big fight about it."

"No wonder you didn't want to be at home." I say.

"I can't avoid it forever."

"Maybe you should go on your own first," I suggest. I have some experience with this. I'd been so young when I saw my mother's name carved into stone—young enough that I'd had to ask my foster mom to take me. Old enough to feel the heavy finality of those words in marble.

"I'm not sure I can," she confesses in a small voice.

"I'll go with you," I offer.

She peeks at me, half her face hidden behind her knees. "You will?"

"If you want," I say quickly. Maybe I shouldn't invite myself to such a private moment.

"I don't want to go alone, and I don't want it to be a spectacle," she says.

"We can go tomorrow." It's too dark now, but I know the

longer she waits the more reasons she'll come up with to avoid it. There's no way I'm letting her go with her dad for the first time. Not if he's just going to stomp all over her broken heart. I don't know him, but I already get the sense I don't like him. Maybe that's just how he works—like those assholes who take pictures of their entire lives to post online. Or maybe everything is a publicity stunt to him. It feels too personal to ask her.

"I don't know how to fix this." She blinks and tears spill down her cheeks. "I don't know how to fix me. I just feel broken."

I reach over, cradling her face in my left hand, my thumb moving to brush off the tears. "The truth is that when something breaks, you don't put yourself back together the same way. You make something new with what's left."

"When do the nightmares stop?" she asks. The question is so small and hopeless that I don't want to tell her the truth—that they're never going to go away. That you just get used to them. That someday it might be all she has left of her mom as time steals away the sound of her laughter or the way she smiled or how she smelled. That someday she might look forward to those nightmares.

"It gets better," I promise her.

"Can I stay here just a little longer?"

I can't say no. I don't want to.

"Okay, but I'm going to make you listen to *The Great Gatsby*," I warn her.

She shifts toward me on the couch, carefully resting her head on my shoulder as though testing it out. I put an arm around her, hoping this doesn't remind her of the last time I did this. If it does, it doesn't seem to bother her. She relaxes against my body, fitting perfectly against me.

I open the book. "'In my younger and more vulnerable years'—see? It's riveting."

She snorts, elbowing me lightly in my ribs before nuzzling back against me. "Keep reading."

So I do.

26

ADAIR
THE PRESENT

"No live music tonight." Jack flashes an apologetic smile. The man oozes charm, but it does nothing to soften the blow.

"This is the Barrelhouse!" I smack the counter. Maybe I'm beginning to feel those shots a bit. "Unacceptable. Actually, I might be able to something about that."

"Oh really?" Jack and Sterling share a look. They think I'm drunk. They're right, but that doesn't mean I'm blowing smoke. "What?"

"A girl has to have her secrets." Pulling out my phone, I send a text.

"Are you going to sing for us, Lucky?" Sterling asks.

I hate the way my old pet name sounds rolling off his tongue, smooth and silky as the bourbon Jack keeps pouring me—with just as much fire hiding under the first taste. I hate that after all these years he can slip back into the way it was between us. I hate that I know it's all just pretend.

I hate that I like the way it makes me feel anyway.

We've nearly finished a bottle when the Calvary arrives. Or maybe I've nearly finished a bottle because Jack is showing no signs of being drunk. In fact, he's as sharp as ever, which means he's the first to spot my friends walking through the door.

"Is that…?" Shock registers on his face when he sees who's entered his bar.

I wave to Poppy and Kai as they scan the crowd. The truth is that I didn't just text them to hook Jack up with a performance for the evening. I needed backup. If a girl is stuck drinking whiskey with her ex-boyfriend, who quite possibly is a sociopath, then she doesn't have a lot of other options than to call in her friends. Kai keeps his head bowed, his cowboy hat tipped down to avoid recognition, but he's unmistakable. He sticks out from the crowd for all the reasons he once thought he'd never fit in. His tight jeans and vintage flannel shirt might look old-school country, but he wears the look like a rock star. As it turned out, I'd been right all those years ago. He was exactly what country music needed exactly when they needed it.

Poppy's always known how to dress the part. Tonight, she's found a cotton summer dress printed with little yellow flowers. Its ruffled skirt ends mid-thigh and showcases her long legs. I used to be jealous of her dancer's body. Her height. The way she seemed to flow across a room. It's strange, but when my girlish body gave over to a slightly more plump version of myself, I'd gotten more comfortable in my skin. Not that I wouldn't kill to move as gracefully as she does

"You look gorgeous," I say as she forcibly hugs me. I don't fight it. Sometimes in friendship, you have to compromise. Poppy is a hugger. I am not. She puts up with my cranky ass, so I let her. This is how being best friends works for us.

"I'm not going to hug you," Kai says with a laugh, spotting my slightly rigid form. "But only if you give me a drink."

"I thought superstars didn't ask for booze," I tease him.

"They don't," Jack interjects, sticking out his hand. "Jack Archer. I'm a big fan."

"You like country music?" Kai asks. It's a test. We all know it.

"Not particularly." Jack passes it. "I'm more of a blues man. But you're not really country—not modern country, at least. I love what you're doing for the scene. It was getting a bit stale. It needed you."

"You're going to make me blush," Kai says.

"Let's dance before I have to give you back to L.A." Poppy grabs his hand and drags him to the dance floor. Considering the lack of live music, there's only a few others on it. Occasionally, someone catches a glimpse of Kai and does a double take.

"I'm going to chat with my boys," Jack says. "I want to make certain they keep an eye on him."

"He's used to it," I say.

"I'd rather play it safe. He's here for a good time not to be harassed." Jack leaves us at the bar to talk to his security team. Now I'm stuck alone with Sterling caught up in memories of the past. That coupled with the amount of whiskey I've drank can only spell trouble.

"I think Kai has gone the farthest of all of us," Sterling says.

I might have agreed before I saw Sterling's condo. I've watched Kai rocket to the top of the music industry since he left Valmont early our sophomore year. He's doing well for himself, but it's nowhere near the level Sterling's achieved. "Sometimes I wish I hadn't hooked him up with a producer at a MacLaine-held record label," I confess to Sterling. "It couldn't have happened to a better guy, but it hasn't been easy. He's had his fair share of people that just want to use him to make a buck or get ahead."

"That's what happens when you're successful," he says.

"He got burned by a few fans. A lot of people look at them as a way to break in to the business. I'm not sure if I should have invited him to a blues bar. I don't want him to feel pressured to sing."

"Jack won't do that," Sterling assures me. "He'll be the first person to hand Kai a guitar if he asks for one, but he doesn't use people. He's not even going to tell you he's starting his own record company. I guarantee it."

"What?" I look around the crowded bar. "How does he have the time?"

Sterling nods like he wonders the same thing. "He's passionate about the industry. He wants to see artists treated with respect. The label is never going to be a huge source of income."

"It doesn't seem like he needs a huge source of income," I point out shrewdly. Jack can't be much older than us, but he owns one of the most established venues in Nashville. I'm as curious about the source of his good fortune as I am about Sterling's. "Does he?"

"He's doing alright." The question rolls right off his broad shoulders.

Another non-answer. I'm not getting clues about either man's wealth tonight. It only makes me question it more.

But maybe interrogating Sterling isn't the route to take. He's never liked answering questions, but he never minds telling a story if you nudge him toward one. "You two have the same tattoo."

I'd noticed Jack's inked forearm when he was feeding me shots. The art is the same. The location is the same. I know it can't be a coincidence.

"We met in the Marines," Sterling says. At last, an answer, but there's a finality to his tone. He knows I'm angling to learn

more about his past and he's warning me to stop talking
about it.

That doesn't mean that I'm going to. "You never told me
about your time in the Armed Forces."

"That's not an oversight."

Before I can press him harder, he stands up and holds out
his hand. "Care to dance, Lucky?"

"If you stop calling me that." I counter his offer. I need to
erect some boundaries—and quickly.

"I didn't mean to make you mad." He sounds genuine.

That only makes it harder to resist the incessant tug of
memories I feel when he's around. I can't bring myself to look
directly at him. I'm not sure I can handle seeing his eyes.
"Look, we can pretend for everyone else," I say, "but let's not
fool ourselves."

Sterling's shoulders square, his jaw tensing before he tips
his head with a terse nod. "Fair enough. We should still
dance," he says, adding, "for the sake of appearance."

If he's going to act nonchalant about this, so can I.
"Let's go."

It's been a long time since I've been out dancing. Stilted
waltzes at charity galas don't count. This is dancing—letting
loose, laughing. Even if my partner is Sterling Ford. I need
more of this. There's no sick father to care for anymore. Ellie's
old enough that I don't have to worry about Ginny leaving her
to cry in her crib. I might not be free of Valmont but my leash
is finally lengthening. This is *life*. The music soaks into my
skin, like the whiskey moving in my bloodstream, and leaves
me no choice but to give in and feel good.

Poppy and Kai join us, him singing along to the song playing. That's when it happens. A girl spots us and begins to
shriek. "I knew it! It is him!"

Kai's eyes close for just a moment as if gathering strength

before he turns on his million-dollar smile. Pretty soon, he's surrounded, signing napkins, and taking selfies. Jack's guys move in to break up the impromptu autograph session, but Kai waves them off. We back away to give the fans more room.

"He claims he hates the attention," Poppy says.

"Bullshit," we both say at the same time.

The truth is, like any famous person, Kai wants privacy every now and then, but he totally feeds off the attention. It drives him, and no one deserves it more.

A chant begins in the crowd and it takes a moment for my whiskey-marinated brain to process they want him to sing. It's about that same time that Kai's hand closes over mine and he drags me to the stage. Sterling and Poppy begin catcalling my name. It's easy to know it's them since everyone else is screaming Kai's.

"Have you lost your mind?" I hiss, trying to escape.

Kai plops his Stetson on my head. "I know you can sing, girl. Now don't break my heart and tell me you don't know my songs."

"Of course, I know them." I tilt the brim up and glare at him. Like I wouldn't know every one of his songs! He presses a microphone into my hands, and I realize he actually wants me to sing with him. On stage. In front of everyone.

Oh my God. The first bars of the song start playing before I can chicken out.

Some blood is thicker than water...

I join in with Kai instinctively, belting his first number one hit.

And there's whiskey hotter than fire.
I know you should treat me better,

But I don't care if you're a liar
Cause some love is sweeter than air.

I took you home to meet my family.
My mama cried when she saw you.
She said that boy won't ever treat you kindly.
Son, some bastards can't stay true.

I don't mean to look at Sterling as the words surge from me, because my gaze travels to him like he's magnetized. People think this song is sad. Maybe if it is if you know better.

I thought our love would last for always,
But you drank me gone one lonely night.
Now I'm drinking to our yesterdays
Cause some bastards can't treat ya right.

Our love is water and it's fire,
So pour another and lie to me.
I'll drink to forget that you're a liar
Cause I need your love to breathe.

There's a reason I can't stop looking at the man in the crowd. There's a reason why no matter how hard I try to keep away, I can't. There's a reason I can't separate desire from hate anymore. This is the only kind of love I've ever known.

And he's the one who showed me it.

27

ADAIR
THE PAST

"Maybe this isn't a good idea," I say for the hundredth time since I picked Sterling up in front of his dormitory. My hand taps the steering wheel, out of beat with the song playing on the radio. That's how I feel: out of sync. I'm not sure that this is going to help.

"You can't avoid it," he says. He reaches and turns off the music.

I'm still tapping the wheel, trying to disperse all the emotions building inside me. "I know."

His hand closes over mine, drawing it away from the wheel. Sterling weaves his fingers through mine and holds it. "It's going to be okay, Lucky."

For the first time his nickname for me doesn't feel like an insult. It feels like a promise. I cling to it along with the rest of his words. Sterling knows because he's been through this. He survived it. I can survive it. I don't know why it comforts me to tell myself this over and over, but it does. I guess I need something to believe in.

"Distract me." The drive to the cemetery is nearly as bad as what's waiting there. I can't stand thinking about it—imagining it—anymore.

He pauses, the pressure of his hand holding mine increasing. I dare a glance over and see his eyebrows knit together in concentration like he's trying to find a safe topic. "In New York, there's a place called Eataly that's half a city block of Italian food and groceries."

"What?" I can't help laughing at his choice. He grins in response. A real smile from Sterling—not a smirk—is like a rainbow coming out from the clouds. Unexpected. Beautiful. Seeing it can't help but brighten the day. "Italy? Like the country?"

"No. E-A-T-A-L-Y," he corrects me. He begins to describe it to me. The fishmonger station piled with crabs and whole fish on ice. Across from that a butcher. The smell of baking bread rising over the crowd and tempting visitors to glass cases full of loaves of every shape and size. Restaurants for pasta and pizza and fish—relaxed or fancy—are tucked around every corner.

"What's your favorite?" I ask. The warmth of his hand seeps under my skin just like the rest of him is starting to.

"I've only ever gotten the gelato and a loaf for Francie," he says. His eyes dart to the window. I've asked the wrong question again, but I'm starting to find my answers in between the ones he gives me. He's told me before that he's poor. A foster kid. He wouldn't have the money to buy all that imported stuff. But I know why he's shared it with me. It wasn't only to distract me. It's because he knows the best distraction is desire. It's wanting something you can't have.

With my hand in his, I realize he might be the only distraction I actually need.

"We'll go there sometime," I find myself saying, "and eat our way through."

"You think you can handle that? You just started eating pizza without a fork," he says.

"I'm all in, baby." I mean it. "So, who's Francie?"

I'm a little scared to ask, because her name's come up before and he didn't like me asking about her.

"My foster mom," he says quietly.

"She adopted you?" I ask.

"Nah." He shrugs like this isn't a big deal but he's careful to avoid looking at me and his hand tightens a little around mine. "I've only been with her a couple of years. It's too late to adopt me now anyway."

Sterling might act like it doesn't bother him, but it does. I have a million more questions I want to ask about how he wound up in foster care and what happened to his parents, but I know better than to ask. He might be relaxing his guard around me but he still has teeth. I don't know what will cause him to bite.

"Well, if she likes good bread, she's alright in my book," I say, turning the topic back to the subject of food.

"Francie loves to cook," he says. "She's taught me how to cook a bunch of stuff."

"Really? I barely know how to make toast."

He arches an eyebrow, his lips twitching. "Somehow that doesn't surprise me, Lucky."

"And why is that?"

"Do you really what me to answer that question?" he asks.

"Nope." I laugh, shaking my head. We both know the answer. "You can teach me how to cook."

"How about I just cook for you instead?"

"Deal."

The rest of the drive is short and filled with more stories about New York. When I turn the Mercedes into Valmont Memorial Cemetery, my mind is on all the places I want to go now thanks to Sterling. The first headstone reminds me why we're here, though. I fall silent and Sterling does the same. We don't speak as I drive slowly down the narrow lanes toward our family's section of the graveyard. There's been a MacLaine buried here since 1810. The moss covered mausoleum bearing the family crest has been full since the seventies. I have no idea what to expect when we reach my mother's grave.

It's not this.

The gravestone is granite with magnolia blossoms carved across the top and a simple inscription:

Anne MacLaine. Beloved Wife and Mother.

It's unlike my father to favor minimalism, but he's done it here. No one consulted me on her tombstone or the funeral or any other arrangements. I don't even know who handled them, honestly. Daddy hadn't been available to do it. Maybe Malcolm?

Who thought they could distill her into six words? Where's the monument she deserves? Or is this just another attempt to prevent unwanted attention? Did Daddy choose it so that no one remembers her? No one asks questions about her death? I want to kick it. I want to cry. I want to fall down and tear up the earth and take my mother back.

Sterling looms behind me, keeping a respectful distance. I need him here next to me. I need to know what to do now. "I don't know what to say."

"What do you feel like saying?" He moves closer until we're side by side, staring down at the resting place of the woman he'll never know and the woman I'll never forget.

"Nothing," I murmur.

"Then do that." His hand finds mine and in his touch, I

find strength. We stand there, leaves blowing all around us, autumn on the wind, until I find my voice.

"I didn't know. You're supposed to get to say goodbye. Life isn't supposed to just snuff you out. She was here and then she was gone—and I don't understand it!"

He waits for me to finish when I finally pause. "We rarely know when we're about to lose someone. That's why it's called loss. You can't plan for it. You just live with it."

"Well, it sucks," I say flatly. I stare at the plain tombstone. "She was so much more than this."

"Tell me about her." He sits, pulling me down next to him.

"She loved old country music and art. You saw her paintings. I've never been able to see them like she did. She saw beauty in everyone, even when they didn't deserve it." My thoughts wander to my father again. I shake my mind free. This isn't about him. It's about her. "She used to say 'some days are diamonds, Adair. Treasure those days.' I didn't understand what she meant, but I do now. I always thought she was complaining about the bad days and how little good days we have. But she was reminding herself that a better day was coming. She just had to look for it and treasure it. I wish I'd treasured my days with her more. I wish I could have said goodbye."

I can't help staring at the small shoots of grass that are growing where they dug up the spot for her coffin. "She's been down there long enough for grass to grow. She's been down there so little, it's still mostly dirt. I'm stuck in this hellish limbo between holding on to her and letting her go."

"You don't have to let her go." Darkness coats his words and I wonder again about his family, but I don't dare bring it up. I wonder if he visits his mother's grave.

"I should have brought flowers," I realize as I stare at the bare grave. "She's dead and I'm still fucking things up."

"Next time," he promises. "Do you think she'd be mad at you?"

I shake my head. "No. She'd hug me and tell me she loved me," I choke on the last bit. She's the only person who's ever said it to me. I strain my memory trying to recall daddy saying it, but I can't. Maybe no one ever will again.

Sterling wraps his arms around me and pulls me into a hug.

"I don't like hugs," I warn him.

"Too bad, Lucky. You're getting one." He doesn't release me and instead of waiting quietly for it to be over, I find myself melting into him. He's warm and solid and real. Sterling for all his bad attitude and quick temper is something I didn't expect: safe harbor. I keep trying to tell myself I'll survive this, hoping I'll find the conviction I need to actually do so. I keep looking for the words—for proof that I can. But it was never about believing in some thing. I know because I found someone to believe in: him.

Adair's friends swarm to the Barrelhouse like moths to a lantern. Soon it's not just Poppy and Kai, it's the whole crew. They're not here to watch Kai perform, they saw him last weekend. They want to bask in some of his attention. The truth is that most of them have been sitting around waiting on something their entire lives: their family's company, a trust fund, an inheritance. In the meantime, everything's been handed to them. They'll never know what it's like to become someone. They were born to someone, which means they've never had to try. And why would they when money means famous friends willing to share the limelight?

The drinks flow as quickly as Jack can pour them. He even assigns a dedicated waitress to our table, but he refuses to take my credit card to start a tab.

"It's on the house," he says, sliding it back to me. "The performance will have us written up in every paper in town— and you better be careful, Sterling, or I really might steal that girl."

My lips curve into a smirk, but my eyes linger on Adair. "You can try, but I wouldn't advise it."

Most of the group is busy doing shots, but I can't help noticing that Oliver Hawthorne has broken off from the crowd. He's dressed in an expensive suit, fresh off whatever job his nepotism has secured. He wastes no time chatting up a single woman at the far end of the bar.

"Keep an eye on that one," I tell Jack. "He's got shifty fingers."

Jack knows exactly what I mean. Oliver won't get any drugs past him tonight. Ava sashays over and links her arms around me. As usual, Darcy is at her heels.

"You sure you don't want something?" Ava asks.

I shrug her off me and force a smile. "Someone has to be the designated driver."

"We have drivers," she says.

"I think it's sweet of you," Darcy says, leaning against me on my other side. They're like a pair of bad pennies—always turning up. They haven't left me alone since they arrived, which I imagine is all part of Adair's plan.

But Adair has gotten quite cozy with Jack's reserve whiskey. She practically sloshes as she pushes herself between me and Darcy.

"Are you hitting on my man?" she says. Her accent, which is usually barely noticeable, deepens to a full southern.

"Your man?" I repeat under my breath, amused despite myself.

"Isn't that what you are?" She turns, forgetting Darcy, and wraps her arms around my neck. "Unless you changed your mind."

I brush a strand of sticky hair from her forehead and let myself pretend she means it. "Never, Lucky."

She's too drunk to care that I just broke the rule she made earlier.

"Good." She gives me a sloppy smile. Then, she lurches

forward and kisses me. She tastes like whiskey and bad decisions, and I want more than a single shot of her.

"Get a room!" Kai whoops.

Adair breaks away from me and giggles. "Is that all you got?"

He doesn't miss a beat. "That's what she said."

"I don't think that works the way you meant it to," Poppy informs him, shaking her head.

"Let's dance." Adair pulls me toward the dance floor.

"I need to talk to Jack for a second," I say, directing her toward her friends. They swallow her whole. Adair never fits in more than when she finally lets go. She's never known what she has, never appreciated what she's got. She's always felt like she's on the outside, but I see what she can't. They're always there, waiting to welcome her inside the inner circle. Most people would kill for that invitation.

Jack's wiping down the counter. It's near close, but he hasn't said a thing to his guests from Valmont.

"They're going to drink all your booze if you're not careful," I warn him. "Moderation is one lesson they'll never learn."

"It's worth it," he says, leaning onto his elbows so no one can hear us. "I've been serving the Wests someone else's whiskey all night. It's the little things."

"I think we might finally get a moment alone with that one." I tip my head toward Oliver, who's broken off from the group again to talk to one of Kai's loitering fans. I've been watching him all night, looking to see if he's up to his old tricks. It seems like he no longer relies on pharmaceutical aids to get women. Someone must've clued him in that money would be enough. That doesn't change what he did years ago. He might not have confessed to being the one who drugged Adair that night. He might not have known she was the target.

He's still on my list.

"I'm on it," Jack says. "You take care of the others?"

"My pleasure."

Considering I don't drink, it's been a long time since I closed down a bar. And closing down a bar in Nashville is a bit of a feat. They stay open well past most cities, even if the hours don't follow the law to the letter. But this is a city built on rebels and whiskey, bootleggers and booze. The party doesn't stop until someone says it does.

Poppy is the first to throw in the towel.

"I need to go home," she announces, peeling off her shoes to rub the balls of her feet. Kai stands behind her massaging her shoulders.

I wave Jack over to let him know he can finally send his staff home. He takes a seat at our hightop while we wait for cars to arrive.

"Thanks for staying open." Kai slaps him on the shoulders and I swear Jack Archer looks like a school girl.

"Where's Cyrus?" I ask Poppy, realizing he never came in.

"Don't you think a better man has replaced him?" Kai asks with a grin.

"He's in New York on business," Poppy says. "Kai is standing in."

"Thought I'd stay in town for a while. We just wrapped my latest record," Kai explains. "I needed a break from it all."

That I get. "I've been to LA before. I completely understand."

"I don't know why you record out there," Poppy says. "There are plenty of studios here."

"Los Angeles is a bit more progressive than here," he says.

"Jack has a record label," Adair blurts out.

"You do?" Kai asks him.

Jack shrugs it off, instantly looking uncomfortable. "It's just a little thing."

"We should talk," Kai says.

"Sure." Jack remains calm. No doubt, he doesn't expect Kai to remember this when he's sobered up. He might be surprised. Kai isn't like the rest of them. He doesn't come from money. He knows what it's like to climb the ladder.

"Take me home," Poppy begs her friends.

"Your Uber is on the way," Kai tells her, checking his phone.

"You're not really going home," Adair whines, pulling on my sleeve. "Everyone is leaving."

Darcy and Ava left hours ago in search of better options when Adair staked her claim on me, Money in tow. No one noticed when Oliver left and no one seems to care now. That's good since Jack orchestrated his exit. I'd be having a chat with him soon.

"I don't want to go home," Adair declares after Poppy and Kai hug everyone goodbye. It's a mark of how intoxicated she is that she enthusiastically returns their embraces.

"You can stay here as long as you want, honey," Jack tells her, "but not much is happening and the kitchen is closed."

"Oh my God." Adair's eyes widen and I immediately sense her drunken brain is hatching a plan. "Hennie's!"

She knows the path to my heart is paved with Hennie's hellfire chicken. "You want to eat at this hour?"

"Did you see how much I drank? Maybe you don't have to take me." She pauses and turns a flirtatious gaze on Jack. "Maybe Jack wants to."

"I don't think so, Lucky." I haul her over my shoulder before she can protest. She laughs all the way back to my car. I tuck her into the passenger seat, saying a prayer for the leather upholstery that she manages to keep the bourbon in her belly.

Adair is all smiles as we drive toward the closest 24-hour Hennie's Hot Chicken. Her feet are up on my dash and she's drumming her thumbs on her stomach to the song on the stereo.

"Remember the first time we came here?" she asks with a happy sigh. "Some days are diamonds..."

I nod, gluing my eyes to the road so that my mind doesn't wander too far back. My brain's been trying to take a permanent trip down memory lane all night.

"When was the last time you had hot chicken?"

"Seriously?" I ask.

"Still can't hack it?"

"Yesterday," I tell her

"Bullshit!"

"Why do you think I finally returned to Nashville?" I dare a glance at her and wish I hadn't. She's silhouetted against the window, city lights painting her hair with glowing neon. She's the answer to my own question.

Adair leans over the console between us, her palm dropping between my legs. Her chin rests on my shoulder. "I thought you came back for me."

"I thought we were going to pretend." I pull into the restaurant's parking lot. I lift her hand from my lap, hoping it doesn't turn her sweet mood sour. "We're here."

Owing to the alcohol content in her bloodstream and the neon skillet blinking orange flames on the sign, she's too distracted to be offended. She's the one always drawing boundary lines, but it didn't take much to blur them. I'd known that much bourbon would, but there's no glory in taking advantage of a situation like this. She lowered her guard tonight, proving she isn't being completely honest with anyone. Not even herself. Adair never has been. But the most action she's getting out of me is whatever she orders off the menu inside.

She leans against me, using my body as a prop, while she studies her options. Finally, she groans. "You know what I like."

"Yes, I do, Lucky," I say darkly. Her breath hitches for a moment and suddenly there's no one else in the world. I force myself to return my attention to ordering food.

She doesn't object when I order one of damn near everything. We cozy up in a corner booth, sitting close to one another because I'm afraid she'll fall out of her seat if I don't put myself between her and open air. A comfortable familiarity threatens to overwhelm me with my arm around her. It's sentimentality—nothing more. When the food arrives, Adair eats like she used to back in college.

"Glad to see you still have an appetite," I say.

"I know. I'm never giving up carbs." She reaches back and pats her ample rear. "But it's catching up to me."

"I like it," I say honestly.

She screws up her nose as she dredges a fry in the ketchup on my plate. "Admit it, I don't have the body I used to have."

There's no way we'd be having this conversation if she were sober. That means she's probably not going to remember it in the morning, so there's no harm in being honest with her.

"I did love it," I admit. "But now?"

"I knew it," she says with a sigh, shoving her plate away and looking defeated.

I grip her chin and tilt her face toward mine. "Now? I want to worship it."

Her eyes flutter open in surprise. "Really?"

"You were hot before. Now you're a goddess."

"That's not a commonly held belief," she says. "The last guy I dated…"

"What?"

"He told me that I needed to go on a diet," she confesses.

"And you believed that dick?" I ask. I wish the guy was here right now so I could wring his neck until he lost a little weight of his own.

"I dumped him," she says brightly. "Nothing comes between me and my French fries."

"Or my French fries, it seems."

"I'm adding to my figure," she says, swiping another from me. "I'm told you prefer me curvy."

I draw her closer. "I do."

"Not that it matters," she hedges, daring another fluttering glance at me. "Because we're *not* sleeping together."

"No, we're not," I confirm.

"Honestly, that seems like a bit of a loss," she says.

"Does it?" I can't help but smile.

"It's not like—"

I cut her off with a kiss. It's not like the one earlier. This one is purposeful and lingering. I savor the softness of her lips under mine, teasing my tongue across hers, until I can't remember why I'm supposed to stay away from her. Pulling away, I try to remind myself. "Don't make this complicated."

"Let's not pretend we've ever been anything but complicated," she whispers and offers me more of her.

29

STERLING
THE PAST

"Things are getting pretty serious between you two." Cyrus shoots a mini basketball at the hoop he's hung over our door.

I look up from my book in time to see him make the shot. "We're friends."

He snorts as he walks over to retrieve the ball. Passing it from palm to palm, he shakes his head as though he doesn't believe that's possible. "I see the way you look at her. And she's got you reading some girly book, too."

"It's for a class," I tell him, dropping the copy of *Persuasion* on the coffee table.

"Sure. That's like your third novel by that chick this month."

"Jane Austen," I correct him. "Not some chick." Cyrus isn't terrible but he's not exactly intellectual. He might be counting how many books I'm reading, but I can't help noticing he hasn't cracked one yet. At least, not while I'm around.

But, unlike some of the other people in Adair's inner circle, he doesn't treat me like the servant class, so I keep this observation to myself.

"Ok, then what are your plans next weekend?" he asks. "There's going to be a Halloween party at—"

"I've got plans," I cut him off. The last thing I need is an invitation to another Valmont party. So far I've managed to avoid them since the night Adair got drugged.

"It's funny because Adair said the same thing when I invited her." Cyrus drops the ball onto his desk and turns on me. "Don't tell me that's a coincidence."

I shrug. "Okay, it's not a coincidence."

"Seriously, man? It's Halloween. I happen to know it's her favorite holiday. Have you even asked her about it?"

"She told me she wanted to skip it." I frown, not sure what to make of this information. On one hand, Cyrus has known her almost her whole life. On the other, like most of her old friends, he doesn't see what she's going through. Maybe it was her favorite before her mom's death.

"So you two are just going to sit around and read books?" he asks, picking up the novel and staring at it like he's never see one before.

Cyrus had come home last weekend to find Adair and I curled on the couch, her nestled between my legs, clothes on, reading books. I think he would have been less mortified if he'd walked in on us naked. He's been acting weird ever since.

"Come on. Convince her to come. Adair's a lot of fun when she loosens up and you can't tell me you're not interested in her."

"I'll talk to her about it." At this point, I'll promise anything to get him off my back. If Adair doesn't want to go to some stupid party, there's no way I'm going to try to talk her into attending. Cyrus must consider this a victory because he grabs his Beats and flops onto his bed.

My phone buzzes and I reach for it, a smile slipping onto my face, when I see it's a text from her about tonight.

Hennie's?

Yes.

Is it okay if Poppy comes? You can bring Cyrus.

I can't think of a better objection than I'd prefer to have her all to myself. Instead, I agree.

"Hey, man." I kick the end of his bed. His eyes jolt open and he lifts one side of his headphones. "Want to go to Hennie's with us?"

"You ever had hot chicken?"

I shake my head.

A wicked grin twists over his lips as he sits upright. "I'll come. This will be worth seeing."

Outside of a sports event, I've never heard so much smack talk as when the three of them start in on what I'm going to think of Nashville's famous dish. It lasts the entire drive to the nearest location. Cyrus continues it as he backs into the glass door at the restaurant.

I block out their taunts and check out my surroundings. Bright, purple high back booths run the perimeter of the space with a sprinkling of tables. The black checkered floor is clean, and glowing neon illuminates a sign hanging in the front window that declares "hotter than hellfire."

"You better go for the mild," Poppy advises me as she orders hers hot. There are five levels of heat: mild, medium, hot, hellfire, and damnation.

"Really? You think I can't handle it?"

"Darling, I'm half-Indian. I can handle my heat." She keeps to my side, and I can't help noticing that she's putting some distance between her and Cyrus. I make a mental note to ask Adair about it later.

"Hellfire," I tell the girl behind the counter. This earns a round of disbelief from the others. They're so loud that a beautiful black woman sticks her head out from the back.

"Why are y'all making such a ruckus?" she asks.

"Sorry, Ms. Palmer," Adair calls. "We brought a Yankee and he ordered his chicken hellfire hot."

"You think you can handle that?" she asks, studying me shrewdly.

"Yes, ma'am," I say. "It's not like they don't have hot food in New York."

"We'll see." She doesn't look convinced of that.

We take our number and find a booth. Adair slides in next to me, and for a moment, Poppy looks like she might try to as well. Finally, she sits next to Cyrus. They're both careful to keep their bodies from touching. It's like there's a line of tape down the center of the seat that only they can see.

"Palmer," I say, "like Darcy?"

"That's her mother, Henrietta. She keeps close tabs on all her restaurants," Cyrus explains.

"I wouldn't be surprised if your chicken comes out damnation hot," Adair warns me. "You don't brag to a Palmer about how much heat you can take."

"Where's your faith in me?" I elbow her gently, and Adair moves a little closer so that our arms and legs brush against each other when we move. Across the table, Cyrus raises an eyebrow that says *friends, huh*?

When it comes to Adair, I'm not making any assumptions.

We haven't exactly decided we're anything more than friends, even if her body keeps sending signals for me to cross the line. Every time I get close, someone interrupts us. Even tonight we have two chaperones. Maybe I'm reading Adair all wrong. Maybe the reason nothing's happened is because she's been so careful to keep herself from being alone with me.

Our order arrives with a bit of fanfare. Ms. Palmer herself brings out a tall glass of milk for me. I make up my mind then that there's no way I'm reaching for it.

"Why's it red?" I ask when they put the plate down in front of me.

Instead of an answer, everyone laughs, but no one louder or harder than Hennie herself. She heads back to the kitchen, shaking her head and howling, muttering *why's it red* the whole way.

No one picks up their food. They're too busy watching me.

"After you," Adair finally says with as much sugar as the sweet tea she insisted I order.

I pick a piece up, say a silent prayer that I don't make an ass out of myself, and take a bite. It's hot—like singe off your tastebuds hot—but it's also delicious. I swallow it. "Not bad."

"Need some milk?" Cyrus asks.

I shake my head and take another bite.

"Okay, you can keep him," Poppy proclaims.

So this was some type of test and I must have passed, because Adair wraps her arms around my neck like she's just been presented with a prize.

"He's all mine," she declares without a hint of reservation.

I don't even think about it. Leaning over, I press my lips to hers. It doesn't matter that her friends are with us or that my mouth feels like I just ate a beehive. I've kissed her a thousand times with my eyes and tasted her words like they came from my own lips, but nothing prepares me for finally having her, even just for this one moment. Nothing ever could. Nothing ever will. I know someday I won't remember what she's wearing or what's said after I finally release her back to the wild world. All I'll remember is the way she sighs into my kiss and this unshakeable feeling of finally finding home.

30

ADAIR
THE PRESENT

I roll over, clutching a sheet to my chest, and stare around the unfamiliar room, my heart beginning to pound as hard as my head. I have no idea where I am. Next to me, the bed is empty. It's been years since I woke up this hungover—or this confused. It doesn't help that blank walls stare back, giving me nothing to ground myself with. No pictures. I look for any clue. One nightstand with no photos. My shoes and jeans on a rug next to the bed. I turn toward the blinding light and realize there's an unbroken pane of windows and it's clearly morning. Outside it's all unbroken blue skies. I'm up high —*penthouse* high. This realization sinks in and then plummets right into a pit in my stomach.

I spent the night with Sterling.

I can recall most of the evening prior to leaving the Barrelhouse. After that, I think hot chicken was involved. The rest? I have no clue. I don't know what's worse: that he brought me home or that I can't remember it?

"Gather your dignity and your panties," I coach myself, "and get out of here."

My phone is charging on the nightstand, which is surprisingly thoughtful for someone who took a drunk woman to bed. I yank it free from the wall and drop the cord on the ground.

I'm not sure who to call. Poppy and Kai are nearby if they're still at her place, but calling Poppy means admitting what happened. I'm not sure I'm ready to do that. There's always Uber—the modern walk of shame. I need to get out of here before he comes back and uses his charm to talk me out of leaving. I'm considering stealing his car when his head pops into the room. I clutch the sheet like a life preserver and glare at him.

"You're up," he says.

"Well spotted." When he doesn't make a move to climb into bed with me, I decide it's now or never. Throwing off the sheet, I scramble for my jeans, ignoring the heat blooming on my cheeks.

"Leaving so soon?" he says dryly. He steps inside the room and leans against the wall. If I wasn't certain his appearance confirms my suspicions. He's wearing nothing but a pair of boxer briefs. I turn my head but not before I get a glimpse of the many assets he has on offer these days.

I can feel his eyes following me, watching as I wiggle on my jeans and adjust my bra. His interest is as shameless as taking me home in the first place. "I can't believe you."

I'm not sure why I trusted Sterling. Because of who he used to be? That's clearly not who he is now. The worst part is that it feels like my fault. I'd been the one to suggest the fake relationship. I'd been stupid enough to pretend that we were together in front of my friends. No one thought twice about leaving me with him last night, even if I was drunk. All because of this little game.

"What do you think happened, Adair?" he asks slowly.

"Let's see," I explode. "I wake up in your bed without my

pants after drinking half the whiskey in Nashville the night before. I think it's pretty obvious what happened."

"Feel free to tell me." He crosses his arms over bare chest, and I try to ignore how his biceps flex into a massive coil at the motion.

"I can't believe you took advantage of me." I'm not angry. I'm hurt. I feel my mask slipping away, revealing the part of me I'll never give him again. I can't help it. It's not that I trusted Sterling before last night. I know he's hiding plenty from me: how he wound up back in Nashville with a bank account capable of buying a million-dollar penthouse, where he's been for the last few years, why he's really come back. I'm not stupid enough to believe it has anything to do with me. Not really. But I never thought he'd stoop to taking a drunk woman to bed.

"You think I raped you?" he asks flatly.

"I mean," I splutter, hating that he's actually said it. "I guess it's not really…"

"Let's be clear," he interrupts me. "If I took you to bed in that state, it's rape."

I lift my chin defiantly, my fingers slipping as I try to lace my shoes. "Yes, it is."

"I agree."

I'm not sure what to say, so I just stare.

"But I didn't sleep with you," he adds. He points to the other side of the bed as though it's proof.

Unlike the rumpled side I woke up on, the sheet over the mattress is smooth with not even the slightest indentation in the crisp bedding. "That doesn't prove anything."

"You were still dressed," he says.

"My jeans were on the floor."

"You took them off. I think you were going to strip completely," he admits, "but you passed out before you did. If

I'm guilty of anything, it's that I didn't stay up and watch you all night to make sure you were okay. I'm sorry for *that*. I slept on the couch with Zeus so he wouldn't keep trying to jump into bed and wake you up."

My jaw clenches, locking my words in place until they're backed up in my throat, scratching for release until it feels as raw as the rest of me. Finally, I manage to force out, "How can I believe you?"

"You'll have to take my word for it." He doesn't look happy that I'm questioning him still.

"You want me to trust you, but how can I? Why should I?" I demand.

"Sometimes you have to have faith in a person," he says in a quiet voice. "You have to ask yourself what they're capable of."

I swallow this sage advice washing down all the retorts crowding on my tongue for their turn to be spoken. "Nothing happened?"

He shakes his head, but instead of looking relieved, he looks disgusted. "That's what you think of me?"

"I don't know what to think of you," I confess. More and more is coming back to me about last night. Sterling laughing at the bar. Sterling feeding me hot chicken. Kissing Sterling. Sterling carrying me into his apartment. I also seem to remember throwing myself at him multiple times. Yeah, now that the memories are coming back, I wish they wouldn't. I hadn't just pulled off my jeans, I'd try to strip for him in a pathetic attempt to get him into bed. I'm the one who should be ashamed.

Instead, I finish tying my shoelaces and search my pockets for a hair tie. I need to get out of here. I can't breathe in the thick air of words unspoken. He'd been a gentleman. I'd been drunk. Nothing changes that I'd kissed him—and that I'd wanted him to keep kissing me.

"I should go," I say, heading for the door but he moves in front of it. His long arms stretch over his head, bracing the doorframe. The light from the living room windows halos his body, casting shadows over the ripples and ridges of his muscular body.

The gentleman is gone. I can't see a hint of him hiding in Sterling's primal eyes.

"You wanted me to fuck you," he says, his voice nearly a growl. "You wanted me to fuck you so that you could hate me. You'd get off on that – screwing someone you hate. Poor little rich girl with no one who loves her. Don't flatter yourself that I'd lay a finger on you. You begged me last night. You were on your knees."

A dangerous flicker in my chest ignites into fire. "I've never begged you for anything."

"Tell yourself that, Lucky. You did and you will again. I know you. I know the only thing you crave more than someone to love you is destruction. You want to be wrecked. You want to be broken." His hand moves to my face, but I don't flinch. I just scowl as he traces my profile with his fingertip. "Isn't that, right?"

"Think what you what," I shoot back. "From now on, no more making this look real. No fake dates. Stay away from me."

I duck under his arms, half-expecting him to stop me. Sterling is true to his word, backing away to let me pass. "You don't even see it do you? I took care of you last night. I kept you safe—and you thanked me by accusing me of something you know I would never do."

"That's where you're wrong." I whirl on him. Zeus pads up

to me and sits at my feet as though he senses now is not the time to jump up for some love. "Don't pretend that I know who you are anymore. Don't pretend that you know me. Stop living in some idealized version of the past. I don't know what you're capable of, and you certainly don't know what I'm capable of."

"Not an apology, clearly."

"Oh, I am so sorry that I jumped to conclusions!" I storm. "It's not like it's that hard to imagine. You did kiss me!"

"So you remember?" he says coolly. "And the rest?"

I take a deep breath and do the last thing he expects, if only to prove him wrong. "Thank you for taking care of me."

"You're welcome," he says tersely.

Zeus pushes his muzzle into my hand and I scratch his head absently.

"But you're right. This thing between us isn't going to work. I can see that now."

"I tried to tell you," I say.

"It was your idea."

"*Pretending*—not actually going out on dates," I remind him. Why does it feel like a moot point?

Sterling stalks toward me, stopping a few paces before he reaches me. "Answer one question for me."

"Why should I?"

"Because you just accused me of taking advantage of you. I figure you owe me," he says.

"Fine," I mutter.

"When was the last time you had that much fun?" he asks.

A half-dozen moments flash to mind. He's in every one of them. "I can't remember."

"That's what I thought." His tone makes me shiver. Sterling sees right through me. He always has.

"I should go." I force myself toward the door.

"I can drive you home," he offers.

"I'm going to meet Poppy," I lie.

Before he can call my bluff, the lock turns and his door swings open. Zeus bounds toward the girl coming through it with a leash in hand. She's gorgeous, leggy, maybe nineteen.

"Hey, boy," she greets Zeus, freezing when she realizes we're here.

I glare at Sterling before forcing a smile onto my face. "You must be the dog walker."

"Um, yeah." She clips the leash on Zeus. "I'm sorry. Should I come back later?"

The question is directed at Sterling, who is looking at me when he answers. "We're all through here, Carly." He looks to her and speaks like I'm already gone. "Zeus has been pacing around waiting for you."

"Did you miss me?" Carly croons.

I slam the door on their conversation. I avoid the bellhop's eyes the entire ride to the lobby. I'm sure a guy who works an elevator for a living has seen his fair share of graceless morning-after exits before.

Digging my phone out of my pocket to call a car, I see I have a missed call. I half-expect it to be Poppy checking up on me after last night's shenanigans, but it's not her. It's Trish, the editor from Bluebird.

The future called while I was busy reliving the past.

That's the problem with Sterling, I can't be the girl he fell in love with. Not anymore. If he knew the truth, he wouldn't even bother trying. I can't keep doing this. I've given up too much. I've lost too much. It's time to move forward. I press the call button.

Trish picks up on the second ring. "I was hoping you'd call back today."

"I'm glad to hear from you," I say truthfully. The universe seems to be sending me a sign. "What's up?"

"Do you think you could drop by the office? I had a chance to look over those edits you sent back to me the other day."

I bite my lip dreading what comes next.

"I love them," she says to my surprise. "You totally understand the author's direction and where she's losing focus. You're exactly what this book needs. I was hoping we could discuss a job."

"Of course," I stammer.

"Excellent. Can you be here before noon? I have phone calls after lunch, so my availability is tight. Otherwise, it will have to wait until next week."

There's not enough time for me to get home and change. Last night's bar attire is not exactly the height of professionalism. Still, there's no way I'm losing this opportunity or waiting longer to move on. I needed a sign. The universe sent one.

"I can be there in an hour."

"Great. I'll see you then."

I hang up feeling more buoyant than I have in months. Now I just have to figure out what to do next. There's no way I can show up to Bluebird smelling like a bottle of bourbon and hot chicken. I haven't even brushed my hair. Being there in an hour doesn't leave me a lot of options though. I could go back up, swallow my pride, and use Sterling's bathroom. But that's a step in the wrong direction. I'm not even sure he'd let me.

Instead, I do what every girl should when she has an emergency. I go to my best friend.

Poppy answers her door in a crimson silk dressing gown, its bell sleeves drape elegantly and little black tassels hang off them. She looks like a movie star from old Hollywood with her hair piled on top of her head.

"How do you look like that and I look like this?" I ask, gesturing to my wrinkled jeans and t-shirt.

"Hair of the dog," she confesses. "Kai made mimosas this morning."

"Day drinking?" She really does belong in Hollywood.

"Just one," she says as we walk through the hall to her bedroom.

"Is Kai still here?" I look around for him.

She shakes her head. "He's a runner now. Los Angeles is a bad influence on him."

"He went for a run?" Maybe they didn't have as much to drink last night as I did. Still, I'm relieved he isn't here. It's not that I don't love him. It's just that it's hard enough to let Poppy see me like this. I don't think I could stand feeling vulnerable in front of both of them.

"Speaking of last night." Poppy scans my attire once more. "It looks like you didn't make it home."

"I told you that on the phone," I say defensively. Poppy had readily agreed to let me raid her closet for my impromptu meeting when I called on my way over. Considering our height difference, my options might be limited, but it's still better than showing up like this.

"You did," she admits, "but you didn't tell me where you were."

"Okay, officer, I confess. I spent the night at Sterling's place."

She bounces on her feet, clapping. "I knew it!"

I glare at her and she immediately freezes like I've hit her pause button.

"I mean, *oh no*!" she stammers, sounding confused. "I don't get it. You've been in love with him for years."

"I have not." I dig in her closet, shoving hangers back and forth like they've offended me, too. "I *was* in love with him."

"Forgive me," she says. "I must have mistaken the fact that

you haven't had a serious relationship with anyone since him for something else."

"That doesn't prove anything except that men are stupid and not worth my time." I should have that put on a shirt. I'd wear it proudly.

"So we aren't happy about this?" she clarifies.

"Nothing happened." I still don't know how to feel about this. I've been so angry at the prospect of Sterling taking advantage of me, where did I get off being insulted that he hadn't? Everything about him is a muddled mess of emotions that I don't have the time or interest to sort through.

"I know he broke your heart," she begins.

I shake my head. "It's not that. It's..."

"What happened?" she asks softly.

I know she's not asking about last night. Poppy Landry is my best friend, the person I call when I need a safe place and a warm smile, but for all that we are to each other, there are parts of me I don't show anyone. Memories too painful to share. "I don't want to talk about it."

She sighs heavily. We've been here before. "Fine. Have it your way. But even if you don't want to talk about it, do you think about it?"

"Every day." My voice sounds far away from me like it's stuck in some other place and time.

"Do you really?" she presses.

"What's the point? I can't change any of it."

"Those who ignore the past are doomed to repeat it," she quotes. "Don't doom yourself. You deserve happiness." She squeezes my hand, knowing that now isn't the time for a hug. Not when I'm wrapped in my shell, afraid to even look in the mirror and see what's staring back at me. Instead, she brushes me away from the closet and rifles through it before finally pulling loose a navy blue wrap dress. "It's too short on me," she says as she pushes it into my arms.

I take it gratefully. She always knows exactly what I need. Right now, I need a dress, some space, and something to look forward to before I find myself lost in memories of Sterling Ford.

31

ADAIR
THE PAST

S terling is afraid of horses. He's not going to admit that, but I can see it. He watches with wary eyes as I check the saddles one more time. I wonder if his second thoughts are going to win out. They're written all over his face. It's a little funny. Adorable even.

Big, bad Sterling Ford has met his match.

"You ready?" I ask him.

"Sure." But he doesn't move, he just stands there with his hands in his pockets.

"We don't have to go riding," I say. "We can do something else. Maybe this needs to be a gradual introduction. You've seen the horse. Maybe you can pet him and then you can sit on him—"

He cuts me off mid-suggestion. "I said I was sure."

"Look, that's how I started. Slowly," I tell him.

"And how old were you?" he asks. My mouth clamps shut and he groans. "Exactly. I'm not a kid. I can handle myself."

"Okay, well, come over here then." I do my best to not insult his masculinity as he attempts to climb onto the horse's back. Once he manages to get on with his feet in the stirrups, he looks even more uncertain. "You okay up there?"

"Fine," he says through gritted teeth. "Let's ride."

"Let me show you a few things first. This is Ember and he's pretty chill." I walk him through the harness and explain the bit. He does a good job of listening and glowering simultaneously.

"What's your horse's name?" He asks, clutching the reins tightly.

"Buttercup," I say. I glare at him when he laughs. "I was twelve when I got her!"

"No judgment." His eyes say he is, in fact, judging me.

I drop a paper sack into my saddle bag and mount Buttercup. With a little encouragement we begin to walk the horses. Sterling settles quickly, looking a bit more at ease, so I increase my pace. Ember, who started life as a child's training horse—a fact I kept to myself— follows my lead.

Even now, despite his scowl, being with Sterling feels natural. Right. Our relationship is moving from one pace to the next smoothly. I only hope it survives me taking him horseback riding.

The land on the rest of the estate is a mix of rolling hills and valleys. I fall into a trot beside him and we ride quietly until we can no longer see the stables or the rest of Windfall. After a few more minutes, we reach my favorite spot. It's mostly an open field, too far from the house to be tended. There's no grass, just a clover field and thousands of yellow wildflowers growing freely. Slowing Buttercup, I dismount and grab her reins. Sterling won't let me help him down. I pretend to focus intensely on tying the reins to a tree and not on his awkward descent.

"What do you think?" I ask, pulling a blanket out of Buttercup's saddle bag and spreading it on the ground.

"I'd make a shitty cowboy," he says truthfully.

I laugh before I can stop myself, covering my mouth when I realize that I actually am laughing at the idea of him as a cowboy and not his joke. But Sterling isn't angry. He's watching me with strange eyes I can't quite read. Then he kisses me.

I'm beginning to anticipate these sudden outbursts of affection, even if I don't know what I do to deserve them. If I did, I might spend all my time triggering this reaction, because kissing Sterling is all I want to do. Well, that and other things, even if we haven't gotten there yet.

When he pulls away, his hand stays on the back of my neck and his eyes blaze. I swear he could burn me alive just looking at me like that. I force myself to turn away before he does. Pulling the paper bag out, I hold it up. "It's starting to get chilly. I figured it might be our last chance for a picnic."

"A picnic?" he repeats.

I don't know if it's a test or if he just thinks this is dumb. I default to the latter as a means of self preservation. "Food. Blanket. Eating outside. Having fun."

"I know what a picnic is." He snatches the bag from my hand and drops onto the blanket.

"Well, you acted like I was speaking in tongues," I complain. So he does think this is stupid. Maybe I'm trying too hard to see Sterling as some romantic figure like Mr. Darcy or Heathcliff.

He reaches up and pulls me into his lap. "Don't be mad, Lucky."

I can't help pouting. Not if he's going to respond to it. "You were teasing me."

"I'll tell you a secret." He tucks my hair behind my ear and whispers, "I've never been on a picnic. That's why I was surprised."

"You've...what?" I've done it again. I'm losing count of the number of times I've stuck my foot in my mouth with him.

"City kid, remember?" he says nonchalantly, but he keeps his head turned from mine. He's missed out on a lot in his life, and it's not all because of growing up in New York.

"It's a stupid Southern thing, I bet. We love our picnics and sweet tea and pageantry." I shrug like I'm over it.

Sterling sees right through me. "It's okay. You don't have to feel sorry for me."

"I hate that I always say the wrong thing," I confess. I'm not exactly sure when I started caring what he thought. Mostly, because I find myself caring so much now that I can't remember a time before I did.

"Make it up to me?" He picks a yellow flower and sticks it behind my ear.

"Anything," I breathe. This close to him, his arms around my waist, sitting in his lap, I'm overwhelmed. I'd do anything he asks.

"Take me on my first picnic?" He kisses the tip of my nose.

"You're an easy date," I tease.

"You have no idea how easy I can be," he says, and I feel him pressing hard against my butt. "I can show you though."

"Mr. Ford, I'm a lady." I pretend to be offended but only to cover how fast my heart begins to beat. We've kissed. A lot. And maybe it's bad luck but every time we start to round a corner, he stops. Sometimes Cyrus comes home. Sometimes he says he's tired.

"Is that so?" He kisses me until I'm breathless.

It takes me a moment to recover. "I suffered through a debutante ball to prove it."

"That sounds dangerous." He's trying not to laugh.

"Two petticoats and a dress that weighed like thirty pounds," I say sourly. "It was."

"I will never question your propriety again." He draws a cross over his heart.

"Believe me, I'd rather be in the stables with the horses."

"There's a whole world between blue jeans and ballgowns, Lucky. It's just waiting for us." His words are more than a promise. They're an invitation. I settle against him and begin to play our game.

"Twenty-five," I prompt him. We'd come up with it accidentally after the first evening we spent talking. I'm not the only one who wants to travel. One of us names an age and we decide where we'll go for our birthdays.

"Australia," he answers.

I've been to half the places he lists but thinking about going with him makes it feel like a brand new adventure.

"The outback?" I ask.

"Great barrier reef," he says. "I just have to learn to snorkel."

I stop myself before I can express surprise that he's never snorkeled. I'm getting better at this.

"You?" he prompts.

"Yorkshire," I say. I tend to be more specific with my choices.

"You've been reading the Brontës again, haven't you?" he asks.

"I think it would be romantic. The moors during autumn, all blustery and cold." I can picture it in my mind. "Wind howling and leaves falling. I think that's the only way to see it."

"When is your birthday?" he asks slowly.

Somehow I've managed to dodge this particular bit of information. Given the nature of the game, it's a small miracle.

But Sterling isn't stupid and I've let too much slip. I take a deep breath. "Promise me you won't make me do anything stupid like a party this year."

"What about our trips?" He's joking but the amusement fades when he sees my face.

"Not this year," I say softly. "I don't want to celebrate anything this year."

"I understand." And I know he's telling the truth. "The year my mom died was terrible. First they took me and my sister away and then they split us up. I remember refusing to leave my room on Christmas morning, even though my foster family bought me presents. I didn't want *their* presents."

He gets it. I don't want to blow out candles or sing. Not this year. Not without my mom there to clap and hide that she's teary-eyed. "My mom cried every year on our birthdays. Happy tears."

Sterling's answering smile is tight-lipped and I wonder if I've said the wrong thing. He's never opened up this much about his past before. I ache to know more about him but I can't risk forcing it. I don't want him to push me away even if it means there are parts of him I'll never know.

A cloud moves over the sun and the air turns from crisp to chilly in an instant. It's like a switch has been flipped, the last remnants of summer swept away. Sterling's mood seems to shift along with it.

"October 31st," I blurt out.

He turns confused eyes on me.

"My birthday," I say. "It's on Halloween. I know. We usually throw a big party and…"

I see him doing the math. Halloween is a week away. We've been playing this game and I've been ignoring the fact that my birthday is creeping closer each time we play.

"Want to watch a movie this year?" he asks. "Eat pizza. I promise no cake."

Tears swell my throat and I swallow against the raw pain.

"Cheer up, Lucky," he orders me. "We don't have to do anything."

"Pizza sounds good." I'm relieved that my voice doesn't crack on the emotions crowding inside me. "And cake might be okay."

"No candles," he promises. He clears his throat. "What else do you do on a picnic?"

He's not going to linger on the topic, and I'm grateful. I need to be more patient with him and his past. He respects my boundaries. I need to do this same for him.

I take the cue and return to our picnic. "Well, when I was little, we'd pick flowers."

He picks another one and puts it next to the first.

"Those are buttercups, by the way," I inform him.

"Ahh, the famous buttercups."

"I was a very original child," I confess with a laugh.

"What else?"

"We'd eat." I point to the bag. Felix made me sandwiches. I paid for them by listening to his well-meaning romantic advice the whole time. "And we'd make crowns."

"Come again?" he says.

"No laughing." I scramble away and kneel near the edge of the blanket. Scattered through the lush green shamrocks, white hop clover grows. I pick a few, careful to keep their stems as long as possible. Settling into a cross-legged position, I hold two up and then carefully tie one stem around the bud of the other.

Sterling watches as I do a few more and then hold up a chain.

"You can also make very fancy bracelets and necklaces," I inform him.

He looks like he wants to laugh but doesn't dare. "Let me try."

It takes him a few tries to get the technique down. A few minutes later, he places a crown of them on my head.

"Princess," he proclaims.

"I told you not to call me that."

"Okay." He plucks a shamrock and puts it between his teeth. He wags a finger at me. "Kiss me and I'll stick with lucky."

"It's only got three leaves," I say, moving closer to him anyway.

"I don't need a four-leaf clover." He drops it to the blanket and brushes his lips over mine. I taste mint. "I have you."

Sterling's body moves over mine, his weight pinning me against the blanket. My legs drop open instinctively and he presses his hips between my thighs. There's multiple layers of denim between us but I feel every inch of him like he's set fire to me.

Sterling? He is the world between blue jeans and ball gowns. His body. His lips. He's not easy. He's hard. His weight shifts again as if to prove it. I've gone places and I've seen things. I've always dreamed of seeing more, and now I'm seeing the whole world in the blue eyes of a boy.

He dips his lips to my neck, travels to my ear, and whispers, "I think I've missed you my whole life."

My heart cracks open and I turn into him, offering him my lips and with it that wide-open spot in my chest. He accepts. I feel it in his touch. A strong hand skims down my shoulder and explores my breast. My nipple hardens as he furthers his study. Then he continues his adventure, slipping his hand to the waistband of my jeans. There's a moment of hesitance as if asking permission. I grab his hand and shove it into my panties.

"Patience," he murmurs with a laugh as a finger begins circling the swollen bundle of nerves he finds.

"Easy for you to say." I buck against him to show just how impatient I am.

"Shut up and kiss me, Lucky."

Our mouths collide as we twine together, his hand between my legs, my arms coiling around him. His tongue wanders past my lips, licks a path along my teeth, journeys deeper until he's my oxygen. We could be anywhere. Any place. Any time. I wouldn't know. There's only him and the need building inside me. Every nerve in my body hones in on his clever fingers until I'm sure the center of the universe hides between my legs, and he's found it.

A subtle tremor builds in my muscles, migrating through me, picking up speed. My eyes close and my teeth clamp down on his lower lip as I explode. My legs snap closed around him, but he continues to seek some hidden place. His fingers delve deeper, coaxing out every spasm, every ounce of mindless bliss until I'm hanging off him too spent for words.

Sterling lays me onto the blanket and draws me against him. I peek to find him watching me with amused eyes.

"What?" I ask suspiciously. Did I do something wrong?

"Your cheeks are as red as your hair," he teases.

I stick my tongue out at him, but I feel myself flush even hotter.

He kisses the tip of my nose. "It's so adorable that I'll forgive you for biting me."

"Biting you?"

He sticks out his lip and I see a faint trace of blood.

"Oh my God!" I bury my face in his neck.

"I was kidding about forgiving you." He presses another kiss to the top of my head. "I took it as a compliment."

I pull back a little to see if he's serious, but his arms tighten like he's holding me captive. "Yeah?"

"Yeah."

"Like your head needed to get any bigger," I grumble, not remotely meaning it.

His barking laugh is so honest, so genuine that I can't help kissing him.

"What was that for?" he asks.

"You don't laugh like that a lot. I like it. I need to reward it."

"Reward, huh?" There's a wicked glint in his blue eyes and I wonder how far he wants to take this. I search for any apprehension inside me and find none. But I didn't really expect my first time to be in a field.

Still, he does deserve some attention of his own. I shove him back and climb on top of him.

"What are you doing, Lucky?" He arches an eyebrow.

"I promise you'll approve." I gather my hair in my hands and twist it into a knot on top of my head, still straddling him. Sterling's eyes hood as he watches me.

"Whatever you're doing, I like the view." He crosses his arms behind his head, relaxing into the afternoon and closing his eyes. I bend down and kiss him, moving quickly down his jaw before shimmying down his long body, leaving kisses in my wake. Everything about Sterling is new, but so is this.

He's undiscovered territory, and I want to escape into him.

A tiny voice in my head reminds me that I have no idea what I'm doing. I lock her away and let my body guide me. When I reach the button on his jeans, I'm glad he's on his back so he can't see my fingers tremble as I undo it. Anxiety clashes with excitement as I unzip his pants and zero in on his dick. I run my hand across it, over his boxers and it grows in size—a feat I would not have thought possible because he already seems so rock hard. Hooking my fingers around the elastic band, I draw them down enough to free him.

I've seen a naked man before.

I've never seen one that looks like this.

I study him for a second, hoping my instinct takes over again.

"Does it pass inspection?" he asks dryly, craning his neck a little to see me.

"Shh!" I hush him. "I'm making a friend."

This earns another laugh. "He's more than a friend where you're concerned. He's your servant."

I dip my lips to cover the broad tip, swirling it with my tongue. Sterling's smart-ass commentary ceases instantly replaced by a grunt of pleasure. The sound inspires me and I try to earn another one, then a groan. I keep going licking and kissing and sucking until he's moaning my name.

"I'm going to…" His warning comes out in pants. Sterling clutches my hair in his hand and bucks against me. I keep my mouth over him, surprised a little as heat floods across my tongue. When he finally goes slack against the blanket, I climb back on top of him. He wraps his arms around me and holds me.

"You really are my lucky charm," he whispers. I can hear the grin in his voice.

"It was okay?" I dare to ask.

He strains his neck so he can look at me. "Better than okay. You've done that before, right?"

I bite my lip, hesitating for a second, before shaking me head.

"You haven't…" Sterling stares at me and I see him realize what I'm saying. "Have you done other things?"

"Some," I say, feeling a little defensive.

"Adair." He says my name strangely. "Are you a virgin?"

"Don't act so surprised," I huff, deciding that being offended looks cooler than being embarrassed. "I told you I'm a lady."

He blows a thin stream of air from his lips as if he's considering what to say to this.

"It's not a big deal," I add, worried that I'm spoiling the moment.

"Yeah, it is," he says, surprising me. "I just…I'm glad you told me."

I want to die. I want to hide. I roll off him and put my arms over my face. He pulls them away.

"Don't do that," he says gently. "It's nothing to be ashamed of."

"Are you sure?" I ask flatly. He's acting like it's a much bigger issue than it is.

"I don't want to push you too far, too fast," he explains. He strokes my cheek gently, his eyes somehow even bluer than normal. "Promise me, you'll tell me if you want me to stop?"

I nod, an ache growing in my throat. I don't want him to stop. Ever. I want every bit of my world to be mixed up with his. My words are small when I answer him. "What do I say if I want you to start?"

"I think you just answered your own question, Lucky." Then his mouth closes over mine and sweeps away everything but him and me and the wide blue sky above.

32

Two hours later and my blood is still up from my confrontation with Adair. Waking up to her was better than any dream, but like dreams often do, it quickly turned into a fucking nightmare.

Zeus watches me from the living room as I pace through the penthouse. He hasn't moved since Carly returned him an hour ago.

"Why did I expect differently?" I ask him. "You know her. Did she treat you like this?"

Zeus whines and tucks his paws over his eyes. Great. Not only am I talking to a dog, he's not listening. I'm not sure why what happened bothers me so much. I don't need Adair to like me—I don't want her to like me. Who cares what she thinks of me?

"Apparently, you do," I answer my own question.

It shouldn't change a fucking thing about my plan. I can't let it. The MacLaines deserve retribution for everything their family has done. The list of their sins is long enough to stretch across half of Nashville. I've been called a mercenary, a murderer, a liar. I'm all those things. But I have a code and so do my brothers. Some lines we refuse to cross.

I should have dumped her at the Eaton last night or driven her back home despite her protests. Sentimentality is for fools and greeting cards. It's not getting the better of me again. And then she acted hurt as she left? As though I'd wounded her. After all these years, she's still chaos—as impossible to withstand as a tornado. One minute she's accusing me of taking advantage of her. The next she's hurt that I didn't? I should know better than to try to make any sense of her. Sanity starts at home and Adair has always lived in a cuckoo clock.

My phone rings and I answer it immediately, half-expecting it to be her. "Yeah?"

"I have a special guest waiting for you," Jack says. "Luca arranged a location for you to meet up."

I'd nearly forgotten that he grabbed Oliver last night for a little chat. "Text me the address."

I hang up and grab my keys. I need to blow off some steam and Oliver needs a wake-up call. The timing is perfect. It's time to cross one name off my list.

The warehouse, tucked into an older, industrial section of Nashville, looks abandoned from the outside. A few windows are broken out, leaving behind their jagged memories. Someone's tagged the receiving dock's door. No one's bothered with this place in a while. No one reputable, at least.

It's times like these that I'm grateful for my stint in the military. Compartmentalization. It's a valuable skill to have at the moment. My thoughts keep jumping to Adair but once I'm inside, in my element, I'll be free of them. Right now, she's a siren song I can't resist.

None of that matters here. Someone cut the bolt on a thick lock and left the chain dangling. It's practically an invitation. Trust Luca to have the perfect spot for a meeting with an unwilling associate. It's a particular talent of the DeAngelos to have their own safe houses in major cities. I shouldn't be surprised that even in Nashville, a city that's largely managed to avoid the attention of organized crime, there's one. There's a lot of money in this town—more than most people realize—and it won't stay unnoticed for long.

"I didn't expect to see you here," I say when I spy Jack in the shadows. In a pair of black jeans and a black t-shirt he blends in nicely, but he doesn't belong here. He wants out of this life. Maybe I'd crossed a boundary asking him to nab Oliver. "You don't have to do this."

"You know that I have a special interest in these sorts of negotiations," he says.

I do know that. Jack loves a minute alone with a man who breaks his moral code. I've been in the room for some of his chats with these monsters. I doubt the men were ever the same. He's doing the world a favor when he takes an interest in these cases, but it was like watching Dr. Jekyll and Mr. Hyde. The Jack that I knew with his easy smile and simple ambitions turns ruthless and cold. It's the same monster inside all of us. It's what bound us together years ago. No matter how far we've come, it's still there. Jack fights his monster. Luca embraces his. Me? I *use* mine.

You don't wind up in a uniform at nineteen without some emotional baggage. We're living proof.

"I'm not staying, but I wanted to personally deliver this piece of shit," he says, sounding somewhat apologetic.

"I understand." More than that, I respect it.

"Luca is already in there. " He tilts his head to a room behind him.

"Did you forget what happens if you leave a cat alone with a mouse?" I ask, looking toward the door behind him.

"He's bored," Jack warns me. "He says you invited him to play, but you haven't provided much entertainment."

"The art of subtlety is lost on him," I say dryly.

"How did last night go after you left?" he asks.

So much for keeping today's events in tidy compartments. "I fed her, put her to bed, and this morning she accused me of attacking her."

"She seems complicated." Jack chooses his words carefully. He always does.

"You were the one asking me if I was having second thoughts," I point out. Maybe now he can see exactly why she made it to the top of my blacklist.

"Have you ever considered that if two people just talked— without lying to each other—they might discover their bullshit stories only hurt themselves?" he asks.

"How wise," I say. "You should write a book."

"I saw the way you looked at her," he says.

"Like I hate her?" I ask.

Jack laughs, but it sounds hollow. "You know it's not true what they say. There is no thin line between love and hate. There's no line at all. It's all mixed up together."

"I can see why you're single."

"Whatever." He shrugs like I'm a lost cause. "Tell yourself what you want. Maybe you do hate her, but you definitely still love her."

"That doesn't change anything." I decided that much as soon as I saw her at the funeral. Adair will never learn. She'll hurt and ruin everyone around her in the name of destroying herself. And they'll pay the price while she remains unscathed. "Look, I better head in there before he eats Oliver for dinner."

Jack grips my hand, bumping his shoulder against mine

before he takes his leave. It's a show of solidarity and support. He might be walking a different path than Luca and I now, but we'll always be brothers. Even if he questions my endgame.

There's no doubt in my mind that Oliver deserves what's coming to him though. When I scribbled the original list down on a redeye from London to Dulles, I'd penciled his name at the bottom of the notepad. At the gala, he'd moved himself to the top. Too much money. Not enough consequences. A particularly off-putting brand of privilege. Like too many in Valmont, he sees the world in categories. Namely two: those that belong at the top of the food chain like him and everyone else who is there for the taking. I know where I'm seen on that ladder, even now. None of them realize it's an illusion. Money doesn't keep them safe. It might buy time, but karma always finds her mark and the bitch calls me to make them pay.

Luca hands me a latte when I step into the room.

"I thought we should commemorate our first day on the new job," he says. We toast our paper cups.

"It's good to be back in the office," I say dryly. "I see you got the place in order."

"When you have a talent, you use it," he says with pride. His tastes tend toward the theatrical. Why bother with simple revenge when you can make it a spectacle? That seems to be his modus operandi. Traditionally, his family relied on old school methods of persuasion and punishment: breaking legs for nonpayment, disappearing members that rat them out. Luca brought a flair to the operation that made him in demand throughout the entire syndicate.

The scene is set before me, perfectly laid out to deliver maximum impact for our message. He's placed an old bed with a rusty metal frame against a crumbling wall. Its mattress is covered in stains I'd rather not think about. The guest of honor is handcuffed to it, stripped to his underwear. There's a bag over his head. Jack brought him here from the bar with it on. Oliver's got no idea who took him or where he is. All he can go on is the dank smell of mold and the sound of scurrying rats all around him. He's spent the whole evening frightened and helpless. There's a certain poetry to it. In truth, he deserves worse.

"You sure you don't want me to kill him?" Luca asks loudly. He picks up two baseball bats and hands me one.

There's a whimper from the black bag.

"That won't be necessary this time. I'm sure that after our chat, he is going to be a good little boy." The trouble in working with an assassin is that they always want to kill the target. I guess it never feels like the job is complete until they have. Not that Luca doesn't follow a code. He does. It's just a bit looser than Jack's.

Jack is trying to balance out his karma. Luca doesn't care about that. He embraced his dark side a long time ago. Now he's going straight to hell on a full-ride scholarship.

"Mr. Hawthorne," I call, circling the end of the bed. He strains toward the sound of my voice. I can imagine what he's thinking. He's wondering if this is a ransom situation or if he's about to die. I enjoy letting him wonder. I enjoy letting him worry. He's never had to before and that's how someone like him rots from the inside out. No one's been around to pluck him from his lofty spot at the top of the tree. The world thinks he's shiny and perfect—a good apple. I know what lurks on the inside: the worms and decay. "It's a crime to drug women. Don't you know that?"

"I haven't done that," he protests in a muffled voice.

I smash the bat against the metal rails and he cries out, shaking in his cuffs. I wait for him to stop screaming. "Try again."

"I have money."

Luca laughs at this. "Join the club. Now answer the teacher or we'll have to take minutes away from recess. *It's a crime to drug women. Don't you know that?*"

"I know," Oliver says.

"That's better. Are you having a good time, Mr. Hawthorne? Now, be honest," I urge him.

His head shakes. "Please. I have a family."

"A brother," Luca says. "I think we might have to talk to him at some point."

"Oh, I'm sure we will," I confirm.

"Leave him out of this," Oliver demands.

"See this is what you don't seem to be comprehending," I say, moving closer and pressing the top of the baseball bat to his chest. "*You* don't get to make demands. You don't order people around. Other people do not exist for your whims. If I want to go and have a little chat with your brother, I will."

"Don't," he pleads. He's starting to get the message.

"I didn't hear the magic word." Luca runs his bat along the top of the slats, and Oliver shrinks down as though he can hide.

"*Please*," he says.

"It looked painful to say that." I imagine he's never used the word before. "You spend your life thinking you can buy whatever and whoever you want. Not anymore. I know about the drugs."

"I haven't done that for years," he insists. "I was just a stupid kid back then."

"This is my courthouse, and I'm the judge. There's no statute of limitations here," I tell him.

"I'll do anything." He tugs against his handcuffs.

"We're not going to kill you." I'm starting to get annoyed with Oliver's pessimism. It's getting in the way of my lesson. Next to me, Luca's grin droops. I guess he was hoping I'd change my mind. "At least not yet. I believe in second chances."

"I promise, I'll never do it again," he says quickly.

"What you're feeling now is nothing compared to what they felt. You're not a man. You're an insect. Do know what happens to insects, Mr. Hawthorne? They wind up under a boot. You don't want to meet me if I have my boots on." I let that threat linger until he knows I mean it. "And you're going to donate one million dollars to the women's clinic at Valmont University."

"How am I going to explain why I'm doing it?" he asks.

"Tell them it's reparations," I say coolly.

"That would ruin my life!"

"Just like you ruined theirs. You're still not getting it, are you? This is getting off easy. You're not in real danger unless I let my friend here take over," I add just to see him tremble. "You've only lost control for one night of your life. One night spent helpless, but still safe. No one's hurt you. No one's violated you. The most you've lost is your dignity. You deserve to lose a lot more. *You'll make the donation.* Say what you want about why, but we're watching you."

"Otherwise, have you ever considered joining a monastery?" Luca asks. "It might be your safest option if you don't make that donation."

"I'll do it," Oliver says, sounding defeated "Just let me go."

"It's a pleasure doing business with you," Luca says before knocking him out with the knob of his bat.

"You could've just kept the hood on." Not that he's going to take my notes on this.

"And listen to him bitching the whole way?" Luca shakes his head. "He deserves a headache, at least. You let him off too easily."

"I have a lot of people to teach around here," I remind him. It's better not to draw too much attention to our revenge business before it's off the ground.

"Fair enough."

It takes both of us to drag Oliver's limp body to the back of Luca's BMW.

"Roomy trunk," I comment as we arrange him inside it.

"It really does have best in its class cargo storage," Luca agrees. He shoves Oliver's legs in and slams the lid shut. "Jack told me you left with Adair last night."

"So?" I ask.

"Jack likes her," Luca says.

"It's not Jack's place to like her," I growl.

"He also predicted you would react that way."

"What about you?" I say, feeling betrayed. "Do you want me to reconsider?"

"I do not have a horse in this race, brother, but you do," he says. "What's it worth for you to win?"

"Everything."

"Have you ever been to the Kentucky Derby?"

"Have you?" I ask. What the fuck is he on about now?

"The horse that wins doesn't always survive the race."

"Are you threatening to shoot my horse?" I ask flatly. I see the point he's making. Apparently, he's taking Jack's side.

"Are you willing to pay that price?"

"I don't know," I admit.

"Because the reason he's in here"— he taps the trunk —"is because of her."

"So?"

"Are you really prepared to do the same thing he did?"

Adair's betrayed face flashes to mind. She's lost faith in me already. She didn't care about who I was then or how little she knows about me now.

"I don't kid myself about the kind of man I am. Someday someone will come for me," Luca says. "And I'll deserve it. I know who I am. I know what that means. Do you? Does she?"

"I'm not sure it matters. She's made up her mind about me." This thing with her isn't a black and white. Adair exists in the gray.

"Then change her mind."

Maybe it's that simple to Luca's lizard brain, which seems to work in binaries, but Adair isn't so easily swayed. "How would you suggest I do that?"

"Send her flowers. Be romantic. Take her on a date or some shit."

I look from him to the trunk that holds a man we just shoved inside it. "Are you really giving me romantic advice right now?"

"I have layers," he says, pretending to be offended. "And, word to the wise, so does she."

"You know an awful lot about her for spending one evening with her." I don't want him to be right, but he might be.

"Women and torture aren't all that different. You just gotta find the right button to press." He shrugs and opens the driver's side door. "Speaking of, where do you want me to dump this piece of shit?"

I'm too preoccupied to come up with an answer. "I trust you."

Luca slides into his car, a slash of a smirk on his face. "You sure about that?"

He takes off before I can process that I might regret giving him free rein. It's too late now and I have other things on my mind.

Like hair the color of wildfire and emerald-green eyes that see right through me. I love her. That's how this started. That's how it ends.

33

The library is dead even for a Saturday. I guess the weekend combined with Halloween means normal people are on their way to parties. They probably don't have to maintain an insanely high GPA like I do. Given how much time I've been spending with Adair, I'm falling behind in a few classes. Enough to worry me. There's still plenty of time to get my grades up. At five, I pack it up and head back. Adair is coming over in an hour, so I'm surprised when I spot her white Roadster parked in front of my building. She's still inside, singing to some song only she can hear.

I poke my head in and startle her.

"Sorry." I hold up my hands in surrender. "Didn't mean to scare you."

"Where were you?" She asks barely concealing the suspicious way her eyes rove across me like she's looking for clues.

"The library. I needed to catch up."

She scrunches up her freckled nose. "You went to the library on a Saturday."

"Not all of us have a dad to write a tuition check," I snap. I instantly regret it. She flinches like I bit her. I know she doesn't mean to be a snob. She's actually remarkably kind in comparison to some of the people I've met in Valmont. "Sorry. I'm just stressed. You want to come in? We can order some food. I tracked down some cupcakes and I promise not to sing." I'd actually swiped them from the cafeteria earlier today. She might not want to celebrate her birthday, but I'm not going to let her ignore it entirely. Baby steps. Next year will be easier.

She pauses and I wonder just how badly I fucked up. "Actually..."

Fan-fucking-tastic, Sterling. You've screwed up her birthday.

"My dad had to go out of town this morning. I thought we could go to my place."

Other than the time we went riding, she's never invited me to her house before. I assume she doesn't want to deal with her father's disapproval. I can't blame her.

When I don't answer immediately, she clears her throat.

"I thought we could be alone," she says.

"Cyrus is out at some party."

"What if he comes home?" she presses.

"He won't bother us," I begin.

Adair lets out a frustrated shriek that stops me. Her cheeks flush and she glues her eyes to the steering wheel. "I mean alone *alone*."

"Oh." This processes more slowly than it should. It's not like I've never slept with someone. I've banged plenty of chicks back home. But this is different. Adair is different.

"We don't have to," she says quickly, misreading my hesitance. She unbuckles her seat belt and reaches for the door handle. "We'll just hang out. I just thought..."

I grab her hand before she can open the door. "Of course, I want to be alone with you."

I pray I've averted crisis. For all her confidence, I sense she needs a little encouragement.

"Cool. Um, we can go now if you want."

"Let me drop my stuff off." I hold up a finger. "I'll be right back."

I brush my teeth in my room and consider grabbing extra clothes. That seems a little too presumptuous so I settle for changing into one of my nicer shirts—a long-sleeved white thermal that Francie sent in a care package. It's nicer than the hoodie I'd been wearing but still casual. It's not every day someone like Adair MacLaine asks you to take her to bed. I grab her present and stick it in my pocket, so she won't complain. She told me not to get her anything and it's not like it's anything special. But I couldn't ignore her birthday entirely.

She's drumming the steering wheel nervously when I come back.

"You want to drive?" She asks when I get into the passenger's seat. "I...I don't want to."

"Okay," I agree slowly. Jumping out, I round the car to open her door before she can beat me to it.

As soon as she steps out of the car, I'm glad I changed. Usually, we hang out in jeans on the couch. Tonight, Adair is in a tight black dress that stops so short the length should be illegal. Long sleeves cover her arms but the neckline dips down between her breasts. She's piled her hair on top of her head, a few strands fluttering freely around her face. Her skin is bare but her lips are glossy. If I had any doubt what she meant about being alone, I don't anymore.

I rush to the other side of the car to help her into her seat —and also, so I can savor another few seconds of her in this outfit.

It's not until we begin to drive that I realize she's shaking.

"Are you okay?" I slow the car a little.

"Yeah," she says quickly. "I'm just a little cold."

"I should tell you it was a bad idea to wear that dress then, but I'm glad you did, Lucky."

She preens and maybe its enough to warm her up because the trembling fades a little. When I pull past the guard station at Windfall, ignoring the security officer's disapproving glare at finding me in the driver's seat, she directs me to bypass the circular drive and head toward the pool house.

"I thought your dad wasn't home," I say as we pass the main house.

"He's not." She chews her lip for a second. "I'm not allowed to have boys in my room."

I try not to laugh and fail. "Is he going to find out?"

"There's cameras all over this place," she tells me.

I cast a concerned look at her. "Maybe we shouldn't…"

"He won't check the pool house cameras. It's too cold to swim and I told him I was going to a friend's for a party."

"Wait." Something terrible occurs to me. "It's your birthday."

"Yep."

"And your dad left town?"

She nods.

"Are you upset?"

"He's been home for like two of my birthdays. It's not a big deal."

I had a shit father before he went to prison, one I didn't really want around either—and that's how I know she's lying. It doesn't matter how much they disappoint you, you never stop hoping they'll finally show up for you.

"He doesn't know what he's missing." I mean it. I know it's true.

Before I can process it, she's unbuckled and climbed into

my lap. It's easy enough given how short her skirt is. It bunches at the waist and I get a glimpse of heaven between her legs. Whatever nerves were bothering her earlier aren't anymore. She wriggles a little, her eyebrows furrowing. "Um, is there something in your pocket?"

For a second I think it's a really stupid joke then I remember her present. I dig it out, inspecting the package to see if she accidentally squished it.

"Your birthday present." She starts to protest but I stop her. "Don't get excited, Lucky. It's just something that made me think of you."

Adair wraps her long arms around her neck, ignoring the tiny package. It's already dark and in the moonlight, I can't see the green of her eyes or the red of her hair. But I see her perfectly. I want to bury my face in her neck and breathe in that scent that I only know as Adair.

"Do you know what I want for my birthday?" she whispers. "You."

"I'm all in, Lucky." My mouth finds hers as she presses closer and I have to remind myself that it's cold and that the first time I fuck her is not going to be in a car. But I can't stop myself from tasting what's to come. I slip my hands up her thighs and cover her mouth with mine. I'm beginning to question my earlier decision not to take her right there, against the steering wheel, when something explodes overhead.

Adair rears up and my arms circle her protectively. Then the second firework lights up the night sky, illuminating a tent for a split second.

"Fuck," she mutters, figuring it out before I can.

Lights burst on and a crowd of people scream "surprise!"

We scramble apart and I help her pull down her skirt before anyone can get a better look at us in the dark.

"I said no parties," she says. "You didn't…"

"I had nothing to do with this," I swear.

Our conversation is cut short as her friends descend upon the Jaguar. There's not an ounce of shock on their faces over our indelicate entrance. Adair looks less than thrilled as she's led toward the tent. She casts a frantic look over her shoulder and yells, "Later! Find me!"

It's not a promise. It's a command. She really didn't want a party.

Since this is Valmont it's not just a party though. Making my way to the tent, I discover a dozen large heaters set up strategically to keep everyone warm. Pink lights are strewn along the tent, casting the entire space with a rosy glow. In the corner, there's a bar and a man in a white jacket serving drinks. I work my way through the crowd to her. She reaches for me, grabbing my hand.

"Don't let go," she says, holding it tightly.

That's easier said than done when her friends start wishing her a happy birthday. They come from every direction, hugging her one at a time before passing her to the next person. It's impossible to keep hold of her but I stay close by. No one notices how she flinches each time. They're oblivious to her pain.

"Are you surprised?" Poppy glows with excitement, completely oblivious to Adair's obvious discomfort.

"I am," Adair says in a strained voice.

"You didn't think we would forget your birthday?" Poppy continues, grabbing Adair's hand and leading her into the crowd of people. They part to allow Adair to see the giant cake on display in the center of the tent. It's shaped like a horseshoe and nearly as tall as I am. They don't do anything halfway in Valmont.

"Sorry, man." Cyrus appears beside me and bumps my shoulder. "I know you thought you were getting her to yourself tonight." He holds out a bottle of whiskey. "Peace offering?"

"No thanks." I turn him down, wondering if I should intervene on Adair's behalf.

"Poppy knew her mom usually planned her birthday parties, so she thought she should step in," he explains.

"You two seem to be getting cozy." I bypass telling him that Adair didn't want a party. I'm beginning to understand these things are never about what the guest of honor wants. It's all for show.

He follows my eyes to where Poppy is forcing a glass of champagne on Adair. "Me and Poppy? I don't know. I've never really..."

"She's gorgeous. She's rich," I say flatly. "She's a lot nicer than most of the people here."

"Is there such a thing as too nice?" he asks. "I don't think I could ever live up to her expectations."

"I've seen the way she looks at you," I say. The truth is that Poppy Landry won't ask him to live up to any expectations. She's blind to his faults. He's not a bad guy, but I suspect she's too good for him.

"She is hot," he agrees after a moment.

It's good to see him really weighing the benefits.

"Money and Oliver are here," he says, pointing to the pair.

"What are they supposed to be?" I ask checking out their wildly colored suits and gold chains.

"Pimps," he tells me. "I'm going to go say hello."

There's no way I'm spending a minute with those two dickheads acting like they're hot shit. "I should check on Adair."

"Catch you later." Cyrus nods and heads toward them.

Weaving my way through the throng of people, I lose sight of her. For the next hour, the party-goers swarm like locusts, drinking, dancing, and blocking me from reaching Adair every time I see her. I finally spot her with Poppy standing by the cocktail bar. She says something to her and then darts toward the pool house.

I force my way though the crowd. This might be my only chance to get her alone. It's dark inside but there's a light on in the bedroom down the hall. Not only did I get her alone, we might be able to pick up where we left off before her friends descended on us.

I'm nearly to the door when I hear voices.

"You better spill," someone says.

Adair's voice answers. "There's nothing to spill. Nothing's happened."

"Have you told him you're a virgin?" Someone asks. Darcy maybe?

Apparently, her sexual history is common knowledge. I have no idea why she acted so weird about it now. I guess part of me thought the confession meant it's a big deal to her. Now she's chatting about it like it's just a burden.

This conversation is none of my business. I wish I hadn't come in after her. I hesitate before peeking through the cracked door. Adair is spread on the bed. Ava and Darcy sitting cross-legged on opposite sides.

"Shut up, Darcy. It's not something I brag about," Adair says.

"Does your daddy know you're dating him?" Ava asks.

I have no interest in their malicious gossip, and Adair doesn't need me to save her. She can take care of herself. I turn to leave when Adair responds.

"Of course, he doesn't." The laugh I've grown to love sounds hollow—cruel even.

A pit opens in my stomach. I taste acid on my tongue. I don't want to hear anymore. This isn't my conversation. But my feet betray me, refusing to move. Instead, I cling to the shadows, out of sight but still able to hear them.

"It's not a bad deal," Darcy says. "Ride him for what he's worth. I mean, it's all he has to offer, right? Then use him to get your dad to back off."

"I'll get right on that," Adair says.

I can't move. I'm stuck listening to her piss all over me.

"When you're done you can pass him around," Ava suggests. "My dad will flip the fuck out. He never cares what trash Money is banging, but, God forbid, I bring someone like that home. Double standard."

"Mine, too."

"Sterling isn't really into dating," Adair says.

"So? He's on scholarship, right? Who do you think is paying his tuition?" Ava asks. "Those of us writing checks. He owes it to us."

"Exactly," Darcy agrees.

"You haven't even graduated," Adair says.

"The point is that he can be useful and fun. Don't forget to share," Ava tells her.

"I won't."

I can't listen a minute longer. I'm glad her friends got their way. I'm glad she's finally shown me who she really is. I just wish it wasn't too late, because she got her hooks into me already. I love her fire—that unreachable piece of her that can never be tamed. The part of her I know will destroy me.

Pushing my way through the crowd, I ignore Cyrus waving to me from across the lawn. He's with Poppy and it looks like they're both reconsidering their relationship. The last thing I need is to watch those two make out all night. It's easy to pretend I don't hear them. The party is loud. Despite the October chill, more than a few people have stripped down and jumped in the pool. I leave the bedlam behind me. The farther

I get from the patio heaters and tent, the colder the night becomes. The music and shouts fade behind me as night swallows me. I should have grabbed my jacket. There's no fucking way I'm going back for it. When I reach the front drive, I stop and stare at the house for a minute. Every light is on. The party probably spilled inside a long time ago. All this house for what? A couple rich assholes? Why had I ever believed she saw something in me? She came from this. I barely own my last name.

I shove my hands in my pockets and start down the long drive. I'll be frozen by the time I reach campus, but, at least, I'll be numb. In my head, a list starts to form. I need to go to campus housing and request a new room. Cyrus is fine. It's not his fault. But I don't want to see any of them again. Then I lay low, focus on my work, finish the fucking year. By then, I'll have forgotten her and she'll have moved on to whatever plaything she spots next. Maybe she'll even grow up and go to London like she wants.

I hope she does.

Because then she'll be far, far away. From me. From them. From whatever's turned her into this raging bitch.

"Sterling!" she calls from behind me.

I turn to the sound of her voice. Fuck, I am just her little lapdog, aren't I?

"Where are you going?" she calls when I keep walking.

I don't answer. I keep walking.

There's a pause and I think she's given up. But then I hear her soft plea, "Don't leave me. You promised you'd stay."

I want to keep walking. I want to pretend I don't hear the anguished request. Instead, I turn and follow the scattered pieces of my heart leading me back to her.

34

ADAIR
THE PRESENT

I flow into Windfall that afternoon, still in shock over today's turn of events. When I woke up in Sterling's bed, I hadn't known what to think. I left feeling worse, confused and unsure where my past ended and my present began. Then destiny dropped a present in my lap: a job.

It's embarrassing to think it's my first real job. I've volunteered for years, but it's not the same. Bluebird offered me a small salary that I don't need *yet*. But it's the first honest money I've ever made. I know exactly what I'm going to do with it. Half to the shelter. The other half saved in a college fund for Ellie. I won't pretend her future is safe with MacLaine Media on the line. I'm not sure that Malcolm or Ginny are ready to admit that, and I can't trust them to think about anyone but themselves. I won't let her wind up like me, completely dependent on her father or any man.

A towering arrangement of magnolia blossoms wobbles into the foyer. I peer around it to find Felix holding the vase.

"These are beautiful," I murmur as he places them on a table. I lean down to breathe in their creamy vanilla aroma. It's the slight tang of lemon hiding under it that I love though.

My mom always told me to wear magnolia perfume because Southern women might be sweet but they still know how to bite.

Felix hands me a card with a wink. "It looks like you have an admirer."

My fingers tremble as I take it. Most men send roses. There's one man that knows I love magnolias. I can't bring myself to break the seal. I'm not sure what I want that card to say.

And there's other things I need to confront. "I want to talk to you about Ellie."

We've been avoiding each other for the most part. Since daddy put Felix in charge of Ellie's inheritance, Felix has continued to serve as the family butler. We can't keep pretending that the will didn't change things.

The smile slips from his face, but he nods. "I thought you might."

"There's some things that we should discuss," I begin.

"You can do that with me," Malcolm interrupts before I can tell Felix my plans. It's not like him to be home this early. His shirt sleeves are rolled to his elbows. Judging from his bloodshot eyes, he's already on his second drink of the afternoon.

"Tough day at the office?" I ask.

"No, long night followed by an even longer morning," he says. Clearly, he didn't appreciate me sending him home to his wife and daughter yesterday. He lists a bit on his feet, and I worry he'll tip over on the marble floor.

"Maybe you should slow down before dinner," I suggest.

"Care to tell me where you've been?" he asks.

I slip the envelope into my purse and brace for impact. There's no way I'm explaining myself to him. Malcolm may think he can replace our father as head of house, but I'm done living under a man's thumb. "I'm an adult. I don't owe you an explanation."

"Exactly! I don't care where you were last night," he spits back. He lowers his voice so that it won't echo in the foyer. "You could afford me the same courtesy in the future."

"I'm not the one who's married," I say, "and cheating on his wife!"

Felix shows no sign of surprise at this revelation. He busies himself with arranging the blossoms. As usual, he's here blending into the background. He's always been more than a keeper of the kitchen and schedules and party plans. He's a keeper of our secrets. Our own professional guardian hired by our mother to watch over us. I often think mom would be disappointed in us, because I know Felix is.

"Goddammit, Adair!" Malcolm storms to daddy's office and I'm right behind him. He points behind me. "Shut the door."

I do so because, unlike Malcolm, I know that Felix is listening. And where Felix is, Ellie is usually nearby. She doesn't need to hear us argue.

"What are you freaking about out about now?" I ask.

"I got a call this afternoon from Trish McHugh at Bluebird Press," he tells me. "She wanted to touch base with me about business given our father's passing. By the way, she sends her condolences."

My hand finds the smooth side of the bookshelf and I lean into it.

He continues, his eyes hard and dark like our father's would be if he were here. "She also wanted to make certain that there's not going to be an interruption of ownership given that she just hired a new editor."

"I don't see how any of this involves you," I say. "Daddy left Bluebird to me."

"Did you tell her that?" he asks. "I can't imagine there are many Adairs out there with English degrees looking for editorial jobs in downtown Nashville."

I shrug, trying to act casual. "You might be surprised. It's not like there's a lot of work for English majors."

"Don't sass me," he says, channeling Daddy even more. I half-expect him to whip off his belt and drive the point home.

Not that I would let him. Not that anyone will ever touch me that way again. I push away from the bookshelf, forcing myself to stand firmly on my feet. I will not back down to him. Not today. Not ever. "You mind your business and I'll mind mine. I know what I'm doing."

"Says the slut getting in bed with Sterling Ford," he says.

"You have no idea what's going on. You don't even know who he is." I let one man slander Sterling in this office before. I won't do it again.

"And you do?"

"Do you know what's going to ruin you?" I step toward him to deliver one final blow before I leave him and this house and this life behind. "The same thing that ruined daddy. Your fucking pride. Your arrogance. You can't see beyond your own shadow because you're too certain of every move you make."

"That arrogance built us this company."

"That arrogance lost us this company and killed our mother," I explode.

Malcolm gives a disgusted shake of his head. "You'll never forgive him for that will you?"

"Why would I? He never apologized." How can he still not understand?

"You're selfish and spoiled. You never understood sacrificing for the good of the family."

"I haven't sacrificed?" I ask softly. Doesn't he see that being here now is proof that I've given up everything for this family? "All I care about is this family. Can you say the same?"

"Why don't you say what you really mean? I've never cared about the right members of this family." Hate drips from his words as slow and sticky as molasses. It's in his blood. He was born poisoned with it.

"Felix took care of you and El—"

"I don't have as liberal of view of who is a MacLaine as you do."

"I can't do this anymore." I shake my head. It's swimming with all the mistakes we've made. Mistakes we keep making. It's too much. "I can't just sit by and watch you cling to this lie about what the MacLaine name means. What it stands for."

"So, you're going to pick up a hammer and start destroying it yourself?"

"Sometimes it's better to tear down what's broken than to waste time fixing what can't be saved." I wait for him to respond. When he doesn't, I walk to the door.

He finds his voice as my hand touches the knob. "If you walk out of this house, don't come back."

It's not the first time I've heard that in this room. But it's going to be the last.

"This was never my house. It's not yours either. Wear your crown, rule your false empire, but don't forget that it's all made of glass."

I leave Magnolia Lane, passing by houses that would open their doors for me in a heartbeat. I'm always welcome in Valmont, but everything here has a cost. I've been in debt to this place and this life long enough. Later, I might regret leaving with nothing but the Roadster and the bottle of champagne I'd brought home to celebrate my new job.

There's nothing to celebrate. Now that Trish knows the truth, she won't want me there. But she'll feel obligated to keep the boss or scared that I'll fire her. I never wanted a pity job. I wanted something of my own.

It's all I'll ever want.

I drive toward Nashville with no destination in mind. By the time I realize where I'm headed, I'm nearly there. I don't know why I drove here. It's like Sterling is a planet and I'm caught in his orbit. I can't move away from him. I can't find my own path. Maybe I don't want to. Maybe I should stop fighting it.

I pull into the parking garage at Twelve and South to consider my options. I can check into the Eaton, which would be reasonable. I can call Poppy. Another rational option. I can drive around and pretend that I know where I'm going. Less rational, but still more reasonable than running to him after this morning. I turn off the car anyway.

Don't let a day be coal, I hear mom saying. *Turn it into a diamond.*

Maybe that doesn't just apply to days. Maybe it applies to people, too.

Everything in my body tells me this is the right place to be. I don't want to trust Sterling. I don't want to need him. But I can't deny that he's the only person who's ever truly understood me. Maybe that doesn't make us friends. Maybe some people wouldn't call that love. It's the only kind I've ever known, and right now, I need someone who sees me.

I'm nearly to the parking garage's elevator when I remember the card in my purse. I know it's from him, just like I knew this moment was inevitable when he showed up in the rain at my daddy's funeral. The crash. The collision. The inescapable force that draws us together time and time again.

In the cement parking garage, the overhead lights flicker as I slip out the card.

Four simple words scrawled in familiar handwriting.

Four simple words that answer my questions. Four simple words that don't belong to another soul. They're ours and always have been. Sterling doesn't need to say I love you. That's not what mattered to us then. It's not what matters now. Reading the card makes it easy to press the call button on the elevator. I watch every floor light up, my certainty build with each.

Zeus is at the door before I manage to knock. I can hear him whining with excitement. Sterling's voice follows from inside, commanding him to calm down. He opens the door before I reach it. For just one moment our eyes meet, and it's the closest I've ever felt to coming home.

"I knew the flowers would..." The words die from his lips when he stops to really look at me. I know he sees the tear stains on my cheeks and my red nose. I know he sees what's under that, too. Pain and defeat and exhaustion. He's at my side then, leading me to the couch. I sit. He stands. "What happened, Lucky?"

The story falls out of me in pieces. I don't cry. I just speak absently, staring beyond him while trying to see a future that might never be in reach. When I finally get to the part where Malcolm tells me to get out, Sterling takes a seat next to me on the couch. Zeus lays his massive head on my knees. I'm not sure which one looks more concerned.

"You can stay here," he says without hesitation.

"I'm not sure that's a good idea." I know that because I want to stay, and I don't have the best instincts of late.

"I meant what I said earlier today. I know it came out shitty," he adds when I startle. "I'm not taking this farther then you ask me to. What I mean is that I don't expect anything if you stay."

Maybe I'm an idiot, because I believe him. There's a million reasons not to trust him. It's stupid considering I don't know where he's been all these years and who he really is anymore.

And none of that matters.

Because he's Sterling and I'm Adair and some things—even when they don't make sense—are meant to be.

"I'm sorry," I say in a quiet voice.

His eyebrow arches. "For what?"

"Do you want the whole list?" I ask. "It could take a while."

He hesitates. A tempest rages in his blue eyes, pulling him in every direction. Pushing him toward me and wrenching him away. I wish I could be his calm—the safe place he seeks instead of the storm. His Adam's apple slides drawing attention to the stubble peppering his jawline. I've been so busy thinking about the boy I used to know that I didn't see the man in front of me. Now that I do, I see what I didn't before: I see what drives him.

And it breaks my heart.

"I shouldn't have come here. I don't know why I came here," I say, the words tripping on my tongue, caught in the confusion that clouds me.

"That's what we do," he murmurs. He's so close that I swear I feel him on my skin even though we aren't touching. "We run back to each other."

We did once. We broke each other then. We rebuilt ourselves, but why? So we can destroy each other again?

I push and he pulls and *we* break— and maybe that's why we'll never fix us.

Or maybe it's because last time, he didn't run back. I didn't rebuild. We've lived shattered lives and told ourselves it made us stronger.

"Why did you leave?" I search his face for the answer I've needed for years.

Sterling brushes a thumb over my lower lip. His touch is a lightning strike and there's nowhere for me to hide. Fire ignites on contact, traveling through me and exploding into flames. He moves closer, his breath warm and sweet on my face. "Why did you stay?"

Getting answers from him requires admitting my own secrets. That's not something I'm willing to do—not even for him.

"No questions," I say, forcing myself to add, "it's not part of the arrangement."

"I can't seem to keep track of all the rules." He withdraws his hand, and I miss him instantly. I ache for him.

I reach for his hand and bring it back to my face. Turning my cheek into it, I plant a kiss on the mound of his palm. "Okay. How's this? We break one rule for every new one I make."

"What rule are we going to break first, Lucky?" And then he's kissing me, because he knows which rule we can't follow a second longer.

We tear the walls we've built down and step into the wreckage together. I've been suffocating behind my barricades for years, and he's air. He's life, not destruction. He's beautiful chaos upending my world and setting me free.

I'd forgotten how good he tastes.

Strong arms slide under me and lift me. We move together instinctually. My legs wrap around his waist. My arms tangle around his neck. We're on a bed and I don't remember getting there. Only him. Only this. He's not a boy. He's a man. I feel the proof of it on my fingertips. I fumble for his belt, but he pushes my hand away and smiles. It's unguarded. Vulnerable. Stripped to show he's here with me. All of him. He lifts my arms and pins our clasped hands over my head. When his mouth meets mine again, he lingers with slow lips. He whispers into the kiss. "This is just the first course, Lucky. I want to take my time. I need to savor ever fucking inch of you. I need to taste you."

Sterling's attention slides along my neck, his lips murmuring wicked promises as he descends. Fabric snaps and I'm vaguely aware that he's ripped something off of me. My dress falls open and finally — blessedly – my skin meets his. He pauses at my stomach and suddenly, I'm painfully aware that I'm not the girl he fell in love with. I know what he sees: the tiny, silvery lines and soft skin. I shrink, trying to hide my flaws but there's nowhere to run.

"Don't you dare hide," he says in a gruff voice. Sterling lifts his head from his devotions and blue eyes pierce through me.

"I know I don't look…I know I'm not the girl you… before…" I struggle to put words to my sudden and crippling self-awareness.

He kisses my belly. "I don't want that girl. I want you. I've never wanted any one like I want you right here and right now." Pushing onto his hands, he brings his face to hover over mine. "The only thing I ever needed was more of you and, Lucky, I got my wish."

We collide, crashing into one another. Drawn by some invisible force neither of us can resist. Giving into it unleashes a savage awareness of each touch until our bodies entwine like our hearts. There's never been anyone like him. I moan as he slips inside me, as he stretches me, as he releases me.

Sterling pushes deeper, carefully, allowing my body to adjust to his size. "You feel even better than I imagined."

"Been imagining it, huh?" I murmur.

"And you haven't been thinking about this?" He lifts an eyebrow and plunges fully inside me. I writhe with delicious fullness under his smug gaze.

"Guilty," I groan. My fingernails sink into his broad shoulders for leverage as he rolls his hips languidly against my cleft.

"I'll punish you later," he teases but I don't miss the dark flash in his eyes. Another reminder that I've only caught glimpses of the man he's become. A curated collection of portraits—the pieces he allows me to see.

I want to see all of him, but that will take time. But it starts here. It starts now. His teeth sink into my shoulder and I whimper, circling against him faster. Sterling clutches my hip and forces me back to the slow, deep rhythm.

"A few things have changed," he says through gritted teeth. "I'm in control now. I'm going to make you feel so fucking good, but you're going to have to let go and finally give in."

His words unlock some hidden door in the wall I've built —one I didn't know existed. Maybe I'd lost that part to him. Maybe no one else ever found it because it opens for him alone. Maybe he holds that key.

Because for once I don't fight him, I do exactly what he says. I open my mind like I've opened my body and allow him to fill me entirely.

I'm drawn to Sterling, because he's part of me. Separately, we don't work and maybe we aren't perfect together, but we are whole. That's the messy truth of it. Wholeness isn't neat or orderly. It's give and take. It's accepting all the parts of each other. I don't know why he left. I don't know why I stayed. I only know one thing. Together our beautiful chaos makes sense. Maybe just to us. But that's all that matters.

"That's right. Give in," he coaxes. "You belong to me."

His words thrust into me and take control. I am his. I

always have been. But he's mine, too. I tighten around him, my body forcing him to give me as much of him as he's taken from me. His forehead presses to mine, slick with heat. He moves faster. He plunges deeper. He thunders, roaring into me and I shatter beneath him.

This time I don't care how much of me he's taken.

He can have it all.

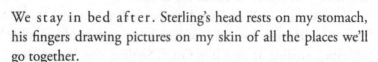

We stay in bed after. Sterling's head rests on my stomach, his fingers drawing pictures on my skin of all the places we'll go together.

Neither of us seem in a hurry to leave the bed yet. That is until he hears my stomach growl.

"Hungry?" He turns his head to gaze up at me.

I run my hand through his tangled hair. "A little. But I'd rather stay here with you."

He pushes up to give me a kiss. Then he winks, and I melt a little. "That's a problem, because you're going to need your strength. It's still early."

"It's a predicament," I agree. "Maybe later..."

I reach for him when a wet black nose pushes between us depositing a leash.

"Okay, boy," he says as if this settles matters. "Someone needs a walk, huh? And my girl needs food." He grabs the leash and climbs out of bed. He's got his pants half-on when Zeus jumps into bed beside me. Sterling pauses, "You aren't allowed on the bed."

Zeus pushes his nose under my shoulder, flattening himself as he tries to hide.

"I can see you," Sterling says, buttoning his jeans.

Undeterred the dog begins to lick my cheek. I giggle,

scratching his head. "I take back what I said about him listening to you."

"You're going to spoil him." Sterling clips the leash on him and tugs him away gently. "Sorry, boy, she's spoken for."

Zeus doesn't seem to mind the rejection now that a walk is imminent. He tugs on his leash.

"Why don't you order something?"

"I don't have my phone," I say. "I guess I could get dressed and go find it."

"That would be a tragedy. I'd prefer you remain naked until I return." He pulls his out of his pocket and tosses it to me. "Pass code is 0822. Order anything you want. I won't be long."

"Anything?" I ask. "I'm pretty hungry."

"I'll take that as a compliment," he calls as Zeus drags him away.

I pull the sheet against me and sit up in bed. It takes me a second to find the food delivery app. As I scroll through the options, a text alert from Sutton flashes at the top of the screen.

I don't mean to look. I don't mean to read it. It's just there for me to see—and now I can't *unsee* it.

Five words change everything. Five words erase everything. Five words shatter this pretty illusion that I let myself believe.

I love you, too.

I can't stop my finger from pressing it—from reading the rest of the conversation. I don't know who Sutton is, but it doesn't matter.

> Forget that bitch. Come home.
> I miss you

> I miss you, too.

> I'm not going to win this time,
> am I?

> Not this time. I love you.

> I love you, too.

The phone falls to the bed as my world falls apart. Getting out of his bed, I open the nightstand drawer. It's in there, on top, just like I knew it would be: *The Great Gatsby*. I don't bother looking at the other books stored there. I turn to the last page and tear it out, ripping up all but the final line. I leave it on the pillow like a note and sprinkle the remaining pieces on the sheets.

He'll know what it means.

The rest comes automatically. I gather my dress from the floor and tie it the best I can with its ripped belt. Shoes. Purse. Out the door. Press the elevator button. I make it to the car before it hits me. I left something behind and I can't go back for it. Closing my eyes, I decide to leave it for him to clean up. It's useless to me now: my broken heart.

ACKNOWLEDGMENTS

Last year life handed me a huge surprise and everything changed. As it turns out, that doesn't just happen in books. Everything got put on hold when I welcomed my little girl, Sophie, to the world. She wrote this book with me, so I have to thank her first. Sophie, I didn't know I needed you, but I'm so thankful to be your mommy.

A huge thanks to Louise, my rockstar agent, and the team at The Bent Agency. I don't know what I would do without you! A special shout-out to Victoria, who tries to keep me on track—a feat about as possible as herding cats.

Thank you to my foreign teams for all the hard work you do getting my books to readers all over the world.

Thank you to my amazing assistants, Natasha and Shelby. I could not do this without you. Seriously, thank you!

Thank you to Rebecca for excellent proofreading!

To my amazing reader group, Geneva Lee's Loves—thank you for standing by me when I pushed this book's release. Thank you for becoming part of my family. Thank you for being as excited about Sophie as I was! You are the best. Thank you to the members of Team G (Elsi, Heather, Christina, Karen, Jami, Michell) for always lifting me up.

This book is dedicated in memory of Trish, who didn't get to read it. I'm so glad you are no longer in pain, but you will be forever missed, my darling friend.

To my author friends who inspire me every single day—thank you for showing me what kickass women can accomplish.

To my readers—thank you for going on this new adventure with me!

And to my family, you are my reason for everything. Elise, you're my best friend, my sister, my business partner. Thank you for whiskey dates and bath bombs. To my kids, remember this is how mommy is going to pay for your therapy. Just kidding. Mostly.

And to Josh—thank you for speaking my language fluently.

GENEVA LEE is the *New York Times*, *USA Today*, and internationally bestselling author of over a dozen novels, including the Royals Saga which has sold two million copies worldwide. She lives in Poulsbo Washington with her husband and three children, and she co-owns Away With Words Bookshop with her sister.

Visit her online at
GenevaLee.com